METRO KINETIC

METRO KINETIC

BRIAN BOWYER

NEW YORK | LOS ANGELES

Jacket design by Don Noble

Jacket Copyright © 2024 by Winding Road Stories

Interior Design by Winding Road Stories

ISBN#: 978-1-960724-34-2 (pbk)
ISBN#: 978-960724-35-9 (ebook)

Published by Winding Road Stories

www.windingroadstories.com

Also by Brian Bowyer

OLD TOO SOON
FLESH REHEARSAL
AUTUMN GOTHIC
ALIVE UNDEAD
GRINDING ROAD
PERPETUAL DREAD
SINISTER MIX
APOCALYPSE
ROAD HARVEST
ROAD NARROWS
KILL FACTOR
SHELF LIFE
WRITING AND RISING FROM ADDICTION

CHAPTER 1

In the Rosira, on the sixteenth floor, eight-year-old Sydney closed her bedroom door and locked it. Her mother lay asleep in the living room with a needle stuck in her arm, and her father was on a rampage after snorting the white powder that always made him act like a maniac.

Friday had been her last day of second grade. Now it was Tuesday and Sydney already wished that summer break was over. Perhaps she would ask her grandparents—who owned this apartment, anyway—if she could go live with them the next time they visited from the Hamptons.

She turned her TV on. It was tuned to a cartoon channel. A cat chased a mouse across the screen.

Moments later, her father pounded on the door. "Sydney! Open this door! Right now!"

She didn't want to see him, but knew if she didn't open the door, he would kick it in again—and then that creepy superintendent would have to come up here and patch another hole in her bedroom wall.

Sydney opened the door. Her father glared down at her with wild, bloodshot eyes. His thick, disheveled hair framed his emaciated face.

He wrapped a bony hand around her throat and shoved her

down onto the bed. "What have I told you about walking away from me when I'm talking to you?"

"I'm sorry, Daddy! It won't happen again!"

"You're goddamn right it won't." He unbuckled his belt and yanked it from the loops around his baggy pants. He grabbed the front of his pants with his other hand to keep them from falling to the floor.

He approached the bed holding his pants up, the belt raised high above his head. "I'm gonna whip you like a goddamn slave."

"No, Daddy! Please!"

"I'm gonna teach you to respect authority if it kills me."

"No! Please, Daddy! No!"

As he cocked his arm to bring the belt down, Sydney saw her mother enter the bedroom pointing a handgun at his back.

"Drop the belt, Dexter, or I swear to God, I will shoot you dead."

Sydney watched her father turn around to face her mother, who wore a sleeveless yellow dress. The needle was no longer stuck in her arm. She swayed on her feet but managed to keep the gun aimed at his chest by holding it with both hands.

"Bitch," her father said. "You don't have the goddamn balls to shoot me."

"I mean it, Dexter. Drop the belt, or I swear to God I'll shoot."

"Go ahead," Dexter said. "The gun's not even loaded."

"I don't believe you."

"It's true. You think I'm stupid enough to leave a loaded gun in the apartment with you around? Go ahead. Pull the trigger."

Sydney watched her mother close her eyes and pull the trigger. The dry-firing click of an empty gun shattered the silence.

"Bitch!" her father shouted, infuriated. "You really would have shot me!" He rushed her and grabbed her by the hair of her head.

"Say goodbye to your mother, Sydney. She's taking a long trip down to the pavement."

"No!" Sydney screamed. She rose from the bed and followed him down the hall as he dragged her mother into the living room. "Don't hurt her! Please! Let her go!"

But Dexter did not let her go.

Sydney watched in horror as he dragged her mother toward the sliding door to the sixteenth-floor balcony.

3

Chapter 2

Samantha had heard bad things about the casting director, but he seemed okay to her. Framed black-and-white photos of dead actors hung from his office walls. Beyond the window behind his desk, she saw a quadrangle of garden space with a wooden bench, a couple of wire chairs, and a clogged birdbath full of dark Manhattan rainwater. His office occupied space on the first floor of an old building in the midtown theater district.

"That was a great audition," he said. "Have a seat."

With two empty chairs in front of his desk, Samantha selected the one on the left. Samantha thought her audition on the fourth floor had gone well. "Thanks," she said, staring at the clock on the wall.

"Are you in a hurry?"

She met his gaze. "Not at all."

"I noticed you were looking at the clock. Perhaps you have somewhere else to go?"

"No." She glanced at the clock again. "Well, just my drawing class, but I still have plenty of time to get there."

"Drawing class?"

"Yes. Life drawing."

"You're learning to draw?"

"Oh, no. I've been drawing my whole life."

"Then why are you taking a drawing class?"

"For practice," Samantha said. "Just like an athlete or a musician has to practice to maintain a level of excellence. Does that make sense?"

"I suppose."

"Plus," she added, "taking a class is cheaper than hiring an artist's model."

"So, when you say life drawing, you mean figure drawing, right?"

"Yes."

"Sketching nude models?"

"Yes."

He clasped his hands together on his desk. "How old are you?"

"Twenty-two."

"Are you a student?"

"No, not anymore. I just graduated from college, actually."

"Four years?"

"Yes."

"Here in Midtown?"

"No. Upper West Side."

"What did you study?"

Samantha looked at the clock again. "Art history. English lit. American studies. Creative writing and visual arts. And acting, of course."

The casting director leaned back in his chair. "My father was a playwright and a stage director. And his father was a theatrical producer. I've spent most of my life surrounded by important people in this business. Therefore, I tend to look for more than just competence in the actors I audition, and you certainly have more than just competence, Samantha. I believe that what you have will carry you very far in this business—provided, of course, that you get one of those *lucky breaks* that even the best actors are often dependent upon. Do you understand what I'm saying to you?"

"Yes... I think I know what you mean."

He smiled. "I'll do something for you, if you'll do something for me."

She stood up. "Listen, no disrespect to you, or anything, but I'm not even remotely attracted to men."

He cocked his head. "You only date women?"

"Yes. I hope you'll still consider me for the part, though."

He nodded, but the look in his eyes told her all she needed to know. "Of course. I'll be in touch if you're chosen for the role."

"Okay. Thanks for auditioning me."

Samantha exited the office and reentered her uncertain future.

CHAPTER 3

Tonight, Christina found herself in The Pit, a death-metal club on the west side of Jersey City, New Jersey—what her father called *the wrong side of the tracks*. She was there with a guy she knew from high school, who played bass in a thrash band called Catastrophe. They were playing three sets at The Pit. She had nothing better to do on a Saturday night, only two weeks left until summer break. With eleventh grade almost over, senior year would soon arrive.

She didn't like Catastrophe, and she didn't really like their bass player, either, but she had agreed to come to the club with him because her father had been drinking whiskey when she left. Christina's mother was dead, and her father often beat her—and worse—whenever he had whiskey in his system.

She noticed a girl watching her after the beginning of Catastrophe's second set. The girl was leaning with her back against the bar, smoking a cigarette. No one was supposed to smoke inside The Pit, but people did, and the owners never said anything. Her arms were crossed, and the cigarette dangled from her lips. She had thick dark hair and wore a motorcycle jacket. Christina thought she looked like a movie star.

She appeared to be about Christina's age, which—technically—was too young to even be *in* The Pit, but (like the smoking) the owners felt some things were better left unsaid about paying customers.

Christina looked away, toward the stage, at Catastrophe. The two guitar players frantically banged their heads to the loud, aggressive music. The bass player swirled his head on his neck, his hair making circles in the air. The drummer was so fast he appeared to be a blur of perpetual motion. The singer's voice growled like a caged animal.

And then the girl was standing right beside her. "I'm Kenzie. What's your name?"

"Christina."

Kenzie smiled. "It's nice to meet you, Christina."

Kenzie's eyes were the brightest, bluest eyes she had ever seen. "Likewise," she said, returning the smile.

"Listen, I only stopped in here to get a drink, and you look like you're enjoying this band even less than I am. What do you say we go someplace else?"

Christina nodded. "Let's do it."

Kenzie drove some kind of a vintage hotrod. As black as her motorcycle jacket, and with thick shiny chrome, Christina thought the car would have looked more at home on a showroom floor in another era. She took Christina to a cocktail lounge on the other side of town. The high-class side. *The right side of the tracks.* Kenzie swept her inside to a table with a candle on top of it. The shadows around them moved in time with smooth piano music.

"You're not from around here, are you?" Christina said.

"No. Fort Lee, originally. I'm only in Jersey City because I'm thinking of attending the university here."

"How old are you?"

"Eighteen," Kenzie said. "You?"

"Seventeen."

Kenzie used her fake ID to purchase shots of rum until the club closed. From there, they pulled over near a park to watch the sun rise.

"How long do you think we'll have to wait until the sun wakes up?" Christina asked.

"It might be a little while," Kenzie said, sliding her hand along Christina's thigh. "But time seems to move faster when I'm with you."

When Kenzie leaned in to kiss Christina, her senses felt alive for the first time that she could remember. The touch of Kenzie's hand on her bare skin, easing closer, made her entire body feel the heat of all the stars that lit the sky before dawn.

Against Christina's wishes, the sun did rise, causing her to open her eyes. She was in the back seat, curled up in Kenzie's arms. They had only slept an hour since the last time they had sex, but now they were both wide awake.

"My dad," Christina said, "will be so mad at me."

"For staying out all night?"

"Yes."

Kenzie lit a cigarette. "We could go to my hotel room."

"I would love that," Christina said.

Kenzie started the ignition and eased her foot onto the gas pedal, fueling Christina's relief. She was now safer in the arms of a stranger than she would ever be at home with her father.

Chapter 4

In Jersey City, one of the guidance counselors at Isaac's high school called him into her office.

"Isaac, I don't know how to tell you this," she said. "Your mother was in a terrible car accident. She's at the hospital, and they don't know if she'll survive. Are you driving yet?"

"Yes," Isaac said. "I mean...I have a driver's license, but I don't have a car."

"Come on. I'll take you to the hospital."

Isaac's mother survived, but the accident left her paralyzed from the waist down. Unable to work, she quickly spiraled into a depression. His father left twelve years ago, when Isaac was four years old. Now—at sixteen—he knew he would have to get a job.

The next day, he walked into a restaurant a few blocks from their house. He asked if they had any work. They told him it was a tough job, but they needed someone to wash dishes. Without saying a word, Isaac walked into the kitchen and grabbed the apron hanging on the wall next to the grill. The owner nodded.

One day between shifts, Isaac went to his high school and waited out front for the final class to let out. He saw Joanna coming down the steps and remained there until she walked up to him. A year older than Isaac, Joanna seemed to be from another, more exotic place entirely.

Like him, she was a musician, but more accomplished. She played bass for a rock band called Animosity, and the reasons for which she had decided to spend time with him recently were—to Isaac—utterly baffling. Perhaps the universe had simply sent him some good luck to compensate for his mother's catastrophic accident. So far, he hadn't even kissed her. He didn't want to do anything that might push her away.

"Hey, Isaac," she said, falling in step with him as he turned and started walking. She looked dejected, as Isaac had expected. "Did you skip school again today?"

"No, I quit."

"Seriously?"

"Yes. Maybe I'll get a GED later, or something. It's no big deal. Anyway, I heard about what happened to Sebastian. That is so messed up."

Sebastian—the rhythm guitar player in Animosity—had been killed in a drive-by shooting the night before.

Joanna nodded. "Yeah, but we know who did it. Two piece-of-shit Mexicans. Hunter and Eli are going to kill them tonight. Animosity is more than just a band. We're a movement. A resistance. We're a family."

Hunter and Eli—as Sebastian had been—were both in their early twenties. Hunter was the vocalist and lead guitar player. Eli played drums. Joanna, at seventeen, was the youngest member of Animosity.

She lit a cigarette. "Would you like to be a part of our family?"

Isaac stopped walking, turned, and looked at her. "You mean

join the band?"

"Yes. We need a rhythm guitar player now, and you already know most of our songs. I messaged Hunter and Eli about it earlier, and they want you to be in the band."

"They do?"

"Yes. Will you do it? Will you join Animosity?"

"I guess."

Joanna smiled. "Excellent! Welcome to the family. I'm going to miss your hair, though. But those are the band rules."

Isaac shrugged. "It's only hair."

He went home and shaved his head. He would do anything Joanna asked of him.

CHAPTER 5

Outside, after the audition, Samantha checked her phone. It was just past noon on a warm Tuesday in June. The sky was blue. Traffic choked the streets, and pedestrians crowded the sidewalks on both sides of the avenue. She hailed a cab and climbed in with her portfolio bag, then rode two miles up Amsterdam to the Upper West Side, arriving at her drawing class—in a studio near the corner of Park and 81st Street—with a few minutes to spare.

Inside, on the first floor, perhaps twenty other artists either stood or sat in a circle in front of easels or with sketchpads on their laps. Samantha took her sketchpad and a pencil from her portfolio bag and sat down on a cold metal folding chair.

When the teacher—a frail-looking older man—led the model to the platform at the front of the room, Samantha was stunned by the young woman's beauty. She had long auburn hair and bright green eyes. The teacher introduced her as Aubrey.

The name fits her, Samantha thought.

Wearing an opaque gown, Aubrey stepped behind a privacy screen to disrobe. Then she stepped up onto the platform naked to take up poses for drawing. She began with a few quick poses for the artists to draw warm-up sketches. The poses and sketches got longer until Aubrey took a fifteen-minute break.

When she came back out, the poses lasted about ten minutes each. Two hours later, after a final pose that lasted about twenty minutes, the class ended.

Samantha put her sketchpad in her portfolio bag and left.

Outside, the temperature had risen. Samantha checked her phone: 3:06 p.m. She elected not to hail a cab. Instead, wanting to bask in the sunlight, she walked along the avenue.

She went to Third Avenue for cigarettes and across town to Lexington Avenue for vodka—not because she couldn't get cigarettes and vodka in her own neighborhood, but simply because she wanted to enjoy the city.

Later, as she approached the building in which she lived—the Rosira—she saw a group of people gathered around a parked car with a crushed roof. Two police cars were double-parked in front of the building, their roof lights flashing blue and red.

Samantha quickened her pace, as traffic on the avenue slowed to a crawl. People opened windows in the Rosira and poked their heads out to look down. The day-shift doorman came out of the building with a white blanket and handed it to a police officer.

"Dead," someone said. "I thought she was just a bird, at first, like a giant eagle or an owl swooping down."

"Everyone get back," one of the police officers said, and Samantha saw a woman lying dead on the sidewalk in a sleeveless yellow dress.

The cadaver was still recognizably human, but if Samantha had ever seen her in the building before, she certainly didn't recognize her now. The skeleton had snapped and folded. The cracked pelvis had compressed into the rib cage, and the spinal column was now a spike that impaled the head. The arms and legs were twisted with shattered bones. Although the woman did not appear to have landed on her head, the stress of impact had nevertheless shot upward through her body, rearranging the facial bones until she resembled something in an abstract painting.

The cop covered the corpse with the blanket, which reddened in several places as it settled.

Samantha looked away, and then a woman said, "Do you live here in the building?"

She turned her head and saw Aubrey—the model from the life-drawing class—standing maybe two feet away. "Yes," Samantha said.

"Which floor?"

"Top."

Aubrey smiled. Her bright green eyes sparkled in the sunlight. Her long red hair was pulled back in a ponytail. "The penthouse?"

Samantha nodded.

"I live on the second floor," Aubrey said. No longer dressed in the opaque gown, she now wore a black sweater and blue jeans.

Samantha looked down at the blanket-shrouded corpse on the sidewalk. "Did you know her?"

"No. I just moved here. You?"

Samantha shook her head. "No, I didn't know her."

"Well," Aubrey said, "you've already seen me naked. Would you like to come up to my apartment? I could make us a pot of coffee."

Samantha withdrew the bottle of vodka from the bag she was holding. "I have a better idea."

Aubrey cocked her head. "Are you inviting me up to the penthouse?"

"Maybe I am," Samantha said.

CHAPTER 6

Christina shuddered as Kenzie brushed fingertips across her upper thigh, the memories of last night stirring the heat inside her again.

"You know I've fallen in love with you, Christina."

After making love all day long, they lay naked on the bed in Kenzie's room, as the setting sun cast beams of scarlet light through the hotel window.

"You have?"

"Yes," Kenzie said. "I'm already madly in love with you."

Christina kissed her on the lips. "I'm already in love with you, too."

They took a shower together. As the water cascaded over them, Christina wrapped her arms around Kenzie and didn't want to let her go, no matter how cold the water got.

Afterward, while getting dressed, Christina checked her phone. "God, my dad will be so pissed."

"Should I take you home?"

"No. I wanna go visit my mother's grave."

Kenzie cocked her head. "Your mother's dead?"

"Yes."

"I'm sorry to hear that."

"Your fake ID," Christina said. "Is it good enough to work in a liquor store?"

"Of course."

"If I give you some money, will you get us a bottle of rum, and then take me to the cemetery?"

"Sure," Kenzie said.

At a nearby liquor store, they went in half on a bottle of rum. Then Kenzie drove them to Garden Grounds Memorial Cemetery on the other side of town.

Night covered the cemetery by the time they reached the open gates. Kenzie parked outside the fence in case anyone closed the gates while they were inside.

Lamps posted along the walkways provided whatever illumination the calm starry night didn't. Christina led Kenzie through a maze of narrow paved lanes between tombstones to her mother's grave.

Kenzie saw the name on the tombstone, then looked at the dates of birth and death. "Damn. Not even forty. And she's only been dead for a year."

Christina nodded. "She was thirty-eight."

They sat down on the grave and opened the rum.

Kenzie lit a cigarette. "So how did she die, anyway?"

Christina took a drink. "Car accident. Her brakes failed, and then her car crashed into a bridge abutment. Although, technically, I suppose you could say my father killed her when he told them to take her off life support."

Kenzie blew a smoke ring. "I'm sorry for your loss."

Christina shrugged. "In my father's defense, she *was* on a ventilator, and they told us that her brain was already dead. I just wish he would have waited a day or two, at least. Leave a little time for a miracle, or something. Do you know what I mean?"

"Yes, I know what you mean."

"Are you an organ donor?"

"I don't remember," Kenzie said. "Let me hit that rum."

Christina handed her the bottle. Kenzie took a drink and gave the bottle back.

"My mother was an organ donor," Christina said.

"Oh yeah?"

"Yes. A team came in and started harvesting her organs right after my father said to pull the plug. I read some reports from the transplant center later. Her corneas went to a blind girl in New York. Her kidneys went to a teenager in Wisconsin. Her liver went to a schoolteacher in Minnesota. I don't remember the rest. They only gave us vague demographic and geographic information."

"Well," Kenzie said, "your mother certainly doesn't need those organs wherever she is now."

Christina took a drink. "Wherever she is now? What are you talking about? We're sitting right on top of exactly where she is now."

Kenzie shook her head. "No. Those are just her bones in the box below."

"So what are you saying? You think my mom died and went to Heaven?"

"I don't know where she went. But she definitely went somewhere."

Christina took another drink, and then gave the bottle to Kenzie. "So you believe in souls? Human spirits?"

Kenzie took a drink. "Of course."

"What about haunted houses, and stuff like that? Do you believe in ghosts?"

"Of course I do. Don't you believe in ghosts?"

Christina shrugged. "I don't know. I've never seen a ghost. Have you?"

Kenzie took a last drag off her cigarette, and then flipped it aside. "I've been seeing ghosts my entire life."

"Do you see any here tonight, in the cemetery?"

"No." Kenzie took a drink. Then she put the lid on the bottle and leaned it against the tombstone. "The only thing I see tonight is you." She pulled Christina closer to kiss her, and slid her hand under Christina's shirt.

They made love on Christina's mother's grave.

CHAPTER 7

I saac sat on the front porch of his mother's house, waiting for Joanna. He watched evening settle over the city like the wings of a raven. As soon as she pulled up in front of the house in her father's car, he put his guitar in the back and got in on the passenger's side.

"Oh my god!" she said. "Your head looks amazing!'

He smiled. "You like it?"

"Yes! It looks like a fucking bullet!"

"Should I go back in and get my amp?"

"No," Joanna said. "You can just use one of Hunter's amps."

She drove them to where Hunter lived in a small house a few blocks up the street. Hunter's house—like most of the others on the street—existed on the cusp of dereliction. Eli was already there. She parked behind Eli's car.

Isaac grabbed his guitar. They heard Eli banging on his drums. Isaac had been inside the house several times, and he knew that Eli's drums were in Hunter's living room. He followed Joanna to the front door and she rapped on the window so they could hear her.

Hunter opened the door. At six-four, he was a foot taller than Joanna and about six inches taller than Isaac. He wasn't wearing a shirt, and his heavily-muscled body was covered with tattoos—the largest of which was a swastika on his chest. He also had swastikas tattooed on both sides of his head. He took a drink of beer from the bottle he was holding. "Come on in."

Isaac followed Joanna into the living room.

They jammed. Afterward, all of them were happy that Isaac was now a member of the band. It was as if it was meant to be.

Later, shortly before midnight, Joanna told Isaac, "Come on. I'll take you home. I have to get my father's car back soon."

"No," Hunter said. "I'll take Isaac home later. Isaac's going out with me and Eli tonight. Tonight, Isaac becomes a *true* member of Animosity."

"Okay," Joanna said. "I'll see you guys tomorrow."

Hunter went to the kitchen and grabbed three beers. Then he came back into the living room. Isaac sat on the loveseat. Hunter handed him a beer. Then he handed Eli a beer and sat down beside him on the couch. He opened his beer and took a drink. "You ever killed anyone, Isaac?" Hunter said.

Isaac took a drink. Then he shook his head. "Nope. Can't say I have."

"You heard what happened to Sebastian, right?"

Isaac nodded. "Yeah, he was killed in a drive-by shooting."

"That's right," Hunter said. "Two piece-of-shit Mexicans annihilated him. Shot him about thirty times. Only good part about the whole thing is that Eli and I know who they are, and where the motherfuckers live. We *were* going to go over there and kill them both tonight. And we're still going over there, but you're coming with us. And since you're the one replacing Sebastian in the band, you're going to be the one to kill the motherfuckers."

Hunter put on a pair of leather gloves. Then he retrieved a semiautomatic pistol from beneath the sofa and placed it on the coffee table. "The gun's untraceable," he said. "Avenge Sebastian's death and you'll take his place as a true member of Animosity."

Isaac turned his beer up and finished it quickly. Then he set the empty bottle next to the gun on the coffee table and stood up. "Not happening. But thank you for the beer."

"You don't want to be a member of the band?"

Isaac shook his head. "Not enough to kill two people I don't even know."

Eli said, "Joanna's not gonna be happy to hear that."

Isaac shrugged. "That's too bad."

"Joanna likes you," Hunter said. "Have you fucked her yet?"

Isaac grabbed his guitar and started heading toward the door. It wasn't too far of a walk back to his mother's house. "No. We're taking it slow."

"You shouldn't have any problems getting it in," Hunter said. "I definitely stretched her out real good for you."

Eli laughed, and then Hunter started laughing, too.

Isaac left. They were still laughing when he closed the door behind him.

CHAPTER 8

The foyer was empty, and when Aubrey followed Samantha into the Rosira's lobby, they saw an old man mopping the floor.

"Hello, Oliver," Samantha said.

He looked up from the floor and regarded them both, frowning. "Hello, Samantha. Who's your friend?"

"This is Aubrey."

He nodded. "It's nice to meet you, Aubrey."

"Likewise," Aubrey said.

Oliver cast his gaze to the sidewalk beyond the lobby windows. "Terrible what happened out there. She fell from the sixteenth floor."

"Damn," Samantha said. "Only two floors beneath me."

"Yes. Did you know her?"

"No, I did not."

Oliver shook his head. "She had a beautiful daughter."

"Had?" Samantha said. "Is her daughter dead, too?"

"Oh, no. Sydney is still alive. Eight years old, I think. The husband is still alive, too. Not a very nice man, I can tell you that much. You'd be well advised to steer clear of that man."

"We'll keep that in mind," Samantha said.

Then she and Aubrey rode the elevator up to the penthouse.

"Nice place," Aubrey said, as soon as they stepped inside.

Samantha shrugged. "Thanks. It's my mother's, actually. She lives in Jersey. She doesn't cross the bridge very often. How do you take your vodka?"

"Straight's fine with me," Aubrey said. "Or mixed. Doesn't matter."

The living room featured a minibar with an under-the-counter refrigerator. From the refrigerator, Samantha retrieved a bottle of soda and held it up. "I mix mine with this. Is that okay?"

"Perfect."

Samantha mixed two drinks, and then handed one to Aubrey. "Wanna go sit on the roof?"

"Can you give me a tour first? Where is your room?"

Samantha led her down the hallway into her room. Aubrey stepped in behind her and wrapped her arms around Samantha, kissing her neck.

"Maybe the roof can wait," Samantha said.

They made love, and Aubrey found the sex delectable. *And wet,* she thought. afterward. *The sex had been incredibly wet.* Lying on the bed, she imagined wet lace settling on their flesh like snowflakes but softer, more delicate.

"We need more drinks," Aubrey said.

They got up, got dressed, and went back into the living room, where Samantha mixed them each another drink. Then Aubrey followed her outside through a glass terrace door onto the rooftop.

Night had fallen on the city. The lights of skyscrapers were aglow. Central Park was visible only a few buildings away.

"You have a much nicer view," Aubrey said, after each sat down on a patio chair near the rooftop's side.

Samantha sipped her drink. "I like it out here, especially at night. With the light pollution, there's almost never any stars to plague me with their mysteries."

"Maybe that's why that woman died today," Aubrey said. "Maybe she ran out of stars to wish upon. So your mom lives in Jersey?"

"Yes. Fort Lee."

"How old are you?"

"Twenty-two."

"I'm twenty-three," Aubrey said. "Are you a student?"

"No, not anymore. As a matter of fact, I just graduated."

"From art school?"

"Yes. Now, I'm actually working."

"Doing what?"

"All kinds of stuff," Samantha said. "But graphic design, mostly. And digital advertisement. I'm also trying to get into acting."

Aubrey sipped her drink. "That's awesome. My brother's an actor in Los Angeles."

"Oh yeah?"

"Yes. Mitchell. He's two years older than me."

"Is there anything I would have seen him in?"

Aubrey shook her head. "I doubt it. No movies yet. He was in two plays that no one's ever heard of, and he's done some work in TV and radio, but so far, that's about it."

"Maybe he'll get his big break soon," Samantha said.

Aubrey nodded. "Maybe. I hope so."

Samantha sipped her drink. "So what about you? You must do more than pose nude for sketch artists."

Aubrey cracked a smile. "I've done some acting in my time—if we're counting porn. And some modeling, of course. But my passion is dancing."

"Dancing?"

"Yes. As a child, I took ballet lessons at Miss Llewellyn's on the Upper West Side. According to rumor, Miss Llewellyn was a fortune teller, with gypsy blood running through her veins. After my first lesson, she told me I was a natural, that I had a future in ballet, and I've been dancing ever since."

"So now you're a ballet dancer?"

Aubrey shook her head. "No. I grew up to be an exhibitionist, so now I'm dancing at Gino's Cabaret."

"Gino's? The strip club? Here on 72nd?"

"Yes."

"I'll have to go see you sometime. You can give me a table dance."

"Oh, I'll give you more than that," she said as she straddled Samantha's lap.

Samantha smiled. "Good to know. Are you ready for another round?"

"Of drinks?"

"Of me."

"I am," Aubrey said.

She was drenched before they could finish their drinks and return to the bedroom.

CHAPTER 9

D ays of poetry; nights of music and invention.

Christina hadn't been home in six days. Kenzie kept an acoustic guitar in the trunk of her car, and she had started teaching Christina how to play. At night, they took turns playing it on the Jersey Shore while campfires burned as they passed bottles of rum back and forth.

Tonight found them on the shore at Point Pleasant Beach, about an hour south of Jersey City.

"You have a good ear for music," Kenzie told her. "And you're an excellent singer, too."

Christina smiled.

"Soon," Kenzie added, "you'll be playing guitar as good as I do."

"I seriously doubt that," Christina said. "You're a wizard with that guitar. I don't know why you're thinking about going to music school. You don't need it. The school should hire you as a teacher."

Kenzie shrugged. "I may not even go. It was just a thought. You know, to major in piano, or something. I don't know."

Christina took a drink. "How do you have all this money, anyway?"

Kenzie did not respond; instead, she just looked at her.

Christina lit a cigarette. "Listen, I don't mean to pry, but you never talk about yourself. Are your parents rich, or something?"

"My mother is, but it's not her money I'm spending. And you're not the only one with a dead parent, by the way."

"Your father's dead?"

"Yes. He died ten years ago, when I was eight."

"Oh," Christina said. "I'm sorry. I didn't know." She held Kenzie's face and kissed her gently.

"Of course you didn't. And there's no need to apologize. Anyway, he left me some money when he died, but I didn't get it until recently, when I turned eighteen. Now I'm just thinking that maybe he would have wanted me to go to school with some of the money, or something. I don't know."

Christina shrugged. "You'll figure it out."

"Eventually. Let me hit that rum."

Christina handed her the bottle. Kenzie took a drink and gave the bottle back.

"We should just start a rock band," Christina said.

"You think so?"

"Yes. I can be the singer. I mean, you have all those guitar riffs, and I have notebooks full of poetry we could use for song lyrics."

"You do?"

"Yes."

"I didn't know you wrote poetry."

Christina took a drink.

"Where are your notebooks?" Kenzie said. "At your dad's house?"

"Yes."

"Can we go get them?"

"I don't know." Christina checked her phone. "It's really not that late. I mean, if Dad's asleep, I can just run in there and get them. But he might still be awake."

"It's an hour drive back to Jersey City," Kenzie said. "He might be asleep by the time we get there."

Christina nodded. "Maybe. I guess it's worth a shot."

Chapter 10

I saac found his mother in the kitchen before he went to work. Her wheelchair was backed into a space between the oven and the refrigerator. She held a cigarette in one hand and an ink pen in the other. A book of crossword puzzles lay open across her lap.

He gave her a kiss. "Goodbye, Mother. I love you."

"I love you, too. I hope you have a good day at work."

"Thanks. I'll bring you something to eat when I come home."

Pasquale's was a little Italian restaurant half a block from his mother's house. The kitchen was cramped even with only three employees on first shift: Isaac, who washed dishes, prepped food, and swept the floor; and Pedro and Rafael, the two Mexican line cooks.

For the past few minutes, Isaac had been listening to Pedro and Rafael talk about two of their friends getting murdered the night before. Their friends—two Mexican brothers named Fernando and Miguel—had been shot to death during a home invasion.

"A few people," Pedro said, "saw two white dudes fleeing the scene. Couple of skinhead motherfuckers. One of them had swastikas tattooed on his head."

"That's fucked up," Rafael said. "Fernando and Miguel were some good dudes, man. I'm going to miss them."

"And speaking of skinheads," Pedro said. "What's up with that haircut, Isaac? You look like a fucking Nazi, bro."

"I'm not your bro," Isaac said. "And you look like the reason my paychecks are so low. Fucking government takes half my money to pay for your goddamn kids."

"What did you just say to me?"

Isaac spun around from the dish tank and faced Pedro. "You heard me, motherfucker. Somebody has to take care of all those kids you never see."

Pedro got right up in Isaac's face. "I should beat your fucking ass, you racist piece of shit."

"Touch me and you're a dead man," Isaac said.

Pedro slapped him across the face.

Isaac saw several knives within arm's reach, but at that moment Pasquale—the owner—walked into the kitchen.

"What the fuck's going on back here?" Pasquale said.

"Nothing," the three of them replied simultaneously.

Pasquale eyed all three of them suspiciously. Then he told Isaac. "You have a phone call."

Isaac followed Pasquale to his office. The telephone looked about as old as Pasquale himself.

"Line two," Pasquale said. Then he left the office to give Isaac some privacy.

Isaac lifted the receiver and pressed LINE 2. "Hello?"

"Hi, Isaac," Joanna said. "I hope I didn't get you in trouble by calling you at work."

"Nah. It's cool."

"I messaged you several times, but you never messaged me back."

"Sorry. I've been too busy working to check my phone."

"That's what I figured. Anyway, why didn't you go with Hunter and Eli last night?"

"I think you know why."

"But I thought you wanted to be with me."

"I do want to be with you."

"Well, last night would have been a perfect initiation into Animosity."

"Do I have to be in the band to be with you?"

"Animosity is more than just a band, Isaac. It's a way of life. And I'm a package deal."

"I'm sorry. Are you mad at me?"

"No. Can I stop by your mom's house later and talk to you?"

"Sure," Isaac said. "But I'm working late today, so I won't be home until after seven o'clock."

"Okay," Joanna said. "I'll see you later."

Isaac's mother was eating the lasagna he brought home from Pasquale's when the doorbell chimed just before eight o'clock.

"That's Joanna," Isaac said. "I'll let her in."

"Girls," his mother said, "are nothing but trouble."

Isaac got up and left the kitchen. He crossed the living room and opened the front door.

Joanna followed him into his bedroom and sat down on the edge of his bed. Isaac sat down beside her.

She looked into his eyes. "Do you know why I came here tonight?"

"You said you wanted to talk to me."

Isaac nearly gasped when Joanna shot forward to kiss him deeply. It was the first time they had kissed. "I do," she said. "But I want us to have sex first. It's time to take our relationship to another level."

Isaac watched her take her clothes off. Her beautiful body was covered in tattoo ink, mostly images of snakes and swastikas that never saw the sun.

Isaac turned off the bedside lamp and took his clothes off as

Joanna took charge. The sex only lasted three minutes with Isaac pausing several times to delay the inevitable. His face felt red in the darkness as they lay naked atop his sheets.

"Was that your first time?" Joanna said.

"No. But I haven't been with very many girls. What about you?"

She lit a cigarette. "I've been with a lot of guys. A lot of girls. Do you have an ashtray?"

Isaac turned the lamp back on and found her an ashtray. Then he got up and got dressed. "Be right back."

He left the room. He passed his mother's bedroom in the hallway. Her door was closed, which meant that she was in there.

He went to the kitchen and looked in the cupboard, where they kept the liquor. His mother knew that he drank, and she was okay with it, especially considering the fact that he paid for everything now. There was a bottle of tequila, a bottle of vodka, and a bottle of whiskey. He grabbed the whiskey and took it into his bedroom.

Joanna was dressed again and sitting on the edge of the bed. "I want some of that," she said.

Isaac took a drink and handed her the whiskey. Then he turned on the radio at low volume for background noise and sat down beside her. They took turns drinking from the bottle.

"I just came from Hunter's," Joanna said, "and he says you're still going to have to kill someone who isn't white if you want to be in Animosity."

"I'm not going to kill some random motherfucker just to—"

"So you don't want to be with me?"

"You didn't let me finish."

"Sorry."

"That's okay. Anyway, I'm not going to kill some random motherfucker just to be in a rock band. However, a stupid prick I work with slapped me earlier today, and now I'm going to kill him."

"Is he white?"

"No. Mexican."

"Awesome!" Joanna said. "If you kill a Mexican, you can be in Animosity!"

"Fine," Isaac said. "Do you have a gun?"
"No, but I can get one. Come on. Let's go talk to Hunter."

CHAPTER 11

Every night at nine o'clock, in Los Angeles, Mitchell walked through a back alley behind the building in which he lived, past a smelly ravine and an old church that was now used as a flophouse for prostitutes, down past rows of small stores that were mostly barbershops and liquor stores and pharmacies, and found a seat on a stool at the bar in a little nightclub called The Never Better Lounge.

Mitchell was in love with the bartender. Her name was Marla. She was about his age, in her mid-twenties, and—like Mitchell—she had never been married. Also like him, Marla didn't have any kids. He knew her from both the lounge and from around the neighborhood, as she lived not far from his building in an apartment with her brother and her brother's wife.

Mitchell knew that he was a good-looking man. Women liked him, but he rarely liked them back. He didn't have time for women. He spent most of his time either looking in a mirror and practicing his lines, or driving from one audition to the next.

He had plenty of money in the bank. He didn't have to work for a living, but he knew he would one day be an actor. When women asked him what he did for a living, he told them he *was* an actor.

The only women he saw with regularity, however, were the hookers in the brothels that he frequented. Until recently, the prostitutes had been enough to please him. But then he had fallen in love with Marla, and now he wanted her.

According to his oracle bones (the skeleton of a turtle that had been telling him the future since Mitchell was a child), Marla would be his lover soon.

"She isn't here tonight," the man tending bar told Mitchell. "She called in sick."

He appeared to be about forty and Mitchell had never seen the man before. "Marla isn't here?"

The man rolled his eyes. "I just told you that. What can I get you?"

"A gin martini." Mitchell knew his night was now ruined by Marla's absence, so he figured he might as well get drunk.

Several drinks later, he found himself sitting with a woman at a table in a corner of the lounge. She appeared to be at least ten years his senior. Despite her age, he thought she was still somewhat attractive. He was pretty sure she had told him her name at some point, but he couldn't remember it.

"It's rare that I ever get out of the house these days," the woman said, "with my mother being so sick. Do you know what I mean?" She took a drink of whatever it was she was drinking. Her cocktail glass had a little umbrella in it.

Mitchell sipped his martini. "You still live with your mother?"

"I moved back in with her to take care of her. Early-onset Alzheimer's disease." The woman finished her drink. "Speaking of which: I'd better get back and check on her." She stood up. "You should come with me."

He took another drink. "Seriously?"

"Sure. She's probably just sleeping, anyway. All she ever does anymore is sleep. We can listen to music."

"Listen to music?"

"Yes. You like music, don't you?"

He shrugged.

"And drink," the woman said. "I have a bottle of scotch. Do you like scotch?"

Mitchell shrugged again. "I guess scotch is okay."

"Good. You can give me a lift. I don't like walking home alone, anyway."

"I'm on foot," Mitchell said. "I only live a couple of blocks away."

The woman smiled. "Then come on. You can walk me home. My mother's house is just down the street."

Mitchell finished his drink and walked the woman home.

The ranch-style brick house was painted white with hunter-green shutters. It stood behind a white picket fence. The front lawn featured a sycamore tree. Lights were on inside throughout the house. The woman unlocked the front door with a key, and Mitchell followed her inside.

She led him into the kitchen. "Have a seat."

Mitchell sat down at the kitchen table.

She pulled a bottle of scotch from the cupboard and then sat down across from him. "Do you want a glass? I normally just drink from the bottle."

He shook his head. "I don't need a glass."

They each took two drinks from the bottle. Then she said, "How old are you, anyway?"

"Twenty-five. You?"

She ran fingers through her hair. "Take a guess."

In the bright light of the kitchen, she looked a little older than she had looked in The Never Better Lounge. He figured she was probably about fifty. "Thirty-eight," he said.

She smiled. "Forty-six. I'm old enough to be your mother. And speaking of mothers: I'd better go check on mine. Be right back."

She left the kitchen and returned moments later. "She's sound asleep. You wanna go listen to music in my room?"

"Sure."

The woman grabbed the bottle, and Mitchell followed her into a bedroom at the end of a hallway.

"My mother's room is on the other side of the house," the

woman said, "so we don't have to worry about waking her up. Have a seat."

Mitchell sat down on the edge of her bed. The woman took a drink and handed him the bottle. Then she turned on some jazz music and sat down beside him. "Do you have any family?" she said.

Mitchell shook his head. "Not in L.A. My mother's dead, and my father's on the east coast."

"Any brothers or sisters?"

"A sister. Aubrey. She lives in New York City."

"Any kids?"

Mitchell took a drink. "No. You?"

"No. There's only my mother. My father died a few years back. His life insurance paid off the mortgage. I'll inherit the house when she dies."

"It's a beautiful house."

"Yes. My father was an accountant. My mother was an interior designer before she got Alzheimer's disease."

Mitchell took a drink and handed her the bottle. "So you don't have any children?"

"No. I was unable to have children. That was why my husband left me, because he wanted kids, and I couldn't give him any." The woman took a drink. "I don't blame him, though. I don't blame him one bit for leaving me."

"I'm sorry to hear that."

She ran fingers through her hair. "It is what it is. I'm very lonely, though. I've been very lonely and troubled for quite some time."

She continued talking, but Mitchell tuned her out and thought about Marla. He hoped she was okay. He was worried about her. He hoped she would be well enough to be back behind the bar tomorrow night. He decided to tell Marla he was in love with her the next time he saw her.

The woman handed him the bottle. He took a drink.

"Sometimes," she said, "when I'm drunk and very depressed, I have fantasies about killing my mother to end her misery, and then killing myself to end my own."

"Oh yeah?"

"Yes. But I'll never do it, of course. They're just bad thoughts, is all. The bad thoughts never last long. Nothing lasts forever but broken lasts a very long time."

Mitchell set the bottle on the floor. Then he retrieved a pair of blue disposable gloves from his jacket's interior pocket and put them on.

"Are you going to kill me?" the woman said.

Mitchell shook his head. "Of course not."

"Then why the gloves?"

"Other than prostitutes, I haven't had sex with a woman in a while."

"Seriously? A man as good-looking as you?"

"Yes. I haven't had time for women. I've been too busy with my work."

"What do you do?"

"I'm an actor."

"Are you rich and famous yet?"

"Rich? Yes, I guess you could say that. But I'm not famous yet. I will be one day, though. One of these days I'm going to be very famous."

"And you always wear gloves when you fuck the hookers?"

"Yes. Condoms too, of course. But I also like the gloves. I don't like the feeling of my fingers touching them."

"But I'm not a prostitute."

Mitchell shrugged. "I guess it's just a habit, at this point."

The woman laughed. "I like you. I really do. But I don't even feel like having sex. I just want to be held. Will you hold me? You can leave the gloves on."

"Sure," Mitchell said.

They stretched out next to each other on the bed. She lay with her back against his chest, and he held her with the gloves on.

"This is nice," she told him. "All I want is a body to hold, and a soul to love forever."

"Yes," Mitchell said, but he wasn't thinking about the woman in his arms. He was thinking about Marla.

"If you think about it," the woman said, "staying alive is basically just keeping all the water inside you from leaking back into the ground."

She said more, but Mitchell wasn't listening. He couldn't stop thinking about Marla. He was looking forward to seeing her again and telling her that he loved her, but he was also nervous about professing his love for her. The last thing he wanted to do was come on too strong and scare her away. But Marla knew who he was. She knew his name. It was not like they were total strangers. And his oracle bones had told him that she would be his lover soon, so there was probably no reason for him to be nervous in the first place.

At some point, the woman had started snoring, but she woke up when Mitchell let go of her. He rose from the bed and took a drink of scotch while she looked up at him. Then he said, "Will you sell me the rest of this bottle? I have liquor at home, of course, but this scotch is hitting the spot."

"You can just have it."

Mitchell nodded. "And for that, your generosity will be rewarded." He retrieved his wallet from his back pocket. His wallet contained three things only: his driver's license, his bank card, and a whole lot of hundred-dollar bills. He pulled the cash out, counted off ten of the bills, and placed them on her nightstand. "There's a thousand dollars," he said. "Have a nice night."

The woman's eyes were already closed, but she managed a smile. "Thank you," she said. "You're very sweet." Then she started snoring again.

Mitchell left.

He walked home.

He drank some more of the scotch and thought about Marla. He knew he wouldn't be going to sleep anytime soon, so he decided to go for a drive.

He wasn't worried about getting a DUI. If a cop pulled him over, he had plenty of bribe money in his wallet. That was one of the reasons he always carried so much cash around. If not for cops and drug dealers, he probably wouldn't even keep cash in his wallet.

Although he did enjoy putting a lot of money in Marla's tip jar every night. And it had felt pretty good being able to give that woman a thousand dollars in cash for the rest of the scotch earlier. He liked doing nice things for good people whenever he could.

Mitchell drove around the city with a smile on his face. He often thought there was no hope for modern society, that it would descend into a cesspool of hatred and greed, but then he encountered someone like that kind woman who was taking care of her sick mother at the exclusion of her own happiness, and he found it possible to believe in the decency of human beings again.

His good mood didn't last, however. As he drove deeper into the city, a profound sadness settled in, and his perception of the encounter with the woman who was taking care of her sick mother started to darken. He remembered what she had said about her fantasy, and how she often thought about killing her mother and then killing herself. Frowning, Mitchell shook his head. She was a nice lady, and she didn't deserve to be forced to harbor such morbid fantasies. She deserved better.

He decided that it was time to do something nice for a good person—to perform an act of kindness and of mercy.

Mitchell always kept a gun in his center console, but he went home and got another one that had a silencer attached to its barrel. Then he drove back to the house that the woman shared with her sick mother.

He had not locked the door when he left, and it was still unlocked when he returned. As soon as he stepped into the living room, he heard someone moving around and whistling tunelessly in the kitchen. He followed the noise and found an old white-haired woman—undoubtedly the kind woman's sick mother—standing at the kitchen sink with her back to him. He announced himself by saying, "Hello there, dear lady."

She stopped whistling and turned off the running water. Then she turned around and faced him. She did not look at all surprised to see him.

Mitchell raised the gun and shot her between the eyes, blowing her brains out the back of her head. The silencer reduced the gunfire to only a mild report. She collapsed to the floor and lay motionless on her side. Her eyes were open. Wearing a fresh pair of disposable gloves, Mitchell closed them.

The kind woman was still passed out in her bedroom.

Mitchell put a bullet through her brain, giving her a graceful escape by killing her instantly. Her death had been as quick and as painless as the death of her mother. "I hope you have some peace now," he said, "whatever the hell your name was."

Before he left, Mitchell took the thousand dollars from her nightstand and put it back in his wallet. If Marla felt well enough to work tomorrow night, he would put it in her tip jar.

Chapter 12

I n Gino's Cabaret, Aubrey stood in a darkened area behind the stage, awaiting her cue.

Moments later, the DJ announced: "And now, ladies and gentlemen, please welcome to the stage, in her last set of the night, the green-eyed Mistress of Fire—Auburn of the Inferno!"

The first notes of her music came pounding out of the speakers, a rock song cranked so loud the lyrics were distorted, but she figured it didn't matter because probably no one else in the club had ever heard the music she listened to, anyway. She pulled back the velvet curtain, approached the pole at center stage, and the six or seven men seated near the front whistled and cheered. The men who came here seemed unable to get enough of her body, and often treated her like a goddess.

She enjoyed stripping not only because she was an exhibitionist, but also because it allowed her to set her own schedule and pay her bills without tapping into the reserves—money she had been stockpiling ever since the murder of her mother—that Aubrey kept stashed away in a savings account.

Her last set ended fifteen minutes later, and Aubrey disappeared behind the curtain.

The next dancer, a skinny girl with black hair who called herself

Ambrosia, brushed past her in the backstage area. "How are they?"

Aubrey shrugged. "Not bad."

"Cool," Ambrosia said, then went onstage as another song began.

Aubrey walked down a narrow corridor to the dressing room, where she changed into her street clothes, before stopping by Gino's office to tip out.

Then she left.

Outside, the night was warm. The lights of Manhattan were aglow.

She checked her phone to see what time it was (12:07 a.m.) and saw an unread message from Samantha: *You get off at midnight, right? I'm getting ready to open a bottle of vodka. Wanna help me finish it?*

Leaving now, Aubrey wrote back. *Need to stop by my apartment. Meet me in the lobby.*

She headed east on 72nd Street, arriving at the Rosira soon thereafter, still high on the hash she had smoked with Gino before her final set. Approaching the main entrance, she admired the building's brick-and-limestone facade, and the details in the scrollwork on the columns beneath the front awning.

There was no one in the foyer. Then Samantha greeted her in the lobby with a kiss.

"Hi," Samantha said. "Did you miss me?"

"Of course. Do you feel like getting high?"

"I do."

Past a bank of mirrors in the lobby was the stairwell door, and they took the stairs up to Aubrey's apartment on the second floor, where she changed shoes and grabbed a small bag of cocaine from her bedroom. Then they rode the elevator up to Samantha's penthouse on the eighteenth floor.

Fifteen minutes later found them doing shots of vodka on patio chairs on the rooftop, pleasantly high.

"It's a beautiful night," Samantha said.

Clouds drifted past the moon, and all of Manhattan suddenly

brightened, as if a veil over the city had been lifted.

"And the moon's full, too," Aubrey said. "So there will be more murders, rapes, and suicides. All sorts of madness."

"Do you believe that's true?"

"It is true. The oceans—dragged by the moon's gravity—rise and fall about four feet twice a day, and humans are about seventy percent water, so it pulls us, too. According to police statistics, there's way more activity in emergency rooms on nights when the moon is full, and of course most nurses will tell you that a lot more babies are born when the moon's full, too."

"I do remember reading," Samantha said, "a recent study about how the water in our brains was affected by the moon just like the tides of the sea, which makes sense, when you think about it, since the majority of the brain is made up of water."

"Yes," Aubrey said. "Maybe that vodka will help."

Samantha handed her the bottle. Aubrey took a drink and gave the bottle back.

Then they both heard what sounded like a woman's scream from somewhere down below, near Central Park.

"Perhaps the madness," Aubrey said, "has already begun."

Samantha took a drink. "Did you know that Central Park used to contain slaughterhouses?"

"Yes, I did know that. And back in the day, West 39th Street was nicknamed Abattoir Row."

"Is that right?"

"Yes. It was the center of Manhattan's slaughterhouse district, where cattle was delivered by boats and trains before being turned into beef for New York dinner plates. There was even a cow bridge, built above the street, for the cattle to march to the slaughterhouses without disrupting traffic."

"That's fascinating."

Aubrey nodded. "Yes. Even more fascinating was the cow tunnel."

"Cow tunnel?"

"Yes. Cattle brought into Manhattan on Hudson River barges were herded through a tunnel under 12th Avenue to the abattoirs on West 39th Street."

"Wow," Samantha said. "Same planet, different world."

Aubrey shrugged. "Yeah, pretty much. Let me hit that vodka."

Samantha handed her the bottle. Aubrey took a drink and gave the bottle back.

"It really wasn't that long ago, in the scheme of things," Samantha said.

"Nope. Not even two hundred years."

"Things change so fast."

Aubrey nodded. "Yes. The only things that don't change are the old people complaining about how things are always changing."

Samantha took a drink. "I'm ready for another line."

The coke was on a glass table between their patio chairs.

"Me too," Aubrey said. "Then I'll be ready for you."

CHAPTER 13

"Some nights," Christina said, in Kenzie's car on the passenger's side, "only songs by dead musicians will suffice."

They were parked up the street from her father's house, waiting for him to turn out the lights. She hoped to sneak in and grab her notebooks without a confrontation.

They had opened another bottle of rum and were chain-smoking cigarettes, listening to music on Christina's phone because the stereo in Kenzie's car only had a radio. According to Kenzie, the car was over fifty years old and had once belonged to her grandfather.

Christina flipped her cigarette out the window. "My mother once told me that burdens, eventually, make life easier. That they're heavy at first, but over time, they become lighter. And then one day, the burden is no longer even a burden, but simply one of the things that made you strong."

"Sounds like your mother was a strong woman."

"She was," Christina said. "I've decided to forgo my senior year."

"Seriously?"

"Yes. When summer's over, I'm not going back to school."

"Your father," Kenzie said. "He hurts you a lot, doesn't he?"

Christina nodded. "I have to get away from here."

Kenzie took a drink. "We can leave right now, if you want to."

Christina shook her head. "No. Not tonight. I have to pack some clothes and grab my notebooks. Plus, I'll need a few hours of sleep. Can we leave tomorrow?"

"Sure, baby. Want me to wait out here? While you go in and get your things?"

"No. If Dad's still awake, there will probably be an argument, and I may as well get it over with. Just go on back to the hotel without me, and I'll text you in the morning."

"Okay, baby. I love you."

"I love you too."

They kissed. Christina watched Kenzie drive away before she entered the house.

The living-room light was on. Christina's father sat on the sofa. He took a drink of whiskey, then set the bottle on the coffee table.

"Well, well, well," he said. "Look who decided to finally come home."

Christina said nothing and headed toward her bedroom.

"Where the hell you been, anyway?"

"I've been out."

"Out? For six goddamn days?"

"Yes."

"Who the hell you been out with? Have you found yourself a boyfriend?"

Christina turned to face him. "No. A girlfriend. Her name is Kenzie."

"A girlfriend?" Her father took a drink. Then he set the bottle back down and stood up. "You're a fucking lesbian whore. And if I ever see this Kenzie slut, maybe I'll kill her ass, like I killed your mother."

Christina crossed her arms. "What are you talking about?"

"Your mother's car crash. It was no accident. I poked a tiny hole in her brake line, causing a slow leak." He smiled. "I didn't know when she would die, but I was hoping you would be in the car, too, you little whore."

Christina put a hand on a hip and cocked her head. "You know,

I've often wondered if that's what really happened. Thanks for telling me. It's good to know."

She went into her room. She closed the door behind her and locked it.

Moments later, her father tried the knob. Then tried it again. After a brief silence, his foot crashed the door open, slamming it against the wall. "So, you like to lick pussy now, huh? Fucking cunt."

He wrapped a meaty hand around her throat and gave her a shove. The backs of her legs hit the bed and she fell back onto the mattress.

Then her father was on top of her. "Goddamn lesbian whore. You wanna be a whore? I'll treat you like a fucking whore."

"Get off me!"

"Daddy's little whore," he said, leering. She could smell the whiskey on his breath, and she could see drops of it glistening in the hair on his chin and neck. "You've been a bad girl, Christina."

She squeezed her legs together, trying to keep his pawing hands from invading her.

"No! Please!" She shook her head, and tears spilled down her face.

"Get off her, old man, or you're going to be a *dead* old man."

Kenzie's voice. Christina saw Kenzie standing at the foot of the bed. She had not heard the car pull up outside. Nor had she heard Kenzie enter the house or her bedroom. But there she was, nevertheless, aiming a pistol at her father's back.

Her father rose from the bed and turned around. "You must be Kenzie. Are you the dyke who's going to take my daughter away from me?"

"Yes," Kenzie said. "Christina is coming with me."

He shrugged. "So be it."

Christina had by then sat up on the bed.

Her father turned to look at her. "I really do wish you had been in the car when your mother died."

He turned to Kenzie and tried to put a hand on her shoulder, but she rammed the butt of the gun into his forehead, making him bleed.

"She's all yours now," he said, staggering out of the room.

"I didn't even know you had a gun," Christina said.

Kenzie shrugged. "There's a lot about me you don't know."

Christina rose up off the bed. "Fuck leaving tomorrow. Let's go right now."

"Are you okay?" Kenzie said. "You look as if you've just seen a ghost."

Christina ran fingers through her hair. "My mother's death. It was no accident."

"Your father killed her?"

"Yes. Sabotaged her brake line. He just confessed it to me."

And then Christina's father appeared in the bedroom doorway. She saw with horror that he held what was probably his favorite handgun: a Ruger Blackhawk .44 Magnum revolver. She knew he always kept the gun loaded with hollow-point bullets.

He stepped into the room and aimed the gun at Kenzie's chest. "I changed my mind, bitch. Christina's not going anywhere." Then he pulled the trigger.

Christina screamed and closed her eyes as the gunfire's report filled the bedroom. She heard her father squeeze the trigger five more times as he unloaded the .44 on her girlfriend.

Then she heard him say: "What the fuck?"

Christina opened her eyes.

Kenzie stood maybe two feet in front of her father, unscathed. There were six holes in the wall directly behind her, as if the bullets had either swerved around her, or passed right through her body.

"What are you?" her father asked Kenzie. "A fucking ghost?"

"No," Kenzie said. "It wasn't my time to go, old man."

"Fuck it," her father said. "I must be drunk. I'm going to bed." Then he slowly staggered out of the room again.

Kenzie asked Christina, "Are you ready?"

"Yes."

She packed some clothes and grabbed her poetry notebooks, but she was completely out of words.

Chapter 14

E li was at Hunter's house when they got there. The two of
them sat on the sofa, drinking beer, as though they had
never left. Isaac had brought the whiskey with him, so he was
drinking on that, but Joanna had stopped drinking because she
was driving.

"We need a gun," Joanna said. "Isaac is going to kill a Mexican."

Hunter looked at Isaac. "Is that right?"

Isaac took a drink and didn't say anything.

"Yes," Joanna said. "So now he can be in Animosity."

Hunter returned his gaze to Joanna. "I see you two lovebirds
are holding hands. Does that mean you've consummated the
relationship?"

"Yes," Joanna said. She looked at Isaac, smiled, and squeezed
his hand. "Isaac and I are officially now an item."

"How sweet." Hunter put on a pair of gloves. "I'll go get you
a gun. Be right back." He got up and left the room. He returned
moments later with a handgun and another pair of gloves. "Here,"
he said, handing Isaac the gloves. "Put these on first.'

Isaac did.

Then Hunter handed him the gun. "Three-eighty," Hunter said.
"It's loaded, but the safety is on. It's untraceable, so just throw it
away when you're finished."

Isaac shoved the gun into the waistband of his jeans at the small of his back.

Joanna looked at Isaac. "Are you ready?"

He nodded.

"Go wait for him in the car, Joanna," Hunter said. "I want to have a few words with him in private."

"Okay," Joanna said. Then she went outside. Moments later, they heard her get in the car and close the door.

"How does my dick taste, Isaac?" Hunter said.

Eli laughed, and then Hunter started laughing, too.

Isaac left. They were still laughing when he closed the door behind him.

Joanna drove. Isaac rode on the passenger's side. He couldn't get Hunter's words (*How does my dick taste, Isaac?*) or the sound of his and Eli's laughter to stop ringing in his mind. His anger only increased after every drink of whiskey.

Joanna stopped at a red light. They were still only a few blocks from Hunter's house. She turned the stereo down, lit a cigarette, and cracked her window. "I don't know why you're mad. You knew we used to date, and that we still fucked occasionally. It's no big deal." The light turned green. She took her foot off the brake pedal and stepped on the accelerator. "Besides, I won't be fucking him now that you and I—"

BAM!

Someone driving an SUV ran the red light at the intersection and crashed into the driver's side of Joanna's car. The impact carried her body to Isaac instantly and knocked the wind out of him. It took him about a minute to catch his breath. Unless he was in shock, he didn't feel any broken bones. The whiskey was still between his legs and he was surprised that the bottle hadn't broken.

Joanna wasn't moving at all. Wasn't breathing. He was sure she was dead. He shoved her lifeless body off of him and got out of the car.

He hadn't even been injured. He had heard stories about drunk people surviving catastrophic car crashes because the booze kept their bodies loose. Maybe that was it. He took a drink of whiskey and walked over to the mangled SUV.

The man driving and the woman on the passenger's side looked just as dead as Joanna. He could see where their heads spidered the windshield.

A dog lay on the road beside the SUV with its guts hanging out. Its hind legs were broken. Isaac didn't know what kind of a dog it was, but it was pretty. The poor creature made pitiful noises and frantically licked its dangling entrails, but when it saw Isaac looking down at it, its tail started wagging. Isaac pulled the gun out and fired one bullet through the dog's head, killing it instantly. He put the gun back in his waistband.

Isaac sensed movement around him as people got out of their vehicles. They began shouting and milling around the scene. He thought that maybe the crash had been a sign from the universe that he was not supposed to kill Pedro tonight. Besides, Pedro lived all the way over on the other side of town, and he didn't feel like walking that far. He didn't even feel like killing Pedro anymore.

He turned around and walked back to Hunter's house. He hadn't locked the door when he left, and it was still unlocked when he got there. He withdrew the gun from his waistband. Then he opened the door and stepped into the living room.

Hunter and Eli still sat on the sofa, drinking beer. "That was fast," Hunter said. "Did Joanna drop you off?"

Isaac lifted the gun and shot Hunter in the head first. Before Eli could even gasp, Isaac shot him in the head as well, killing them both instantly. Then he put the gun down on the coffee table.

Walking, halfway to his mother's house, he took the gloves off and tossed them aside.

When he got home, his mother sat in her wheelchair in the kitchen, smoking a cigarette and looking at a crossword puzzle.

"You're home early," she said. "Where's your girlfriend?"

He took a drink of whiskey. "I don't have a girlfriend. Girls are nothing but trouble."

She looked up at him and smiled. "It's about time you listened to something I said."

"Goodnight, Mom. I love you."

"I love you too."

Isaac went into his room and closed the door.

The next day, Isaac smoked a joint before work and was fried by the time he got to Pasquale's. Pedro and Rafael were already there, chopping vegetables in the kitchen.

"Damn, Isaac," Rafael said. "Your eyes are red as fuck, dude."

"Oh shit," Isaac said. "I forgot to put some Visine in."

Isaac carried Visine with him everywhere he went. He took a bottle from his pocket, unscrewed the plastic cap, and placed the cap in his mouth between his lips like he always did. He leaned his head back, raised the bottle above his eyes—and hiccupped. When he hiccupped, he accidentally sucked the plastic cap down into his pharynx or his larynx or maybe even his trachea. All he knew for sure was that he was choking. He tried to dislodge the cap from wherever it was stuck, but it wasn't happening. He couldn't get any air in or out of his body whatsoever. Isaac found the idea of surviving last night's car crash only to choke to death on a plastic Visine bottle cap laughable, and he actually smiled. But he began beating his chest, nevertheless.

Pedro and Rafael looked over at him.

"Are you choking, dude?" Rafael said. "Man, you're turning fucking *blue*."

Isaac nodded and kept beating his chest.

"Oh shit," Pedro said. "He *is* fucking choking." He then ran over to Isaac, wrapped him in a bear hug from behind, and began performing the Heimlich maneuver.

After a first abdominal thrust, then a second, the bottle cap dislodged from wherever it had been stuck and flew out of Isaac's mouth across the room.

Pasquale walked into the kitchen. "What the fuck's going on back here?"

"Nothing," the three of them replied simultaneously.

Pasquale eyed all three of them suspiciously. Then he told Pedro, "You have a phone call."

Pedro followed Pasquale out of the kitchen.

Rafael resumed chopping vegetables.

Isaac shock his head at the absurdity of everything and began loading the dish tank.

Chapter 15

"Hi, Mitchell," Marla said, when he sat down at the bar. "Gin martini?"

The lounge had only opened about ten minutes ago. It was just past noon, and he didn't see anyone else inside.

Mitchell nodded. "Make it strong. And I'm glad you're back. I missed seeing you here last night."

She put a cocktail napkin on the bar. Then she mixed his drink and set it down atop the napkin.

Mitchell gave her a hundred-dollar bill. "Keep the change."

Marla didn't bother opening the cash register; she simply put the money in her pocket. "You're hitting the booze early today."

Mitchell sipped his drink. "Had a ten a.m. audition. Nothing else to do, now. So I figured I'd go ahead and start drinking."

"How'd the audition go?" She kept sniffling like she had a cold or something, but then he noticed the powder on her nose.

He shrugged. "Went well enough, I suppose. You have something on your nose."

She turned around and examined her face in the mirror that spanned the wall of bottles behind the bar. She wiped her nose with a cocktail napkin and threw the napkin in the trash.

Mitchell sipped his drink. "Are you feeling better?"

"What are you talking about?" She turned back around and

faced him.

"Someone told me you called off sick last night."

"I wasn't sick. I just didn't want to be here. I hate this fucking place."

"You do?"

"Yes."

"Then why do you work here?"

"Because of you, now. Mostly."

Mitchell suddenly began feeling warm and fuzzy inside. "I love you. I've been trying to work up the courage to tell you that I'm in love with you."

Marla rolled her eyes. "I'm serious. The only reason I haven't quit is because of the way you tip me like a madman every night. I hate my life, and I hate my brother and his wife. I'm trying to save enough money to move out of their apartment, but it isn't working. I'm thinking about robbing an armored truck."

"An armored truck?"

"Yes. Everyone always talks about robbing banks, but that's fucking stupid. You almost never get away with it and even if you do, you only get a few grand. Just whatever's in the teller drawers. Unless you rob the vault. But if you rob an armored truck, especially after they've already picked up all the money from all the vaults in the local banks, you're going to get a fortune. Probably have to kill the drivers, though. But who gives a fuck?"

Mitchell finished his drink. "The best time to do it would be on whatever day of the week the local banks are shipping money to the Federal Reserve."

"Exactly." Marla took Mitchell's empty glass and set it on the counter behind her. "Would you like to try a shot of my moon juice?"

"Moon juice?"

"Yes." She poured out two shots from an old water bottle with no label on it. "I brew it myself."

Mitchell said, "You go first."

She swallowed hers in one gulp, then grimaced, and her eyes filled with tears. "Your turn," she said, pointing at the other shot glass.

Mitchell drank his and coughed. He felt his eyes water, too. "What the fuck is that shit? Goddamn battery acid?"

Marla laughed. Then she handed him a cocktail napkin. "Your nose is bleeding."

Mitchell dabbed his nose with the napkin and it came away red. Marla took the napkin from him and put it in the trash. Then she poured them shots of moon juice until the water bottle was empty. Whatever the moon juice was, it had a mild hallucinogenic effect. Mitchell liked the way it made him feel.

"You actually like this place?" Marla said.

Mitchell shrugged. "It's okay."

She threw away the empty bottle. "I don't mind it in the daytime. Nobody comes here in the daytime."

"Would you mix me another gin martini, please?"

"Sure."

She made the drink and handed it to him. He gave her another hundred-dollar bill and she put it in her pocket.

"I take it you're rich," she said.

He shrugged.

"And since you're rich, you probably won't help me rob an armored truck, will you?"

He shook his head. "Probably not. But I can help you get your own apartment, if you want. Since you hate living with your brother and his wife."

"Wait a second. You said you loved me, right?"

"Yes."

"Did you mean that?"

"Of course I did, Marla. I love you more than anything."

"Are you married?"

"No."

"Any kids?"

"No."

"So you live alone?"

"Yes."

"Then why don't I just come and live with you?"

Mitchell started feeling warm and fuzzy again. "You would do that? You would come and live with me?"

"Yes! Can I quit my job?"

"Of course you can."

"Yay! I'm very easy to take care of. All you'll have to do is buy me alcohol and cigarettes and feed me once in a while. I'll be the cheapest pet you've ever owned."

Mitchell finished his drink. "I'm ready to leave when you are."

Marla grabbed a bottle of gin and her moon juice. She walked out with Mitchell without even locking the door.

CHAPTER 16

Aubrey lay naked on her living-room sofa, enjoying the breeze from the screened window as it drifted across her body, still damp with sweat from exertion. As almost always after exercising, her body felt good and strong. The temperature today—a Friday—was perfect: warm, soothing. She stretched. Her muscles expanded and then relaxed as tendrils of the summer breeze reached beneath her to the small of her back arched against the sofa.

Hearing laughter outside the window, she got up and looked down. She saw the old janitor—Oliver—and the creepy superintendent—Lucas—smoking cigarettes on the sidewalk one story below. She watched them until Oliver turned, walked away, and headed west. Lucas remained standing where he was, in front of the building, staring across the street, unaware of her standing nude at the window a floor above.

While visiting her brother in L.A. recently, her bedroom window in his apartment had faced nothing more interesting than a trash compactor. She had missed New York City. With this window, she could observe yellow cabs and black limos pull up through the circular drive to the main entrance, watch people come and go while listening to snippets of conversation and the sounds of traffic, the noise of gunfire and backfires drifting from elsewhere in the city, and the ambulance, fire-engine, and police sirens wailing through the streets that personified—for Aubrey—all the drama and beautiful urgency of New York. With a second-floor front apartment in Manhattan, she had a view of the entire world.

Behind her, on the coffee table, her phone chimed, alerting her to a text message from Samantha. *Hi!* she had written, presumably up on the eighteenth floor. *Getting ready to go to another audition. Wish me luck!*

Good luck! Aubrey wrote back. *I have some errands to run, so I'll be gone for most of the day. See you tonight!*

She took a shower, got dressed, and took the stairs down to the lobby. Outside, she hailed a cab to the financial district.

Alexander walked out of 47 West Street where he worked for Nolen and Nolen as a finance manager. He saw the young woman immediately. She was standing across the street, leaning against a lamppost, smoking a cigarette. He had seen her there previously several times the past few weeks. Today she wore a black skirt and a blue top that accentuated her breasts. She was beautiful, and appeared to be the same age his daughter would have been had his daughter not been killed ten years before.

Alexander had been planning to approach her from the first moment he saw her, but that had been over a month ago, and he still had not yet worked up the courage to do it.

He watched a car pull up to the corner where she stood. The passenger-side window came down. She discarded her cigarette and leaned into the car for a few seconds, then stood up again, and the car pulled away.

Alexander crossed the street and stopped by the lamppost. She looked up at him but didn't say a word. Suddenly nervous, he cleared his throat. "Young lady, there is something I want you to do for me."

"I may be young," she said, "but I'm no lady. And what took you so long, anyway?"

His nervousness increased, and he wished he had taken a Valium before leaving work. "What do you mean?"

"Never mind," she said. "What is it?"

He ran fingers through his salt-and-pepper hair. "What's what?"

"The thing you want me to do for you. What is it?"

He needed to settle down and get himself together. This was, after all, a business proposition. "Can we go somewhere and talk?"

"Listen," she said. "I'm losing business talking to you. Why don't you come back when you're ready to do some business?"

"I want you to be my daughter for the evening."

She laughed, and her laughter reminded him of his daughter's laughter before she had died. "Do you want me to call you Daddy?"

He nodded. "Yes. Call me Daddy."

"Okay, Daddy." She batted her long eyelashes. "Do you have any money?"

He retrieved a silver money clip from his pocket. He withdrew three hundred-dollar bills and put them in her palm. "I'll pay you more as we go along."

She put the bills in her purse and hooked her arm through his. "As you wish, Daddy. Lead the way."

They turned and started up the street. "I had a daughter once," Alexander said. "Her name was Aubrianne. For the rest of the night, I'll call you Aubrey."

"Thank you for such a lovely name, Daddy. But if you're keeping me for the rest of the night, I'm going to need at least five thousand dollars."

"Fine. There's a bank just up the street. I'll pay you there. Then we need to go shopping and get you some clothes."

In the restaurant, conversation hummed over the sporadic clinking of silverware and the clatter of saucers and plates. Aubrey and Alexander were seated at a table near the front of the room. The maître d' had spoken to Alexander by name when they came in, which he suspected had impressed Aubrey even more than the designer clothes he had bought for her. The outfit she had been wearing was in the back of his Mercedes in the parking lot.

They ate in silence. After their plates were taken away, they shared a bottle of expensive champagne.

Alexander said, "You look ravishing."

She smiled. "Thank you, Daddy. But you still haven't told me what it is that you want me to do."

He poured more champagne into his glass. "I want you to spend the weekend at my house in Putnam County."

Aubrey cocked her head. "Putnam County?"

"About sixty miles north of the city."

She thought about it. "The whole weekend will cost you another ten thousand dollars."

"Money isn't a problem. I have cash in a safe at my house. I'll pay you when we get there."

She batted her eyelashes. "Whatever you say, Daddy."

He smiled. "You're a wonderful daughter, Aubrey."

She looked at his hand. "You're not wearing a wedding band."

"No. My wife died ten years ago."

She licked her lips. "You must be so lonely."

"Yes. I have a son, but I rarely see him. He lives on the west coast."

"Is that right?"

"Yes. In Los Angeles."

"Oh, I *love* Los Angeles," Aubrey said.

Alexander nodded. "So do I. And I hope you'll love my house in Putnam County." He raised a hand to signal the waiter. "It's time to hit the road."

Alexander drove.

Just outside of Manhattan, Aubrey lit a cigarette on the passenger's side. She cracked her window. "Tell me about your son."

Alexander turned the radio off. "His name is Mitchell. He's twenty-five. How old are you?"

"Twenty-three."

He nodded. "I thought you looked the same age his sister would have been."

"Your daughter would have been twenty-three?"

"Yes."

"Were she and Mitchell close?"

"Yes. Extremely. He hasn't been the same since she died."

"What happened to her?"

"Her mother killed her," Alexander said. "She found out that Mitchell and Aubrianne were having sex, and it drove her crazy."

Aubrey discarded her cigarette and closed the window. "When was this?"

"Ten years ago."

"Didn't you say that your wife died ten years ago?"

"Yes. She killed Aubrianne, and then she killed herself."

From her purse, Aubrey retrieved a breath mint and put it in her mouth. "Personally, I never understood why people freak out over incest."

"Oh, it wasn't the incest that freaked her out," Alexander said. "In fact, she had been molesting Mitchell for years."

"She was fucking her own son?"

"Yes. When she found out that he was also fucking his sister, she went insane with jealousy. She shot Aubrianne in the head, then got in bed beside her and blew her brains out. When I came home from work, Mitchell was in bed with them both. I had to pry him off their corpses. He didn't speak for years after that."

"Why didn't she kill Mitchell?"

"We'll never know," Alexander said. "She didn't leave a note."

Night had fallen when they arrived in Putnam County. Alexander drove them up a long private road to his house on a hill overlooking the river. Outdoor lanterns illuminated the property. He parked in a circular drive near the front and killed the engine.

"This place is massive," Aubrey said.

They got out and entered the house. Alexander led Aubrey to his library. Throughout the spacious chamber, the heads of dead animals gazed at them blindly from the walls.

He gestured to a sofa in one of the armchair-furnished reading areas. "Have a seat."

Aubrey sat down on the sofa, then looked up into the glass eyes of a bison. "Are you a hunter, Daddy?"

"No. I'm not much of a reader, either. The library was furnished when I bought the house."

"That's too bad," Aubrey said. "Reading is one of life's greatest pleasures."

"Ah, so you're a literate whore, are you?"

"Don't be mean, Daddy. Books helped me through a lot of troubled times in my youth."

Alexander opened a minibar beside the sofa. "Care for something to drink?"

"Yes, please."

"We have wine, whiskey, vodka—"

"Vodka, please," Aubrey said.

He filled two lowball glasses with vodka, handed one to Aubrey, and then joined her on the sofa. He raised his glass. "To you," he said. "My daughter, back from the dead."

They drank.

"You still owe me ten thousand dollars," Aubrey said.

Alexander set his glass on the marble-and-granite coffee table. "My safe is in the basement." He stood up. "Shall we?"

Aubrey set her glass on the table and rose from the sofa. "After you."

Alexander led her to a bookcase. "Remember those old movies with the mansions that have secret passageways?" He pushed a button concealed behind a copy of *Rosemary's Baby* by Ira Levin, and a door disguised to look like part of the wall opened onto a hidden staircase. He turned a light on. "Ladies first."

Aubrey started down the stairs. Alexander closed the door behind them and followed her down.

In the basement, he led her down a stone-walled hallway, opening four doors along the way.

At a fifth door—metal, like the rest—he tapped a numerical sequence into a keypad, unlocking it, and she followed him into a large bare room with cinderblock walls, a concrete floor, and a ceiling that appeared to be made of steel. Along the back wall stood a tall black safe that was shaped like a refrigerator.

He led her to the safe. "I keep most of my money in the bank, but I like to keep cash in the house, too, just in case."

He unlocked the safe with two separate keys. Then he opened it, withdrew some money from within, and spun back around.

"Here's ten grand," he said, handing her two black-banded bundles of five thousand dollars in hundred-dollar bills.

Aubrey put the money in her purse. Then she pulled out a gun, aimed it at his chest, and put some distance between them by taking several steps in reverse.

"Is this a joke?" Alexander said, staring into the muzzle of the handgun pointed at his chest. It appeared to be a 9mm, or a .380 automatic, perhaps.

"No, it's not a joke. And I didn't just happen to be standing by that lamppost. I've been staking out your office at Nolen and Nolen for over a month."

Alexander looked at the gun again, and then back into her eyes. "Mind if I ask why?"

"Because I needed some money, and I figured I could get some from you." For a split second, she glanced past him to the stacks of cash piled inside the safe. Then she returned her gaze to Alexander. "And it looks like I figured correctly, too."

"Okay. So this is a robbery. I get that. But why me? I mean, out of all the people in New York City, why have you been staking *me* out for over a month?"

"You haven't figured it out yet?"

"No. Enlighten me."

She smiled. "Because you really *are* my father, *Daddy*."

"What the hell are you talking about?"

"I'm your daughter," she said. "I'm Aubrianne."

"That's impossible. My daughter has been dead for over a decade."

"No. Mom didn't kill me, and she didn't kill herself. And it wasn't Mom who had been molesting Mitchell—it was you. And you molested me, too. You raped us both for years. When Mom finally told you that she was going to the police, you decided to kill all three of us. But Mitchell was always your favorite and I guess that's why you decided not to kill him."

"But I killed you."

"No. You broke Mom's neck, but all you managed to do to me was give me whiplash. I pretended to be dead. You fell for it."

Alexander smiled. "You're a cunning little bitch. I'll give you that."

"Thank you. I learned from the best."

"You were still alive when I strapped you in the car."

"Yes. It was dark out. You let the car roll into the lake and ran away Thanks for leaving the back window open. I climbed out and swam to shore."

"I should have checked for a pulse," Alexander said. "That was back when I was drinking way too much. You never would have gotten away with it had I not been drunk."

Aubrey nodded. "That's probably true."

"So where have you been all this time?"

"All over America. I was a prostitute for a while. I started turning tricks when I was thirteen."

"Why didn't you go to the police?"

Aubrey shrugged. "I don't know. I was afraid you might hurt Mitchell if I did. Plus, going to the police isn't my style. Besides, I liked being a prostitute. It satisfied my raving nymphomania. But I'm not a prostitute anymore. Now I'm a stripper. Well, I *was* a stripper. After tonight, I'll probably be retired."

"Does Mitchell know you're still alive?"

"Yes, although it was several years before I contacted him. When I did, I made him promise to keep it a secret from you."

"And he certainly kept it a secret. I don't talk to Mitchell often, but he never once told me that he had been in contact with you."

From her purse, Aubrey produced a taser with the hand not pointing the pistol at his chest, and he found it encouraging; perhaps she didn't intend to murder him, after all.

"There's over two million dollars in the safe," he said. "All cash. Just take it and go. You deserve it."

"What you never understood," Aubrey said, "is that the three of us loved each other deeply. But we all hated you. My earliest memory is being raped by you. According to Mom, you started raping Mitchell and me when we were babies."

Alexander shook his head. "That's not true. I didn't touch either of you until you were two."

Aubrey laughed. "Ah, okay. Well, that was awfully considerate of you, waiting until we were two."

Then she shot him with the taser.

The pain was immediate, and Alexander felt his muscles freeze before he dropped to the floor. He never lost consciousness, however. He saw his daughter approach him, get down on her knees, and rip apart his button-up shirt.

He looked down. The two conductive wires from the taser were still attached to the probes embedded in his chest.

Aubrey grabbed the dartlike electrodes and yanked them out of his flesh. Then she ejected the cartridge that housed the electrodes and tossed the wires aside, effectively turning the taser into a stun gun. She held it up in front of his eyes; a blue electric arc flowed between its two small prongs.

"Speaking of what we deserve," Aubrey said, "here's a token of my appreciation." Then she jammed the electric arc into the crotch of Alexander's designer pants.

He screamed but not for long. The pain from the electric charge rendered him unconscious.

Alexander woke up naked, flat on his back, along the wall across from the safe. The concrete floor was cold against his skin. He tried to get up, but each wrist was handcuffed to an old, cast-iron radiator's floor brackets to either side. His crotch seared from the taser, and his mouth was gagged with what felt like a bundle of cloth.

Seconds later, Aubrey stepped out of the safe with a suitcase. She approached him. As she drew near, he recognized the suitcase. It was a piece of his own luggage from the closet in his master bedroom up on the first floor.

Aubrey stopped a few feet away from him and looked down, smiling. "If I play my cards right," she said, "this two million dollars will last me for quite some time. I'm taking your car, too, by the way. I'll probably just leave it on the side of the road, once I'm back in Manhattan. Or be like you, and put it in a lake. Who knows? I might even hand the keys to a bag lady."

Alexander tried to speak, but the gag in his mouth prevented him from forming intelligible words.

Aubrey bent down and lowered the gag until it hung beneath his chin. "Try again."

"I said you can't just leave me here. The secret passageway—no one knows where it is. No one will ever find me down here. I'll starve to death."

Aubrey shook her head. "Nah. Even if I left the door to the passageway open, which I absolutely am *not* going to do, the odds are good that no one would come all the way out here looking for you. Not in time to save your life, anyway. But don't worry: you'll die of dehydration long before you starve to death."

She bent down again to raise the gag.

"Wait, Aubrianne! Please! I'm begging you!"

"Begging me? Let me tell you something, *Daddy.* You're lucky I'm in a hurry. You're lucky I have a woman I love in the city waiting for me. What I would really like to do is get medieval on your ass. I'm talking about scooping your eyeballs out with a spoon, and making you eat them. And cutting your fucking dick off, and making you eat that, too. And then ripping your balls off, and putting those in your empty eye sockets. And that's just for starters. But, like I said, you're lucky I have a woman I love in the city waiting for me, and I'm in a hurry to get back to her. So I'm just gonna leave you here to die. Enjoy the rest of your agonizing life."

She put the gag back in his mouth and walked away.

Time passed, but not much, and then Aubrey returned. Alexander hoped that perhaps she had decided to let him go. She still carried the suitcase, and her purse still dangled from a shoulder, but she also now held a plastic bag like the ones he kept in a kitchen cabinet after trips to the grocery store.

She set the suitcase and her purse on the floor. Then she pulled his blowtorch out of the bag and held it up.

"I was headed for the door," Aubrey said, "when I saw this blowtorch just sitting on your kitchen counter, and I took it as a sign from the universe that I needed to torture you to death."

Unbelievable, Alexander tried to say, but the gag prevented him from doing so. As an avid meat eater, he often cooked steak dinners for himself several nights per week, and used the blowtorch to sear the crust of a steak after cooking the meat to a perfect temperature.

And now my daughter will use it to cauterize my wounds, he thought, *so I'll stay alive longer while she tortures me.*

Aubrey set the blowtorch on the floor. From the bag, she retrieved a steak knife and a spoon, and set those on the floor, also.

"I know I said I was gonna retire from stripping, but I'm gonna perform one last time, just for you." She smiled, and added, "I don't wanna get blood all over my clothes."

Aubrey stripped naked, moved her clothes to a spot on the floor about fifteen feet away, and then came back to Alexander. "Remember what I said about rearranging your eyeballs and your testicles?" She grabbed the steak knife, the spoon, and the blowtorch, then got down on her knees in front of his face.

"Our bodies return to earth," she told him. "Our souls return to the universe."

Alexander closed his eyes, but she forced them open.

His last night was the longest of his life.

Samantha sat drinking vodka on the rooftop when her phone chimed at almost two a.m. She checked her phone and saw a new message from Aubrey: *Sorry I'm late. My errands took a lot longer than expected. You still awake?*

Of course! Samantha wrote back. *Come on up!*

A few minutes later, Aubrey stepped into the penthouse. Samantha closed the door and locked it.

"Let me hit that vodka," Aubrey said.

Samantha handed her the bottle. Aubrey took a drink and gave the bottle back.

They kissed.

"I missed you," Samantha said.

"I missed you, too."

"I was worried about you! I messaged you several times, but you never answered."

"I forgot to grab my phone before I left."

"Seriously?"

Aubrey paused, and then shook her head. "No, that's not true. I don't wanna lie to you. It's a long story, but I left my phone at home intentionally. Let's just say I went to a place where I didn't want a tracking device in my pocket."

Samantha took a drink. "Say no more. Can we do it now?"

"Absolutely."

She grabbed Aubrey's hand and pulled her toward the bedroom.

CHAPTER 17

"So where do you want to go, anyway?" Kenzie asked her. "New York? Chicago? L.A.?"

Christina lay beside her on the bed in Kenzie's hotel room. "I don't know. But we can't go anywhere, yet."

"Why not?"

"Because we have to go back to my dad's house first."

"We do?"

"Yes. After he fired his gun at you last night...and I still don't know how he missed, by the way. I mean, you were standing right in front of him, and he fired six times, and all six bullets went into the wall right behind you—"

"Like I told him," Kenzie said, "it wasn't my time to go."

"I guess. Anyway, after that, I was in such a hurry to get out of there, I forgot to grab my shoebox beneath the bed."

"Shoebox?"

"Yes. There's a bunch of old photos of my mother in there."

Kenzie sat up on the bed. "You wanna go get it now?"

Christina checked her phone: 7:49 p.m. "I'm sure Dad's still awake, but it's a Saturday night, so he might be at the bar. If not, I'll have to sneak in later tonight."

Kenzie grabbed her keys and the bottle of rum they were drinking. "Only one way to find out."

"Fuck," Christina said, when she saw her dad's car parked in the driveway. "I guess he didn't go to the bar tonight. And all the lights are still on, too, so he's probably still awake. I'll have to sneak in later tonight to get the shoebox."

Kenzie drove them up the street and turned left at a stop sign. "Do you like acid?"

"Yes, I do. Why? Do you have some?"

"No, but I might be able to get some, back home, in Fort Lee. It's only about thirty minutes away."

"I can get some acid right here in Jersey City," Christina said.

"Seriously?"

"Yeah." She pulled her phone out. "I'll shoot Isaac a text."

"Who's Isaac?"

"Kid I went to school with. A year younger than me. Sixteen, I think. His mother was in a car crash. Last I heard, he was working in a restaurant."

"Did his mother die in the crash?"

"No. Just paralyzed, I think."

"Damn," Kenzie said. "That's even worse."

To Isaac, Christina wrote: *Thinking about taking a trip. You know anything?*

Moments later, her phone rang. "Hello? Yes. Just me and my girlfriend."

Kenzie turned the radio down.

Christina continued speaking into her phone. "Yes. Oh, okay. Yeah, I know where that is. We're not that far from there, actually. Okay. We'll be there in a few."

The call ended. She put the phone back in her pocket. "He's on foot. Leaving Silvio's house now."

"Silvio?"

"Older dude. Friend of ours. Lives behind a warehouse. Isaac wants us to pick him up out front."

"Cool," Kenzie said. "Show me the way."

Christina guided her downtown, and then beyond, to the city's old industrial district. They passed old factories and mills full of machinery that hadn't been touched in years.

Christina saw Isaac standing in front of the warehouse as soon as they pulled into the parking lot. The sun had already set, and the purple twilight was fading, but she recognized him by his oversized hoodie. "That's him," she said, pointing him out to Kenzie.

Moments later, he climbed into the car behind Christina on the passenger's side.

She turned around and looked at him. "What's up, Isaac? It's been a minute."

"Yes, it has." Then he yanked his hood off.

"Holy fucking shit!" Christina said. "You shaved your fucking head!"

He smiled. "Yeah. About a week ago, actually. Do you like it?"

"I don't know. I mean, you went from having all that hair to being completely bald. I guess it's just gonna take some getting used to. Anyway, how much acid you got?"

"Three hits."

"Three hits? That's all?"

"Yeah, for now. I'm supposed to be getting more in about an hour. Are you two in a hurry?"

"No. And this is Kenzie, by the way. Kenzie, this is Isaac."

"Nice to meet you, Isaac," Kenzie said.

"Likewise." From his hoodie's interior pocket, Isaac retrieved a cellophane packet. "I'm taking one of these hits myself, but you can just have the other two."

"For free?" Christina said.

"Yep." From the cellophane packet, Isaac retrieved three blotter tabs and put one in his mouth. Then he handed Christina the other two.

"Thanks!" Christina said, putting a tab in her mouth and giving the other one to Kenzie, who immediately followed suit.

"Don't mention it. If you like it, I'll sell you some later, when I get more. I'm sure you'll like it, though. And this is some fast-acting acid, by the way."

"Oh yeah?'

"Yes. Only takes about fifteen minutes to kick in. It's pharmaceutical-grade LSD. No strychnine or speed mixed in, but it definitely kicks in fast. You wanna smoke some weed, while we wait?"

"Sure!"

Isaac lit a joint. They passed it round and round, waiting for the acid to kick in. After they finished the joint, they each took a drink from Kenzie and Christina's bottle of rum.

The acid hit Christina subtly at first, ghostly sensations like tiny spiders climbing up and down her spine, the tingling of phantom limbs she didn't even know existed. Then it kicked in full-force. Her whole body lit up, and her mind awakened to an elevated awareness that always seemed new to her, no matter how many times she had dropped acid.

"Our brains are neon," Isaac said, "and they're spinning like little planets above our heads."

"Dude," Kenzie said, "you're fucking stupid."

"I'm tripping," Christina said. "I need to get out of the car."

They all got out and started walking. The sky was black. Full night had fallen. As they left the warehouse behind, the street grew even shabbier. Most of the buildings were old row houses of rotting wood and brick crumbling into ruin.

"Seemingly vacant structures," Isaac said, "with only God knows what living inside them."

"No," Christina said. "They're galleries of sorrow, displaying everything that the people who used to live there wanted, but never got—all those dead dreams they tried and failed to achieve."

A delivery truck pulled up to a stop sign in front of them. Two men in ski masks with machine guns jumped out screaming at them in a foreign language. They confiscated their phones, and then forced them into the back of the truck. Once they were all inside, the door slammed shut behind them, and they settled down with a pile of other hostages. Some of them were crying;

others laughed and talked excitedly.

Minutes later, the truck stopped and the door slid up. The hostages were herded out onto a loading bay. Then they were ushered through a gauntlet of screams and artificial fog into the flashing, multicolored lights of an otherwise darkened auditorium.

The place was packed. The audience was full of people chanting, yelling, or screaming. Men in ski masks with machine guns blocked the exit doors.

Christina had heard rumors about audience-abduction concerts before, but had never expected to find herself in the middle of one right here in Jersey City. *Then again*, she thought, *the craziest stuff always goddamn happens when I'm on acid.*

"We can make our way to the front!" Isaac yelled. "Follow me!"

Christina looked at Kenzie and shrugged. Kenzie shrugged back and took Christina's hand. Together, they followed Isaac down to the front of the stage.

A large man in a ski mask with a machine gun walked up to a microphone at the front of the stage. There was a drum set behind him. A wall of amplifiers lined the back of the stage. In front of the amplifiers were several electric guitars. There were a couple of bass guitars, too. There was also a synthesizer, and even a turntable.

The man turned on the microphone and launched into a furious tirade, but feedback mangled his voice, and Christina couldn't understand his words. Thunderous applause erupted throughout the audience nevertheless.

The man waited until the crowd was quiet again. Then he approached the speakers along the front of the stage and waved his machine gun at the audience, screaming at the top of his lungs.

Isaac turned to Kenzie and Christina. "What the fuck is he saying?"

The man with the machine gun heard Isaac. He walked right up to him and shot him through the head. His gun must have been set to semiautomatic fire, because only one bullet came out when he pulled the trigger, but that bullet blew Isaac's brains out the back of his skull and all over the people behind him.

Then he pointed the gun at a boy to Christina's left and screamed, "Get on stage, you piece of fucking shit!"

The boy needed no further prompting. He took the stage, sat down behind the drum set, and picked up a set of sticks. Then he began playing a groove in 4/4 time.

The man with the machine gun smiled and started banging his head.

The crowd went crazy.

The man returned to the front of the stage and waved his gun at the crowd again. The audience parted and ejected a young female with a mohawk. The man aimed his gun at her, and then pointed at one of the guitars. Some people in the front lifted her and passed her up to the stage. Crying, she strapped on a guitar. Wet mascara sparkled on her face beneath the spotlight. The man turned on her amp, but she didn't know how to play. Godawful noise came out of her amp when she hit the strings. The man shot her in the face. Her head exploded and her body hit the floor. Feedback shrieked.

Most of the audience screamed; the rest cheered and applauded.

Kenzie turned to Christina. "I'm going up."

Christina nodded.

Kenzie took the stage. The man aimed his gun at her but didn't pull the trigger. She strapped on a guitar. Then she began playing some riffs and licks over the groove that the boy was still providing with the drums.

The man started laughing and jumping up and down, delirious with excitement. Then he went back to the front of the stage and waved his gun at the audience. This time, a teenage boy with blue hair was ejected. The man aimed his gun at the boy and pointed at a bass guitar. The boy shook his head. The man shot him in the face. Then he grabbed a woman in the front row by her hair and dragged her onto the stage. Crying, she strapped on a bass, but she didn't know how to play, and he shot her in the face, too.

The crowd screamed as Kenzie and the drummer continued to play their instrumental tune.

Four more kids got their heads blown off before the man finally aimed his gun at Christina, and pointed at a bass. Already a decent guitar player, Christina figured it wouldn't be too difficult to sound halfway decent on a bass. *Besides,* she thought, *there's a first time for everything.* She took the stage and strapped on a bass.

Kenzie, riffing in open E, smiled at her and winked. Christina gave her a thumbs-up and turned on a microphone.

CHAPTER 18

"Awesome apartment!" Marla said, as soon as they stepped into the living room.

Mitchell locked the door behind them. "If you want to move into a bigger place, just let me know. You and I can live anywhere we want."

"No," Marla said. "This is perfect."

Mitchell stopped halfway to the kitchen and turned around. "We have the gin, but I have wine, whiskey, vodka, beer—"

"What are you having?"

"I think I'll have some whiskey."

"Whiskey's fine with me."

"How do you take it?"

She shrugged. "Straight from the bottle, usually."

Moments later, Mitchell joined her on the sofa with a bottle of Maker's Mark.

"Can we have sex first?" Marla said. "That moon juice always makes me horny."

"Sure." He took a drink and set the bottle on the coffee table. Then he took her into his bedroom.

It was the first time he had made love to a woman without wearing a condom and disposable gloves in quite some time. Afterward, he said, "My oracle bones told me that you and I would end up being together."

Marla sat up on the bed. "You have oracle bones?"

"Yes."

"That's awesome! What do you use? Like, the shoulder blade of an ox? Or a turtle shell, or something?"

"Hawksbill turtle. A sea creature. I've been using the entire skeleton since I was a child."

"Where did you get it?"

"It was a gift from my grandfather."

"Can I see it?"

"Not right now. Maybe some other time. Soon, I'm going to take you to Vegas and make you my wife."

She smiled. "Can I pick the date?"

"Of course you can."

"Yay! I'll choose a good astrological date for us. Maybe there will be a time soon when our ruling planets are aligned."

"I'm ready to drink some whiskey," Mitchell said.

"Me too."

They got up, got dressed, and went back into the living room.

Marla took a drink of Maker's Mark. "Do you believe in God?"

"Sometimes I do. Sometimes I don't."

"Same here. I do most of the time, though." She set the bottle on the coffee table beside an ashtray that was shaped like a seashell. "Once upon a time, I was a Catholic, but not anymore. I haven't considered myself a Catholic for a very long time. I used to fuck the priest in the cathedral my mother took me to when I was a child."

Mitchell took a drink. "Is that right?"

"Yes. It's a common misconception that Catholic priests only rape little boys. Trust me: they rape little girls, too. Although in my case, it was the other way around. He didn't molest me. I molested the priest. And then it turned into a love affair that lasted for a couple of years."

Mitchell lit a cigarette. "How old were you?"

"Seven when I met him. He was fifty. I broke up with him when I was nine. That was when I quit being a Catholic. I never went back to the cathedral."

"Your mother stopped making you go?"

"Yes."

"Did she find out about your affair with the priest?"

"No."

Mitchell blew a smoke ring. "That's fascinating."

"The priest was a fascinating man. He had these awesome theories about light. He thought that light was the source of all information, that it determines any and all possible outcomes, that it streams at perfect angles to align certain events in space and time. He also said he reflected light with mirrored bowls of holy water to summon aliens from outer space."

"So why did you break up with him?"

"I met another man." Marla lit a cigarette. "I fell in love with my fourth-grade teacher."

"Oh yeah?"

"Yes. His name was Mister Sammons. His first name was Drexel, but I wasn't allowed to call him that, in case I messed up and called him by his first name in front of other people. He was an alcoholic and he would give me vodka all the time. He kept it in his desk, his car, his jacket, pretty much everywhere. There was a cloakroom in the back of the classroom. He kept a sleeping bag in a cardboard box in a corner of the cloakroom and covered it with old newspapers and magazines. He would lock the door between classes and pull the sleeping bag out and take naps until the bell rang, always still drunk from the night before and already drinking. Needless to say, he and I had a lot of sex in that cloakroom."

Mitchell finished his cigarette and extinguished it in the ashtray. "So why do you hate your brother, anyway?"

"He used to rape me when we were kids, and then he—"

"Wait a second. Where was your father at, back when your brother was raping you?"

"I don't remember my father. He left when we were young. Told my mother he was going out for cigarettes. Never came back."

"My favorite author," Mitchell said. "Stephen King. Same thing happened to him. His father told his mother that he was going out for smokes, and he never came home."

Marla took a drink. "I love Stephen King. My favorite is *Pet Sematary*. What's yours?"

"Probably *The Shining*."

Marla lit a cigarette. "I like that one, too. Anyway, my brother used to rape me when we were kids, but that's not the reason I hate him. The rape was no big deal. I could just close my eyes and pretend to be someplace else until it was over. The reason I hate my brother is because he killed the only girl I was ever in love with."

"You were in love with a girl?"

"Yes. Her name was Gwyneth."

"And your brother killed her?"

"Yes. I couldn't prove it, of course. But I know he killed her."

"How do you know?"

"I just do."

Mitchell took a drink. "Why did he do it? Was it jealousy?"

"Probably. And there was undoubtedly a little bit of spite involved, also."

"Spite?"

"Yes. He and my mother both hated lesbians."

"Hated lesbians?"

"Yes. We're not from the city. We're from a small town upstate. Very conservative community. And my mother was more conservative than most. She never found out about Gwyneth, but she would have been more distraught to learn that I was having sex with another girl than she would have been if she had found out I was having sex with the priest and my fourth-grade teacher."

Mitchell took a drink. "That is so fucking weird."

"Tell me about it. Anyway, I had never been with another girl before, and I had to keep the affair a secret from my mother. I tried to keep it a secret from my brother, too, but he went to the same high school that Gwyneth and I did, so it was impossible."

"Is your brother older or younger than you?"

"Older. One year. Gwyneth was one year older than me, too.

She and my brother were seniors that year. I was still a junior. She transferred from another school in the middle of October that year, and whenever I saw her in the hallways, my head spun and my bones felt like liquid mercury flowing inside my body."

"That's how I feel whenever I look at you," Mitchell said.

"She stopped me in the hall one day after geometry and asked me for directions to another classroom. After I told her, she put a hand on my arm and thanked me. The touch of her skin on my flesh was like a shock of electricity. It didn't hurt, but I jumped back on instinct and dropped my textbooks. She apologized. Then she giggled and walked away. Her smile reminded me of orchids in bloom."

"Orchids in bloom," Mitchell said. "That's beautiful."

Marla finished her cigarette. She stubbed it out in the ashtray and drank from the bottle of Maker's Mark. Then she continued her story.

"I didn't know it at the time, but my brother saw us in the hallway. That night, he told me that I was probably infected now because the lesbian had touched me, as if her sexual preference were contagious."

"How did your brother know that she was a lesbian?"

"Rumors at school. According to the rumors, Gwyneth had transferred to our school because students at the other school taunted her about it."

Mitchell shook his head. "High-school kids can be so mean."

"Yes. The next day, my brother and some of his friends began taunting Gwyneth out in the open, but whenever they thought that no one was looking, they pawed at her like a pack of rabid wolves. I told them to leave her alone, but they ignored me."

Mitchell took a drink. "Goddamn hypocrites."

"After school, I would go to a little forest at the edge of our neighborhood. Most of the trees had been chopped down to make way for power lines, but a few of them survived. I would sit on the ground and write poetry in my notebook. I would also scribble messages to the elements, and then tear them out and toss them to the wind."

"What did the messages say?"

"Basic stuff, mostly. *Where do you come from? Where are you going? I hate it here. Take me with you.* Just a bunch of simple stuff like that, mainly."

Mitchell was smiling with a faraway look in his eyes. "That's beautiful. Do you still write?"

"Occasionally."

"Can I read your work sometime?"

"Sure. It isn't very good, but I don't mind. Anyway, that became my favorite thing to do after school, to go sit alone in the forest and write poetry and letters to the elements. One day, when I was sitting by the stream, I looked over and saw Gwyneth sitting beside me. I had not heard her approach, or even sit down beside me on the ground. It was like she had just materialized out of thin air, or something. She told me that she had been following me to the forest for several days in a row after school, ever since I had told my brother and his friends to stop taunting her about her sexual preference."

Mitchell took a drink and handed her the bottle. "I'm sure she appreciated that," he said.

Marla took a drink and set the bottle on the coffee table. "Yes. She also told me that she had been gathering my letters to the elements and reading them every day after I left. She told me that she hated that town, too. Then she told me that she had left a message for me, but that I had probably been too busy staring at my notebook to notice it. That was when she pointed to the ground, and I looked down. Three simple words, *I like you,* had been spelled using pebbles on the ground right in front of me by the stream."

Mitchell smiled. "That's amazing."

"I asked her if it was true, and she said yes. I told her I liked her too, and that I thought she was beautiful. She told me she thought that I was beautiful, too. And then she kissed me. It was sweeter than anything I had ever imagined. I told her that I was nervous, because I had never been with a girl before, but she told me not to worry, and we made love. After that, we were inseparable."

"Then what happened?" Mitchell said. "Did your mother find out?"

"No. My brother did, of course, because everyone at school knew we were lovers. I mean, it wasn't hard to figure out. And he threatened to tell my mother a couple of times, but he never did."

"Did his friends start taunting you at school the way they taunted Gwyneth?"

"Yes. The entire school did, basically, but we didn't care. We had each other, and that was all we cared about. Gwyneth said she was leaving town right after graduation. Said I could either leave with her right then or wait a year to graduate and then join her in the city one year later. I told her that I was leaving with her when she did. I had never been happier."

"And then what happened?"

"She graduated. We were supposed to leave that night, but we ended up getting drunk and decided to leave the next day. She spent the night at my mother's house."

"Your mother let her spend the night?"

"Yes. She didn't know we were lovers. She just thought we were best friends."

"Ah, okay."

"So anyway, she passed out on the sofa like she always did, and my brother covered her body in fentanyl patches while she was passed out."

"Fentanyl patches?"

"Yes."

"Holy shit. Fentanyl's, like, a hundred times stronger than morphine."

"I know. She never had a chance."

Mitchell took a drink. "As little as a quarter of a milligram of fentanyl can be lethal."

"Yes. According to the toxicology report, there were well over a hundred micrograms per liter in Gwyneth's blood when she died."

"Jesus Christ. Where did your brother get the fentanyl patches?"

Marla shrugged. "My brother's a drug dealer. Did I tell you that?"

"No."

"Well he is, and he was a drug dealer then, too. It was a small town, but just like any other small town, you could find any drug you wanted on the street."

"And your brother was never caught?"

"Nope. Her death was ruled an accidental overdose. But I knew my brother did it, even before he basically admitted it to me."

"He told you he did it?"

"More or less. He left not long after graduation and moved here to the city. But right before he left, he looked right at me and told me that it was too bad what happened to my *girlfriend*. And then he winked. And then he laughed. And then he left."

"Sounds like a confession to me."

Marla took a drink. "I graduated the next year, but I had no ambition to do anything or get involved with anyone at all. I got a job waitressing at a local restaurant to pay for my drugs and alcohol."

"Did you just keep living at your mother's house?"

"Yes, until she got sick and died a few years later. I saw my brother at her funeral for the first time since he had moved to the city. He acted as if nothing bad had ever happened between us, and he asked me what I planned to do with my life. I told him I had no idea. He suggested I come to the city. Told me I could stay with him and his wife until I got on my feet. And here I am."

"Which I for one am very happy about." Mitchell raised the bottle of Maker's Mark. "To fate."

"I want to kill my brother," Marla said, "for what he did to Gwyneth. I want to kill his stupid wife, too."

She took a swig of her moon juice and handed Mitchell the bottle.

They drank, made love again, and then resumed drinking.

Eventually, they fell asleep.

CHAPTER 19

Aubrey's hair on the pillow, red like the morning sun beyond the eighteenth-story window. Samantha's own hair was wet; she had just stepped out of the shower five minutes before. There was a half-full bottle of vodka on the nightstand, and she grabbed it, took a drink, and smiled, content to just stand there and watch Aubrey sleep, feeling truly alive for the first time in her life. She still did what she had done before—worked at home doing graphic design and digital marketing; left the apartment to go to acting auditions and art classes—but did everything now with a happy serenity of knowing that Aubrey was by her side.

On the bed, Aubrey opened her eyes, and Samantha marveled at the gold within the green of her irises. "What time is it?" Aubrey said.

"Almost eight."

Aubrey sat up, stretched, and ran fingers through her hair. "Five o'clock somewhere. Let me hit that vodka."

Samantha handed her the bottle.

Aubrey took a drink and gave the bottle back. "You've already showered."

"Yes. I was trying not to wake you."

"You didn't." Still naked, Aubrey rose from the bed. "I need to take a shower. You mind if I shower here?"

"Of course not, baby. I'll be on the rooftop."

In the shower, Aubrey ran the water first hot, and then cold. She stood motionless beneath the downpour, waiting for her head to clear, trying to make sense of yesterday's events. She had murdered her father, and still believed in her heart that he had deserved it. But not only had she killed him, she had tortured him to death; moreover, she had done so with a savage glee.

Am I a monster? Aubrey thought.

In retrospect, she saw herself yesterday as a lunatic from a nightmare, a homicidal maniac with a knife in one hand and a blowtorch in the other, her naked body stained red as a butcher's apron after a long day at a slaughterhouse.

She scrubbed her flesh vigorously with Samantha's body wash, and then shampooed her hair, deciding then and there to just come clean and tell her girlfriend exactly what had happened yesterday. She loved Samantha and didn't want any secrets between them. And if her girlfriend loved her as much as she claimed to, then hopefully she would feel the same way, too. But Samantha was an actress. Could anyone truly know when an actor was being sincere, and not acting?

It's gonna take more than a shower, Aubrey thought, *to derail this train of thought.*

She turned the water off. Using both hands, she pressed water out of her dripping hair.

She got out and toweled off. She brushed her teeth and evacuated her bladder. In the master bedroom, she put on last night's clothes.

Then she joined Samantha on the rooftop. Her girlfriend sat on a patio chair, facing Central Park. Aubrey sat down on the patio chair beside her.

"Feel better?" Samantha said.

"A little bit." She held her hand out for the vodka bottle.

Samantha handed her the bottle. Aubrey took a drink and passed it back.

"Yesterday, while you were gone," Samantha said "I went for a walk to kill some time, and I never realized how many doves were in Central Park."

"I read somewhere that it's filled with the abandoned doves of failed magicians."

Samantha took a drink. "That makes sense."

"And speaking of yesterday," Aubrey said, "I have a confession to make."

"Oh yeah?"

"Yes, because I don't want to lie to you anymore."

"What did you lie about?"

"Those errands I said I had to run. There were none. Yesterday, I went to my father's house and tortured him to death."

Samantha cocked her head. "Tortured him to death?"

"Yes. Yesterday, I murdered my father."

"Why?"

"Because he killed my mother ten years ago."

"Damn," Samantha said. "I'm sorry. I didn't even know your mother was dead."

Aubrey nodded. "He killed her ten years ago, and then he tried to kill me. I've been wanting to kill him ever since. Yesterday, I finally did it."

Samantha lit a cigarette. "Ten years. What a crazy coincidence."

"What are you talking about?"

"My father committed suicide ten years ago."

Aubrey shot her a look. "I didn't know your father was dead."

"Yep. Hanged himself ten years ago. I was twelve. My little sister was eight."

"Damn. I didn't even know you had a little sister."

Samantha handed her the vodka bottle.

Aubrey took a drink and gave the bottle back. "What's your sister's name?"

"Kenzie."

"Does she live with your mother, in Fort Lee?"

"Yes. Well, as far as I know. She's eighteen, now. I haven't talked to her in a while. Last I heard, she was thinking about going to music school."

"She's a musician?"

"Yes. A really *good* musician, actually."

Aubrey cast her gaze across the street, toward Central Park. "Do you think I'm a monster? For murdering my father?"

Samantha took her hand. "No. If you think he deserved it, that's good enough for me."

"Thanks. I was hoping you would feel that way."

"I love you," Samantha said.

"I love you, too."

"Would you like to go feed the doves? I bought a jar of breadcrumbs yesterday."

"Yes," Aubrey said. "I would love to."

CHAPTER 20

Like a dream, Christina thought.

Ever since the acid had kicked in, almost everything about this night—being abducted and forced into the back of a delivery truck; getting herded into this packed auditorium; witnessing the executions of Isaac and other members of the audience—it all seemed like a dream. The only thing that felt real was her performance: singing, playing bass, and creating music on this stage while her girlfriend played guitar and a boy she had never met before played drums. She smiled while she sang, happy despite the madness of her predicament, for Christina had never felt more at home anywhere than right here on this stage.

Eventually, however, the show ended, and they were herded back outside onto the loading bay. Soon thereafter, the delivery truck dropped them off at the stop sign where they had been abducted. Their confiscated phones were not returned. They made their way back to Kenzie's car in front of the warehouse and got in.

"I'm sorry about your friend," Kenzie said, starting the engine. "What was his name again?"

"Isaac."

"Isaac. Right. Seemed like a nice kid."

From the floorboard, Christina grabbed their bottle of rum. She uncapped it and took a drink. "We're gonna have to get new phones tomorrow."

"Yes."

"And I don't have the money for a phone, so I'm gonna have to rob my dad tonight."

Kenzie turned the car around. "I'll buy you a new phone, baby. It's no big deal. You still wanna go get the shoebox, though?"

"Yes."

Fifteen minutes later, Kenzie parked along the street in front of Christina's father's house.

"All the lights are out," Christina said. "I'll be right back."

She got out and went inside.

The interior was dark, silent. She grabbed a flashlight from the kitchen and took it into her bedroom, where she filled a duffel bag with some clothes, an extra pair of shoes, and the shoebox containing the photographs of her dead mother.

She took the flashlight back into the kitchen. Then she wrapped her right hand in a dishrag and used it to grab a claw hammer from the utility drawer.

Her father was passed out—snoring and reeking of whiskey—when she stepped into his bedroom. Moonlight through the window illuminated his face. His mouth was open. She tried to slap him awake a couple of times, but he never budged.

Christina raised the hammer. "This is for my mother." Then she brought the hammer straight down onto the center of his forehead. She was pretty sure the first blow killed him, but she kept swinging the hammer until nothing remained of his head and face but a bloody, unrecognizable mess.

She left the hammer and the dishrag on the bed. Then she went back outside and got in Kenzie's car.

"You killed him," Kenzie said, behind the steering wheel. The engine was still running.

Christina nodded. "Yes. How did you know?"

"There's blood all over your face, and in your hair. You'll have to get rid of those clothes now, too."

"I brought more," Christina said, tossing her bag into the back.

Chapter 21

J ack raised his glass of whiskey. "To the baby."

Elaine's labor was scheduled to be induced at nine a.m. tomorrow. The baby was a boy and they had already named him Carl.

Elaine smiled at Jack from across the table. "His first year of spring."

"What are you talking about?"

"Human life expectancy," Elaine said, "is eighty years. Well, slightly more for a woman. A little less for a man. But for simplicity, we'll say eighty years. Eighty divided by the four seasons is twenty. So the first twenty years of life is spring. After that, ages twenty to forty is summer, forty to sixty is autumn, and then sixty to eighty is winter. You and I are in the summers of our lives."

Jack swallowed a drink. "So if life was like a football game...you know, with four quarters—anything after eighty would be overtime."

Elaine shrugged. "Yes, you could say that." Then she raised her glass of water. "To the baby."

She knew Carl was abnormal when he was born. Jack cut the cord and Carl screamed silently until the nurse dislodged whatever had been stuck inside his throat. Then his mouth opened wide and his loud voice filled the hospital room. To Elaine, Carl's cries sounded like knives being raked across sheet metal.

"He's beautiful," the nurse said, but she wouldn't make eye contact with Elaine.

Jack wouldn't look at her, either. He was simply staring at a wall, looking dumbfounded. Elaine thought he was probably thinking the same thing: Their baby was downright hideous

They took Carl home and he sucked Elaine's tits dry. Then Jack went to a store and bought some formula and Carl ate every bit of it. They ordered pizza for dinner and Carl kept trying to stick his face inside the box.

His head seemed abnormally large to Elaine—already bigger than it had been just that morning. He had been born bald two days before, but he had already grown some black hair at the base of his fat neck. Elaine shuddered just looking at her son and wondered if there had been some sort of mistake.

Carl refused to sleep in his bassinet. He would scream and cry until they put him in bed with them. Then he refused to let Jack sleep in bed with him and Elaine. He would scream and cry until Jack would get up for a shot of whiskey or a cigarette, and then Carl would immediately become quiet and act peacefully. After that, Jack just started sleeping on the couch.

Carl grew every night. Every morning, Elaine would wake up and see him lying on the bed with his diaper burst open. By the fourth day, his penis was easily the size of a grown man's. He grew to fifty pounds within a week and seventy halfway through the next, with a full head of black hair and several scattered teeth that didn't look like baby teeth at all.

Carl called Elaine *baby* when he was three weeks old. She was breastfeeding him, and he pulled her nipple out of his mouth with a fist. Then he smiled up at her and she noticed a few more of those evil-looking teeth. "Baby," he said.

"Yes," Elaine said. "You're Mommy's little baby."

Carl shook his head. Then he smiled again. "No. You're *my* little baby. I'm Carl. You're baby."

A part of Elaine was horrified, and another part was proud of her infant son for speaking in complete sentences.

He never talked around Jack, however—only Elaine. For the most part, Carl barely acknowledged the fact that his father even existed.

One morning, Jack said, "He looks just like your brother."

Elaine's brother—Lucas—was a building superintendent in New York City, and liked Lucas at all.

He took a shot of whiskey. "I'm starting to think you fucked your creepy brother."

Elaine just shook her head. "Don't be silly."

CHAPTER 22

Mitchell woke up first. He looked beyond the bedroom window and saw that night had fallen. Beside him on the bed, Marla lay whispering in her sleep. He couldn't make out what she was saying, but he knew that—for the rest of his life—the voice he needed to hear was hers, whispering in the night.

He got up, went to the bathroom, and brushed his teeth. He took a quick shower and shaved. Then he went back into the bedroom and saw that Marla was awake. She was sitting up on the bed holding the bottle of Maker's Mark.

"We're almost out of whiskey," she said.

"We'll get more," Mitchell said, putting on the same clothes he'd been wearing earlier.

Marla took a drink. "Mind if I take a shower?"

He put a hand on his hip and cocked his head. "This is where you live now. You're going to be my wife. You don't have to ask my permission for anything."

Marla took a shower. When she came out of the bathroom, Mitchell sat drinking from a bottle of vodka at the kitchen table.

"Ready to go get your stuff?" he said. "From your brother's place?"

She nodded. "I don't have much. Just some clothes and my laptop. Let me hit that vodka."

He handed her the bottle, and she took a drink.

"We need to get more whiskey, too," she said.

"Were you serious about wanting to kill your brother and his wife?"

"Yes."

"Then you should probably leave your cellphone here."

Marla cocked her head. "My cellphone?"

"Yes. They're tracking devices."

"I don't have a cellphone."

"You don't?"

"No. I can't afford one. And I'm not really going to kill them, anyway. I would like to, but it's just a fantasy."

Mitchell stood up. His jacket was hanging on the back of his chair, and he put it on. Then he pulled his car keys from a pocket of his jeans. "Ready when you are."

She took another drink and set the bottle on the table. "Do you have a cellphone?"

"Yes, but it can't be traced to me."

They took the elevator down to the first floor and went outside. They saw no other people in the parking lot.

"Want my jacket?" Mitchell said.

"No. It's a beautiful night."

"Every night is beautiful. Do you love it as much as I do?"

"Of course I love the night," she told him. "I'm made of stars, as are we all."

They got in his car and went to a nearby liquor store. He bought two fifths of whiskey. He put one in the trunk and cracked the other one open behind the steering wheel. Then she guided him to the building in which her brother and his wife lived.

Mitchell parked in front of the building and killed the engine. "Which floor?"

"Second. Right there on the end." She pointed to a window through which he could see the flickering light of a television.

"Is it cool to take the liquor in?" He took a drink.

"Sure. Let me hit that."

He handed her the bottle, and she took a drink.

"My brother's a big guy, though. He's even bigger than you are. And he's fucking crazy, too. Never can tell what he's going to do. Really just depends on whatever fucking drug he's on. If it's heroin, he might be nodding off and drooling all over himself. If it's meth, he might be jumping up and down on the goddamn coffee table. But he's usually harmless. Just thought I should tell you that."

They took the stairs up to the second floor. Her brother and his wife lived in 2G. When they reached the door at the end of the hallway, she handed him the bottle and unlocked the door with a key. Then she opened the door, and he followed her inside.

Her brother and his wife were seated on a sofa, playing a video game on a big-screen TV, but her brother paused the game and stood up as soon as they stepped into the living room. He was one of the biggest men Mitchell had ever seen. His head nearly touched the ceiling. His arms were about the size of Mitchell's thighs. His wife's eyes—like her husband's—appeared to be ready to pop out of her skull.

"This is my fiancé," Marla told them. "We're going to Las Vegas and getting married."

"Tonight?" her brother said.

Marla looked at Mitchell. "Yes. I'm pretty sure our planets are aligned."

Mitchell smiled. Then he took a drink from the bottle of whiskey.

"Can we go?" her brother said. "We're tripping on acid. We love to go to Vegas when we're tripping." He looked down at his wife. "Ain't that right, baby?"

She nodded, smiling and clawing at her face. "Yes. The lights of Vegas are awesome when you're tripping."

Mitchell checked his watch. "It's almost midnight. Driving at night, it usually takes me about four hours to get there. If we leave now, we'll be there before the sun rises over the desert. I'm ready whenever."

Her brother was still staring at Mitchell's wristwatch. "Is that a Rolex?"

"Yes."

"Goddamn, man. That is a beautiful fucking watch."

"Thank you."

Marla looked at Mitchell. "Come on. I need to pack my suitcase."

He followed her into the kitchen, where she grabbed a couple of trash bags, and then he followed her into a bedroom.

She took a suitcase from a closet and put some clothes in it. She put her laptop in one of the trash bags and put it on top of the clothes. She took the other trash bag into the adjoining bathroom and put her toiletries in it. Then she put the toiletries in her suitcase and zipped it closed. "Everything I own," she said. "I pack light."

Mitchell smiled. "You're going to be my wife."

"Yes," Marla said. "Let's hit the fucking road."

Mitchell drove. Marla rode shotgun. Her brother rode behind her, and his wife rode behind Mitchell. They loaded up on booze and smokes before leaving the city. Then, after about forty miles east on I-10, it was a straight shot north on I-15 all the way to Nevada.

Because Marla's brother and his wife were tripping on acid, they drank beer instead of whiskey. Mitchell had to keep stopping the car so they could relieve themselves on the side of the road.

It was after five in the morning before they crossed into Nevada. The sun rose about twenty minutes later. Mitchell took a dirt road off the interstate and parked near the base of one of the mountains that surrounded them on all sides.

"Why are we stopping here?" the brother's wife said. "Vegas is still a few miles away."

"Life's too mysterious," her husband said. "Don't take it serious." Then he began cackling maniacally.

Mitchell—looking at the wife in the rearview mirror—took a drink of whiskey. "For the scenery," he said. "One of my favorite spots is up ahead, and I wanna show it to Marla. Plus, I figured you two would need to piss." He handed the bottle to Marla, and she took a drink.

The wife finished her beer and lit a cigarette. "Works for me. I'm ready to stretch my legs, anyway."

The four of them got out of the car and set off into a stretch of desert. It wasn't yet six a.m., but the temperature was at least eighty degrees.

Marla's brother looked at Mitchell. "Aren't you burning up in that fucking jacket?"

Mitchell shook his head. "No. I'm okay."

They walked in silence for a while, and then stopped when they saw eight words scrawled in red across the face of a rock wall: *None of you will leave this place alive.*

"Trippy," the wife said. Then she looked at her husband. "Can we smoke some weed? This acid's starting to wear off a little bit."

"Sure." He finished his beer, tossed the can off the large flat rock that all four of them were standing on, and sat down. His wife sat down beside him. He retrieved a bag of weed and a pack of rolling papers from a pocket of the knee-length camouflage shorts he was wearing. His T-shirt was already soaked with sweat.

Marla and Mitchell did not sit down. She handed him the bottle. He took a drink and gave the bottle back. Then he looked over at the eight words scrawled across the face of the rock wall. "Whoever wrote those words was fifty percent prophetic."

Marla's brother looked up at him. "What the fuck are you talking about?"

"The dead are whispering on the wind. They're speaking to us. Can't you hear them?"

"There is no fucking wind," Marla's brother said.

His wife looked up at Mitchell. "Dude, you're fucking loco."

Mitchell pulled a pistol from a holster beneath his jacket. Marla saw a silencer attached to the semiautomatic's barrel. "Gwyneth is speaking from beyond the grave," Mitchell said.

Marla's brother shot his sister a look of confusion, and then looked back up at Mitchell. "Is that right?"

"Yes."

"And what exactly is Gwyneth saying from beyond the grave?"

Mitchell took a few steps to the left, until he stood next to the woman, who still sat beside her husband. He raised the gun to the side of her head. "Gwyneth says to tell your wife goodbye." Then he shot her through the head, blowing her brains out the other side of her skull, and all over her husband's face.

Marla started jumping up and down, delirious with excitement, then leaned over and put her face in front of her brother's blood-soaked face. "HOW DOES IT FEEL NOW, YOU PIECE OF FUCKING SHIT? HOW DOES IT FEEL TO LOSE THE WOMAN YOU LOVE?"

Her brother said nothing; he continued putting marijuana into a rolling paper—as if nothing unusual had occurred.

Marla picked up a jagged chunk of stone and smashed it against the side of her brother's head. Mitchell heard a crack that may have been the sound of the man's skull splitting open.

Her brother slumped over on the rock. His wide-open eyes were still bright with acid and awareness. Fresh blood oozed from his temple and commingled with his dead wife's blood on his face.

Mitchell stood over the man and aimed the gun at his head.

"No!" Marla said. "Let me do it! I want to be the one who kills him."

Mitchell shrugged. "Okay." He pulled a revolver from his jacket's interior pocket and aimed it at her brother. Then he gave the semiautomatic to Marla. "Knock yourself out."

She aimed the pistol at her brother's face. "For Gwyneth, you piece of fucking shit." She squeezed the trigger at close range and the bullet seemed to separate his eyes.

"Can I have my gun back?" Mitchell said.

She handed him the gun. He returned the pistol to its holster and the revolver to his jacket's interior pocket.

They walked back to the car and got in and Mitchell started the engine. They passed the bottle back and forth the rest of the way to Vegas.

CHAPTER 23

S amantha found herself in a constant state of arousal whenever Aubrey was around. They lay naked on Aubrey's bed, in her apartment on the Rosira's second floor. Both were still wet from hours of sex, with little else to do but exchange life stories and share bottles of vodka in between bouts of lovemaking. When not exploring each other's bodies, they confessed secrets to each other.

The suitcase containing two million dollars was stashed in Aubrey's walk-in closet.

"What are you gonna do with all that money?" Samantha said. "It's probably not a good idea to keep that much cash in the apartment."

"I'm not sure yet," Aubrey said. "I thought about putting it all in a safe-deposit box, but those things aren't insured."

"Is that, like, one of those boxes that you keep in a bank's vault, or whatever? And they give you your own personal key?"

"Yes. There's two keys, actually. You get one, and the bank keeps the other. It takes both keys to open the box."

"And they're not insured?"

"No. I looked into it. You can purchase your own insurance to cover theft, fire, terrorist attack, or whatever, but if the stuff in your box turns up missing for any reason, you're basically shit out of luck."

Samantha took a drink. "Damn. You'd be better off buying your own damn safe."

"Yeah. I'll probably just do that, and then start putting the money in my bank account, one small deposit at a time. I'm also thinking about giving some to my brother."

"Oh yeah?"

"Thinking about it, even though Mitchell doesn't need it. I mean, he inherited money when Mom died, and he'll inherit even more, now that our father's dead. Let me hit that vodka."

Samantha handed her the bottle.

Aubrey took a drink and gave the bottle back. "Wanna go shopping for a safe?"

"Sure." Samantha capped the bottle and set it on the nightstand.

Aubrey rose from the bed. "Let's go take a shower first."

Chapter 24

After tossing her bloodstained clothes in a dumpster, Christina chopped her hair short and dyed it blue.

"It looks good," Kenzie told her, standing behind her in the hotel bathroom, looking at Christina's hair in the mirror. "Hopefully, whenever they find your father's body, they'll think whoever killed him abducted you. But you'll have to stay off your old social media accounts forever."

"I'll create new fake accounts," Christina said. 'With a fake email. I'm still gonna need a new phone, though. I use a phone for a whole lot more than just social media."

Kenzie took a drink from the bottle of rum she was holding. "I'll get two new phones, with two separate lines, and give you one of those."

"Thanks, baby."

"You're welcome." Kenzie kissed Christina's forehead. "And then I'm thinking we just need to lay low for a while. Maybe go stay at my mom's house in Fort Lee, or my sister's place in New York."

Staring at Kenzie's reflection in the mirror, Christina cocked her head. "I didn't know you had a sister."

"Yes. In Manhattan."

Christina turned around to face her. "What's her name?"

"Samantha."

"Is she older than you?"

"Four years older. She's twenty-two."

"I've always wanted to see New York City," Christina said.

Kenzie nodded. "Cool. After we get our phones, I'll send her a message and let her know we'll be there soon."

CHAPTER 25

One morning, when Carl was two months old, Elaine had to dig splinters from his penis with a sewing needle because it got stuck between two wooden bars of his playpen.

Jack sat across from them at the kitchen table, drinking whiskey. "I was watching videos on YouTube earlier," he said, "about freakishly large babies. I saw one about a girl who looked like she was twelve, but the parents claimed she wasn't even a year old yet. The girl was wearing a diaper that the father had made out of a tablecloth. So, I mean, it *does* happen. Some babies just get freakishly big. But, other than being freakishly big, the little girl seemed perfectly normal. Carl doesn't seem normal. He seems like some kind of a monster."

While Elaine still worked on his penis with the sewing needle, Carl glared at his father and hissed.

Jack took another shot of whiskey. Then he laughed, but there was no humor in it. "I think he understood what I just said."

He did, Elaine thought. *Carl understands everything we say.*

They took Carl to a doctor. Carl didn't speak, pretending to be dumb as he pretended around his father. The doctor weighed Carl. He was up to eighty pounds with his third month still two weeks away.

"What the heck are you feeding him?" the doctor asked. He seemed—like Jack—to be revolted by Carl's appearance, but Elaine thought her baby boy was growing into a handsome little man.

"Carl eats pretty much whatever he wants to," Jack said.

The doctor shook his head. "He should not be eating table food."

He told them to make sure Carl got plenty of exercise. Then he sent them home.

That night, while Elaine gave Carl a bath, his penis got hard and poked up out of the water.

Jack walked in to blow his nose and saw Carl's erection. "Boy's got a bigger pecker than I do. I bet your creepy brother's got a big old pecker, too. Maybe you and Carl should go live with Lucas, in New York City."

Elaine shot her husband an angry stare. "You're insane."

Jack walked out and slammed the bathroom door.

CHAPTER 26

When Marla woke up, Mitchell was already awake. He sat at a small table beside the bed on which she lay. His hair was wet. He wore blue disposable gloves and was cleaning one of his guns.

She sat up on the bed. "Where are we?"

"Sleazy motel on the strip."

"So we're in Vegas?"

"Yes. What's the last thing you remember?"

"Blowing my brother's brains out, pretty much. I was fucking drunk. Must have blacked out. Did you take a shower?"

"Yes. The water pressure's not bad."

"I need a shower. And I'm fucking thirsty, too."

Mitchell pointed to a bottle on the table. "I just opened the whiskey."

Marla shook her head. "Not yet. I seriously need to hydrate before I start drinking whiskey."

"Your brother," Mitchell said. "Was he the first person you ever killed?"

"Yes. And I take it his wife was *not* the first person you ever killed."

"No. Not even close."

She nodded. "That's what I thought. The silencer was pretty

much a dead giveaway."

Mitchell took a drink. "Sorry for the cheap motel. I know you deserve better, but this place lets me pay with cash and no ID. And they have no cameras. I didn't want to leave any evidence that we were here. I mean, it might be a while before the bodies are found, but still . . ."

Marla rose from the bed and stretched. "I suppose we can't get married in Vegas now."

He shook his head. "I figured we could spend the night here, and then head back home tomorrow. Besides, we have the rest of our lives to get married."

Marla glanced at the window. The curtains were closed. "What time is it?"

Mitchell looked at his wristwatch. "Almost six p.m. Sunset's at eight."

She smiled. "Nice gloves, by the way."

"Latex," he said. "I never leave home without them."

Marla saw her suitcase on the floor. She picked it up and set it on the bed. "Did I carry this in, or did you?"

"I did, after you fell asleep."

"Thanks." She opened the suitcase. "Have you slept at all?"

"Yes. Couple of hours. I don't sleep much."

Marla took her toiletries into the bathroom and closed the door. Fifteen minutes later, she emerged from the bathroom with wet hair.

"Feel better?" Mitchell said.

"Yes. I drank about a gallon of tap water, and now I'm ready to drink some fucking whiskey." She put the bag of toiletries in her suitcase. Then she joined Mitchell at the table by the bed.

"Are you hungry?" Mitchell said.

"Not yet. You?"

He shook his head. "Not yet. I wanna get drunk before I eat. We'll go out and find some dinner later."

"Works for me."

Marla lit a cigarette and set it in the ashtray on the table. "This place must be sleazy. I didn't think you could smoke indoors anywhere anymore."

"Seems that way, doesn't it? Most places, anyway." Mitchell lit a cigarette. "I slipped some cash to the chick at the front desk, when we got here, and told her we'd be smoking. The cash made her happy. She even gave me the ashtray."

"Cool."

"I turned the TV on while you were sleeping, but I turned it off. There's only about five channels, and all of them are porn. Want me to turn it back on?"

"No thanks. I'm good. I had to kill a couple of cockroaches in the shower."

"Me too."

Marla blew a smoke ring. "So how many people have you killed, anyway?"

"I don't know."

"Ten? Twenty?"

"Oh, no. Certainly more than that."

"A hundred?"

He shrugged. "I don't know. If I had to guess? Over the years? Maybe four hundred. Five hundred. Something like that."

"Holy shit!" Marla finished her cigarette and put it out. "So what are you? A serial killer? An assassin? Something like that?"

Mitchell put his cigarette out, too. "Well, technically, if you kill two people, you're a serial killer, so I suppose you could say I *am* a serial killer, but I'm not like most normal serial killers."

Marla laughed. "Ah, so most serial killers are normal. I see."

Mitchell shook his head. "That's not what I meant. What I'm trying to say is that I don't kill people for the same reasons that most serial killers do. I just like doing nice things for good people."

"What the fuck are you talking about?"

Mitchell took a drink. "I dream of a perfect world. And perfect people with perfect health. A perfect society with perfect laws, perfect justice, perfect equality for everyone."

Marla said nothing. The sounds of two people having sex in the room next door were easy to hear through the thin walls.

Mitchell took another drink. "I can't change the world, of

course. And I can't change society. But I like doing nice things for good people whenever I can."

"By killing them," Marla said.

"By removing imperfect people from the prisons of their misery. Whenever I see these sad, imperfect people, I'm filled with unspeakable despair. But when I kill them, I set them free. Their suffering is over, and my sorrow is lifted."

Marla took a drink. "Until the next time."

He smiled. "Sometimes the best thing you can do for someone is kill them."

She shook her head. "Dude, you're fucking wacko." Marla kissed him.

They drank until the fifth was empty, and then opened another one.

Around ten p.m., Marla said, "I'm starving."

"Me too."

They left in Mitchell's car.

The night was hot. Casinos, hotels, and restaurants dominated both sides of downtown's neon-lined avenues. They chose a restaurant called Irishman's Flat. Mitchell ordered trout and a bottle of beer. Marla ordered veal and a glass of wine. They ate. Mitchell paid for the food and tipped their waitress generously.

"I'm ready to drink some more whiskey," Marla said. "And smoke a cigarette. But first, I need to use the bathroom. Be right back."

She went to the restroom. When she came back out, Mitchell looked as if he had seen a ghost. "What's wrong?"

"My sister killed my father," Mitchell said.

Marla cocked her head. "What?"

"My sister. Aubrey. She messaged me while you were in the bathroom. Said she killed our father."

"Seriously?"

"Yes. I mean, she didn't come right out and *say* it. She was speaking in code, but it was easy to figure out what she was talking about. She said she killed our father, and that she had some money waiting for me in Manhattan."

"Why did she kill him?"

"Long story. Aubrey hated our father. And a part of me hated our father, too. But I also loved him. And of course, I love my sister, but now I'm thinking I might have to kill her."

He rose from the table. "You ever been to New York?"

"No."

"You feel like riding clear across the country with me?"

"I guess."

"Maybe we'll get married," Mitchell said, "while we're there."

She smiled. "Maybe so."

CHAPTER 27

On the Rosira's second floor, Aubrey's doorbell rang. "Probably the superintendent," she told Samantha, who sat next to her on the living-room sofa, going over the script of a play she had auditioned for recently.

At the front door, staring through the one-way peephole, she saw not only the superintendent—Lucas—but the old janitor—Oliver—standing next to each other out in the hallway. Aubrey opened the door.

Lucas—tall, menacing, and of an indeterminate age—held a clipboard. Oliver—in his seventies, but still spry; not short, but shorter than Lucas—held a toolbox.

"Hello, gentlemen. Come on in."

The two men entered her apartment.

Aubrey closed the door and locked it. "Can I get you something to drink?"

Lucas shook his head. "No thank you."

She looked at Oliver. "What about you?"

He smiled. "No thank you, dear. I'm okay."

Lucas looked down at his clipboard. "I understand you have a safe that needs bolted to the floor."

"Yes."

"Where is it?"

"In my room. Right this way." She led the two men into her bedroom, where the safe stood empty in a corner with its door open.

"Big safe," Lucas said. "How'd you get it up here?"

"They delivered it. They used a dolly to get it up here."

Oliver, still holding the toolbox, approached the safe and bent down for a closer inspection. "Yep," he said. "Already has its own bolts and mounting holes. Want me to bolt it down right here, or in your closet?"

"Right there's fine," Aubrey said. "I need my closet space."

Oliver nodded. "Will do." From his toolbox, he retrieved a power drill and drilled four anchor holes into the floor through the mounting holes in the base of the safe. Then he inserted the bolts through the base and tightened the nuts on top of the bolts, securing the safe to the floor. "You're all set."

"Thank you very much," Aubrey said.

Lucas shot her a look. "You could keep a couple of small children in that safe, if you wanted to."

Aubrey cocked her head. The suitcase containing the two million dollars was locked up in the spare bedroom. "Is that right?"

He shrugged. "It's big enough. That's all I'm saying."

She smiled. "I'll keep that in mind."

In the living room, Samantha still sat on the sofa, perusing the playscript.

Aubrey led the two men across the room to the front door, then unlocked and opened it for them. "Thanks again."

As the men were leaving, Oliver turned around to face her. "You're new to this city, aren't you?"

"Yes."

The old man smiled. "I thought so."

Then Lucas, too, turned around to face her. "This whole city's new, actually. In the scheme of things."

"You think so?"

He nodded. "Absolutely. Compared to many cities around the world, New York City is still a goddamn infant."

"Can't argue with that," Aubrey said.

"I mean, the river's old," he said, gesturing in what Aubrey knew was the direction of the Hudson River. "And the land itself is as old as any land on planet Earth. But New York City is still a goddamn baby."

"Thanks again," Aubrey said.

The two men left.

Aubrey closed the door and locked it.

"That superintendent is creepy," Samantha said, after Aubrey sat down next to her on the sofa.

"Yes. He certainly is."

Samantha set her playscript on the coffee table. "Anyway, Kenzie messaged me a few minutes ago."

"Your sister?"

"Yes."

"What did she say?"

"Said she and her girlfriend are coming to visit us soon. I told her a little about you, and she's looking forward to meeting you."

Aubrey nodded. "Cool. I'm looking forward to meeting her, too. And her girlfriend."

"I've never met her girlfriend," Samantha said. "Her name's Christina. She's seventeen. A year younger than Kenzie. But if Kenzie likes her, I'm sure I'll like her, too."

"I'm ready to start drinking," Aubrey said. "Do you have any vodka in your apartment?"

"Plenty."

They rode the elevator together up to the penthouse.

CHAPTER 28

In Fort Lee, Kenzie parked in front of her mother's early-Victorian mansion.

"Wow," Christina said. "What a house."

Kenzie's mother greeted them in the great room, swirling the contents of a cocktail glass with a swizzle stick.

"Hello, Kenzie. Who's your friend?"

"*Girlfriend*," Kenzie corrected. "This is Christina."

"It's nice to meet you, Christina. I'm Emma Kinkade."

"Likewise," Christina said. "You have a beautiful house."

"Thank you." Emma turned to her daughter. "How was Jersey City?"

Kenzie shrugged. "I don't know. I met Christina there, so it wasn't *all* that bad."

"Will you be attending the university there?"

"No. It's a long story, but we're done with Jersey City."

"Is that so?"

"Yes. I tried to call you about an hour ago, but I just got a new phone, and knew you wouldn't recognize the number."

Emma pulled her phone out, swiped the screen, and held it up for Kenzie to see. "Is this the number?"

Kenzie stepped forward to look at the screen. "Yep. That's it."

"I'll add it to my contacts," Emma said. "Have you talked to your sister?"

"Yes. As a matter of fact, we're on our way to visit Samantha now. Just wanted to stop and grab a few things, before we head to New York. And I've decided not to go to music school, by the way."

"Good." Emma sipped her drink. "You don't need it. Music school would be a waste of your time and talent."

Christina said, "I told her the same thing! I've been telling her we should form a rock band, when we get to New York."

Emma looked at Christina. "So you're a musician, too?"

"Yes. Well, kind of. Kenzie's been teaching me to play guitar."

Kenzie laughed. Then she told her mother, "Christina's being modest. She's one of the best singers I've ever heard. If we start a band, she's going to be the vocalist."

Emma turned to Christina. "Sing something for me."

Christina sang the first few lines of a song she had written recently.

"Damn!" Emma said, after she was finished. "That was fantastic!"

"Thanks," Christina said.

Kenzie told Christina, "Come on. You can help me pack."

Christina followed Kenzie to her room.

CHAPTER 29

W hen Carl was six months old, he walked into the kitchen one night and opened the refrigerator. Jack and Elaine sat at the table, playing cards. Carl closed the refrigerator. Then he stood on his tiptoes and opened the freezer door. The freezer was where Jack kept his whiskey. After that, Jack started keeping Carl downstairs in the basement.

"He doesn't like the basement," Elaine told Jack one day, when Carl was eight months old. "He gets lonely down there. And scared. And cold."

Jack took a drink of whiskey. "I'll turn the heat up for him. And give him a couple more blankets."

She wanted to protest, but Jack often got violent and beat her when he was drinking, so Elaine said nothing and walked away.

On the night before his first birthday, Carl fell asleep on the living-room floor in front of the TV. Jack, drinking whiskey on the couch, had not yet taken him downstairs to the basement for the night. When he noticed that Carl was sleeping, he got up and staggered into the master bedroom.

Elaine lay on the bed in her bra and panties, reading a novel.

Jack stretched out beside her on the bed. He took the novel out of her hands and set it on the nightstand. Then he raked a hand through her hair and began kissing her neck.

"Not tonight, Jack. I don't feel good."

"But we haven't had sex in months."

"I'm sorry," Elaine said. "I have a headache."

"Well, apparently your head's not hurting too bad to read one of those stupid romance books."

A sound drew their attention to the bedroom doorway.

Carl stood in the doorway. "I'm hungry."

"You're always goddamn hungry," Jack said. "I'm taking your stupid ass down to the basement."

"No!" Carl took off running.

Jack got up and took off chasing Carl.

By the time Elaine caught up with them, in the kitchen, Jack had Carl by the hair and was opening the door to the basement.

"Leave him alone!" Elaine shouted. "Let him go!"

Jack spun around from the open door and released his hold on Carl. "Or else what, bitch? What the fuck are you gonna do about it?"

A red rage rose up inside Elaine. Without even thinking about it, she raised both arms and gave him a hard shove. Jack's eyes widened as he tumbled backward down the stairs. He flipped two or three times on the way down before his head smacked the cinderblock wall with a resounding thud at the bottom. His skull cracked open. Blood covered the wall. Jack lay motionless on the concrete floor in a broken heap.

"He's dead," Carl said.

"Yes." Elaine closed the door and locked it. "I'll tell the police he got drunk and fell down the stairs. Then we'll go visit my brother in New York City. It's about time you met your uncle Lucas, anyway. But first I need to feed you. I know you're hungry."

Carl followed his mother into her bedroom.

Elaine had a seat on the bed and Carl sat down on her lap. Elaine pulled a breast out and Carl licked her nipple. His diaper burst open and he had a massive erection.

"I love you, son."

"I love you too, baby." Carl put a hand down her panties.

Elaine reached over and turned off the lamp.

CHAPTER 30

The elevator doors slid open, and Lucas stepped out onto the eleventh floor. The woman from 11B stood in the hallway, yelling at a man—her boyfriend, presumably—as he headed toward the stairway.

"That's right, motherfucker!" the woman shouted. "Get your sorry ass outta here, and don't *ever* come back!"

The man did not reply, allowing his footsteps down the stairs as he descended to be his only response.

The woman turned her gaze to Lucas. She wore a torn nightgown, and no bra. She clawed tangled hair out of her bloodshot eyes and smiled. "Hi there, neighbor! Wait a second. You're the superintendent, right?"

He nodded.

"What's your name again?"

"Lucas."

"Lucas! That's right. I'm Donna. What brings you up here at three o'clock in the morning, Lucas?"

"Noise complaints." He looked down at his clipboard. "Some of your neighbors were complaining about the noise."

"Is that right? Well, I have a few complaints, myself. If you wanna come in for a drink, I'll tell you all about them."

"Okay." Lucas stepped into her apartment.

In the living room, the stench of a filthy litter box hit him immediately. Clothes covered most of the furniture. Unopened bills surrounded an ashtray overflowing with cigarette butts on the heavily-stained coffee table.

From an end table next to the satin-covered sofa, she grabbed a bottle of Jack Daniel's and held it up. "You like whiskey?"

"I do."

She handed him the bottle. He took a drink and gave the bottle back.

"Now," Lucas said, "tell me about those complaints you mentioned."

"Water bugs in the bathroom." Donna took a drink. "And the woman upstairs keeps pouring grease down the kitchen sink. I think she's been flushing her tampons, too, because my toilet keeps clogging up. And I'm sick to goddamn death of killing cockroaches. You need to get an exterminator in here, or something. Also, there's some kind of a giant bird—I don't know if it's an eagle, an owl, or what—that keeps dropping decapitated pigeon carcasses out on the balcony. Is there anything you can do about that?"

Lucas nodded. "I'll see what I can do."

With the hand not holding his clipboard, he retrieved his phone and made a call. "Oliver. Hello. Listen, I know it's late, but Donna in 11B has a clogged toilet. Yes. I'm up here with her now. Can you come up here and take a look at that real quick? Okay. Thank you."

Lucas ended the call. "He said he'll be right up."

"Great!" Donna said.

Oliver arrived soon thereafter, holding a toolbox. When Donna turned around to lead him to the bathroom, Lucas watched the old man withdraw a hypodermic syringe of what he knew was a fast-acting sedative from his jacket's interior pocket and shove the needle into the side of her neck. Oliver pressed the plunger. Donna raised a hand to her neck, but never said a word. Seconds later, her eyes rolled up into her head. Then she dropped to the floor, unconscious.

"Is the hallway empty?" Lucas said.

Oliver set his toolbox on the floor. "Of course. It's almost four o'clock in the morning. I'll come back and get my toolbox later."

Lucas set his clipboard on top of Oliver's toolbox. They wrapped a blanket around Donna and dragged her from the apartment to the freight elevator at the other end of the hallway. They rode the elevator down to Lucas's domain in the basement.

They dragged Donna—still unconscious—past Lucas's apartment, past the laundry room, past the garbage room, past the elevator-motor room, and set her down in front of the door to the boiler room. Lucas unlocked and opened the door. Then they dragged Donna into the boiler room. Lucas closed the door and locked it.

Illumination was dim, but sufficient. There was no one else in the boiler room, but it sounded as if it were full of people. Numerous noisy machines were running: the house pumps; the burner and the blower on the boiler; motors pumping oil and oxygen; the bladder tank; multiple sump pumps gurgling. The room itself was large, hollow, and bricked up, so all noise inside it echoed until everything sounded orchestral.

They dragged Donna past the water pumps, stripped her naked, and strapped her to a mobile operating table parked in front of the boiler. Surgical instruments were arranged on a tray atop a cart next to the table. There was a drain beneath the table in the concrete floor.

Oliver pointed to a steel door in the wall, next to the boiler. "Is this the new incinerator you were telling me about?"

"Yes," Lucas said. "A cremation system, like they have in mortuaries. Wanna see it?"

"Sure."

Lucas approached the steel door, yanked its metal handle, and swung it open. Beyond was a conveyor belt, and the scent of cooked meat came wafting out. Next to the steel door was a digital readout. Lucas pushed a green button. Gas inside the incinerator began escaping under pressure, and orange flames ignited. He closed the door and pushed a red button. The conveyor belt squeaked as it started moving. Numerals on the readout quickly jumped from 300 to 600 to 1200 to 2400. Then he shut the system off and turned around. "Pretty nifty, huh?"

Oliver nodded. "Yes. That will make getting rid of the bones easier."

On the operating table, Donna came awake. "What's going on? Where am I? What's happening to me?"

"You're in the boiler room," Lucas told her. "And I'll let Oliver tell you what's happening to you."

The old man looked down at Donna's naked form on the operating table. "We're going to kill you," Oliver said. "And then we're going to eat you. But first, we're going to torture you for as long as we possibly can."

"Wait!" Donna said. "I have money. A *lot* of money. From my husband's accident."

Oliver cocked his head. "Your husband's accident?"

"Yes."

"You don't *have* a husband. You bring different men home to your apartment every night."

"My husband's dead." Flat on her back, Donna moved her eyes from Oliver to Lucas. "I told you about my husband's accident, right? When I signed the lease? Weren't you in the landlord's office?"

Lucas nodded. "Yes. It was a fascinating story, actually."

"I wanna hear the story," Oliver said.

"My husband melted," Donna told him.

"Melted?"

"Yes. On his thirty-sixth birthday. Michael was older than me. I'm still thirty-three."

"How did it happen?"

"Michael worked at a steel mill."

"A steel mill? In New York?"

"No. Pennsylvania. He was operating the remote control of a ladle belt. The ladle belt was a conveyor suspended high above the floor. It transferred large tubs of molten steel from the melting furnace to the holding furnace. There was an explosion.

High above where Michael was standing, one of the tubs tipped over and dumped five hundred tons of molten steel directly onto his head."

"Holy shit!"

"Once the spill cooled and workers were able to get to him, what remained was more a block of steel than a human being."

"Wow. That *is* fascinating."

"Yes. But at least he died instantly. The coroner told me that Michael probably never felt a thing."

"So there was a lawsuit? A settlement?"

"Yes. I received a large sum of money and moved here, to New York, to start over. And if you'll let me go, I'll give *you* a large sum of money, too. Both of you."

Oliver looked at Lucas. "What do you think?"

Lucas shrugged. "I'm gonna leave it up to you."

Oliver nodded. Then he looked down at Donna. "Gag this fucking bitch."

From the tray of surgical instruments atop the medical cart, Lucas grabbed a ball-gag, shoved the rubber sphere in Donna's mouth, then wrapped the leather strap around her head and buckled it tight.

"I don't want your money," Oliver told Donna. "I'm an old man now, and my needs are meager." He smiled, and added, "The only thing I enjoy more than eating human flesh is torturing young women like you to death."

He walked away, and Lucas followed. They removed their clothes, then came back and loomed naked over Donna on the operating table. From the tray, Lucas selected a scalpel and a retractor. Oliver selected needle-nose pliers and a blowtorch.

"This will be fun," Oliver said. "Just like the good old days."

Smiling, Lucas nodded. "I think I'll start with her face."

He began Donna's slow destruction with the scalpel.

CHAPTER 31

E mma Kinkade looked up from her laptop. The writing had been going so well that it took her a few seconds to recognize the source of the interruption: Her phone was ringing in her pocket. Very few people called her anymore, and she figured it had to be either her agent, her editor, or a solicitor. She took the phone from her pocket, saw her agent's number on the screen, and answered the call. "Hello, Natalie."

"Emma! How are you on this beautiful summer morning?"

"Beautiful?"

"Yes! It's beautiful here in New York. I can't imagine it's all that different across the bridge in Fort Lee."

At thirty-two, Natalie was twelve years younger than Emma. Natalie kept an office on the west side of Manhattan, just across the George Washington Bridge from Emma's house in New Jersey.

"I haven't looked outside yet," Emma said.

"Oh no! Did I wake you?"

Emma took a drink from her bottle. She had started mixing drinks around nine o'clock last night, but had switched to straight vodka after midnight. "No. I haven't been to sleep yet."

"Been writing all night?"

"On and off. My daughter stopped by yesterday."

"Samantha?"

"No. My youngest daughter, Kenzie. She introduced me to her girlfriend. They're headed your way, now. Actually, they should already be there. They left about an hour ago. Said they were headed to Manhattan, to visit Samantha."

"Awesome! Anyway, the reason I'm calling is, I was wondering if—"

"No," Emma interrupted. "Absolutely not."

"You don't even know what I was going to say."

"Yes, I do. You were going to ask me to participate in some vile publicity event." Her latest romance novel was due to launch in a couple of weeks, and she would be expected to publicize its release.

"You should do it for your fans," Natalie said. "All of them are eager to meet the creator of your books. Besides, you're developing a reputation as something of a recluse."

"What did you have in mind?"

Her agent sighed with relief. "A book signing at Mizzoli's, here in New York, in a couple of weeks."

Emma took a drink. "Okay." Then she took another drink. "I'll be there."

Emma woke up that evening and took a shower. Then she mixed a drink and returned to her study. She opened her laptop and finished writing the scene she had been working on that morning. After that, she sat back and looked across the room at her reflection in a mirror between two bookshelves.

I'm forty-four, she thought. *My god, time is flying. And Ryan has been dead for a decade.*

She looked out one of the windows and remembered walking back from a pub to this house with her late husband ten years ago, not long before Ryan committed suicide. The view hadn't changed much. In her mind's eye Emma saw Ryan sitting on the grass, his back against the oak tree at the edge of the property, a notebook open across his lap, working on one of his horror novels or one of his plays in longhand. She blinked and the vision was gone, replaced by images of Ryan hanging from a rope.

She pulled her gaze from the oak tree and looked at one of the bookshelves next to the mirror. One of the shelves bore the four horror novels Ryan published before he died.

Beside one of those books was a reading edition of the only play Ryan wrote that had ever been commissioned, *The Myth of Coincidence*. The play debuted on Broadway not long after he died, and though the play was a success, tragedy and misfortune became attached to the play almost immediately. As far as Emma knew, *The Myth of Coincidence* had not been performed on a stage in almost a decade.

Because it's cursed, Emma thought. *It's a goddamn haunted play.*

She took a drink of vodka. She exhaled, then resumed working on her novel.

CHAPTER 32

M itchell drove. Marla rode next to him on the passenger's side. Eleven hours east of Vegas—and a third of the way through their trip to New York City—they stopped and rented a room in Denver, Colorado. From the hotel, they walked to a nearby restaurant for dinner and drinks.

"Steak," Mitchell said, when the waitress came for their order. "Bloody as hell. Baked potato. Bourbon and Coke."

"Swordfish," Marla said. "Caesar salad. Vodka and ginger ale."

They ate in silence for a while, and then Mitchell said, "Did you know that some lizards spend their entire lives in a tree?"

"No, I didn't know that."

"It's true. Their feet never even touch the ground. And do you know why?"

"No, I don't."

"Fear of death. They're born knowing that everything wants to kill them and eat them, so they spend their whole lives in a tree, with their eyes on the sky, watching out for predatory birds. And look at chameleons, for God's sake. Even a stupid chameleon is so afraid of death that it will actually change the colors of its entire body just to try to stay alive a little while longer."

"Crazy," Marla said.

"Yes. Now compare that to people who kill themselves, or the goth kids with their idiotic death fixations. Some people are just too stupid to live. A lot of them don't have the brains that nature gave a goddamn reptile."

Marla sipped her drink. "Tell me about the first time you ever killed someone."

"Ten years ago. It was dark and I had just come out of a nightclub. I was fifteen years old."

"Wait a second. You were fifteen, and you had just come out of a nightclub?"

"Yes. I was already tall. I looked older than I was.'

"That's funny, because now you look so young."

He shrugged. "Plus I always carried fake IDs. Anyway, I was walking down a dark alley, looking up at the stars, when I almost tripped over an old wino lying in a doorway."

"So you got mad and killed him?"

"I killed him, but I wasn't mad at him. I felt sorry for him. I killed him to put him out of his misery."

"And what did it feel like?"

Mitchell sipped his drink. "It felt amazing. It made me feel like a creature of infinite mercy."

"How did you do it?"

"Bludgeoned him to death. There were a bunch of broken bricks and cinderblocks lying around. I picked up one of the bricks and started bashing him in the face."

"Oh my. Did he scream?"

"No. He never woke up. I bashed his face until there was nothing left of it. By the time I finished, his head looked like a watermelon had exploded."

Marla—finished with her meal—put her fork down and pushed her plate to the edge of the table for the waitress. "I've been suicidal before. Does that make me too stupid to live?"

Mitchell, too, pushed his plate to the edge of the table and held Marla's hand. "No, but I'm glad you didn't kill yourself. Otherwise, I never would have met you."

Marla finished her drink. "Feel like going for a walk?"

"I guess." Mitchell finished his drink, and then paid their bill with cash.

The summer night was warm. It wasn't even 10 p.m. Swarms of pedestrians crowded downtown Denver's sidewalks.

After passing the center of downtown, Marla drifted from the main strip to an empty road between shops, and Mitchell followed. They passed a café, a candle shop, a clothing store, a laundromat, and a bookstore.

As they passed an old, abandoned theater with faded brickwork and boarded-up windows, a man spoke from the shadows in the deeply recessed entrance: "The end is near." His voice was as dry as the nighttime Denver air.

Marla paused, and Mitchell followed suit. Squinting into the gloom, he saw the vagrant seated in the entryway with his legs splayed and his back against the theater door, holding a brown paper bag with a bottle in it. Unwashed, unshorn, and dressed in grimy rags, he seemed less a man than a heap of trash saturated with layers of organic filth. A commingled stench of feces, urine, and body odor oozed out of the doorway.

The vagrant drank from the bottle he was holding, and then repeated himself: "The end is near."

Mitchell nodded. "It always is." Then he drew his silencer-fitted pistol and shot the man once through the head, killing him instantly.

"Are you still gonna kill your sister?" Marla asked. "When we get to New York?"

"I don't know. I haven't decided yet."

They turned and headed back toward the hotel.

CHAPTER 33

On the Rosira's eighteenth floor, in Samantha's penthouse, Aubrey marked the page of her paperback and closed the book. "When will Kenzie be here?"

Samantha set her playscript on the coffee table. "Any minute, probably."

"And what's her girlfriend's name again?"

"Christina."

"Christina, right. And she's a musician, too?"

"A singer," Samantha said. "According to Kenzie, Christina's the best singer she's ever heard."

"And your sister plays guitar, right?"

"Yes. She has some videos on YouTube. Would you like to see one?"

"Sure."

While Samantha grabbed her phone, Aubrey grabbed their bottle of vodka and took a drink. The day was still young, and she was already catching a buzz, but it was only a mild sort of drunk that softened reality's edges, the sort of drunk she most enjoyed that made existence more endurable, despite the fact that time was pushing everyone on Earth closer to oblivion by the second.

Holding her phone up, Samantha scooted closer to Aubrey on the sofa.

Looking at the screen, Aubrey cocked her head. "Wow. You and your sister look a lot alike."

Samantha nodded. "Yes." Then she pressed PLAY.

In the video, Kenzie was playing a green electric guitar. The riffs she played were rock and heavy metal, mostly, but the solos she ripped through were bluesy—slippery and hot with cold undertones. Malevolence filled her melodies, Aubrey thought, the notes and the spaces between them downright haunting. This was not the smooth, polished blues of New York City, but the rough, dirty blues Aubrey associated with places like New Orleans or Mississippi.

"Your sister has an old soul," Aubrey said. "You can hear it."

"I played guitar at first, before Kenzie. I started playing when I was fourteen. I practiced for two years, so by the time I was sixteen, I was pretty decent, but Kenzie started playing at age twelve. She was four years younger, and she blew me away immediately."

"So you quit playing?" Aubrey said.

"Yes. I mean, you either have it or you don't, and it was obvious that Kenzie was the musician of the family, not me. I figured that to keep practicing guitar, for me, would be like polishing a water faucet for hours upon hours and expecting it to improve the water that comes out of the faucet."

Aubrey took a drink. "Or like a chef trying to cook with a lot of recipes, but no ingredients."

"Exactly."

While both still watched the video, a message from Kenzie appeared on the screen of Samantha's phone, and she opened it.

"They're here," Samantha said. "Let's go down and greet them in the lobby."

CHAPTER 34

After several hours of torture, Donna unmercifully died. Lucas and Oliver, both still naked and covered in blood, spread her corpse out over the drain in the boiler room's concrete floor.

Lucas chopped the head off with a machete. Then he pressed the machete's tip into each of the body's major joints, separating the cartilage. He raised the blade and chopped down on those places to cut through cartilage and ligaments. Soon he had the arm pieces, the leg pieces, the torso, and the head all separated. He was aware of Oliver stroking his own flaccid penis while watching him work. He knew the old man had developed erectile dysfunction in recent years, but that every time Oliver observed an act of butchery, it increased his circulation down below.

Lucas grabbed a sharp knife and held the thigh of a leg at an angle against a cinderblock. He sliced the meat from the bone in large fillets. He put the meat in a black trash bag and tossed the bone into the incinerator.

He repeated the process for each of the limb parts, and then the torso. He put the heart, kidneys, and liver in the trash bag with the rest of the meat. He pitched the bones and remaining organs into the incinerator. Then he tossed Donna's head into the incinerator, too.

"I think I'm gonna come," Oliver said. "Is that okay with you?"

Lucas shrugged. "Knock yourself out."

Seconds later—while Lucas watched—the old man moaned and shuddered uncontrollably as a few drops of semen dripped from his still-limp penis into the drain.

"My nephew's coming to live with me," Lucas said.

Oliver shot him a look. "Your nephew?"

"Yes. With his mother."

Oliver cocked his head. "Do you mean they're coming to live *here*, in the building? Or down here with *you*, in the basement?"

"Down here with me. In my apartment. There's plenty of room."

Oliver ran bloody fingers through his white, blood-encrusted hair. "Yes, but won't that interfere with the things we like to do down here?"

"No, of course not. They won't have keys to this boiler room, or anything. Just the apartment. And trust me—my sister knows how sick and twisted I am. So don't worry about it."

"Your nephew," Oliver said. "He's your sister's boy?"

"Yes. Her husband died recently. Fell down some stairs and broke his neck, or some shit."

"I'm sorry to hear that."

"Don't be. He never liked me, and I never liked him. But anyway, according to my sister, Carl is unnaturally large, so don't be alarmed when you see him."

"Unnaturally large?"

"Yes. Apparently, he's only a year old, but already the size of a small adult."

"Holy shit! Is that even possible?"

Lucas shrugged. "It's what my sister says." Still holding the bag of meat, he walked over to his clothes and picked them up. "Ready to go cook some dinner?"

Oliver nodded. "Absolutely." He gathered his clothes and followed Lucas to his apartment.

CHAPTER 35

Two weeks after the phone call from her agent, Emma found herself at Mizzoli's for the book signing in New York. Her table was set up in the romance section of the bookstore, surrounded by staff and fans who all appeared to be at least half her age. She already had half a bottle of vodka in her system, and the bottle of water on her table had more vodka than flavored water in it. Natalie had been there earlier, but she'd already left for a prior engagement, so Emma just sat alone behind her table, scrawling her signature on the title pages of books for the fans who filed past.

Two hours later, after the last of the fans had left and she was busy signing the remaining stock, a man who appeared to be in his thirties approached her table, holding a slim volume in both hands. He'd been waiting for the fans to depart before he approached her. He was tall, thin, and incredibly handsome. He looked like an actor. He also looked familiar, and Emma wondered if perhaps she had seen him in a movie or on TV. He smiled and proffered the book for Emma to sign on the title page, and she saw with a shock that it wasn't one of her books. It was a reading edition of her late husband's only commissioned play, *The Myth of Coincidence.*

"I hope you don't mind," the man said, "but I'm a huge fan of your husband's work, and I'd be delighted if you would sign this copy for me."

Even with the alcohol in her system, Emma's hand shook when she took the book. "No, I don't mind. Who do I make it out to?"

"Thomas," the man said. "Thomas Maxwell."

Emma signed the playscript and handed it back to him. She was glad to be rid of it. Holding it in her hands had brought back the familiar horror.

"I'm a writer myself," Thomas said. "I'm also a journalist, and I was hoping you might consent to an interview."

She was tempted to tell him that she didn't do interviews, that she had nothing she wanted to say about anything to anyone, but something about the man's smile made her relent. Besides, anyone who was a fan of her late husband's work was pretty much okay in her book.

Emma shrugged. "Why not? I'll consent to an interview. But not today. And I'm not coming back to New York anytime soon. How do you feel about coming to my house in New Jersey?"

Thomas smiled. "That would be great."

Emma wrote her phone number on a bookmark and gave it to him. "Give me a call and we'll arrange a date."

CHAPTER 36

Fifteen hours after leaving Denver, Mitchell and Marla stopped for a night at a hotel in Chicago. The downtown hotel was on South Michigan Avenue, but Mitchell parked his car across the street in the underground Grant Park garage.

From the trunk, he grabbed a duffel bag that contained their toiletries and a bottle of whiskey. While approaching the building, the night's wind off Lake Michigan tossed their hair in all directions.

"Congress Hotel," Marla said, staring up at the red letters atop the eleven-story edifice. "It looks old as hell."

"It is," Mitchell said. "It opened for business in 1893. It's actually called the Congress Plaza Hotel. Supposedly, it's the most haunted hotel in Chicago."

"How do you know?"

He shrugged. "I just do. You've never heard of this place?"

"No."

"I've always wanted to stay here," Mitchell said. "Al Capone and his cohorts ran their headquarters and committed gruesome crimes here."

"Al Capone. Was he the mobster they called Scarface?"

"Yes. Evidently, Al Capone's ghost is seen most frequently near his old suite on the eighth floor. Then you've got Peg Leg Johnny the ghost of a hobo who was brutally murdered in the alley behind the hotel. There's also the spirit of a young boy who, along with his sibling, was thrown from a window by his mother, before she jumped to her own death."

"Crazy," Marla said.

"Yes. The most haunted spot, however, is supposedly Room 441, which is believed to be the inspiration for Stephen King's 1408. Have you read that one?"

"Of course. I love 1408. Creepy as hell."

"Hauntings aside," Mitchell said, "perhaps the hotel's most enduring legacy is the fact that H. H. Holmes—America's first serial killer—used to hang out in the lobby, in search of new victims. Then he would lure young women back to his Murder Castle and torture them to death."

The lobby was empty. The middle-aged man behind the front desk, who had pleasant-smelling tonic in his hair and on his mustache, gave each of them a friendly look. His nametag identified him as Benedict.

"Is Room 441 available?" Mitchell asked him.

He shook his head. "I'm afraid not. As you can imagine, it's our most frequently requested reservation."

"I'm glad," Marla said. "I mean, I don't believe in ghosts, but I have no desire to stay in a room that inspired a story by Stephen King."

Benedict cocked his head. "You don't believe in ghosts?"

"No."

"Ghosts are very real," he told her. "I assure you."

"We don't have a reservation," Mitchell said. "Can we still get a room?"

"Of course."

"Great. And since it's late, we'll rent the room for the next two days. Is it okay to pay with cash?"

"Absolutely."

A few minutes later, they took an elevator up to the sixth floor, made their way to Room 602, and stepped inside.

"I'm ready for a drink," Marla said.

Mitchell took their whiskey from the duffel bag, handed her the bottle, and she took a drink. Then she took another drink and gave the bottle back.

She found the television's remote control and turned on the TV. It was set to a news channel. She left it there but turned the volume down low.

"Feels good to be off the road," she said. Then she stretched out on the king-sized bed. "Oh, this is nice. Care to join me?"

Mitchell kicked his shoes off and took a drink of whiskey. Then he sat down next to her on the bed, with his back against the headboard and his feet straight out in front of him, facing the TV. "You don't believe in ghosts?"

"Actually, I do," Marla said. "I just felt like being argumentative with Benedict. But I've never seen a ghost," she added. "Have you?"

"Oh, yes. Many times."

"Awesome! Tell me one of your ghost stories."

Mitchell took a drink, trying to decide which one to tell her. "I suppose I could tell you about the ghost of Adrian Treadway."

"Who was he?"

"A young man who was murdered in a vigilante-style execution, in the town where Aubrey and I grew up, about a hundred years before we were born."

"In California?"

"No. In New York. Our father worked in Manhattan, but he drove about an hour to work and back every day. We actually lived in a small town called Carmel Hamlet, in Putnam County, about sixty miles north of New York City. Anyway, about a hundred years before we were born, there was a young man named Adrian Treadway who supposedly had some sort of mental problems, or something. Like, he was retarded, or some shit, and a bunch of young boys in the area came forth with claims that he had been sexually molesting them."

"So Adrian Treadway was a pedophile?"

"Yes. Allegedly. But apparently his father had a lot of money and paid the authorities to try and keep everything hush-hush.

It didn't work, however. Word got around. One night, a group of men dragged him to a stretch of the old Corbin Line, tied him down to the tracks, then watched a train come along and chop his whole body in half."

"Good for them," Marla said. "Fucking pervert."

"Yes. Soon after his execution, though, stories began circulating that Adrian Treadway's ghost now haunted that stretch of the Corbin Line, with reports of young boys who'd attempted to walk the tracks simply vanishing, never to be seen again. These stories went on for a hundred years, so by the time Aubrey and I were alive, everyone in our town knew about it, and the kids were scared to walk the tracks—even though the Corbin Line had long since been abandoned—for fear of being snatched up by the ghost of Adrian Treadway."

"And you saw the ghost?"

"Yes. I was just getting to that. When I was eleven, I had a sixth-grade classmate named Jared Atkins. He had an older sister named Sherry, and I had a major crush on her. I used to spend the night at their mom's house on weekends from time to time, and Sherry would come in Jared's room and smoke weed with us. She'd let us listen to whatever music she was into, and we'd all tell each other ghost stories. She even claimed to have seen the ghost of Adrian Treadway one time, on the old Corbin Line. She told us that she would take us up there sometime and show us where she had seen him, so maybe we could see the ghost for ourselves. One morning, the phone rang in our house and my dad told me it was Jared. This was during the summer break after sixth grade had ended, and I hadn't spoken to him in a while. I lifted the receiver, and Jared told me that he and Sherry were going up to the old Corbin Line, if I was interested. I told him that I *was* interested. We agreed to meet at noon."

Marla smiled. "You were probably more interested in seeing Sherry than seeing the ghost."

"Oh, undoubtedly. Anyway, the old Corbin Line was only a couple of miles from where I lived. I told my dad to drop me off at the bowling alley. After he drove away, I took a path between houses and climbed a gate into the woods. Jared was already there, waiting for me, holding a duffel bag. 'I brought us a bottle of vodka,' he said. 'Stole it from Mom's liquor cabinet.' I asked him where Sherry was, and he told me that something came up, and she couldn't make it."

"Damn," Marla said. "I bet you were disappointed."

Mitchell shrugged. "I'm sure I was, but I was also happy that he had a bottle of vodka, and we took off walking. Eventually, we hiked down a slope of rocks to the track bed about thirty feet below. The dirt was so barren that the railway lines were exposed, but what was left of the crossties were either broken or rotting, and the rails that dwindled away in a straight line ahead of us were dislodged in a lot of places. A few hundred yards along we encountered thick groundcover, and soon the only sound was the noise of our shoes as we kicked through the foliage. Above us, on both sides, trees and thickets crowded the tops of the embankments. We stopped, passed the vodka back and forth a couple of times, and then walked on."

"Let me hit that whiskey," Marla said.

He handed her the bottle. She took a drink and gave the bottle back.

Mitchell took a drink. "Anyway, we pressed on, with the summer sun beating down on our heads, and then Jared told me a story about the ghost of Adrian Treadway. He said that two guys and two girls had come up there to the tracks a few years back to drink beer, have sex, and camp out, and that no one heard anything from them for a couple of days. Then, suddenly, one of the girls turned up naked at a local bar, rambling about how the ghost of Adrian Treadway had murdered her three companions. Supposedly, the teenage girl's hair had turned snow-white overnight."

"Crazy," Marla said.

"Yes. And evidently it's a true story, because I looked it up later, after Jared disappeared. None of the girl's three friends were ever seen again, and the girl ended up in a loony bin."

"Wait a second. Jared disappeared, too?"

"Yes, right after he told me that story. As soon as he finished telling it, we took a few shots of vodka, and then we took off walking again. The foliage seemed to enclose us, and I remember starting to feel claustrophobic. In front of us, the old Corbin Line cut straight into the distance for as far as we could see. Rails broke through the vegetation occasionally, but you didn't need to see them to know you were following the remains of a railroad. Then we heard laughter, behind us, and turned around fast."

He paused to take a drink.

Marla said, "Laughter?"

He nodded.

"What did you see? After you turned around?"

"Something was approaching us, along the railroad. At first, it was too far away for me to see any detail, but even though it was still a few hundred feet away, there seemed to be something wrong with it. Then I saw that it was a man, because of its size and the clothes that it was wearing. And although it moved slowly, it appeared to be quickly advancing. In the blink of an eye, it seemed to have gotten much, much closer, and we could see it in much greater detail: how a black bandana was wrapped around its face; how the dark hair atop the thing's head looked like a rat's nest; how the ends of its tattered pants dragged the ground; how the body and limbs inside its clothes looked absolutely wasted. The craziest thing about it, though, were its eyes. They glowed a bright, electric blue. Unnaturally bright. They looked like two gas flames blazing in the sunlight. Then, in a booming, demonic voice, the thing clearly called Jared's name."

"Damn!" Marla said. "Then what happened?"

"We ran. There was no talking or screaming or anything. We just ran as fast as we could. I glanced back once and saw that the thing was now even closer, despite the fact that we were running and it was still moving as slowly as before. Impossibly, it was gaining on us. And then it called Jared's name again, in that same demonic voice, only now, because it was closer, the voice was louder."

He paused, took a drink, and handed her the bottle.

She took a drink and gave the bottle back. "Then what happened?"

"After it called his name that second time, Jared shrieked and veered sharply to the left, and I followed. On that side stood an old, rotting shed perched atop a rusted, metal understructure. The windows were boarded over. There was a ladder on the side of the shed that led up to a catwalk and an entry door. Jared climbed the ladder, and I followed him up. The catwalk creaked and I was afraid it would break loose as we made our way to the entry door. Then we barged through the door into the shed's interior. It was dark in there, but not pitch-dark. Some light came in through a window in the back wall that had not been boarded over. Jared slammed the door closed behind us. There was a rusty bolt near the top and he shoved it into place, locking the door. After that, we just backed up and stood in silence for a few seconds, hoping the ghost of Adrian Treadway would leave us alone. But then we heard the creaking of the catwalk outside, followed by that terrible voice calling Jared's name yet again."

"Crazy," Marla said.

"Yes. Jared turned to face me. And he looked horrified, to be sure. Hell, we both were. But he also looked perplexed, as if he just couldn't figure out why this thing had decided to single him out instead of me. We retreated into separate corners, listening to the scratching of claws on the other side of the door. There was a heavy blow, and the door shook violently. Woodwork shuddered as the door started bowing in its frame. I sank to my knees, eyeing the shadow in the gap at the bottom. Jared screamed and told the thing to go away. Then everything got quiet."

"Did it go away?"

"No. Moments later, something punctured the roof. We looked up and saw two giant fingers peel the roof off the shed like the lid of a tin can and toss it aside."

"Holy shit!"

"Yes. The ghost had grown impossibly large. One of its blazing blue eyes gazed down at us from above, so huge that it blocked our view of the clouds and the sky. Then a hand bigger than our whole bodies came crashing down into the shed. I was stricken mute, but Jared screamed. He was still screaming when the ghost of Adrian Treadway grabbed him and took him away."

"Insanity," Marla said.

Mitchell handed her the bottle. She took a drink and gave the bottle back.

Then the TV shut off, the remote control flew across the room, and the bathroom door closed on its own.

Marla looked at Mitchell. "I think the ghosts in here liked your story."

"Maybe so."

They passed the bottle back and forth until they fell asleep.

CHAPTER 37

In the Rosira, on the eighteenth floor, Christina peered out the window of a spare bedroom in Samantha's penthouse and thought she would be happy to never leave New York City. Behind her, on the bed, Kenzie launched into another of their new songs on her acoustic guitar. They'd been in Manhattan for a week, and Samantha had told them they could have this bedroom—one of four in the apartment—for as long as they wanted it.

"*Besides,*" Samantha had added, after Kenzie expressed a desire not to invade her sister's privacy, "*this is our mother's penthouse, so basically this is your apartment, too.*"

And the privacy issue was moot: for the past few nights, Samantha had been staying down in Aubrey's apartment on the second floor anyway.

Christina turned from the window to face her girlfriend. "That strip club," she said, "that Aubrey used to work in. What's it called again?"

Kenzie stopped playing and looked up from her guitar. "Strip club?"

"Yes. She said she used to work in a strip club somewhere near this building, and that one of the bartenders there was a really good drummer. Don't you remember?"

"No, but we definitely need a drummer. Want me to message

145

my sister?"

"Sure."

Kenzie grabbed her phone and sent a text to Samantha. Moments later, Samantha messaged back. "Gino's Cabaret," Kenzie said. "A few blocks west right here on 72nd. The drummer's name is Seth. Wanna go check it out?"

"Sure," Christina said.

They left.

The old janitor, Oliver, was downstairs mopping the lobby while they crossed it. They had spoken with him a few times in the week since their arrival. He looked up at them and smiled. "Hello, ladies. You headed out?"

"Yes," Christina said.

He wiped his brow with a forearm. "It's a beautiful day out there. Enjoy it."

"Thanks!"

They stepped outside.

"He's such a nice old man," Christina said.

"I don't know," Kenzie said. "He sort of gives me the creeps."

They headed west on 51st Street, arriving at Gino's Cabaret soon thereafter. A young, early drunk stumbled on his way out the door as they tried to enter, and then the doorman asked to see their IDs. Kenzie showed him her fake ID, but Christina didn't have one.

"I left my purse at home," she told him. "You want me to wait out here?"

He shook his head. "Nah, that's okay. You can come on in. I'll have to stamp your hand, though, so you won't be able to drink."

"That's cool."

The doorman stamped her hand, and then she followed Kenzie inside the club.

The place was large and dark, with perhaps thirty stools at the bar, and as many tables in front of a stage on which a beautiful woman danced to a rock song Christina had never heard. "I didn't know strippers even *worked* during the days."

Kenzie shot her a look. "You've never been in a strip club?"

Christina shook her head.

"The headliners work the nights," Kenzie said. "The second-tier strippers work the days."

Christina cast her gaze toward the stage. "She doesn't look like a second-tier stripper to me."

Kenzie shrugged. "It's New York City. All the strippers are gonna be gorgeous."

At the bar, they elected to remain standing.

The bartender was a young man with a shorn head and several tattoos. "What can I get you?"

"Are you Seth?" Kenzie asked him.

"No. Seth won't be in until tonight."

Christina said, "We heard he's a really good drummer."

"He is. Why? You've never heard him?"

"No. Is he in a band?"

"No. He *was* in a band called Pandemonium, but they just broke up. I can't believe you've never heard Pandemonium. They used to play all over town."

"We're not from around here," Kenzie said. "Do you have his phone number?"

"Yes, but I can't just give it out. Are you looking to start a band?"

"Yes," Christina said.

"Tell you what: hang tight, I'll give him a call, and I'll let you know what he says."

"Cool," Kenzie said.

He walked off. They watched him make a call. He jotted something on a cocktail napkin. After he disconnected, he came back and handed Kenzie an address. "This is where he lives. I told him two chicks were in here looking to start a band, and he actually sounded pretty excited. He told me to tell you to come on over."

"Thanks," Kenzie said.

"Don't mention it."

They left, walked back to the Rosira, and got in Kenzie's car. They stopped and got a bottle of rum on the way to Seth's address—an old brownstone on a street between Columbus and

Central Park West.

As they approached the building, a guy sitting on the steps of the brownstone said, "You looking for me?" He looked about twenty-five, and wore his long hair tied back in a ponytail.

"Are you Seth?" Christina said.

He stood up and nodded. He was tall and very thin. "That's me."

"I'm Christina, and this is Kenzie. She plays guitar. I sing. We're looking to start a band."

"So I heard. How old are you?"

"Seventeen."

"And I'm eighteen," Kenzie said. "How old are you?"

"Twenty-four," Seth said. "I'm a goddamn geezer."

Christina laughed.

Seth looked down at the brown paper bag Kenzie was holding. "What's in the bag?"

She withdrew the bottle of rum and held it up. "Fake ID," she explained. Then she pointed to the brownstone behind him. "This is your place?"

He glanced over his shoulder as if surprised to see the building still standing. "My father's place, actually, although he's almost never here. He has girlfriends scattered all over the world."

"We heard your band broke up," Christina said. "Pandemonium."

"Yes. Long story."

"Sounds like a metal band."

"We were. What kind of a band are you girls looking to form?"

Christina shrugged. "Rock. Blues. Metal. Just whatever."

"Blues?" Seth cracked a grin. "What do you teenage girls know about the blues?"

"You'd be surprised," Kenzie said. "But we write rock and metal songs, mostly."

He nodded. "Fair enough. Want to come on in and jam? I've got a shitload of musical instruments in the basement. Got a PA system, too."

"Sweet!" Christina said.

They followed him inside. The entry hall had nothing in it but a leather jacket hanging on a hook. The amount of open space stupefied Christina. The entrance hall's emptiness reminded her somehow of a chapel.

The brownstone's next room was large, and they crossed it to another room in which Seth opened a door to an even bigger room. Then he guided them to a steel spiral staircase, and they descended.

At the bottom of the stairs to the basement, Seth pushed open a wooden door and turned on some lights, and they followed him into a huge rehearsal space filled with musical equipment. Old pipes ran above their heads, crisscrossing in places, and all the walls were peeling, but everything else in the room appeared to be in excellent condition.

A massive drum set occupied the center of the chamber. A few sofas lined the walls, but the only other furniture in the room was a long table on which sat a PA system's mixing board with two chairs in front of it. Electric guitars, bass guitars, amplifiers, microphones, effects processors, and speaker cabinets filled the majority of remaining space.

Seth grabbed a pair of drumsticks. Then he sat down on the stool behind the set and launched into a drum solo that lasted about two minutes.

After he finished, Kenzie took a drink of rum. "Dude, that was fucking awesome."

He shrugged. "Thanks. Now it's your turn. Show me what you got."

Kenzie gave Christina the bottle. Then she grabbed a Fender Strat, plugged it into a Marshall amp, and turned it on. She quickly tuned the guitar and began playing one of their songs.

Christina—watching for Seth's reaction to their music—was pleased when he immediately began drumming a perfect beat.

She took a drink of rum and set the bottle on the floor. From several bass guitars, she selected a blue Ibanez, plugged it into a Peavey amp, and turned it on. After tuning the bass to Kenzie's electric, she locked in with Seth's drums and began laying down a heavy groove, feeling more at home than anywhere since the stage during that audience-abduction concert back in New Jersey.

Smiling, Christina turned on a microphone. She closed her eyes and started to sing.

CHAPTER 38

Six-year-old Haley woke in darkness, and she was cold. One of her parents must have come into her room after she had fallen asleep and turned off her bedside lamp. She reached for the lamp to turn it back on, but it wasn't there. Maybe it had somehow fallen off the nightstand while she was asleep.

But then she found that the nightstand wasn't there, either—which was weird. And why was it so cold in here? Her room never got *this* cold. And where were her blankets, anyway? She looked down for her blankets, but she couldn't see anything. She couldn't even see her hands in front of her face.

When she decided to get up and feel her way to the light switch on the wall, she realized that she wasn't even in her bed. She was on a floor, and it wasn't the floor in her bedroom. There was carpet on the floor in her bedroom; this floor had no carpet. There was no carpet on the floor in her parents' bedroom, so maybe that's where she was.

She got up, started tiptoeing around blindly with her arms straight out in front of her, and bumped into something on the floor.

"Haley?" her mother said. "What are you *doing* in here? Your father and I have to go to work in the morning, and you have to go to school. You're supposed to be sleeping."

"I woke up in here," Haley said. "It was dark and I was cold, and for some reason I woke up in *here*."

"I can't see anything," her mother said. "Why is it so *dark* in here?" Haley heard her mother moving around a little bit, and then her mother said: "What the hell?"

Haley's father woke up. "Can you two knock it off? I have to be up at six in the morning." He was quiet for a second. Then: "Am I on the floor? What the hell am I doing on the floor?"

"Something's wrong," her mother said. "I'm on the floor, too. And this is not our floor."

"Jesus Christ," her father said. "You're right. This floor feels like concrete."

"Oh my god," her mother said. "Where *are* we?"

"I don't know," her father said. "Just stay put. I can't see anything, but I'll get up and feel around." Moments later: "I don't feel anything but the walls. They're cinderblock, and I can't find any windows. What's the last thing you remember?"

"Putting Haley to bed," her mother said. "I read her a story, and she fell asleep. I kissed her goodnight, and then I came into our room. You were sound asleep. I read a few pages of the book I'm reading, and then I fell asleep, too."

"And then we all three woke up here," Haley said, "in the dark, and in the cold."

Her father said, "It doesn't make any sense."

They heard footsteps approaching in a hallway, followed by a man's voice: "Do you think the drugs have worn off yet?"

"Probably," another man said. "Time to have some fun."

Then a door opened and light entered the room.

Hours later, in the basement, after slaughtering the family of three, Oliver—still naked and covered in gore—fondled his limp penis while Lucas removed the internal organs from the little girl's carcass. *Haley,* Oliver remembered. *The little girl's name had*

been Haley.

They had snatched the family of three from the Rosira's fourteenth floor and spent the past several hours torturing them to death. Now the mother and father's remains—the edible parts, anyway—were wrapped in paper and stacked in a standalone freezer that hummed in a corner of the boiler room (their bones long since pitched into the incinerator), and Haley's corpse hung upside down from a meat hook above the drain in the floor.

While watching Lucas slice open the dead girl's neck, and seeing the blood spill from her body into the drain, Oliver started to feel a familiar twitch, a fluttering ache inside his scrotum that let him know—despite the fact that his penis was still limp—that he could possibly have an orgasm soon.

Lucas seemed to work as if on autopilot, opening the corpse as if he were field dressing a deer. Using a hunting knife, he made an incision below the breastbone and up to the pelvis, allowing the guts to spill out, and preserving the stuff they liked to eat in plastic bags that they would—in all likelihood—take to his apartment and cook for dinner later.

"Oh my god," Oliver said. "I'm gonna come. Is that okay with you?"

Lucas shot him a look. "I don't give a fuck."

Seconds later, Oliver shuddered and moaned while a few drops of semen leaked from his penis onto his hand.

"My nephew will be here soon," Lucas said.

"The freak?"

"Yes. Possibly this evening."

"What's his name again?"

"Carl. His mother's name is Elaine."

Oliver smiled. "Sweet. I can't wait to meet them."

CHAPTER 39

Emma was done writing for the day. She finished her cosmopolitan and mixed another one. Then she stepped outside and walked across the lawn toward the oak tree.

The evening sun was setting in the west. A squirrel fled at her approach.

When Emma reached the oak tree, she turned and looked back at the house. Nearly two hundred years old, the early-Victorian mansion had twelve bedrooms, a ballroom, a library, a billiards room, and many other rooms that she and Ryan had almost never used. Her first thought had been to sell it after his suicide, but then she changed her mind and decided to keep it.

She heard a noise behind her that sounded like laughter. Turning around, she looked up and thought she saw a pair of boots swaying between some limbs high up in the oak tree, but she blinked and the vision was gone. *Must have been a shadow,* she thought, feeling tears spring to her eyes. *My god, Ryan. It's been ten years and still I miss you.*

To the east, a storm was brewing. A jagged fork of lightning fired off on the horizon, and Emma rushed back to the house.

The doorbell chimed and broke the silence. Emma hurried across the great room and opened the front door. Thomas was even taller than she recalled. He was dressed in all black clothing, and his smile was just as beautiful as she remembered. "I hope your journey here was pleasant," Emma said.

"Entirely. You live in a beautiful house."

"Thank you."

"The perfect environment in which to write."

Emma smiled. "Yes. I like writing here."

She took him to the library—in which there was a minibar—and offered him a drink.

"Whiskey, please," Thomas said. "I like it with soda."

She mixed him a bourbon-and-soda and made herself a cosmopolitan, and then they sat down on a sofa. Once they started drinking, the conversation flowed, and Emma wondered if in fact the interview had already begun, or if the exchange of information was simply easy communication between two people with similar interests.

Eventually, Thomas began recording their conversation with his phone. He mainly asked her questions about her life and her work. He also asked a few questions about her late husband.

After the interview was over, they drank some more while Emma gave him a tour of the house. She stopped before a door in a hallway on the west wing and said, "This is the room in which Ryan wrote. Sometimes I go in there and talk to his ghost.'

"Does he really haunt the room?"

Emma smiled and shook her head. "No. Not that I'm aware of. But I like to imagine that he does."

"Do you mind if I see the room?"

"Of course not." Emma opened the door and they stepped inside.

A writing desk occupied the center of the room. An old computer sat atop the writing desk.

Emma went to a window and pulled open the curtains. Light flooded the room, illuminating dozens of framed paintings.

Thomas began walking around the room, examining some of

the canvases hanging on the walls and stacked against the walls on the floor. All of them bore Ryan Kinkade's signature. "Ryan was a painter? Wow. These are brilliant! No wonder he only gave us four novels. He was always busy painting. Although I suppose four novels is not a low amount for someone who was only thirty-four when he...well...when he died."

"It's okay," Emma said. "You can say it: for someone who was only thirty-four when he committed suicide."

"It must have been hard for you," Thomas said. "Weren't you the one who found his body?"

Emma nodded. "Yes. It was difficult."

"Did he leave a note?"

"No. He didn't have to. He used to say that everything he wrote was just a long suicide note."

Thomas finished his drink.

Emma said, "Are you ready for a refill?"

"I would love one. But I've already had a couple, and I'm afraid one more might push me over the limit. I still have to drive back to New York."

Emma finished her drink. "So stay here and get drunk with me tonight."

"Seriously?"

"Yes. You can sleep in one of the guest rooms, and drive back in the morning. I've been drinking alone for a decade and could use the company. Unless, of course, you already have other plans."

Thomas shook his head. "I don't have any plans. And tomorrow's Saturday, so I don't have any plans for tomorrow, either."

"So you'll stay and get drunk with me?"

Thomas smiled. "Absolutely."

They drank all day and then Emma had Chinese food delivered to the mansion. She could not recall the last time she enjoyed a dinner so much, or such company. Their conversation was effortless. They had many preferences in common, and shared similar interests. They laughed at each other's humor, and she found Thomas's dark, sarcastic wit infectious.

At one point he told her that he had been single for several years, and she felt her heart flutter like a lovesick schoolgirl's.

"How old *are* you?" she asked him, sometime after dinner.

They sat side by side on a sofa in the library. A fire blazed in the fireplace.

"I'm forty," Thomas said. "Four years younger than you."

Emma sipped her drink. "That's crazy. You look much younger."

He smiled. "Thanks. So do you."

"You also look very familiar to me," Emma said.

"Perhaps you've seen me on television."

"Oh yeah?"

He nodded. "Yes. I do some acting in addition to journalism. Stage work in plays, mostly, but lately I've had a few TV parts."

She smiled. "Maybe that's it. I do have a TV on most of the time, for noise. Occasionally, I even glance at it. I fall asleep with it on most nights. Come, I'll show you."

Emma took Thomas's hand and led him to the bedroom. It felt right to have him there, touching her, chasing her loneliness away.

After they made love that night, Thomas spent more nights at her mansion than his own place in New York.

On a Saturday in July, she led him from the library and out across the lawn. It was a hot summer day, and they sought refuge in the shade beneath the oak tree. Thomas pulled Emma toward him and held her.

She looked up into the tree, and he pulled away from her.

"You're crying," he said.

She nodded.

He wiped tears from her cheeks. "I love you, Emma."

"I love you too."

He led her back across the lawn, into the library, and they held each other.

Emma looked out a window, back toward the oak tree, and caught a fleeting glimpse of Ryan's ghost, haunting her still.

She told herself that she was happy for the first time in ten years.

CHAPTER 40

Mitchell drove. Marla rode next to him on the passenger's side. Six hours east of Chicago—and over three-fourths of the way through their trip to New York City—they stopped and got a hotel room in Youngstown, Ohio.

In the room, from Mitchell's duffel bag, Marla retrieved their bottle of whiskey and took a drink. "I saw a club down the street. Avalon Saloon. Wanna go check it out?"

"Sure," Mitchell said.

They dropped their bags and left.

Fiona wasn't hungry, but figured she may as well get something to eat. On her way to a fast-food restaurant, she saw a man with brown hair get out of an SUV. He was parked in front of a convenience store. A little boy with brown hair like his father's got out on the passenger's side. It was nighttime, and though the parking lot was well lit, she couldn't see their faces across three lanes of traffic between her moving vehicle and the convenience store.

Straight ahead, at the next intersection, she made an illegal U-turn as the light turned from yellow to red, then drove back and parked next to the man's SUV. Aware of the fact that she was in the grip of a strange compulsion, Fiona got out of her car on shaky legs and stood staring into the convenience store. The man and the boy were in there, but she couldn't see them for the merchandise displays blocking the windows.

She turned away from the store and leaned against her car, trying to compose herself. After the crash that killed her family (which happened not long after she got out of rehab for alcoholism), her AA sponsor told her there was a name for the strange compulsion that currently seized her: searching behavior.

Psychologically, she could accept that Josh and Denny were lost forever. Emotionally, however, she remained convinced she would see them again. Sometimes, at home, she expected to see them in a room whenever she entered it, always more shocked by the room's emptiness than she would have been to discover that her husband and son were with her again. She often saw them in a mall, or in a park, or on a playground, always at a distance, walking away from her. She usually let them go, but occasionally felt compelled to follow.

Fiona turned away from her car and went to the store's entrance. Opening the door, she hesitated, knowing she was torturing herself. The emotional collapse that would inevitably ensue when this man and boy proved not to be Josh and Denny would only make her want to drink alcohol. She took a deep breath and entered the store, nevertheless.

To her left, the cashier—a young man with a shorn head—smiled at her and nodded. Ignoring him, she passed the first, second, and third of five aisles, then saw the man and boy at the end of the fourth aisle.

They stood before a cooler full of energy drinks, with their backs to her. Fiona stopped in the middle of the aisle, waiting for them to turn around. The man wore a white shirt, blue jeans, and black tennis shoes—as Josh had often worn. The little boy—Denny's size—wore a red shirt, gray pants, and tennis shoes similar to his father's.

With clenched fists, she heard herself say, "Josh? Denny?"

The man and the boy turned around. They were not Josh and Denny, just as she had known they would not be.

"Sorry," she said. "I thought...when I saw you standing there...I thought..."

The boy cocked his head. "Are you okay?"

"Don't let him go," Fiona told the father. "Whatever you do, don't let him out of your sight. They disappear."

She left, intending to get some food, even though she still wasn't hungry. She could take the food home and eat it later.

Two blocks up the street, however, she repeated one of the mantras she heard so many times in rehab: "Relapse is a part of recovery."

Fiona stopped at Avalon Saloon.

They walked in and Mitchell did a quick scope of the place. Avalon Saloon was not too crowded, and no one seemed to be paying attention to anyone else. Everyone was focused on their drinks or looking down at their phones. He chose a table by the door and gestured for Marla to sit down.

"I'll go get us some drinks," Mitchell said. "Whiskey?"

"Sure."

While Mitchell stood at the bar waiting for the drinks, he noticed the young woman on a stool to his left. A miserable expression occupied her pretty face, as if she had just finished a hard day at work, or if perhaps a man or a woman in her life were driving her crazy. Six shot glasses stood in a line on the bar directly in front of her: four were empty; two still contained what Mitchell thought was probably vodka. She held a bottled beer in her right hand.

"Bad day?" Mitchell asked her.

She looked up at him. "Relapse is a part of recovery."

"Is that so?"

The woman shrugged. "I don't know. Just something they tell you in rehab."

The bartender returned with Mitchell's drinks. Mitchell paid with cash and told him to keep the change.

Then he told the woman, "I'm Mitchell, by the way. What's your name?"

"Fiona."

"Fiona. Lovely name. Listen, Fiona, my girlfriend and I are new in town, and we don't really know where anything is. Why don't you join us at our table? We can pay for your drinks, and maybe you can give us a few ideas about what to do around this place."

Fiona shrugged. "There isn't much to do in Youngstown." She knocked back her two remaining shots in rapid succession. "But I missed my meeting earlier and could use the conversation." Still holding the bottle of beer, she rose from the stool.

"Great!" Mitchell said, and led her to his table, where he handed Marla one of the two whiskeys. "Marla, this is Fiona. Fiona, this is Marla, my fiancée."

Fiona nodded. "Nice to meet you."

Marla sipped her whiskey. "Likewise."

Mitchell and Fiona sat down.

Mitchell told Marla, "Fiona says there's not much to do in this town."

"Well," Fiona said, "I guess there *is* stuff to do. Just depends on what you like. There's a nice Italian restaurant called Nicolinni's that Josh and I used to go to, if you like Italian food."

Mitchell smiled. "We'll keep that in mind."

Fiona sipped her beer. "And there's a drive-in theater not too far from here, if you don't mind driving to Warren. It's only about twenty minutes away. Josh and I went there a few times before we got married. We always meant to take Denny there, but just never got around to it."

Marla said, "Denny's your son?"

"Was," Fiona said. "He and Josh died in a car crash last month."

"Oh my god! I'm so sorry to hear that!"

Fiona nodded. "Yeah. It happened a week after I got out of rehab."

Mitchell sipped his whiskey. "What were you in rehab for?"

"Alcoholism."

"Here in Youngstown?"

"Yes. Neil Kennedy Recovery Center. I was in there for twenty-eight days. Longest I've been sober since childhood. I went in at the end of April, got out in the last week of May, then Josh and Denny got killed in the first week of June."

"How awful," Marla said.

"Yes. They were on their way to a baseball game in Cleveland, but never made it. A drunk driver crossed the median on the highway and struck them head-on. They died instantly."

"I hope the driver died, too," Marla said.

Fiona shook her head. "Nope. He was barely even injured."

"That's usually the way it goes," Mitchell said. "Seems like the drunk drivers always survive the accidents."

Fiona sipped her beer. "Yes. And he had six prior DUI convictions, too. They charged him with DUI manslaughter this time, and vehicular homicide, but nothing's gonna bring Josh and Denny back."

Mitchell sipped his whiskey. "That's some messed-up irony, right there. You go to rehab for alcoholism, and then a drunk driver kills your family when you get out."

"Yeah. And the *really* ironic part is this: They never would have had the money to go to the baseball game if I hadn't gone to rehab in the first place. I mean, we weren't exactly poor. They could have afforded to go to the game, but they never would have. See, before I went to rehab, I was spending about two hundred dollars a week on alcohol. Well, after a week out of rehab, we had two hundred dollars extra, and Josh had always wanted to take Denny to a baseball game. When he mentioned us going to Cleveland, I told them to go without me. I mean, I was only a week out of rehab, you know? I didn't feel strong enough in my sobriety to be in a crowd of people yet. Plus they sell beer at those baseball games, so I told them that I would just stay home and relax. I wish I had gone now, of course. I wish I had died with them in the car crash."

"I'm so sorry for your loss," Marla said.

Fiona shrugged, sipped her beer, and looked away.

Mitchell sipped his whiskey. "You said you missed a meeting earlier. Were you talking about an AA meeting?"

"Yes, but it's no big deal. They have meetings there five nights a week, and there's another place I go to on weekends. I fell off the wagon tonight, but I'll get back on it tomorrow. Just like they always say in rehab: relapse is a part of recovery."

"I've never been to an AA meeting," Mitchell said.

"You should come! Both of you! We meet in the basement of a church just down the street. Cornerstone Baptist. You can't miss it. There's free coffee. Plus donuts. And you'd get to hear some pretty cool stories, too. It's kind of fun, actually."

"What time are the meetings?" Marla said.

"Eight p.m."

"And you'll be there tomorrow night?"

"Yes. Definitely."

Mitchell sipped his whiskey. "Perhaps we'll see you there."

"Cool." Fiona finished her beer and rose from the table. "Suppose I'd better get home, before I get too drunk to drive. It was nice meeting you."

"Likewise," Marla said.

Fiona left.

Mitchell asked Marla, "Ready to go back to the hotel? We still have plenty of whiskey in the room."

She nodded.

They finished their drinks and left.

Fiona woke up Friday morning and brushed her teeth. She was thirsty but didn't have a hangover. She started a pot of coffee.

Then she poured the few beers that she kept in her refrigerator for emergencies down the drain.

I'll be okay, she thought, *if I can just make it until eight o'clock. If I can make it to the meeting tonight, I'll be fine.*

Marla woke up. Mitchell sat beside her on the hotel bed, facing the TV. It was tuned to a news channel. She sat up and stretched. "What time is it?"

"Almost noon."

"Was housekeeping in here?"

"No. I booked the room for another day, after you passed out."

"So we're not getting back on the road yet?"

"No. Not yet. Maybe tomorrow."

"Have you decided if you're going to kill your sister?"

"No. Not yet. I guess I'll figure it out when we get to New York."

Fiona parked in front of the church, ten minutes early. She took a Winston from her pack and lit it with the orange flame of a Bic lighter. Cigarettes were still something she would allow herself for the time being, although she knew she needed to quit those too, one of these days. But first things first. Or, as all the literature said, one step at a time.

While she smoked, Fiona considered what she might have for dinner after the meeting. *Maybe a pizza,* she thought. It occurred to her that she had not eaten pizza since Josh and Denny died, perhaps because pizza had been the one food the three of them ate together more than anything. They used to order half of each pizza with everything, and the other half with pepperoni and cheese, for Denny.

Maybe I'll order it the same way tonight, for old times' sake. I could light some candles. Try to watch a movie, perhaps. And not drink alcohol.

Finished with her cigarette, she dropped it into a soda can sitting in her cup holder. According to the dashboard clock, the time was 7:57 p.m.

She got out and took a deep breath of the warm evening air. To the west, the lowering sun was changing from orange to red.

Fiona went inside the church and headed down to the basement.

Marla passed out around six p.m., but Mitchell couldn't sleep. They'd been drinking whiskey all day long, but he didn't feel drunk at all. He felt restless, more than anything—perhaps due to round-the-clock news coverage of unrest in the Middle East. *What else is new?* he thought. *They've been fighting over there for a thousand years and will fight for a thousand more.* He thought about changing channels but decided against it. Marla liked listening to the news; she claimed it helped her sleep.

Mitchell rose from the hotel bed at seven-thirty, fully dressed. Beyond the window facing west, the July sun was blazing, and he knew that about ninety minutes of daylight still remained. He put his jacket on nevertheless to conceal his shoulder rig, which featured a holster, a leather harness, and a spare-magazine carrier. The pistol—a Glock 19 9mm—hung beneath his left arm. He knew the gun was loaded, but he took it from its holster and ejected the fifteen-round magazine anyway: brass cartridges gleamed. Smiling, he locked the magazine back in place and shoved the pistol into its holster.

Then he rode the elevator down to the first floor and stepped outside. He took off walking.

The group sat around a large room in the basement, eating donuts, drinking coffee, and telling each other stories. Fiona didn't speak much, just listened, and was edging into a doze when Mitchell—the man she had met in the bar last night—walked in. She wondered where his fiancée was. *Marla?* She was pretty sure the woman's name had been Marla.

Then Mitchell drew a gun from a holster beneath his jacket, and chaos ensued.

Marla was still asleep when Mitchell returned to their hotel room. He took a few shots of whiskey, then kicked his shoes off and stretched out next to her on the bed.

On TV, newscasters yapped about a disease and vaccinations, but Mitchell tuned them out, pleased that he had managed to light a candle in the darkness of humanity. *Fourteen candles, specifically,* Mitchell thought, for he had been counting.

Smiling, he closed his eyes. He fell asleep almost immediately.

Marla woke up, grabbed the remote, and pressed INFO to check the time: 9:06 p.m. To her right, Mitchell snored beside her on the bed.

She got up, staggered into the bathroom, and brushed her teeth. Then she came back out, sat down on the bed with her back against the headboard, and opened the horror novel she had found in a department store a few towns back.

She sipped whiskey from the bottle while she read, not stopping until—perhaps an hour later—a breaking news alert on TV interrupted an interview she had not been paying any attention to whatsoever. She looked up at the screen and saw an attractive female reporter standing in a church's crowded, benighted parking lot. The emergency lights of first responders swirled behind her.

"Good evening. I'm Hannah Roberts, and I'm here tonight in Youngstown, Ohio, where a tragic mass shooting has occurred. I'm told that more than a dozen are dead on the scene. The shooting victims were attending an Alcoholics Anonymous meeting in the basement of the church behind me, which is Cornerstone Baptist."

The camera pulled back and panned to the right, revealing a sad-faced man wearing a police officer's uniform. "With me now," Hannah Roberts continued, "is Officer Byron Webb of the Youngstown Police Department. Officer Webb, what can you tell us at this time?"

The cop looked at the camera, and his sad expression transformed into a face of anger. "What I can tell you, Hannah, is that some spineless, gutless, cowardly piece of human filth walked into this church tonight and ended the lives of fourteen good men and women who were only trying to better themselves. These people died for no reason whatsoever. It's sickening." He pointed a finger at the camera. "But I've got a message for whoever did this. We're going to find you, and we're going to make you pay. You can take that to the bank."

To Marla's right, Mitchell laughed.

She turned her head. "Good evening. Did you sleep well?"

"Yes, I did. Let me hit that whiskey."

She handed him the bottle.

He took a drink and gave the bottle back. "You ready to hit the road?"

"I am," she said.

They packed their bags and left Youngstown behind.

CHAPTER 41

On Aubrey's sofa, Samantha perused a playscript. She'd been staying in Aubrey's apartment on the Rosira's second floor ever since Kenzie and Christina began crashing in the penthouse on the eighteenth floor a couple of weeks ago.

To her left, Aubrey closed the novel she was reading and set it on the coffee table. "It's almost noon, and we haven't started drinking yet."

Samantha laughed. "I know, and I'm about *ready* to start drinking, actually."

Beyond the window, July sunlight glinted off the buildings across the street.

"It's so pretty out there today," Aubrey said. "We should go for a walk."

Samantha set her playscript on the coffee table. "Let's take the subway to Coney Island. We can drink vodka while we walk along the boardwalk."

"Great idea!" Aubrey rose from the sofa. "I have some water in the fridge. I'll empty a couple of bottles, and fill them with vodka. Be right back."

She headed toward the kitchen, and the doorbell rang.

"Probably my sister," Samantha said. "She told me she and Christina might stop by."

Aubrey went to the door and opened it. "Hi, Kenzie. Hi, Christina. Come on in."

Seconds later, Samantha watched her sister and Christina enter the living room.

Christina walked right up to her, holding a bottle of rum. "I'm going to marry your sister, as soon as I turn eighteen. Do I have your blessing?"

Samantha shrugged. "If you want that crazy bitch, you can have her."

Kenzie—with an electric guitar's gig bag strapped across her back—extended a fist toward Samantha, and pointed to the floor with her middle finger. "Can you hear this, or should I turn it up?"

Smiling, Samantha rolled her eyes.

Aubrey said, "You two wanna go to Coney Island with us?"

"Can't," Christina said. "We're on our way to Seth's, for band practice. We've only been jamming for a week, and he's already got us a couple of gigs lined up, so we have to rehearse. And, oh my god, he is *such* an amazing drummer. Thanks for hooking us up with him."

Aubrey nodded. "You're welcome. So, it's just the three of you? The band's a trio?"

"Yes," Kenzie said. "Me on guitar. Seth on drums. Christina plays bass and sings."

Samantha said, "Do you have a name yet?"

"Screamweaver," Christina said. She took a drink of rum.

"Screamweaver," Aubrey said. "I like that."

Kenzie told Samantha, "We recorded a couple of songs. I'll send them to your phone."

"Thanks!"

Soon thereafter, Kenzie and Christina left for band practice.

Then Aubrey filled two empty water bottles with vodka, and Samantha rode the elevator with her downstairs to the first floor.

Oliver was mopping the lobby while they crossed it. "Enjoy this beautiful day," he told them.

"Thanks," Aubrey said. "We will."

Samantha took a drink of vodka and inhaled the warm summer

air, wanting the alcohol to obliterate all negativity from her thoughts, and it mostly did.

They took off walking. 72nd Street was busy, as always. They passed a vegetable store, a butcher shop, and a Chinese restaurant, then waited at the corner of 69th for a limo to pass by, and they crossed the street. They passed a drugstore, an ice-cream parlor, and a couple of bars. They saw an old wino tap dancing for the amusement of passersby on the center strip of fenced-in grass that divided Broadway.

At Columbus Circle, they boarded a subway and rode the D train all the way to Coney Island in a straight shot, arriving in just under one hour. By two o'clock, they held hands and sipped vodka on the boardwalk.

They walked until Aubrey's phone chimed, alerting her to a text message, at which point they stopped and she released Samantha's hand to check her phone. "It's a message from my brother," Aubrey said.

"Mitchell?"

"Yes. Says he'll probably be in New York in a couple of days."

While Aubrey responded to the message, a painting caught Samantha's eyes in glimpses as people passed before them on the boardwalk.

"What are you looking at?" Aubrey said, after she put her phone away.

"That painting." Samantha pointed. "Over there, leaning against the wall."

Aubrey looked in that direction, squinting. "Oh, wow. That looks awesome. Let's go check it out."

They cut across the boardwalk, weaving between pedestrians, until they stood in front of the canvas, which was framed.

The painting depicted a nude, pregnant woman standing before a benighted window, facing the viewer, sawing her own arm off with a hacksaw. Beyond the window was a clear view of a spiral galaxy in outer space.

"Damn," Aubrey said. "That is a stunning piece of work."

Samantha nodded. "Do you think it's for sale?"

To their right, a young woman in front of the wall between the sidewalk and the beach rose from a crouch and approached them. "You wanna buy the painting?"

She didn't exactly look homeless, but Samantha wouldn't be surprised if the young woman slept in an old bus or on the sofas of friends who hadn't disowned her yet. Her clothes looked okay, but her hair was a mess, and she was thin to the point of emaciation. Her sunken cheeks and the dark rings beneath her eyes accentuated her unhealthy appearance.

"Yes," Samantha said. "Did you paint this?"

The woman looked down at the canvas. "Yes, I did."

"It's exquisite. How much do you want for it?"

The woman shrugged. "Just give me enough to score some heroin, and you can have it."

"How much do you need?"

The woman shrugged again. Then she ran a hand across her filthy, matted hair. "A hundred bucks would be okay, I guess. I'm Lydia, by the way."

"Nice to meet you, Lydia. I'm Samantha. And this is my girlfriend, Aubrey." From a pocket, Samantha withdrew a twenty-dollar bill. "I hardly ever carry much cash anymore. Wanna follow us to an ATM?"

Aubrey reached into her purse. "I'll pay for it."

Samantha started to protest, but then remembered how much cash Aubrey kept in her bedroom safe. "Thank you, baby," she said.

Aubrey gave Lydia some money. "Here's a hundred." Then she asked Samantha, "Do you like heroin?"

"Sometimes."

"You wanna do some with me?"

"Sure!"

Aubrey asked Lydia, "Will you get us some heroin, too, if I give you the money?"

"Yeah, I can do that."

Aubrey handed Lydia some more cash. "Here's another hundred. How far do you have to go to get it?"

"Not far. Just down the street, actually. I get it from a guy in the building where I live."

"Cool. You want us to just wait here?"

Lydia thought about it, and then shook her head. "Nah. Why don't you just come back to my place? You can wait in my apartment, while I go get it."

"Works for me," Aubrey said.

Samantha grabbed the painting, then she and Aubrey followed Lydia to an apartment building a couple of blocks away, next to the subway station.

Lydia's apartment was on the ground floor. "Just make yourselves at home," she told them. "I'll be right back." She left.

In the living room, Samantha leaned the painting against the coffee table, then she and Aubrey sat down on the sofa. "This place is a lot cleaner than I expected," Samantha said.

Aubrey found the remote control. She turned the TV on, flipped to a station playing music videos, and set the remote back down. "Maybe it's her parents' place, or something," Aubrey said.

Samantha sipped vodka from her water bottle. "Maybe so."

Lydia returned soon thereafter. She closed the door behind her, locked it, and gave Aubrey a small bag of white powder. "Let's get high in the kitchen."

Aubrey rose from the sofa. Leaving her painting in the living room, Samantha followed them both into the kitchen.

Lydia gestured at the kitchen table. "Have a seat."

Samantha looked around. Like the living room, the kitchen was clean. There were no dishes in the sink, and the silver refrigerator looked like a newer model.

From a cupboard, Lydia retrieved three unopened hypodermic syringes and set them on the table. From a cabinet by the stove, she grabbed a box of Q-tips and set it next to the syringes. She withdrew three spoons from a cutlery drawer and set those down, too. Then she filled a glass with water and joined them at the table.

While Lydia prepared her own dose for injection, Samantha watched Aubrey open a syringe and saw that it already had a needle attached. Aubrey dumped some heroin out of their bag and split it up into two hits. She drew some water from the glass with the syringe and pressed it out into one of the spoons. She stirred up some of the powder with the water in the spoon and cooked it over a cigarette lighter's flame. She cooked the shot until it hissed, put the lighter down, and drew the shot through a Q-tip into the syringe. Then she flicked air out of the syringe and handed it to Samantha. "All yours, baby," Aubrey said.

Samantha knew the needle was new but sterilized it with the cigarette lighter anyway. Then she found a vein and injected herself. The euphoria was nearly instantaneous, and a pleasant warmth spread throughout her body.

Soon thereafter, once all three had gotten high, Aubrey and Samantha followed Lydia back into the living room. Lydia sat down on the loveseat. Samantha sat down next to Aubrey on the sofa. An old hip-hop video was playing on TV. Aubrey said, "Music was so much better back in the day."

Samantha looked down at the painting still leaning against the coffee table—and realized that the pregnant woman sawing her own arm off with a hacksaw resembled the artist seated to her right. "Is this a self-portrait?" she asked Lydia.

"Yes, and it's also the last painting I'll ever do."

"It is?"

"Yes," Lydia said. "I killed Wayne yesterday, and they're going to know it was me as soon as they find him. After I killed him, I came here and painted that last night."

"Who's Wayne?" Aubrey said.

"My ex-husband. He filed for divorce while I was in jail. I was locked up for six months, and just got out a few days ago. This isn't my place, by the way. Mom just said I could stay here, until I got back on my feet. But that's not gonna happen now, of course."

Samantha said, "Why'd you kill him?"

"Because he starved my daughter to death."

"Damn," Aubrey said.

"Yeah. We had a one-year-old daughter, Felicity. I hadn't seen her in six months. When I went over there yesterday to see her,

I found her dead in her crib."

"Oh my god," Samantha said. "I'm so sorry."

"I had been so excited to see how much she had grown in the past six months, but she couldn't have weighed much more than the eight pounds she had weighed when I gave birth to her. It was sickening."

"How awful," Aubrey said.

"Yeah. And she hadn't been dead long, either. I mean, maybe if I'd gotten there sooner, someone could have saved her, but I doubt it. She was lying naked, flat on her back, covered in flies. Her rancid crib was stained black and speckled with toxic mold. Her whole body was speckled, too. I didn't know if it was fungus, or just part of the decomposition process, but I picked her up and kissed her goodbye nevertheless. Then I went in the bathroom and grabbed the straight razor Wayne always shaved with. I found him nodding off in the bedroom with a needle stuck in his arm. He was so wasted that he barely knew what was happening when I practically sawed his head off with the straight razor."

"Maybe you can plead temporary insanity," Samantha said.

Lydia shrugged. "Maybe so. Anyway, I'm glad you like the painting. I have to use the bathroom. There's some beer in the fridge, if you want some." She got up and walked away.

Samantha looked back down at the painting. To her left, Aubrey's phone chimed, alerting her to a text message.

Aubrey checked her phone. "It's Mitchell." She spent the next several minutes exchanging messages with her brother.

Then they watched videos and drank vodka until their water bottles were empty.

"I suppose we should head on back," Samantha said.

Aubrey rose from the sofa. "I need to pee before we go. I'll go check on Lydia. I think she may have passed out." She walked away. Moments later, she returned. "Baby, will you come here for a second?"

"Sure." Samantha followed Aubrey to the bathroom.

Lydia lay naked in the tub, already dead, her sightless eyes still shiny as polished glass. Red streams of blood flowed from the slices in her forearms and drifted through the water. A straight razor lay atop her clothes on the floor next to the tub.

"I'll just pee at the subway station," Aubrey said.

"Yeah. Me too."

Samantha grabbed her painting. They left the door open behind them.

CHAPTER 42

On a Thursday in July, Oliver stood waiting when Lucas's sister led her son into the Rosira. He watched them enter the lobby with a mixture of bewilderment and disbelief. Lucas had told him that his nephew was tall for his age, but Carl—supposedly only a year old—already towered over his mother.

Oliver recognized Elaine from a photo Lucas had shown him, but he had never seen a photograph of Carl. Perhaps the behemoth standing next to her in a long trench coat, a wide-brim fishing hat with a neck flap, and a black mask that concealed everything but his eyes wasn't her son. Maybe Carl still sat out front in a taxicab, or something.

He approached them. "Hello, Elaine. It's a pleasure to meet you."

With one hand pulling an upright carry-on and the other holding a suitcase, she stopped at the sound of her name, and looked at him. "You must be Oliver. Lucas told me you would show us to the apartment."

He nodded. "Yes. Lucas is currently dealing with a plumbing issue in 8B. You know how it is. A superintendent's job never ends." Then he looked up into the eyes of the giant standing beside her. "Is this your son?"

"Yes, this is Carl."

Oliver smiled. "It's nice to meet you, Carl. Your uncle is looking forward to meeting you."

Carl, holding a suitcase in each massive fist, did not respond.

Elaine said, "Carl doesn't talk much, so don't be offended. He's just shy."

"Oh, I'm not offended." Oliver thought of an old Aztec tale about a baby who explodes from his mother's body as a fully-grown man and goes on to become a god of war. "The apartment's in the basement. Follow me."

CHAPTER 43

Emma set her phone down. "Kenzie started a band."

Thomas—likewise naked—lay next to her on the bed. Beyond her bedroom window, a nighttime rain fell on Fort Lee, New Jersey.

"Kenzie," Thomas said. "That's your youngest daughter, right?"

"Yes. She's eighteen."

"And your oldest daughter—what's her name again?"

"Samantha."

"Samantha, right. And she's twenty-two?"

"Yes. She's the one who wants to be an actress. Kenzie's staying with Samantha in Manhattan."

"Kenzie's band," Thomas said. "Is it a rock band?"

"I'm guessing. I mean, she didn't specify. But yeah, I'm sure it's a rock band. Her girlfriend's the singer. Christina. One year younger. I met her before they left. Nice girl. Great singer, too, by the way."

"Cool. Has Samantha had any luck with the acting that you know of?"

Emma shrugged. "Not sure. I know she auditioned for a few plays recently. Would you like a drink?"

"Sure."

Emma got up and crossed the room to the minibar. The muted TV provided faint illumination. "I'm in the mood for bourbon and soda. Is that okay with you?"

"Fine with me."

She mixed them each a drink, then came back to bed and handed Thomas a glass.

He sipped his drink. "Perfect. And speaking of plays, I want to talk to you about *The Myth of Coincidence.*"

Emma cringed. "What about it?"

"Well, I know you think the play is haunted...that the ghost of your late husband somehow—"

"It *is* haunted! Listen, I don't know if it's Ryan's ghost that haunts the play, or something else entirely, but the play is haunted, and I don't want to talk about it. *The Myth of Coincidence* makes me sick to my stomach."

"Fine," Thomas said. "But we're going to have to talk about it, eventually."

Emma sipped her drink. "I don't wanna talk about Ryan, or his play. And I don't wanna talk about my writing, either. Let's talk about *your* writing, for a change."

"My writing?"

"Yes. When we first met, you told me that you were an actor and a writer, but you never talk about your writing. Why is that?"

Thomas shrugged. "I don't know. I mean, you've written a gazillion bestsellers, and I've only written one."

"Wait a second. You wrote a bestseller?"

"Yes, a few years back."

"I didn't know that! Was it fiction?"

"No. Valencia Rizzo's authorized biography."

"Valencia Rizzo?"

"Yes. Ever heard of her?"

"No, I don't think so. Who is she?"

Thomas sipped his drink. "She *was* a famous musician. Well, slightly famous, anyway. The book became a bestseller after she died."

"How did she die?"

He shot her a look and smiled. "Maybe you should read the book. A revised edition was published after she died."

Emma laughed. "Just tell me the story. I'll read the book later."

"Are you sure? It's a pretty long story."

"Of course I'm sure." Emma sipped her drink. "Besides, we have all night."

"Okay." Thomas took a deep breath. "It begins and ends with music, so I guess I'll start there. My obsession with music began when I was two. I don't remember life any other way. My obsession with Valencia began the first time I saw her in concert when I was thirteen. That was the year my sister committed suicide."

"I didn't know you had a sister who committed suicide."

"Yes. She hanged herself, just like your late husband. Anyway, Valencia had been one of my sister's favorite musicians, and I went to the show mainly for the spirit of my sister. Valencia was only eighteen at the time. She was opening for some goth-rock band and blew them off the stage. Few outside of the underground had even heard of her, but those who heard her knew that she was going to be huge. Five years later, when I was eighteen and Valencia was twenty-three, my band opened for her band in New Orleans. After the show, she and I broke into a cathedral and made love until six o'clock in the morning. We also drank a lot of whiskey. Sometime during the night, she asked me why my sister committed suicide."

"And why *did* your sister commit suicide?" Emma said.

Thomas shrugged. "Why else? Unrequited love."

"Ah." Emma sipped her drink. "Love will make you do some crazy things.'

"Yes. Anyway, Valencia never did achieve crossover success, but that's because Valencia wasn't a pop star. What she was—unquestionably—was the premier vocalist of her time. And she had mastered just about every instrument imaginable. Her work encompassed goth, industrial, jazz, opera, rock, blues, and every period of classical music—and yet it transcended them all. Her fans were legion. All throughout her twenties, Valencia headlined shows and sold them out all over the world. She released at least one album each year of that decade; sometimes two. Only a few of her albums went platinum, but all of them went gold, and the overwhelming majority of critics loved her music. When she was thirty, Valencia fell in love with a woman named Miriam and pretty much vanished from the public eye. But she and I remained great friends and stayed in touch. I loved Valencia like a sister."

"Were you jealous of Miriam?"

"No, of course not. I was happy for Valencia."

"So you're a musician, too?"

"Yes, but I abandoned my pursuit of a music career while in my early twenties. I switched to literature and journalism. I took a job in New York as a writer for a corporate magazine. By the time I was thirty, I had already published several books and novels."

"That's impressive," Emma said.

"Thanks."

"Tell me more about Miriam."

Thomas sipped his drink. "They were the same age. Miriam was Valencia's lover, life partner, and sometimes collaborator, but she committed suicide when they were thirty-two. Miriam's death devastated Valencia. She suffered a breakdown so shattering it landed her in a psychiatric hospital for a couple of years."

"Damn. That's terrible."

"Yes. She left the hospital at age thirty-five. Soon thereafter she wrote and recorded *Cannibal Valentine*, an album that many fans and critics considered to be her masterpiece. She started touring again, too. Her performances were still full of rage and terror, but her post-breakdown voice was even more mesmerizing than before. She toured for over two years. After the tour ended, Valencia paid me—the most accomplished critic of her work—a lot of money to write her authorized biography."

"Was that a difficult book to write?"

"In a way. I worked on the book for over a year, and it was published about a year after I finished it. Then I just sort of expected to hear that Valencia had committed suicide before the age of forty. But that didn't happen. Instead, much to my surprise—and to the surprise of many—she fell in love with and married a much older man."

"An older man?"

"Yes. She was thirty-seven when she met him, and he was seventy. His name was Enzo Lore, and he was an obscure, avant-garde, country-music performer. He had also published several of his own novels and books of poetry. He was tall, thin, and had a full head of thick white hair. He wore it long and kept it tied back in a ponytail. He looked more like fifty-five than seventy, but their three-decade age difference was still noticeable because Valencia looked like she was still in her twenties."

"Did you read any of his books?"

"I tried, but I couldn't finish them. The stuff he wrote just wasn't my cup of tea. The man could definitely write, however. There was no denying the fact that Enzo was a good writer. And though I don't like country music at all, there was also no denying the fact that Enzo was one hell of a singer, songwriter, and guitar player. Eventually, during a phone conversation, Valencia told me that she wanted me to meet him, that she thought I would like him."

"So you met him?"

"Yes, in their hotel room after a show one night in New York. And Valencia had been right: I did like him. He seemed even younger in person than he did in photographs. He was shooting heroin and drinking whiskey when I met him—and the man had already had a liver transplant. I just shook my head, laughing, when he offered me a syringe. 'Nah, man. Thanks,' I told him. 'But I will take a shot of that whiskey.' We drank and talked about music all night long."

"Then what happened?"

"Enzo and Valencia made an album together. It was a weird, country-goth opera that surprised me by being better than I thought it would be. They went on tour together, and the music sounded even better live. They didn't play to large crowds in huge stadiums, of course, but they had a lot of fun performing in small clubs all across America. Then Enzo got sick. 'He needs another liver transplant,' Valencia told me. 'Plus a lot of his other organs are failing. We're going overseas. Enzo knows a magician who can help us.' So they left, and Valencia called me when they got back to America. 'Enzo is better,' she told me. 'It was a radical procedure, but the magician said he's going to be fine.' And Enzo *was* fine, evidently. Apparently, they both were. Happy, healthy, and whole. According to Valencia, the radical procedure had involved black magic."

"Black magic?"

"Yes, according to Valencia. Anyway, they recorded a new album together and went on tour. Word of mouth spread, and their popularity exploded after the public heard about the black magic. They didn't play in small clubs for long. Soon they started selling out arenas. But while all of that was going on, I fell in love with and married a woman named Ashlyn. Five days after our one-year anniversary, Ashlyn died in a car crash."

"Oh no!" Emma said. "I'm so sorry. I never even knew you were married."

"Yes. I was devastated. I dove into my work and an endless stream of Tennessee whiskey."

"Then what happened?"

"Time passed." Thomas sipped his drink. "And then Valencia sent a message to my phone: *Enzo is sick again. You should come to Florida. We would love to see you.* Enzo and Valencia had moved to Florida a few years before. She had given me their new address in a previous conversation. I messaged back: *I'll be there tomorrow.* Then I went online and booked a flight to Panama City Beach."

"So you went to see them?"

"Yes. They lived in a seaside villa just outside Panama City Beach, a rambling fortress of marble that looked more like something you would see in Rome. Statues of gods and goddesses rose from colorful flowers in the gardens. Frozen nymphs and satyrs frolicked in the waters that splashed in numerous fountains."

"Sounds beautiful," Emma said.

"It was. Enzo and Valencia had been standing side by side outside the front entrance of the main house when I arrived. Both of them looked wasted, but Enzo appeared to be on the verge of passing out while he stood there. I followed them inside, and they led me to my room. I put my suitcase down and opened it. I hadn't packed much: clothes enough for three days; a bag of toiletries; my laptop; a few bottles of whiskey. I grabbed a bottle and followed them into the living room. They sat down on the sofa. I sat down on the loveseat and took a shot of whiskey. Enzo injected himself with heroin. Not long after that, he passed out. Valencia was also high on heroin, but it didn't make her sleepy the way it did Enzo. She had a faraway look in her eyes and was smiling dreamily. She told me she was glad I came. Then she told me that Enzo had Alzheimer's disease, and that because dementia was the one thing the magician couldn't fix, they had decided to end their lives."

Emma sipped her drink. "They decided to kill themselves?"

"Yes. Valencia told me that she fell in love with Enzo's words before she fell in love with his music, that she read one of his books and his words lit a fire inside her all the way down to her soul. She said nothing she had ever read affected her like Enzo's poetry. When she finally met him backstage after a show in Shreveport, he had the saddest eyes she had ever seen. Everyone he had ever cared about was gone. His friends. His family. His heroes. All of them were dead, and she fell in love with him instantly. She said it was very bizarre, and very intense, and they had been together ever since. Then she told me they were performing in the city that night, and asked me if I was coming to the show."

"What did you say?"

Thomas sipped his drink. "I told her I wouldn't miss it."

"Did you go?"

"Yes. The show was in a goth club called Nocturnica and I may have been the only person in the audience not wearing leather and chains. Enzo and Valencia took the stage dressed in black. They had no backing band. It was just Enzo with an acoustic guitar and Valencia with a piano. Both had microphones. They sounded phenomenal, but Valencia was a goddess. Her majesty was that of a thousand gravestones. Her voice emanated apocalypse."

"Sounds like a hell of a show."

"It was. Enzo and Valencia kissed at the show's conclusion. Then they opened each other's throats with straight razors. They collapsed onto the stage and bled to death in each other's arms. Witnesses in the front row saw them both mouth the word *forever* before they killed each other. I didn't see any of that, however."

"You didn't?"

"No. I just read about it later. I left halfway through their last song of the night, while they were still alive and singing to each other with love shining in their eyes. I walked out hoping that I could be close to someone else again."

Emma finished her drink. "I hope you feel close to me."

"I do," Thomas said. "But soon we'll need to talk about *The Myth of Coincidence*."

Chapter 44

Mitchell drove. Marla rode next to him on the passenger's side. After traveling for most of the night, they arrived in Manhattan as the sun rose over New York.

Marla turned the radio down. "I'm hungry. Can we get some breakfast?"

Mitchell found a diner on East 19th Street. The place was packed.

"Crazy," Marla said. "It's only six o'clock in the morning."

Mitchell shrugged. "It's the city that never sleeps."

Their hostess gave them a table by the front windows, and they sat down.

As they studied their menus, a waitress approached their table. "Are you ready to order yet?"

"I'll have the waffle combo," Marla said.

The waitress wrote it down. "Fried eggs or scrambled?"

"Scrambled, please."

"Skillet potatoes or hash browns?"

"Hash browns."

"That comes with three strips of bacon, or sausage links."

"Sausage links, please. And a large coffee. Extra cream and extra sugar."

The waitress turned to Mitchell.

"That sounds good," he said. "I'll have exactly what she's having."

The waitress walked away.

Fifteen minutes later, with a sausage link on his fork, Mitchell told Marla, "I read a story recently about a couple who got married, but instead of exchanging rings, they bit the tips of each other's ring finger off and swallowed them."

She looked up from her plate and smiled. "How romantic."

"I thought so, too. Supposedly, they soaked their fingers in ice for thirty minutes, and then bit down together on the count of three."

"We should do that," Marla said, "whenever we get married."

"I agree."

They finished their breakfast. Then Mitchell drove them to the Empire Hotel on West 63rd Street, and they checked into a room on the seventh floor.

From Mitchell's duffel bag, Marla retrieved their bottle of whiskey and took a drink. "What time is it?"

Mitchell checked his phone. "Almost eight a.m."

"God, it's so *early*."

"I know. We should probably try to sleep, but I don't think I can with all this coffee in my system. Let me hit that whiskey."

She handed him the bottle, and he took a drink.

Then he set the bottle on the dresser by the bed. "Feel like going for a walk?"

"Sure."

They rode the elevator down to the lobby and stepped outside.

"My first time in New York," Marla said.

The July morning was warm, sunny, and the streets were not as busy as Marla had been expecting. They passed by several storefronts, upscale boutiques, a few eateries, and a museum before Mitchell stopped in front of an old-fashioned barbershop with red, white, and blue colors twisting in a barber's pole next to the front entrance.

"I think I need a haircut," he said. "What do you think? You think I need a haircut?"

Marla shrugged. "I don't know. I mean, I guess..if you want one."

"I think I do," he said, and she followed him inside, feeling as if she had stepped onto the set of a sitcom, perhaps, or maybe an old black-and-white movie.

The small, two-seat shop featured a pair of chrome hydraulic barber chairs—both of which were empty. The blue-and-white checkerboard floor was spotless. Blue tiles ran halfway up the walls before turning into gray, vintage wallpaper. Glass product bottles lined a bookcase behind the counter. The classic smell of aftershave permeated the air, and posters offering hairstyles forty years out of fashion graced the walls.

Off to the side, in an otherwise empty waiting area, an old man sat reading a newspaper, and Marla couldn't remember the last time she had seen anyone actually reading a newspaper. THE NEW YORK TIMES was printed in the masthead on the newspaper's front page.

Mitchell said, "I didn't even know they made those things anymore."

The old man looked up and smiled. His teeth were so perfect Marla thought they were probably false.

"Newspapers, I meant," Mitchell added.

The old man nodded, setting the paper aside. "I knew what you meant. I'm Bill. You looking for a haircut?"

"Yes, I am. Is this your place?"

"It sure is."

"A barber named Bill," Mitchell said. "Has a nice ring to it. I'm Mitchell, by the way. And this is Marla, my fiancée."

Bill nodded at Marla. "It's nice to meet you."

She smiled and nodded back. "It's nice to meet you, too."

Bill got up and headed toward the barber chairs. "Right this way."

Mitchell followed Bill, but Marla remained standing where she was.

"You may as well come on over, too," Bill told her.

"Okay."

Both hydraulic barber chairs faced a single mirror. Mitchell took the one on the left, and Marla sat down to his right. "These are nice," Marla said, running her fingers down the barber chair's smooth, vinyl, nautical-blue armrests.

"Thanks," Bill said. "These same chairs have been in this place for as long as I can remember. My father passed this shop on down to me about forty years ago, and I never felt the need to upgrade."

Mitchell said, "Is your father still alive?"

"Lord, no. His ticker gave out a long time ago. Right after my mom died, actually. It was cancer that killed her, and then he had the heart attack. My own wife died not long after that."

"Oh no!" Marla said. "What happened to your wife?"

"Passed out drunk, puked in her sleep, and choked on her own vomit. I was passed out right beside her. When I woke up, she was already cold and blue."

"That's grim," Mitchell said.

"Yeah. She and I were chronic alcoholics. I still am, of course. I'll go to my grave a goddamn alcoholic. Speaking of which: you mind if I have a sip before I get started on your hair?"

Mitchell shook his head. "Not at all. As a matter of fact, I guess you could say that Marla and I are chronic alcoholics."

Bill nodded. "Kind of hard not to be, in this crazy world."

"You got that right," Mitchell said.

From one of the nicest decanters Marla had ever seen (gold-leaf stopper; intricate starburst inlays cut into the glass), Bill poured amber liquid into one of four lowball glasses in the decanter set and took a sip.

"What are you drinking?" Marla said.

"Apple-pie moonshine. My late wife's recipe. I make it upstairs in my apartment."

"You live upstairs?" Mitchell said.

"Sure enough. She and I never had kids. Been living alone up there ever since she died."

"What's the recipe?" Marla said.

"A gallon of apple juice, a gallon of apple cider, two cups of white sugar, two cups of brown sugar, four cinnamon sticks, a pinch of apple-pie spice, a bottle of one-ninety grain, and a bottle of hundred-proof vodka."

"Damn! That sounds potent!"

"It is. Wanna try some?"

"Sure!"

He poured her a glass, and she took a sip.

"Goddamn. That's delicious." She handed Mitchell the glass. "Here. Try this."

He took a drink and nodded. "Damn right." Then he took another drink and gave the glass back.

Bill grabbed a barber cape and draped it over Mitchell. "Want me to shave your face? I know it's early in the morning, but you already have a five o'clock shadow."

"We just got into town," Mitchell explained. "Been on the road all night, and I haven't had a chance to shave. But no thanks. I'll shave later. Right now, I'll just take the haircut."

"So just a trim, then?"

"Yep. Just trim it up."

For the next few minutes, Marla sipped her moonshine and watched Bill cut Mitchell's hair while the two men talked.

Soon, they began discussing ghosts.

"What about you?" Bill asked Marla. "Do you believe in ghosts?"

"Yes, I do."

"Would you like to hear a ghost story?"

"I would love to."

Bill paused to sip his drink, and then resumed trimming Mitchell's hair. "One of my old buddies and drinking partners, Steve Harper, was a funny guy—so funny that a lot of people, me included, used to tell him all the time that he should be a comedian."

"That's a tough gig, there," Mitchell said. "Comedy. It's awfully hard to make people laugh—especially these days."

"I know. But I'm not talking about telling jokes. Steve would simply make offhanded remarks or basic observations and people would just about fall off their chairs laughing. He cracked me up all the time, and I don't even have a good sense of humor. His wit was scathing, and he could use his humor as a weapon, to be sure, but I found out pretty quickly that he also used it as a diversion from his own personal demons."

"Was Steve an alcoholic?" Marla asked.

"Oh yes. He battled the booze for years. Always talked about quitting, but never did. His wife was dead, his kids were out of state, and just about every time I saw him, he was plastered out of his mind. Then he came in here one day asking me to shave off his beard—which just about floored me, because in all my years of knowing him, I had never once seen him without his beard."

Bill paused to sip his drink, and then resumed trimming Mitchell's hair. "He was wearing a suit, too, by the way, which was something else I had never seen him do. So I asked him why he was all dressed up and wanting to lose the beard all of a sudden, and he told me that he had a function to attend."

"A function?" Mitchell said.

"Yes. He wouldn't be more specific. Anyway, I asked him if he wanted a drink before I got started, and he told me no, that his drinking days were over. And of course, I had heard him say that shit at least a hundred times, so I didn't really pay it much attention. I just grabbed my clippers and started cutting big old clumps of gray hair off his face and watching them fall to the floor. After I finished, and he was shaved all the way down to his skin, I told him that he looked like a goddamn kid again. Then I asked him if that function he mentioned was a dinner date with a female, but he just smiled, shook his head, and held up the hand still wearing the wedding ring his dead wife had given him. Right before he left, he turned to me and said, 'I want you to know how much I appreciate you being my friend for all these years. You always were my favorite.' After he left, I looked down at that gray pile of his facial hair on the floor, and it occurred to me that—if Steve decided to keep shaving—it might be the last time I ever saw his beard again, so I decided to just leave it there for a while, figured I'd sweep it up off the floor later, at the end of the day."

Bill paused to sip his drink.

"Then what happened?" Marla said.

"Well, the shop was empty after Steve left, so I walked over there to my chair, sat down, and picked up the newspaper. I hadn't had a chance to read it yet that morning, and I decided to start with the section I hated most: the obituaries. That's one of the hardest parts about getting old—seeing all your friends in the obituaries. That, and all the goddamn funerals. Anyway, I got about halfway down a page and froze, because I couldn't fucking believe what I was seeing. The obituary said that Steven Ray Harper, age seventy-seven, had passed away three days before, and that his funeral would be held that very day at Crestwood Funeral Home at two p.m."

"Crazy," Marla said.

"Yes. Hell, for a second there, I thought I might be *going* crazy. I mean, I had just shaved his beard off a few minutes before, and now I was looking at his picture in an obituary."

"Did he have a beard in the picture?" Mitchell said.

"Yes, but it was a youthful picture of Steve, back when his beard was brown, instead of gray. So I got up, came right back over here to where you're sitting, and saw Steve's beard still on the floor."

"Did you sweep it up?" Marla said.

"No. I closed the shop and drove over to the funeral home, where I heard his kids talk about how young their father looked without his beard, and where I listened to a preacher talk about things that had nothing to do with Steve's life, and it occurred to me that none of those people in attendance even knew who Steve really was, that I was the only one there who was going to miss his humor, and who knew what a good man he was, and who understood how much he had loved his wife."

Bill paused to sip his drink, and then resumed trimming Mitchell's hair.

"Then what happened?" Marla said.

"I came back here to the shop—and saw that all that facial hair on the floor from Steve's beard had vanished while I'd been gone. Then it dawned on me that his kids had waited until the day of his funeral to run his obituary."

"He may have been afraid you would have missed it," Marla said, "and found a way to come pay you a final visit."

Bill shrugged. "Maybe so." Finished cutting Mitchell's hair, he brushed the barber cape off, and then removed it.

Mitchell rose from the chrome, hydraulic chair. "How much do I owe you?"

Bill told him a price.

Mitchell gave him twice that amount. "Keep the change."

"Thanks."

"Don't mention it. There *is* one more thing I wanted to ask you, though, about Steve's ghost."

"Go right ahead."

"When you came back here, after the funeral, and Steve's beard was gone, did you check the security cameras? To see if maybe his ghost showed up on film?"

Bill shook his head. "I ain't got no cameras in this old shop."

Mitchell nodded. "I didn't think so." From the holster beneath his jacket, he drew the silencer-fitted pistol and aimed it at Bill's face. "You're too good for this cruel world. Go be with your friend." Then he shot Bill once through the head, killing him instantly.

Marla looked away. "Are we gonna go see your sister?"

"I don't know. Maybe later. I'm ready for a nap."

"Me too," Marla said.

Chapter 45

Eighteen floors above Manhattan, the four of them sat on patio chairs near the rooftop's Broadway side. Aubrey and Samantha shared a bottle of vodka. Kenzie and Christina shared a bottle of rum. To the west, the sun was going down beyond Central Park.

"Where's the show tonight?" Samantha asked her sister.

Kenzie looked up from the guitar she'd been strumming. "I don't know. I can't remember." She turned to Christina, who was jotting down lyrics in a notebook. "What's that place called again? Venus?"

"Mercury." Christina said, without looking up from her notebook. "Mercury Performance Hall, on the Lower East Side."

Aubrey, with an arm around Samantha's shoulders, said, "Damn! A lot of famous bands have played there. And what is this? Your second gig?"

"Third," Kenzie said.

"Third, right. But still...how'd you manage to land a gig at Mercury?"

"Seth booked it for us," Christina said. "He has a lot of connections. We're opening for a band called Noctourniquet."

"Seth's already there," Kenzie said. "Setting up his drums and the PA. We have to meet him there for soundcheck at nine o'clock."

Aubrey checked her phone. "It's almost eight o'clock now."

"I know," Kenzie said. "Are you coming to the show?"

"Yes. What time do you take the stage?"

"Ten o'clock."

Aubrey nodded. "Cool. My brother's in Manhattan, by the way. I'm gonna try to get him over here tomorrow so you all can meet him."

CHAPTER 46

S miling at the dead baby in the oven, Elaine could only shake her head. *Some things never change*, she thought.

The kitchen in her brother Lucas's basement apartment beneath the Rosira was spacious, and though equipped with modern fittings, it still retained an old-world charm: stone-flagged floor; beamed ceiling; wainscoted walls hung with pots and pans. A solid-oak table at least ten feet in length dominated the center of the room.

But none of that currently mattered. All that mattered right now was the sight of the dead baby in the oven. She could tell it had been a boy because its genitals were still on display in the baking pan.

"Baby?" *Carl's voice, behind her.*

She turned around and looked way up into the eyes of her giant son. "Hi, Carl. I didn't even hear you come in here. And yes, your uncle Lucas likes to eat babies from time to time."

"Can I eat some of the baby?"

"Oh, I don't know. Your uncle might get mad if I let you eat some of his baby."

Lucas entered the kitchen. "Nonsense," he said, after evidently overhearing some of their conversation. "If Carl wants to eat the baby, he can have it."

"Are you sure?"

"Of course. I can always get more."

"Carl," Elaine said. "What do you say to your uncle?"

"Thank you, Uncle Lucas."

"You're welcome."

CHAPTER 47

W hile they drank bourbon in the great room, Thomas told Emma, "We need to talk about *The Myth of Coincidence*."

They were seated on a sofa. A TV was on, but muted. Jazz music emanated from the stereo.

Emma sipped her drink. "What about it?"

"I think the play should be performed again."

Emma's heart started pounding and she suddenly felt dizzy. "I don't think you know what you're saying."

He smiled. Then he reached over, took her hand, and squeezed it. "Emma, I'm not superstitious."

"Neither am I. But Thomas, superstition has nothing to do with *The Myth of Coincidence*."

Thomas squeezed her hand again. Then he said, "Surely you don't believe the play is haunted."

"I don't know how else to explain everything that happened."

He released her hand. "It was crazy, to be sure. But all of it was coincidence, Emma. Surely you know that."

"The play opened on Broadway just a week after Ryan died, and right after the curtain fell on opening night, the actor playing the part of Ryan collapsed on the stage and died instantly. Massive heart attack."

Thomas took a drink. "A tragic coincidence."

"The actor was twenty-four, the same age as Ryan when he died, with no known prior heart conditions."

"Coincidence," Thomas insisted.

"The play was staged again a month later, and one hour after the opening night's performance, the main actor was struck by a cab outside the theater and killed instantly."

Thomas took a drink. "Coincidence."

"The play was staged again the following year, and about an hour after the opening night's performance, the leading actor was shot and killed by a stray bullet during a drive-by shooting while walking home. The bullet struck him in the heart. He died instantly."

Thomas nodded. "Yes. Another tragedy, but it was also just another coincidence."

Emma took a drink. "Three deaths in a row, and all of them so soon after Ryan's suicide. Well, I just couldn't take it anymore. I didn't want anything else to do with the goddamn play, so I decided to pull it."

"Yes," Thomas said. "But then another agent persuaded you to permit the play to be staged two years later."

Emma nodded. "Yes, he did. I never should have listened to him, but—like you—he believed the whole thing was a coincidence, and I let him talk me into it. The play was staged, and five minutes after the opening night's performance, the main actor fell down a set of stairs backstage and broke his neck. He died instantly."

Thomas took a drink. "That was the last time the play was ever staged."

"Yes. Four opening nights, followed immediately by the four tragic deaths of the leading actors. After that, I wanted nothing more to do with it. I sold the rights to the play, and as far as I know, it hasn't been staged anywhere since."

"It hasn't," Thomas said. "But I want to change that."

"What are you talking about?"

"Well, actually it's my *father* who wants to change that, and I'm going to help him."

Emma took a drink, and then repeated herself: "What are you talking about?"

"My father is the producer who bought the rights to *The Myth of Coincidence* from one of your former agents all those years ago. He's in his sixties now, and he thinks the time is right to stage the play again. He put a company together, and it's been in rehearsal for months now. And I'm the lead actor. I'm playing the role of Ryan Kinkade."

Emma suddenly felt frozen as she stared at Thomas beside her on the sofa. "Unbelievable," she said. "I mean, I believe you, but this is unbelievable."

"Emma, when I first approached you, I only wanted you to sign the book and consent to an interview. I never planned or expected to fall in love with you. Please don't hate me."

"I don't hate you, Thomas. I'm madly in love with you. And that is why I'm begging you not to do the play. Please, Thomas. Don't do it. I do not want to lose you. Please don't do that godforsaken play."

"Emma, the play is going to be phenomenal. And I want to prove to you that the deaths were nothing more than coincidence. Me doing the play will free you from this ridiculous superstition."

"Thomas, I'm begging you. Do not do the play. There's already been four deaths. If you do the play, you'll be the fifth. And then I swear to God, I'll fucking kill myself."

Thomas finished his drink. He set his empty glass on a coaster and rose from the sofa. "I have to go. There's a final rehearsal in the morning. The play opens tomorrow night."

Emma finished her drink and stood up. "Please don't do it. I'm begging you."

Thomas grabbed his jacket. "I'd ask you to come, but I know you won't, so I'll call you after the play is over. My father knows who you are, of course. I gave him your number and told him to call you if anything happens to me. But nothing will happen to me. You'll see. I love you."

"I love you too."

He left.

Emma went into the library and mixed another drink. Then she carried her glass to a window and looked out at the oak tree.

The next day, the day of the play's opening, Emma woke up and drank all day long. She knew this would be her last night. Death was the only relief left, and she wanted to consume as much alcohol as possible before she killed herself.

That night, she sat at her desk in the library and stared out a window at the oak tree in the moonlight. She had stopped mixing drinks earlier in the day and now drank vodka from a bottle, waiting for Thomas's father to call her and tell her that Thomas was dead. She knew there would be no other outcome. And then, after Thomas was dead, she would have no other reason to go on living.

Emma smiled at the rope on her desk. She had already fashioned a noose and believed that her death would be perfectly fitting.

She saw something moving out on the lawn. It looked like a man walking toward the oak tree. She stood up, swaying, and nearly knocked her chair over. She staggered to the French doors and opened them. Then she stepped outside into the night.

Lightning fired off on the horizon, and a low rumble of thunder followed the flash. Dark clouds moved across the sky directly overhead, intermittently blocking the moonlight.

She saw motion beside the oak tree and approached it. When she reached the tree, there was nothing there, but she thought she heard laughter on the wind. "Ryan?" she said. "Ryan? Are you there?"

There was no answer but the wind, and she no longer heard the sound of a dead man's laughter.

She needed a drink and realized that she had left her bottle in the library. While heading back toward the open French doors, she heard her cellphone ringing, and realized that she had left it, too, on her desk beside the bottle and the rope.

Her phone had stopped ringing by the time she returned to the library. She picked the phone up and saw that she had missed a call from a number with a New York area code. It was not Thomas's number. *Probably his father*, she thought. *Undoubtedly calling to tell me that Thomas is dead.*

She took a drink of vodka. Then she checked the time. It was after eleven o'clock. The play would have ended over an hour ago by now, and still she had not heard from Thomas. She took another drink and thought: *Thomas is already dead.*

She grabbed the rope and the chair and carried them outside to the oak tree.

Lightning flashed. Thunder roared. Storm clouds raced across the sky, but no rain had yet begun to fall.

She placed the chair beneath a thick branch, stood up on the chair, and tied one end of the rope around the branch. Then she placed the noose around her neck.

She was just about to kick the chair out from beneath her when she heard Thomas yell her name. She looked across the lawn and saw him standing in the light of the open French doors. She had given him a key to the mansion, and he had evidently chosen to drive over and see her after the play rather than call her. "Emma!" he repeated. "No! Don't do it!" He started sprinting toward her across the lawn.

"I told you," he said, when he reached her. He had stopped about three feet in front of her, smiling.

He pulled his phone out and looked at the screen. "Over two hours now, and I'm still alive. See? All those other deaths were just a coincidence."

As soon as he finished speaking, an electric-blue bolt of lightning struck the top of his head. The strike was catastrophic. His eyes blew out of his head, and his hair and clothing went up in flames. Emma could smell him burning, and felt the heat from three feet away. When the second bolt struck him, there was nothing left of Thomas but the scorched end of a shoelace that a gust of wind quickly blew away.

Coincidence? Emma thought. *I don't think so.*

She kicked the chair out from beneath her as rain began to fall.

CHAPTER 48

On the Rosira's sixteenth floor, eight-year-old Sydney prayed to whatever gods were listening that her father passed out before he came into her room. Ever since throwing her mother off the balcony a month before, Dexter—she tried not to even think of him as her father anymore—had been coming into her room and molesting her. He usually came alone, but occasionally brought other men into her room with him, and they not only did things to *her*, but—even worse—made *her* do things to *them*, which made her feel lower than the lizards living beneath her grandparents' back porch in the Hamptons.

She missed her mother terribly, and often thought of jumping off the balcony to be with her in Heaven.

She turned her TV on. It was tuned to a cartoon channel. Dinosaurs chased cavemen across the screen. Moments later, Dexter started pounding on her door.

"Sydney! Open this door! Right now!"

The door was locked, and she knew if she didn't open it, he would probably kick it in—and then that creepy superintendent would have to come up here and patch another hole in her bedroom wall. Maybe if she pretended to be asleep, her father would simply go away, would stagger back to his own bedroom, and pass out.

No such luck. Seconds later, Dexter kicked the door in. It crashed open and slammed against the wall. He stood glaring at her with wild, bloodshot eyes.

"Little bitch." He unbuckled his belt and approached her. "I'm gonna teach you a thing or two about gratitude."

As he approached her, Sydney rose from the bed and tried to run around him, but he grabbed her before she made it to the door. He shoved her forehead against the wall and pinned her there. She cried out, but he pushed her harder against the wall and covered her mouth. "You're gonna learn some hard lessons tonight," Dexter said.

Tears escaped Sydney's eyes, despite her best efforts to control her fear.

"Oh, yes. You're gonna learn some hard lessons if it takes all goddamn night." He slid a hand around the front of her body and forced it down her pants.

She felt his breath on the top of her head and closed her eyes. "Please, no," she said, through clenched teeth.

He laughed and pressed himself harder against her backside. "Nobody tells me no," Dexter said.

Desperate, Sydney found just enough leeway to thrust an elbow back with all her strength directly into his groin. Dexter let out a pained shout and doubled over. She spun around and saw fury on his face as he caught his breath.

"Little bitch!" he yelled, and then lunged for her.

She sidestepped his attack, dashed around him, and fled her bedroom. Then she sprinted down the hall, crossed the living room, and rushed out into the sixteenth-floor hallway.

Dexter followed.

Having finished their nightly inspection of the recently-unoccupied 16D's ongoing renovations, Oliver had just followed Lucas out of the apartment when the little girl (Sydney, eight years old; he remembered her name and age) from 16A came running out of her apartment into the hallway. Seconds later, her father—Dexter—followed her out. He held his pants up with one hand and a leather belt in the other.

"Little bitch!" Dexter yelled. "Get back here!"

Oliver recalled that Dexter's wife—Sydney's mother—had supposedly jumped off the balcony about a month ago.

Lucas told Dexter, "Stop yelling. You'll disturb the other residents."

"Sorry about that," Dexter said. Then he told his daughter, in a lower tone of voice, "You need to get your ass back in the apartment—now."

Sydney looked up at Lucas, but then turned to Oliver. "You have to help me. My dad is going to kill me."

Lucas said, "Going to kill you?"

Ignoring Lucas, she continued speaking to Oliver: "He pushed my mom off the balcony, and now he's going to kill me, too."

Dexter shook his head. "She has a wild imagination. Everyone knows my wife committed suicide."

Lucas nodded. "Yes, I know her death was ruled a suicide. However, now that your daughter claims she's afraid you're going to kill her, I'm obligated to contact the police."

Dexter said, "Are you fucking kidding me?"

"No, I'm not. But it's just a formality. Nothing to worry about. We *will* have to fill out some paperwork, though, while we wait for the police, so I'm going to need you both to come down to my office in the basement."

Dexter shrugged. "Fine. I have nothing to hide."

Oliver smiled at the eight-year-old, and then gestured to the left. "Right this way."

He and Lucas led them to the freight elevator.

Sydney had never been inside the freight elevator, and as soon as she stepped into it, she felt as if she had traveled back in time. The freight elevator was *so old*. The Rosira's passenger elevators—which she had been in many times—all featured mahogany paneling and brass buttons, but the freight elevator had corroded bars instead of walls, and its lone bulb cast light on peeling plaster in the elevator shaft as they descended.

When they reached the basement, the largest man Sydney had ever seen greeted them in the hallway. He wore a trench coat, a wide-brim hat, and a black mask that concealed everything but his eyes.

"Carl," Lucas told him, "this is Sydney. We need her father to fill out some paperwork, so take Sydney to your mother. Tell Elaine I said to make her something to eat."

When Carl extended a hand, Sydney—suddenly afraid—was hesitant to take it.

"It's okay," Oliver told her. "Carl's a big baby. He won't hurt you."

No worse than my own father, Sydney thought.

She placed her palm in Carl's fist and watched the two men lead her father down the hallway.

"This way," Carl said, pointing in the opposite direction.

Sydney thought he sounded like a monster in a movie but turned and started walking by his side. He led her past large machines that seemed like gear-brained robots to Sydney—machines with steel cables, spinning wheels, and iron pendulums swinging back and forth.

"Don't get too close to the machines," Carl told her. "They're dangerous. If you get too close, you could lose an arm."

Despite his gargantuan size (and movie-villain voice), Sydney found her fear of the giant rapidly diminishing. Within moments, she had developed an odd level of comfort around him that surprised her.

Soon, Carl stopped and put a code into a keypad next to a door, and then opened it. "The motor room," he explained. "Last I checked, my mom was passed out on the sofa."

They stepped inside, and the door closed behind them.

Straight ahead, a woman lay sound asleep on a sofa, her loud snores blending into the noise of the machines that surrounded her. Sydney saw more of those rotating wheels, spinning cables, and steel pendulums swinging back and forth.

"Uncle Lucas knows the names of all these machines," Carl said. "I don't know anything about them."

Remembering that his uncle had said Carl's mother's name was Elaine, Sydney pointed to the woman on the sofa. "Is that your mother? Elaine?"

"Yes. She drinks too much. She wakes up, drinks, and goes back to sleep for a while. Wakes up, drinks, and goes back to sleep again. That's all she does, all day long. All night, too."

Sydney looked around. "I bet we could play some fun games of hide-and-seek down here."

"Hide-and-seek?"

"Yes."

"What's that?"

Sydney leaned her head back and looked up at the giant. "You've never played hide-and-seek?"

"No. What is it?"

"A game. One player's the hider, and the other's the seeker. While the seeker closes their eyes and counts to a hundred, the hider runs and hides. After the seeker opens their eyes, they try to go find the hider. Wanna play?"

"Sure, but I'm too big to hide. I'll be the seeker."

"Okay. Close your eyes and start counting. Don't open your eyes until you get to a hundred."

Carl closed his eyes. "One, two—"

Sydney fled the room.

From the main hallway of dim fluorescent lights and scuffed laminate flooring, she dashed into a darker hall of peeling plaster walls to either side, and a maze of ceiling pipes overhead. Garbage cans lined the hallway, and she crouched behind one, with her back against the can, facing a wall with glass-encased electric meters for the apartments upstairs. Behind the glass, tiny wheels spun.

He'll never find me here, Sydney thought.

But Carl did find her, and it didn't take him long.

"That was fast," Sydney said. "Are you sure you counted to a hundred?"

"Yes. I counted fast."

"Okay." Sydney rose. "I'll go hide again. Close your eyes."

Carl closed his eyes. "One, two—"

Sydney took off down the hallway and pretended she was flying through outer space, where the stars smelled like elevator grease, and the asteroids passing by resembled garbage cans.

She ducked into a room full of pulleys and furnaces, and Carl found her. She dashed into another filled with valves and pipes, and Carl found her in that room, too. After he found her in yet another room full of wires and more pipes from which hissing steam rose, Sydney said, "I just can't hide from you! How do you find me so fast?"

Carl shrugged. "Easy. I can smell you. All I have to do is follow my nose."

"Do I smell bad?"

"No. It's just your own scent. There's nothing wrong with it. And playing hide-and-seek with you has been the most fun I've ever had in my whole life."

Sydney cocked her head. "How old are you?"

"Not very. I'm younger than I look."

"I'm hungry," Sydney said. "Do you have any food?"

Carl nodded. "Of course. We never run out of food. Follow me."

He led her into a kitchen larger than the kitchen in her father's apartment up on the sixteenth floor. This kitchen looked much older, too. A long table occupied the center of the room, and numerous pots and pans hung from the walls.

"Have a seat," Carl said, gesturing at the table.

Sydney sat down.

From an old refrigerator, he withdrew a tray of pre-sliced meat. "Are you a vegetarian?"

"No."

"Good. All of us are big meat eaters down here. Do you like sandwiches?"

"Yes."

He set the meat on the table, along with a loaf of bread.

"Do you have any ketchup?" Sydney said.

"Of course." He grabbed some ketchup from the refrigerator, and then joined her at the table.

They ate.

"What do you think?" Carl said.

Sydney swallowed a bite of her sandwich. "This meat is delicious."

Moments later, Elaine staggered into the kitchen with a bottle of Grey Goose vodka—the same brand Sydney's mother used to drink, before her father threw her off the balcony.

Looking at Sydney, Elaine told Carl, "I see you found yourself a little girlfriend."

"Her name is Sydney," Carl said. "Uncle Lucas told me to bring her to you, to make her something to eat, but you were asleep, so I made her a meat sandwich."

"Oh, I'm sure she likes the meat, if you catch my drift." Elaine took a drink. "We all know how much little girls love the meat—especially the meat big boys like you have between their legs." She took another drink. "Let me ask you a question, Sydney. How old are you?"

"Eight. I'll be nine in September."

"See? That's an awfully bold statement. How do you know you'll even be *alive* in September?" Elaine took a drink. Then she set the bottle on the table and staggered to the sink. When she turned back around, she held a butcher's knife. "How do you know I won't take this knife and saw your goddamn head off long before September comes around?"

"Mom," Carl said. "Leave her alone."

Elaine shot him a look. "You shut the fuck up. I'm not talking to you. And don't worry, I'm not gonna hurt your little girlfriend. I'm just trying to make a point. All of us could be dead before September."

Sydney thought of her mother and nodded. "You're right, Elaine. I'll be nine in September—if I'm still alive."

Elaine cocked her head. "How do you know my name?"

Carl said, "Uncle Lucas told her."

"I see." Elaine put down the knife. "Speaking of whom," she told Carl, "go get your uncle Lucas. Tell him I need to ask him something. Sydney can stay here with me and keep me company."

Carl rose from his chair. "Don't hurt her."

Elaine rolled her eyes. "Goddammit, Carl, I done told you I'm not gonna hurt your little friend. Now go get your uncle Lucas. Sydney and I are gonna have us a heart-to-heart."

Carl looked down at Sydney. Then he turned, and she watched him walk away.

Carl stepped out of the basement apartment and turned left, walked down the hallway past the laundry room, the garbage room, the elevator-motor room, and then stopped in front of the door to the boiler room. When his uncle told him they needed Sydney's father to fill out paperwork, Carl knew that really meant her father would soon be dead.

Using the key his uncle gave him, he unlocked the door to the boiler room and stepped inside. He closed the door behind him and locked it. Straight ahead, past the water pumps, Lucas and Oliver stood looking down at Sydney's naked father, who lay strapped to a metal table in front of the boiler.

Carl approached them. As he drew closer, he saw that Oliver's pants were pulled down low: the old man fondled his flaccid penis with both hands while watching Lucas torture the father with pliers and a blowtorch. The father's scalp was gone, as were his eyes, his teeth, and his tongue. Carl could tell he was still alive, though, by the rise and fall of his chest, and the bubbles in the blood that oozed from his ruined mouth.

Lucas looked up at Carl and smiled. "Want me to cut his heart out? So you can eat it?"

"No thank you, Uncle Lucas. I just ate a meat sandwich."

"Oh god," Oliver said, still stroking his limp penis. Then he looked up at Carl. "I think I'm gonna come. Is that okay with you?"

Before Carl could answer, Lucas said, "We don't mind. Go right ahead."

Seconds later—while Carl watched—the old man moaned and shuddered uncontrollably as a few drops of semen dripped from his penis into the drain beneath his feet.

"Well, look at this," Lucas said. "I think Dexter finally kicked the bucket."

Carl looked down and saw that Sydney's father no longer breathed.

Oliver pulled his pants up. "All our freezers are full. We don't need any more meat."

"We'll cremate him," Lucas said, setting down his pliers and the blowtorch.

Then he turned, approached the incinerator's door, and opened it. "Carl," he said. "You're a big boy. Pick that son of a bitch up and put him on this conveyor belt."

Carl did. Then he watched Lucas push a green button on a digital readout next to the incinerator's door, and heard gas inside the system begin escaping under pressure as orange flames ignited.

Lucas pushed a red button, and the conveyor belt squeaked as it started moving. Numerals on the readout jumped from 300 to 600 to 1200 to 2400. Once Dexter's corpse was all the way inside, Lucas closed the incinerator's door.

Carl told Lucas, "Mom needs to ask you something."

Oliver wiped his hands on the front of his pants. "She probably wants to know how we plan on killing the little girl."

"Sydney's my friend," Carl said. "We can't get rid of Sydney."

"We have to," Lucas told him. "There's no way we can let her live. But don't worry. Because she's your friend, there will be no torture. We'll make her death as painless as possible."

CHAPTER 49

I n their room on the Empire Hotel's seventh floor, Marla sat down on the bed with a towel around her head.

Mitchell, at the table by the window, took a drink of bourbon. "There's been a change of plans."

"We're not gonna meet your sister today?"

"No, not today. Apparently, her girlfriend's mother committed suicide."

"Damn."

"Yes. Aubrey messaged me while you were in the shower. Her girlfriend's mother was Emma Kinkade, the famous writer."

"Holy shit! I saw that in my newsfeed earlier. They found her hanging from a tree behind her mansion."

"Yes, in Fort Lee, so they're gonna be in New Jersey for the next few days. For the funeral, or whatever. We'll catch up with Aubrey when they get back." He rose from the table and joined her on the bed.

"Let me hit that whiskey," Marla said.

He handed her the bottle. She took a drink and gave the bottle back.

Then she pulled the towel from her head and began fluffing her wet hair with both hands. "You never told me why you wanted to kill your sister."

"I haven't decided if I'm actually *going* to kill her. I told you she killed our father, right?"

"Yes, and that she had some money for you."

"Right. I'm guessing she stole the money from our father when she killed him—money I don't even want. As a matter of fact, I'm going to turn the money down. I just need to see her face to face, to decide if I'm going to kill her, or let her live."

"When I asked you why she killed him, you told me it was a long story."

"It is. Want me to summarize?"

"Sure."

Mitchell took a drink. "Our father sexually abused us when we were young. It went on for years. After our mother finally threatened to tell the police, he killed her. He thought he killed Aubrey, too, but she managed to escape. Years later, she resurfaced in my life, and made me promise not to tell him she was alive."

"Damn."

"Yes. Anyway, here's the thing—a part of me hated our father and wanted to kill him myself. But another part of me loved him more than anything and wanted him to live for many years. Does that make sense?"

Marla shrugged. "I don't know. I guess."

"So a part of me wants to kill her for robbing me of a chance to kill him myself, while another part of me wants to kill her for murdering the father I loved. Then again, *another* part of me hopes that I'll forgive her when I see her, because she's my sister and I love her, and that she and I can live happily ever after. The whole thing's all fucked up, but I definitely need to see her, face to face."

"Let me hit that whiskey," Marla said.

He handed her the bottle. She took a drink and gave the bottle back.

Mitchell took a drink. "Do you still want to marry me?"

She smiled. "Of course I want to marry you!"

"Good." He took his phone from a pocket and looked at it. "Last night, after you fell asleep, I went online and found an ordained minister with a boat."

"You did?"

"Yes. He said he could marry us tonight, while giving us a boat tour of Manhattan."

"Oh my god! That sounds so romantic."

"So you wanna do it?"

"Yes."

"Cool," Mitchell said. "I'll send him another message."

Midnight found Marla nervous in Mitchell's car. *My god*, she thought, fidgety on the passenger's side, *I can't believe we're finally getting married.*

He drove her to Midtown Manhattan, parked in a garage on West 44th Street, and they walked down to Pier 84, where the minister—a Mexican named Raoul, according to Mitchell—had agreed to meet them at one a.m.

They arrived early. A Mexican man showed up late.

"Are you Raoul?" Mitchell asked him.

"No. I'm Diego. Sorry I'm late."

"Where's Raoul?"

"In his boat," Diego said, pointing at a yacht to the west out on the Hudson River.

Lights glowed from most of the boat's windows, which—to Marla—resembled the eyes of jack-o'-lanterns. "I'm getting a bad feeling about this," she told Mitchell.

He turned to Diego, pulled the silencer-fitted pistol from the holster beneath his jacket, and aimed the muzzle at Diego's face. "Are you fucking with us?"

Diego recoiled automatically and threw his hands up. "What are you talking about, man?"

"This could be a set-up," Mitchell said. "For all we know, you're planning on taking our money and killing us both."

"Nah, man. It's not like that. Look, Raoul told me you two wanted to get married."

Mitchell lowered the gun, but kept it aimed at Diego's chest. "We do. But what are you suggesting? That we swim out there to the yacht and get married?"

"No, man. We take *my* boat to the yacht. It's docked right down there." He pointed toward the river.

Mitchell put his gun away. "Fine. We'll go with you, but if I sense foul play, I'm shooting you first. Understand? You first."

Diego smiled. "Dude, you worry too much. Come on. Raoul's waiting for us."

They followed him to his boat, which was small—a single engine—but accommodated three people easily.

Manhattan's glittering skyline and the Statue of Liberty soothed Marla's nerves as they sped over the Hudson to Raoul's yacht. When they reached it, Diego coasted parallel to starboard, shut the engine off, and secured his boat to Raoul's. Then Marla followed him up a ladder, and Mitchell followed them both onto the yacht, where another Mexican man—older than Diego—greeted them on the deck and introduced himself as Raoul.

"This one has a gun," Diego told Raoul, pointing a finger at Mitchell.

Raoul, who stood with his hands behind his back, drew a gun of his own and pointed it at Mitchell. "I don't allow guns on my boat," he told him. "So, on the count of three, I want you to take your gun out, give it to Diego, and do it slowly. Otherwise, I'll put a bullet right between your eyes. One, two, three."

Mitchell reached into his jacket, took the gun from its holster, and gave it to Diego.

"Excellent," Raoul said. Then he asked Diego, "What about the woman? Is she packing heat?"

"I don't know."

"Well don't just stand there," Raoul ordered. "Pat her down."

Diego did. "Nope. She's clean."

"Excellent," Raoul repeated.

"Look," Mitchell said. "We just wanna get married. But if this is a bad time, we can go get married somewhere else. It's no big deal."

Raoul shook his head. "You're never getting married. As a matter of fact, you're never gonna leave this boat alive. We have a vampire below deck, and the two of you are gonna keep her fed for a long time."

"Vampire?" Marla said.

Raoul shot her a look and nodded. He opened his mouth to speak, but never had a chance.

Faster than seemed humanly possible, Mitchell grabbed Raoul's right forearm and right wrist with both hands, spun him sideways, and aimed the gun at Diego. In that split second, long before Diego had a chance to raise Mitchell's gun, Raoul's gun went off. The bullet hit Diego in the face, and his head exploded. He was dead before he hit the deck.

Raoul squeezed his trigger a few more times, sending a few bullets out over the Hudson, but then Mitchell—still holding Raoul's right wrist with his left hand—slammed his right forearm into Raoul's elbow joint from its opposite bending direction, and broke his arm. Marla heard the bone snap over the ringing in her ears from the gunfire. Screaming, Raoul dropped the gun. Mitchell picked it up, blew Raoul's brains out the back of his head, and tossed the gun into the river. Then he retrieved his own gun—which Diego had dropped—from the deck and returned it to the holster beneath his jacket.

"That was easy." He grabbed Diego's keys from the dead man's pocket and held them up. "Now I have to figure out how to drive that boat."

"What about the vampire?" Marla said. "Do you think they really have a vampire below deck?"

"I have no idea."

Marla smiled. "I wanna go check it out."

"Seriously?"

"Yes."

"I don't know," Mitchell said. "That sounds pretty dangerous to me."

"Apparently it wasn't too dangerous to Raoul and Diego. I mean, evidently they were luring people here to feed it. So I say we go tell it that Raoul and Diego are dead, and that if it wants us to bring it sustenance, we'll only do it if it turns us into vampires."

Mitchell cocked his head. "You wanna be a vampire?"

"Yes! If you and I were vampires, we'd both be immortal, and then we could be together forever."

Mitchell shrugged. "I guess we can check it out." Drawing his gun, he pocketed Diego's keys. "But if the vampire fucks with me, I'll blow its head off."

Marla followed him downstairs below deck, where lights glowed in the hallway, the kitchenette, the bathroom, the entertainment salon, and the two empty bedrooms that they searched.

In the aft cabin, however, a young girl sat facing them on a twin bed. She appeared to be about five or six years old, with long black hair, pale flesh, and the brightest, bluest eyes Marla had ever seen. The girl's wrists were handcuffed in front of her, the cuffs linked by a steel chain to shackles on her ankles, the shackles chained to a steel ring bolted into the floor in front of the bed.

"Are you the vampire?" Marla said.

The girl smiled, and Marla noticed that her teeth looked like normal human teeth; she had no fangs. "Is that what Raoul called me? A vampire?"

She spoke with a British accent and sounded—to Marla—like someone who'd been speaking for a lot longer than six or seven years.

"Yes," Mitchell said, with his gun pointed at the floor. "Raoul's dead. Diego's dead, too. Before I killed them, however, Raoul told us that you were a vampire, and that we would keep you fed for a long time."

The girl shook her head. "I'm not a vampire. He just liked watching me eat human flesh. It was a fetish of his. Raoul was a strange individual. He's been bringing me human flesh for many years."

"Many years?" Mitchell said. "You can't be more than five or six years old."

"I assure you, sir, that I am far older than I look."

Marla said, "How old are you?"

"I'm not exactly sure. Somewhere close to six hundred, certainly."

"Whatever," Mitchell said.

"I understand your skepticism, sir, and I'll try to convince you of my tale's authenticity. My name is Alyria, by the way."

Marla found the young girl's words—spoken with such authority—utterly fascinating.

"My father," Alyria said, "was the King of France in the 1400s. King Charles the Seventh."

"I remember reading about him in history class," Marla said. "He was the one whose kingdom Joan of Arc helped to save. And then he let her burn at the stake when the English captured her."

"Yes. Tragic, is it not? And my father wasn't Joan of Arc's only lover—for my mother also shared their bed. She preferred my father over Joan, however. In time, my mother became jealous, and wanted her out of the picture, so she wouldn't have to share my father with Joan anymore."

Marla smiled. "Joan of Arc in a three-way relationship. Quite a contrast to the saintly image she's known for."

"Don't tell me you're falling for this nonsense," Mitchell said.

"My mother became violently sick," Alyria continued, "and my father summoned a woman, a master practitioner of witchcraft, to see if her magic could heal my mother's disease. She said it couldn't, that the illness was too far advanced. My father became furious, and ordered her immediate execution, at which time the woman offered an alternative. If he would spare her life, she would cast a spell, and I—his daughter—would never age and die. He agreed, and she did it, and she was then chained in a dungeon for one year so that my father could determine the validity of her magic. A year passed, and I didn't age, and my father let her go. And the rest, as they say, is history."

"So you're immortal," Marla said.

"No, I'm not immortal. It's true that I'll never age, and that I'm immune to all disease, and that my wounds heal almost immediately. But I *can* die. If my heart was ripped from my chest, or if my brains were blown out of my skull, or if my head was severed from my neck, I would most certainly die. Nothing lasts forever. Not on this side of death's veil, anyway. Not even stars."

"So your mother died," Mitchell said. "And I'm assuming your father died too, eventually. And even though I don't believe one word of your bullshit story, I'll play along and pose a question. After your father died, why didn't you become the Queen of France?"

"My existence was a secret. My father kept me in isolation. I finally managed to escape and disappear."

Marla said, "You were never captured?"

"No."

"How have you managed to survive—trapped in a child's body—for six hundred years? I mean, how have you managed to support yourself?"

Alyria smiled. "The easiest and oldest profession of all: prostitution. I'm sure you're both aware that many men possess a fondness for little girls. Raoul and Diego were but two of many others."

"That's quite a tale," Marla said. "But I believe you."

Mitchell laughed.

Ignoring him, Alyria asked Marla, "Do you believe in human souls?"

"Yes."

"What do you think will happen to your soul when you die?"

"I don't know."

"But you believe in life after death?"

"Yes," Marla said. "Nature wastes nothing. Matter, energy—neither is ever lost. And the human spirit is just a form of energy."

"But where does that energy go?"

"I don't know."

"The truth," Alyria said, "is that I'm ready to die, that I've *been* ready to die for quite some time. Everyone wants to live forever, but give someone the chance, and they would see what I see."

Mitchell said, "And what is that?"

"No end in sight. At least when people die, they die with the hope of something better in an afterlife. And after all these years I'm ready—have *been* ready—to let go, to die and be transformed into something else, or just sleep forever. Believe me, eternal sleep sounds pretty good to me. I'll take anything but this life of which I've grown so very tired."

Mitchell raised his gun. "I'll kill you right now, if you want me to."

Alyria smiled and closed her eyes. "Yes, please. And thank you."

"You're welcome," Mitchell said. Then he shot her once through the head, killing her instantly.

"Think you can figure out how to drive that boat?" Marla said.

Mitchell shrugged. "Shouldn't be hard."

CHAPTER 50

K enzie felt numb, and from the look in her sister's eyes, she knew Samantha felt numb, too. The four of them—Kenzie, Samantha, Aubrey, and Christina—sat in the great room of her dead mother's mansion, drinking from a couple of bottles they passed around. Aubrey and Samantha shared a bottle of vodka; Kenzie and Christina shared a bottle of rum.

From Manhattan, Aubrey had driven them to Fort Lee in her car the night before, with Samantha riding shotgun, while Kenzie and Christina rode in the back. Now, however, because they had been drinking heavily all morning, they waited for the limousine that would take them to Emma Kinkade's funeral service.

Natalie Ogren—Emma's literary agent (and now the executor, Kenzie knew, of her mother's literary estate)—had arranged the service so that she and Samantha didn't have to.

"I can't believe she's gone," Kenzie said.

Christina nodded. "I'm glad I got to meet her."

Aubrey took a drink. "I wish I could have met her."

Samantha said, "It doesn't seem real."

Fifteen minutes later, they all got out of the limo in front of Rose & Quesenberry Funeral Home and went inside.

The place was packed. A few of the people Kenzie recognized; most she didn't. She was glad Christina was there to hold her hand.

Natalie Ogren was already there. "Hello, Kenzie. Hello, Samantha," the literary agent said. Then she looked at Aubrey and Christina. "Who are your friends?"

"This is my *girl*friend," Samantha said. "Her name's Aubrey."

"It's nice to meet you, Aubrey."

"Likewise."

"And this is *my* girlfriend," Kenzie said. "Christina."

"It's nice to meet you, Christina."

"It's nice to meet you, too."

"Your mother's casket," Natalie said, "is in a chapel on the west wing, but if you don't mind, I'd like to speak to you about a few things first."

She led the four of them into a small room to the left of the main entrance.

"I buried my own mother six years ago," Natalie said. "Ovarian cancer. So she died young, too. About your mom's age. I wish I could tell you that it gets easier with time, but it does not. In a few minutes, you're going to walk into that chapel and a lot of the people in there are going to try to comfort you. They'll try to hug you or shake your hand or pat you on the shoulder, and most of them will say things like, 'It's okay,' or 'You're gonna be all right,' or 'At least she's in a better place.' They don't mean to be insensitive. It's just the only way they know to offer comfort to someone who's beyond *being* comforted right now. So just smile and nod, if you can. Hug them back, shake their hands—just whatever. But I want you both to know that I'll do anything I can to help you through this. And I'm not just talking about today, but moving forward. As the executor of your mother's literary estate, I'm in this with you both for the long haul."

Kenzie nodded. "Thank you."

Samantha said, "We appreciate it."

"You're welcome. Also, as you may or may not know, before your mother died, Emma named me the executor of her will. And it's pretty simple, really. You two are the only beneficiaries. I'll send you each a copy later, but she left everything to the two of you, to be split down the middle, fifty-fifty. The mansion here in Fort Lee, the penthouse in Manhattan, all of her other assets and properties, her fortune in the bank—all of it. So, if it's any consolation, at least there's that."

After the viewing (Emma's casket had been open, and Kenzie thought her mother looked more peaceful in death than she had ever seen her in life, with her face relaxed and her eyelashes resting on her cheeks), the limo took them to Sunset Memorial Cemetery.

Later, after the casket was lowered and everyone else had gone, the four of them stood drinking from metal flasks by Emma's open grave.

"Damn," Christina said, pointing to the left. "What the fuck is wrong with that dude?"

All three looked to the left. About fifteen feet away, past the mound of earth that would be shoveled in on top of Emma's casket, an older man in a black suit stood bashing his head against an oak tree.

"Hey, mister!" Aubrey called out. "Are you okay?"

He stopped bashing his head and turned to face them. Kenzie saw blood smeared across his forehead. Taking a handkerchief from his breast pocket, he began dabbing his brow and approached them. He was tall, and lean, with thick, slicked-back gray hair. Kenzie thought he looked like an aging movie star.

"Sorry about that," he said. "Diversion technique. Lately I've been having these blinding headaches."

"That sounds terrible," Samantha said.

He nodded. "Yes. I'm Walter Maxwell, by the way. Does my last name ring a bell?"

Samantha shook her head. "No. And I'm Samantha."

"Yes, I know who you are." Then he looked at Kenzie. "And I know who you are, too. First of all, I would like to express my condolences to you both on the loss of your mother."

"Thank you," Kenzie said.

He grimaced, and then smacked himself upside the head with his left hand several times.

"You should probably get those headaches checked out," Samantha said.

Nodding, he squeezed his eyes shut for a couple of seconds, and then opened them. "Yes. They're becoming quite debilitating, actually. Anyway, my son—*Thomas* Maxwell—was in a romantic relationship with your mother. *Now* does my last name ring a bell?"

"No," Kenzie said.

He looked at Samantha. "What about you?"

Samantha took a drink of vodka from her flask. "No. Mom rarely discussed her personal life with either of us."

"I see," Walter said. "Well, here's the deal: my son is missing."

"I'm sorry to hear that," Samantha said.

Walter smacked himself upside the head a few more times. "So you haven't seen him?"

"No. I don't even know what he looks like."

He looked at Kenzie. "What about you?"

She took a drink of rum and shook her head. "I've never even heard of Thomas Maxwell."

"Perhaps I should backtrack a bit," Walter said. "Years ago, I bought the rights to a play with a bad reputation from one of your mother's former agents."

"You're a producer?" Samantha said.

"Yes. The play was written by your father, shortly before his suicide."

Kenzie said, "*The Myth of Coincidence.*"

He nodded. "Are you familiar with the play?"

Kenzie took a drink. "I've never read it, but Mom always told us the play was haunted."

Walter punched himself twice in the temple with his right fist. "A lot of people thought the play was haunted. It was staged exactly four times, and each time, the leading actor died immediately after the opening night's performance.'

"And you bought the rights to the play anyway?" Samantha said.

"Yes. I didn't believe in hauntings, or curses, but your mother apparently did, and when I heard through the grapevine that she was selling the play for cheap, just to get rid of it, I purchased the rights and sat on the play for years. A few months back, I decided the time was right to stage the play again. So I put a company together, and my son chose to play the leading role"

"And now he's missing," Kenzie said.

"Yes. Your mother didn't want him to take the role. She was afraid he would die like the previous four actors who took it. But he was fine. After the opening night's performance, he took a cab here from New York to show her that he was okay, to prove to her that the four deaths were nothing more than coincidence, and to free her from what he felt was a silly superstition. And then he just disappeared. We know he arrived at Emma's mansion because the cab driver verified dropping him off there, and he used a credit card to pay the fare. Now we can't find his phone or anything else. It's like he vanished off the face of the earth. It makes no sense."

"I don't know what to tell you," Samantha said.

Walter smacked himself upside the head a couple of times. "And then your mother just so happens—on that very same night—to hang herself from the same tree your father did ten years ago. It doesn't make sense. Something's amiss. And I think you girls had something to do with it."

"Are you insane?" Kenzie said. "We don't even know your son."

"And we weren't even *here* when Mom died," Samantha added. "We were in New York. We only came to Fort Lee for the funeral."

Walter dabbed his bleeding forehead with the handkerchief, and then slapped himself. "This isn't over. You two haven't heard the last from me."

He turned, and they watched him walk away. He was still slapping himself as he crossed a slope toward the crest of a low hill and disappeared.

That night, in Emma's library, Kenzie pulled a reading edition of her late father's play from one of her dead mother's shelves and held it up.

"Is that the play the old man was talking about?" Christina said.

"Yes. *The Myth of Coincidence.*"

"I'd like to read it. Can I take it back to Manhattan?"

"Sure." Kenzie handed her the play. "You can have it."

"Thanks. And what's that old man's name again?"

"Walter Maxwell."

"Right. Walter Maxwell. He seemed dangerous to me. Are you worried about him?"

Kenzie shook her head. "Not at all."

Christina said, "The whole thing's crazy."

At the French doors, Kenzie pointed to an oak tree bathed in moonlight at the edge of the property. "That's the tree, by the way."

"That your mom hanged herself from?"

"Yes. And my dad, ten years before."

"Some people," Christina said, "believe there's a genetic component to suicide."

"Is that right?"

"Yes. Sort of like the Hemingway Curse."

"Hemingway Curse?"

"Yes. You know how the Kennedy Curse came with assassinations? The Hemingway Curse was all about suicides."

"Are you talking about Ernest Hemingway?"

"Yes. The famous writer who blew his brains out, like, a hundred years ago, or some shit."

"I've never read any Hemingway," Kenzie said.

"Me neither. But I watched a documentary about the Hemingway Curse. After his father committed suicide, Hemingway wrote that he would probably go the same way. And he did, of course, but it wasn't just him and his dad. He also had a brother, a sister, and a granddaughter who committed suicide. So that makes five, but I'm pretty sure there were seven confirmed suicides in the family—and possibly more."

Kenzie took a drink from their bottle of rum. "Well, you don't have to worry about me. I will never kill myself unless something happens to you."

"Same," Christina said. "I love you."

"I love you, too."

The next day, they went back to Manhattan with Aubrey and Samantha.

CHAPTER 51

B eneath the Rosira, after feeding Dexter's corpse to the incinerator, Carl followed Lucas and Oliver from the boiler room back to his uncle's basement apartment.

"Elaine?" Lucas called out, in the kitchen. "Where are you? Carl said you needed to talk to me." When there was no answer, Lucas turned and looked up at his nephew. "Your mother probably took the little girl downstairs to the bomb shelter."

Carl said nothing, trying to think of a way to stop them from killing Sydney.

"Bomb shelter?" Oliver said.

Lucas nodded. "Yes. I built myself a bomb shelter in the sub-basement. You know, in case of a terrorist attack. I built it according to government specifications. Come on. I'll show you."

He led them to a door between the sink and the refrigerator, then opened it and started down some stairs. Oliver followed him down, and Carl followed them both into the sub-basement, bending low to keep his head from scraping the ceiling as they walked past cartons of bottled water and canned food stacked along the walls to an open metal door that looked like a meat locker's door. Then he followed his uncle and the old man into a concrete enclosure colder than the rest of the sub-basement.

In the center of the small room, Sydney stood bound, gagged, and naked atop a plastic toolbox. Elaine sat in front of her on a folding chair with her legs crossed, smoking a cigarette. She had tied two lengths of rope around Sydney's wrists and looped them over steel hooks driven into wooden beams along the ceiling. On the floor next to Elaine's feet lay a crowbar, a fire extinguisher, and a knife with a serrated blade.

She picked the knife up by its handle and turned to Carl, and her brother, and the old man. "You're all here," she said. "Finally."

Fear and desperation filled Sydney's eyes. It sickened Carl.

"I'm gonna kill this little bitch," Elaine told her son. "But don't worry. I'll find you another friend soon."

"No!" Carl shouted, and heard a sob catch inside his throat.

His mother laughed, and he felt something snap. Then a curtain of blood-red fury descended, and he blacked out.

Sydney needed to pee, but she was determined not to pee where she stood—nude, bound, and gagged—atop a toolbox in a concrete room. She wanted to avoid the humiliation of standing in her own waste for as long as possible. Also, she didn't want to give Elaine the satisfaction of seeing her lose control of her bladder. Carl's mother was clearly insane. Elaine watched her with a sinister smile on her face, and with eyes that seemed not a woman's eyes at all, but the multifaceted eyes of a spider.

In her eight years of life, Sydney had never before felt totally lost. Frightened, yes. Often terrified—especially after her father threw her mother off the balcony, and while hiding beneath her bed, waiting for him to enter her room (either alone or with other men) and violate her. But she had always kept a map in her mind, with a destination marked if only vaguely, and had believed that if she could just survive until her teenage years, she would run away and start a new life without him.

Not anymore, though. She no longer had a map. Her life had become a horrifying maze of funhouse mirrors, and she was trapped in its infinite chambers, with no one to turn to, and no hand to hold.

Sydney closed her eyes, knowing she would soon be dead. Her only hope now was that Elaine would kill her quickly and send her to Heaven to be with her mother.

"You're all here," Elaine said. "Finally."

Sydney opened her eyes.

Carl, Lucas, and Oliver had entered the concrete room.

Elaine still sat on the chair, but now held a knife. "I'm gonna kill this little bitch," she told her son. "But don't worry. I'll find you another friend soon."

"No!" he shouted, and she laughed. Carl lunged for his mother.

Sydney watched his eyes become vacant, as if someone had switched him off. In a blur of motion, he sent a massive fist crashing down onto the top of Elaine's head. The wet crack of her skull shattering filled the room like a shotgun blast. Ribbons of blood sprayed into the air, throbbing in time with his dying mother's heartbeat.

"That was my sister, you son of a bitch!" Lucas screamed. "I'm going to fucking—"

His final words were cut short by the collision of his and Oliver's skulls. Carl's enormous hands clapped together, sending blood, shards of bone, and chunks of dripping meat into the air. Their bodies hit the floor as gore splashed all over Sydney's body.

Carl turned to face her, splattered in scarlet, and smiled. The lights came back on in his eyes. "Can we play some more hide-and-seek?"

"Sure. But first I need to pee. Cut me loose."

Carl grabbed his dead mother's knife, sawed through Sydney's ropes, and then tossed the knife aside.

Gathering her clothes, Sydney looked down at the corpses on the floor. "Did they kill my father?"

"Yes."

"Good." She got dressed. "Where's the bathroom?"

"Come on. I'll show you." Carl turned and walked out of the bomb shelter. Sydney followed.

CHAPTER 52

Agony awakened Walter Maxwell from a nightmare.

In the dream, he had been running through a moonlit field as his missing son chased him with a machete, and then—KAPOW!—intense physical pain woke him up. It felt as though he had taken a pool cue to the eye. An eight-ball break; a real sinker. Now it hurt down to his left ear and all down the other side of his neck.

Cursing, he rose from bed, staggered into the kitchen, and began washing his hands under hot water, trying in vain to focus on anything but the pain in his head. Both of his eyes were watering, and one of his eyelids was drooping closed on its own. He turned the hot water off and started pacing around, filled with both misery and anxiety.

He went into the living room, forced himself to sit down, turned the TV on, and then quickly turned it off, wondering if perhaps *The Myth of Coincidence* were haunted after all. He only staged the play once, but ever since that night, his son had been missing and Walter had been afflicted with crippling headaches.

His cat—Tabby—sat at his feet, looking up at him. She always seemed to know when he didn't feel well, sometimes as soon as he did. It was uncanny.

"Do you believe in haunted plays?" he asked the cat.

Tabby cocked her head, regarding him quizzically.

"Right," Walter said. "I don't know, either. I don't know anything anymore."

He stood up, took a deep breath, and walked over to the living-room window, putting a hand over the eyelid that had drooped closed, because it felt as if someone with a knife were attempting to bore into his skull above that eye.

He went back into the kitchen and drank a glass of wine, then began pacing again. The corners of his forehead felt like bone fragments were cracking down to his cheeks and then back up to the tops of his ears. He lost his balance and fell. Then he got up and sat down at the kitchen table.

A hard and sudden crack somewhere between the backs of his eyes and his temples made him shout. His left foot started twitching, and then both legs. He put the skin of an index finger between his teeth and bit down hard enough to draw blood.

Another forceful crack in his head was followed by a snapping sensation, and then it felt like channel-locks were clamping down on his orbital ridge. The pain increased. He began rocking on the chair and bouncing his knees. The activity became so vigorous that he kicked himself in the head with his knees several times. He began grunting to refrain from screaming, tried talking to himself, but was in too much pain. Eventually, he fell off his chair and crashed onto the floor, screaming, and bashing his head against the tiles.

He was still screaming and bleeding the next day when—after neighbors called an ambulance—paramedics took him to a hospital.

The oncologist had an office in a building near the hospital. He was a short man, in his forties (about twenty years younger than Walter), and very thin. He closed his office door and told Walter to have a seat.

After an initial CT scan in the hospital's emergency department, which was followed by an MRI, an immediate appointment with the oncologist had been arranged. Walter had been undergoing more testing for the past hour—and it still was not even noon. Normally he would appreciate the speed with which all of this was happening, but these were not normal circumstances. Under these circumstances, the urgency was horrifying.

The oncologist cleared his throat. "In a case like this, I have found that the greatest mercy is directness. You have a rare and aggressive brain cancer known as diffuse intrinsic pontine glioma, or DIPG. The tumors form on the base of the brain stem and spread like sand. It's inoperable. You probably have about two to four months left. Certainly not much more. I'm very sorry."

Walter said nothing.

"Again, I'm very sorry, but there's nothing we can do. You're terminal. Try to enjoy what little time you have."

Walter said, "Can you give me something for pain?"

"Of course."

The oncologist wrote him a prescription for OxyContin.

An hour later, after stopping by a pharmacy on his way home, Walter opened a can of cat food and dumped its contents into Tabby's bowl.

Then a darkness began somewhere in his mind, perhaps in a place where the cancer lived, and where resentment lived and had for a long time. The darkness in that place revealed to him a future of loss and unimaginable pain that began the night he staged that godforsaken play, *The Myth of Coincidence*.

He blamed its author, who hanged himself ten years ago, and the author's wife, who hanged herself the night his son went missing. And he blamed her daughters, too—both of whom were still alive right here in New York City.

The darkness inside him spread as the cancer spread, turning his whole world black. Around three in the afternoon, it took him into his bedroom to grab the 10mm pistol he kept in his nightstand.

CHAPTER 53

On a Friday afternoon, just to get out of Manhattan, Aubrey and Samantha took a bus out to the Hamptons. It was not a public bus, but a privately-owned luxury liner with free Wi-Fi, spacious seating, and complimentary snacks. The bus also offered complimentary cocktails, but Aubrey and Samantha drank their own vodka from water bottles they brought along in duffel bags. Power outlets allowed them to keep their phones charged during the two-hour ride to East Hampton Main Beach.

They spent the day walking back and forth between downtown and the beach, sipping vodka while eating cotton candy and ice cream.

That evening, they sipped vodka on the shore while parents watched children build sandcastles, and hard-bodied men and women struck poses for one another, and retirees sat beneath umbrellas, soaking up the shade.

Later, as the sun sank out of sight to the west, and the stars came out to the east, over the Atlantic, Samantha's phone chimed, alerting her to a text message. "It's Kenzie," she said, looking at her phone. "They're getting ready to take the stage at a place called Bedlam, on the Upper West Side."

"That's close to our building," Aubrey said. "And they're such a good band. I can't wait until they release their debut album."

Eventually, it was time—nearly midnight—to catch the last westbound bus back to Manhattan.

It was almost two a.m. when they got home. As they approached their building, a man stepped out of the shadows and raised a gun.

The doctor had given him four months to live, and Walter had been prepared to wait outside the Rosira's entrance that whole time for Kenzie and Samantha, but in the end, he did not even have to wait eleven hours. He checked his wristwatch as soon as he saw Samantha on the sidewalk: 1:56 a.m. He wished Kenzie were with her, but he didn't see her younger sister anywhere. *Oh well,* he thought. *One of two is better than none at all.*

Samantha was not alone, however. He recognized the woman whose hand she held as the same woman who had been with her at Emma Kinkade's funeral, so he assumed she had to be Samantha's girlfriend.

Just look at them, he thought. *So young. Probably twenty years younger than my son. When you're that age, you think you know everything, but then you get older and realize you never knew anything at all. They don't see it yet, and they never will, now, but it happens to everyone. Well, everyone who has the luck of growing old. Unfortunately for these two, their time on planet Earth ends tonight.*

Stepping out of the shadows, Walter raised his gun.

Samantha recognized him immediately, and even remembered his name: Walter Maxwell. The man whose son was missing. The man who had staged her late father's play; the play her late mother had always claimed was haunted.

"Wait," Samantha said, choosing to look into Walter's eyes rather than the round, dark muzzle of his pistol. "Let's talk about this."

"There's nothing to talk about," Walter said. "Unless you can tell me where my son is."

Aubrey released Samantha's hand. "Listen, mister," Aubrey said. "She already told you at Emma's funeral: we don't know anything about your goddamn son."

Walter nodded. "Fair enough." Then he shot her right between the eyes, killing her instantly.

Samantha screamed, knowing she would never hold Aubrey's hand again. Then Walter shot her through the head at point-blank range, and she knew no more.

Soon, he knew, there would be sirens, but Walter would not be around to hear them.

Godspeed, Thomas, he thought. *Until we meet again.*

He put the muzzle of the pistol to his head and pulled the trigger.

CHAPTER 54

I was born for this, Christina thought, while singing and playing bass in front of Bedlam's packed crowd on a Friday night.

Every night on stage with Kenzie and Seth felt like the best night of her life. And—she knew—they were only getting started.

The club was open until four a.m., but their performance ended at two.

"Thanks for coming out!" Christina yelled, at their show's conclusion. "We're Screamweaver! Spread the word!"

The audience cheered and applauded.

Then she, Kenzie, and Seth went backstage.

"You coming to our place?" Kenzie asked Seth. "Aubrey and Samantha have some killer cocaine."

"Nah," Seth said. "Going hiking with my girlfriend in the morning. Gonna load my drums and take my ass home."

"You leaving now?" Christina asked him. "Or closing time?"

"Closing time. I wanna drink for a couple more hours."

"Will you just put our stuff in your van? So we can walk on home and get started on the coke?"

"No problem."

"Thanks. Just message us tomorrow, after you're back from hiking, and we'll swing by and pick up our gear."

Seth nodded. "You got it."

They parted ways.

While walking home—the Rosira was only a few blocks west—Christina put an arm around Kenzie's shoulders. "You played great tonight. Your guitar sounded amazing."

Kenzie looked at her and smiled. "Thanks. So did you."

As they approached the Rosira, they saw a small crowd gathered along the street. Two police cars were parked in front of the building, their roof lights flashing blue and red.

"What the fuck?" Kenzie said.

They quickened their pace.

"Dead," someone said. "All three of them. Looks like the man shot the two women before killing himself."

"Everyone get back," one of the police officers said.

Christina looked down—and recognized all three corpses on the sidewalk immediately. Aubrey and Samantha were each dead of a gunshot to the forehead. Walter Maxwell—she remembered his name—was dead of a self-inflicted gunshot to his temple; his pistol lay on the sidewalk next to his body.

"Unbelievable," Kenzie said. "I just buried my mom, and now I'll have to bury my goddamn sister."

Christina took her hand. "Oh God, baby. I'm so sorry."

"Everyone get back," the police officer repeated.

The night-shift doorman came out of the building with some blankets and gave them to the other cop.

"Come on," Kenzie said. "Let's go back to the club. I don't feel like talking to the cops."

"Okay."

They turned and headed east on 72nd Street.

CHAPTER 55

"It's August now," Marla told Mitchell, in their room on the Empire Hotel's seventh floor. "I just realized that. It's August first. July's already over. Time is flying." She lay on their bed staring at the muted TV.

Mitchell, at their table by the window, sat looking down at his phone. "Aubrey's not answering my texts."

"So let's just go see her," Marla said. "I'm ready to meet your sister."

Mitchell looked up from his phone. "Well, she *did* give me the code to get into the building."

"Do you have the address?"

"Yes. It's called the Rosira. Upper West Side. Seventy-second Street."

They left, arriving at the Rosira soon thereafter. They took the stairs up to the second floor, and then Mitchell rang Aubrey's doorbell. No answer. He rang it again; still no answer.

"She might be up in the penthouse," Mitchell said.

"Oh yeah?"

"Yes. Her girlfriend lives in the penthouse, but her girlfriend's younger sister stays there too, or some shit, so she and Aubrey have been bouncing between apartments."

"Cool," Marla said. "Let's go check it out."

They rode an elevator up to the eighteenth floor. At the penthouse, Mitchell pulled his phone out.

"What are you doing?" Marla said.

"Hold on. Gonna scroll through some messages." Moments later: "Okay, Samantha's her girlfriend's name, and Samantha's younger sister's name is Kenzie."

Mitchell put his phone away. Then he pressed the doorbell.

Seconds later, a teenage girl with blue hair opened the door. "Yes?" she said. "May I help you?"

"Are you Kenzie?"

"No."

"Samantha?"

"No, I'm Christina. Who the fuck are you?"

"I'm Mitchell, and this is Marla, my fiancée. We're looking for my sister, Aubrey. Is she in there?"

Christina's eyebrows lowered, and she drew her lips in tight. Her eyes watered, too. Marla thought the blue-haired girl appeared to be ready to cry.

Christina shook her head. "No, Aubrey isn't in here. Listen, I'm afraid I have some terrible news, so you may as well come on in." She took a step back and to the side.

Marla followed Mitchell into the living room, where another teenage girl sat crying on the sofa.

Christina closed the door behind them.

Then she joined the other girl on the sofa and put an arm around her shoulders. "Kenzie," she said, "this is Mitchell, Aubrey's brother. And that's his fiancée, Marla. Would you like to tell them the bad news, or do you want me to?"

Kenzie, still crying, withdrew a tissue from a box on the coffee table. She blew her nose, dropped the tissue in a plastic bag on the floor at her feet, and then looked up at Mitchell. "Your sister's dead."

Marla looked over at Mitchell. There was no change in his facial expression.

"Dead?" Mitchell said.

"Yes." Kenzie blew her nose again. "She and my sister were

murdered in front of the building last night. It's a long story, but a lunatic killed them both, and then he killed himself. I'm very sorry."

Marla saw fresh tears fall from Kenzie's eyes, and then Christina pulled her close for a tighter embrace.

Mitchell drew his silencer-fitted pistol. "Try to remember," he told Kenzie and Christina, "that sorrow can often be a sort of privilege." Then he shot them once each through the head in rapid succession, killing them instantly.

"Jesus fucking Christ!" Marla said. "Was that necessary?"

"Yes. Absolutely. You saw how sad they were. It was sickening. They're both in a better place now. And speaking of a better place, I say we get the hell out of New York."

Marla cast her gaze to the skyscrapers beyond the sliding-glass doors to the balcony. "Where are we going?"

"Vegas," Mitchell said. "We'll head back to Vegas and get married."

They arrived in Las Vegas five days later, after stopping for nights in Cleveland, Chicago, Des Moines, and Denver along the way. Once in Vegas, Mitchell rented a room at the same cheap motel they had stayed in before heading east.

In the room, Mitchell set his box of disposable gloves on the table by the window.

Marla put her suitcase on the floor at the foot of the bed. "Do you think anyone ever found my brother and his wife's bodies out in the desert?"

Mitchell shrugged. "No idea. Maybe their skeletons. That's about it. Damn, that seems like a long time ago, doesn't it?"

"Yes, but it really wasn't. Are you tired? From all the driving?"

"No, but I'm fucking starving." Mitchell checked his phone. "It's almost ten o'clock. You wanna go get some dinner?"

"Sure," Marla said.

They left in Mitchell's car.

The night was hot. Casinos, hotels, and restaurants lined both sides of the avenue. They chose a restaurant called Costa Matteo's and went inside. Marla ordered spaghetti and a glass of wine. Mitchell ordered lasagna and a bottle of beer. They ate. Mitchell paid for the food and tipped their waitress stupendously.

"I'm ready to go drink some whiskey," Marla said "And smoke a cigarette."

They left.

Behind the restaurant, a man pushing a wheelchair opened the passenger door of a van parked next to Mitchell's car. A woman sat on the van's passenger side. The couple appeared to be in their sixties. The man lifted the woman out of the van and placed her in the wheelchair. Both were smiling, apparently happy to be on their way to dinner. The parking lot lay otherwise deserted.

Mitchell, holding Marla's hand, led her past the van to get to his car, but then stopped and began looking around. "I don't see any cameras anywhere. Come on. Let's go say hello."

He led Marla directly to the couple. "Good evening," he said, reaching into his jacket.

The couple looked up at them, still smiling, but neither the man nor the woman said anything.

From the holster beneath his jacket, Mitchell drew the silencer-fitted pistol. "It isn't fair," he told them. Then he shot them once each through the head, killing them instantly.

He turned to Marla. "Are you ready to go drink some whiskey?"

She nodded.

They got in his car and went back to their motel room—where they drank, made love, and each smoked a cigarette.

Then Mitchell said, "I'm going to take a shower. Would you like to join me?"

Marla shook her head. "No thanks. I'm just going to sit out here and keep drinking."

"Okay." He got up, walked into the bathroom naked, and closed the door. Moments later, Marla heard him turn the water on.

She got up and got dressed. Then she grabbed the bottle and sat down at the table next to the bed. She took a drink of whiskey and lit another cigarette.

From Mitchell's box of disposable gloves on the table, she pulled a pair out and put them on. They were size XL, and therefore too big for her hands, but she liked the way they felt, and left them on. They were blue disposable gloves like the kind medical professionals wore. Mitchell had said they were made of latex, but they were not. According to the box, they were latex-free and made of nitrile.

Marla raised the bottle and took another drink. She smoked her cigarette down to the filter and stubbed it out in the ashtray. Then she reached across the table and pulled Mitchell's silencer-fitted pistol from the holster beneath his jacket, which hung on the back of the other chair.

She remembered how good it had felt to shoot her brother between the eyes with this very gun, not long before they left Vegas for New York. *That was for you, Gwyneth,* she thought. *Orchids in bloom. The next time I pull this trigger, it will be for me.*

She had seen Mitchell clean this gun several times since she killed her brother with it, so she doubted her fingerprints were still on it, but she went ahead and wiped it down with the front of her shirt, just in case.

Then she heard Mitchell turn the water off in the bathroom. Moments later, he opened the door and stepped out with a towel around his waist.

Marla raised the gun and aimed it at his chest. "They're nitrile," she said. "Not latex."

Mitchell cocked his head. "The gloves?"

"And they weren't sad. They weren't miserable."

"Huh?"

"They were happy."

"What are you talking about?"

"The woman in the wheelchair, and her husband. You say you only kill people who are sad, or miserable, but they weren't sad, or miserable. They were happy. And they loved each other. You could see it in their eyes. They were just going out for dinner on a summer night in Vegas, and you fucking killed them. For no fucking reason."

Mitchell raised the hand not holding the towel around his waist. "Now just wait a goddamn second. Just look at the quality of life those people were forced to endure. She was imprisoned in a fucking wheelchair, and he was chained to her by the bonds of love. What kind of lives could they have had? Their futures were so limited. They were slaves to a goddamn chair. I did them both a favor and set them free."

Marla stood up and shot him four times in the chest. Mitchell hit the floor in front of the bathroom door, bleeding profusely.

She walked over to stand above him and aimed the gun down at his face. He was still alive, but fading fast. "When you get to Hell," she told him, "tell my brother I said hello." Then she shot him right between the eyes.

Marla turned around. Mitchell's clothes lay on the floor beside the bed. She tossed the gun onto the bed, pulled his wallet from a pocket of his jeans, and took the cash out. She didn't count it, but it was all hundred-dollar bills and probably over ten thousand dollars. She put the money in her pocket.

Then she walked back over to the table and sat down, wondering what the hell she was going to do. The keys to Mitchell's car were on the table, and she had enough money in her pocket to go anywhere in America, get her own apartment, and start over. Or maybe she should just fill the tank up, drive back home to Los Angeles, and ditch the car after she got there. But where was home now, anyway? Her brother's apartment? Her dead brother and his wife's remains lay in the desert outside of Vegas, or if their bones had been discovered, the authorities would undoubtedly want to talk to her. Perhaps it would be best to just return to their apartment and pretend she hadn't seen them. She could simply lie to the police and tell them she woke up one day and discovered that her brother and his wife were gone. She could say it happened all the time. They were drug dealers, anyway. It shouldn't be difficult to believe they had somehow managed to get murdered outside of Vegas.

She would still have to ditch the car, of course, but she knew that the owner of The Never Better Lounge had a brother who ran a chop shop. She could just give them the car and tell them to get rid of it.

Or maybe she should just leave the car here and walk to the nearest bus station. She was not very familiar with Las Vegas, but there had to be a bus station somewhere in the city. She could just pay cash for a bus ticket to Los Angeles—or to anywhere else in America, for that matter.

She took a drink of whiskey. The bottle was almost empty, but there were still a few extra bottles in the trunk of Mitchell's car.

She could also simply call 911. She could say that the four of them were on their way to Vegas when Mitchell stopped the car in the desert, murdered her brother and his wife, and then kept her as a hostage. She could tell the authorities that he took her to New York for a couple of weeks, and then brought her back to Vegas. She could even tell them that she had witnessed him murder the woman in the wheelchair and her husband. She could say that she managed to get his gun while he thought she was sleeping, and that she killed him after he finished taking a shower.

Marla finished the bottle—and decided not to call 911. There were probably too many holes in her story. Plus she didn't trust cops, anyway. Besides, the night was still young, and she was already halfway drunk. She could just drink some more whiskey, sleep for a few hours later, and then leave early in the morning—long before housekeeping came knocking on the door at eleven a.m.

She grabbed the car keys off the table, stood up, and went outside.

To Marla's right, a police officer argued with a woman at the door of the next room over. Marla walked to Mitchell's car, listening. Apparently, someone stole some money from the woman's motel room, and the cop was telling her there was nothing he could do about it. Furious, the woman slammed the door in his face.

Marla cracked open a bottle and took a drink, and the cop headed back to his squad car, which was parked beside Mitchell's car. When she closed the trunk, the cop turned his head and looked at her. "Beautiful night," he said. "And I am so glad my shift is almost over."

The cop appeared to be about ten years older than she was. Mid-thirties, perhaps. He was unusually thin, though. Freakishly thin. Thin to the point of emaciation. He was so skinny that Marla thought he was probably sick. If he *was* sick, however, he didn't appear to be debilitated by his illness. Marla thought his eyes and smile looked kind. She decided that maybe his presence in her life at this moment and this place was a sign from the universe that she should just go ahead and come clean. Well, *almost* clean, anyway.

Marla had left the door to the motel room partially open. She took a drink and then pointed to the door. "There's a dead man in that room," she said.

The cop glanced over at the door, and then returned his gaze to Marla. "A dead man?"

"Yes."

"How did he die?"

She took a drink. "I shot him. I had to."

The cop drew his gun. "Is there anyone else in the room?"

"No."

"Did you call 911?"

"No. It just happened a few minutes ago. I shot him with his own gun. Come on. I'll show you."

The cop followed her into the motel room. He closed the door behind him. Then he crossed the room and looked down at the corpse. "Four to the chest and one to the head."

"Yes. I wanted to be sure that he was dead."

The cop saw the gun lying on the bed. "That's his gun? The one you shot him with?"

"Yes."

"That gun has a silencer on it."

"Yes. I was his hostage."

"His hostage?"

"Yes. He killed my brother and his wife out in the desert, and then he took me hostage."

"What were you doing out in the desert?"

"I don't know. He just drove us there. The four of us were on our way to Vegas from L.A., but he stopped in the desert. He killed my brother and his wife, then took me as a hostage to New York for a couple of weeks. We just got back today. Then he killed a woman in a wheelchair and her husband behind a restaurant tonight."

The cop cracked a smile. "I heard about that earlier. You were with him?"

"Yes. He forced me back here, and I fell asleep. When I woke up, he was just getting out of the shower."

"And you managed to get his gun, and then you killed him. Right? That's your story?"

Marla took a drink. "Yes. That's exactly what happened."

"And you never called 911?"

"No. I guess I panicked."

"You panicked, but you took the time to put on a pair of latex gloves?"

Marla looked down at her hands. "These were his gloves. Not mine. There's a whole box of them on the table. And they're nitrile. Not latex."

"Does anyone else even know that you're in Vegas?"

"No. There was only my brother and his wife, but both of them are dead."

"Put the bottle down on the table, turn around, and put your hands behind your back."

Marla set the bottle on the table. "Am I under arrest?"

"Turn around and put your hands behind your back."

She did, and the cop handcuffed her.

"Do you have any weapons on you?" he said.

"No."

"Do you have a cellphone?"

"No."

He patted her down. "I'll be damned. I thought everyone had cellphones these days."

"Am I under arrest?"

"No, but I *am* going to take you downtown for questioning."

He took her outside and put her in the back of the squad car. Then he drove her to a police station downtown.

He killed the engine. "Be right back." He got out of the car.

Marla heard him lock the doors. Then she watched him walk inside the building.

She needed a drink. The handcuffs were uncomfortable. The cop seemed to be gone for a long time.

When he finally came back out, he wore street clothes and carried a gym bag. He unlocked the car, got in, and set the gym bag on the passenger's seat. Then he started the engine.

"What the fuck is going on?" Marla said.

"My shift is over. I'm officially off duty." He drove out of the parking lot and put the car back on the road.

"So where the fuck are you taking me?"

"No more questions."

"I want an attorney."

The skeletal cop laughed, and Marla saw his eyes when he looked at her in the rearview mirror. His face resembled a makeup-covered skull. "God Almighty couldn't help you now," he said. "Fucking white-trash piece of shit." Then he cranked up the radio so that further conversation was impossible.

He took her to a derelict-looking house at the end of a dirt road somewhere on the outskirts of Vegas. Marla didn't see any other houses around. There was a one-car garage beside the single-story house, and the garage looked just as shabby as the house did.

There was a nice-looking pickup truck in the driveway, however, and the cop parked the police car behind the truck. He killed the engine and grabbed his gym bag. Then he got out and opened Marla's door. "Get out."

"I want an attorney."

He grabbed her by an arm and yanked her out of the car.

Then he dragged her into the one-car garage. Marla thought he was strong for someone who looked like he'd been starving in a concentration camp.

The cop turned on a light. Other than a few tools and some boxes on the sagging shelves, the garage was empty. There was a drain with a metal grate over it in the center of the concrete floor.

"Can you take these handcuffs off? Please? My wrists are killing me."

He set the gym bag on the floor. Then he forced Marla to her knees.

"Why are you doing this to me?"

He pulled a gun from the waistband of his jeans and placed its muzzle against her forehead. "I told you no more questions."

"Listen: there's over ten thousand dollars in my pocket. You can have it."

"I would have found it anyway," he said, "when I go through your clothes later. Now shut the fuck up."

"Listen. Please. Just listen to me. I don't know what—"

BAM!

He smashed the gun against the side of her head so hard she saw stars, and she fell over onto her side, bleeding, with her hands still cuffed behind her back.

"I'm going to strip you naked," he said. "If you say one word, I'll introduce you to more premature pain. Nod if you understand me."

Marla nodded.

The cop set his gun down on the floor. From the gym bag, he retrieved four items: a knife, a roll of duct tape, a collar, and a leash. He placed the four items on the floor.

He removed Marla's shoes, socks, pants, and panties, and put them in the gym bag. He picked the knife up and cut away her shirt and bra, and put those in the gym bag, too. He taped her mouth shut and snapped the leather collar around her neck. The collar had a stainless steel ring on the front of it, and he attached the link at the end of the leash to the collar's ring.

Then he dragged her into the house.

The fattest woman Marla had ever seen sat on a couch in the living room. She had to weigh a thousand pounds at least. Eating fried chicken from a five-gallon bucket, she looked up when the cop dragged Marla into the living room. "Oh my." She smiled grotesquely. "Did you bring me a new toy?"

"Yes, Your Majesty," the skinny cop responded with absolute reverence in his voice.

"Is she local?"

"No."

"Bring her to me."

The cop dragged Marla to the couch and forced her to her knees. Then he handed the fat woman the leash. "Bow your head before the queen," he said.

Marla did. The fat woman's feet were hideous and smelled like rotting cheese.

"She's beautiful," the fat woman said. "I will take great pleasure in destroying this woman's beauty."

"So you are pleased?" the cop said.

"Yes."

"Then may I please have a piece of that chicken? I haven't eaten since those two crackers yesterday, and I am starving."

The fat woman looked up at the cop. "You didn't sneak around today and eat at work?"

"No, Your Majesty."

"Not even a bagel or a donut?"

He shook his head. "No. I drank some coffee, but I haven't eaten anything at all."

Marla could hear the skinny cop's stomach growling, and she doubted that he was lying. She also wondered what kind of strange dark hole in the universe she had managed to fall into.

"Then yes," the fat woman said. "You may have a piece of chicken. Actually, you can have as much as you like. But first, bring me my wheelchair."

The cop left the room. He returned moments later pushing the biggest wheelchair Marla had ever seen. There was no coffee table or any other furniture in the living room to block his path as he pushed the wheelchair right up to the couch. Marla wondered if it was a custom-made wheelchair. She saw electronic control panels on the armrests, and its wheels looked like motorcycle tires.

The fat woman handed Marla's leash back to the skinny cop. Then she used a bariatric walker to move herself from the couch to the wheelchair. "Take her to my torture chamber," she said. "I have to go to the bathroom first."

"As you wish, Your Majesty." The skinny cop dragged Marla into a dark room elsewhere in the house and turned on a light.

The first thing Marla noticed was the drain. The room's floor was concrete, and—like the grate-covered drain in the garage—the drain in the center of this room's floor was covered with a metal grate.

The cop grabbed a fistful of her hair, then yanked her head up until it was level with his waist.

Marla saw what looked like an operating table on one side of the drain. On the other side of the drain was one of those hospital beds like the kind she had seen in ICU rooms.

"I'm going to remove your duct tape," the cop said. "The queen loves to hear her victims scream." He ripped the duct tape from her face.

Marla said, "I have to go to the bathroom. I'm about to piss myself."

He dragged her to the drain. "Go right ahead. You'll be pissing, shitting, and bleeding in this drain all night long."

Squatting over the drain, Marla emptied her bladder, trying to think of something to say that might persuade these two lunatics to release her, but she knew it was useless. *I'm fucked*, Marla thought. *Tonight is the last night of my life.*

The cop pressed a damp cloth across her face. *Probably chloroform*, Marla thought. Moments later, she lost consciousness.

The smell of ammonia woke her up. She opened her eyes and saw the fat woman holding a bottle of ammonia beneath her nose. Marla looked around—and discovered that she lay on the hospital bed in the fat woman's torture chamber. The bed's head frame had been raised so that Marla was in a sitting-up position. Her hands were no longer cuffed behind her back. Leather straps now secured her wrists and ankles to each side of the hospital bed.

The fat woman's wheelchair was parked next to Marla's bed, and she set the bottle of ammonia down on a metal table beside her wheelchair. From the numerous knives, hand tools, and surgical instruments lined up on the table, the fat woman picked up a scalpel. "There's no one here but us to hear you scream." With her other hand, she picked up a blowtorch. "And your screams will be music to my ears."

"I killed a man tonight," Marla said, "because he killed a woman in a wheelchair. And now a woman in a wheelchair is going to kill me."

The fat woman smiled. "I will keep you alive for as long as I possibly can. Long before you die, you will be begging me for death."

Determined not to beg for mercy (she was long past any hope of that), Marla closed her eyes and tried to find a place to hide inside her mind. With the scalpel's first incision, her eyes snapped open, and she screamed.

CHAPTER 56

Autumn struck a match in October as it always did, setting the trees ablaze with fires that provided no warmth. The cool air, Sydney knew, would soon be getting colder. She had turned nine back in September, and she knew also that she and Carl would soon have to head south or to the west or else they would freeze to death. They usually made enough money to stay in motel rooms at night, but not always.

Fortunately, they already had a motel room for tonight. Carl was back in the motel room right now, resting, but today Sydney found herself walking around whatever city this was, looking for the red-light district. She found it with ease. No matter where they went, it was never all that difficult to find a red-light district. She decided to come back later, when the freaks were out prowling in the night.

Sydney passed the city fairgrounds on her way back to the motel. The fairgrounds were crowded with people, thrill-rides, flashing neon signs, and a caravan of trucks and trailers. *Traveling carnival*, she thought, and smiled.

Carl, of course, would have no interest in the carnival, but Sydney did. She had a few dollars in her pocket and decided to buy a ticket. Moments later, she ate pink cotton candy while walking up the midway. She strolled past concession stands, games of chance, and kiddie rides. She saw an Octopus, a Tilt-A-Whirl, and a Zipper. There was a Ferris wheel, a carousel with mythological characters instead of horses, and a funhouse with a maniacally laughing clown waving from the balcony.

And then she saw a sign for a freak show. An arrow on the sign pointed toward a large red tent. There was a banner atop the tent on which was printed: *Dr. Odd's Marvels.*

Sydney approached the tent.

A man stood behind a ticket booth by the front entrance. He was tall, skinny, and bald. His pock-marked face was gaunt and very pale. He appeared to be about fifty, and he wore a white lab coat with a stethoscope wrapped around his neck. He held a wheel of pasteboard tickets in one hand and a bullhorn in the other. "Step right up, ladies and gentlemen, to Doctor Odd's Marvels! You'll be shocked and amazed by the astonishing collection of monstrosities that I have gathered for you! My name is Doctor Odd, and I have traveled to the farthest reaches of the planet to bring back marvels for your enjoyment and entertainment!"

Sydney held up some money to purchase a ticket. There was no one else in line at the ticket booth.

Dr. Odd lowered his bullhorn, looked down at her, and smiled. "My, my, my, little girl. If you ain't the prettiest thing I've seen all day, then my name ain't Doctor Odd. What's your name, pretty girl?"

"Sydney."

"And how old are you, Sydney?"

"Nine."

"I'll tell you what, Sydney: a girl as pretty as you gets in for free." He put a hand on her shoulder to usher her inside. "Just move on ahead and keep to the right."

"No thanks," Sydney said. "I've changed my mind."

"Changed your mind?"

"Yes."

"Are you sure? We have a three-armed man in there. And a two-headed woman. We also have stillborns in there. Do you know what stillborns are?"

Sydney nodded.

"We keep them in bottles," Dr. Odd said. "In formaldehyde. Little shrunken things—cats, goats, pigs. All kinds of stuff. We also have stillborn *human* babies in there. And a werewolf. And a sasquatch. Would you like to come inside?"

Sydney shook her head. "Not interested."

Dr. Odd frowned. "Because I touched you? Because I put my hand on your shoulder?"

"No. That didn't bother me at all."

She took off walking toward a concession stand where she bought more cotton candy. By the time she finished eating it, the sun had set. *Almost nighttime*, she thought, and smiled. To the east, the first stars of twilight started sparkling.

Still hungry, Sydney left the fairgrounds and walked to a nearby restaurant. She went inside and ordered some fries to go. She took her fries to a nearby park and ate them at a picnic table. Then she stretched out on the ground and fell asleep.

When she woke up, the park was empty. Night had fallen and stars dotted the sky. Sydney took off walking. Soon thereafter, she found herself in the red-light district.

She had not been there long when a hand came down on her shoulder. Spinning around, Sydney looked up at the smiling face of Dr. Odd. She saw mischief in his eyes, and he no longer wore the lab coat or the stethoscope.

"Well, hello there, Sydney. I didn't expect to see you again—especially in a place like this. What's a pretty little girl like you doing in the red-light district?"

Sydney shrugged. "What else? I'm trying to make some money. Do you like little girls?"

Still smiling, Dr. Odd cocked his head. "Well, I suppose you could say I like little girls *and* little boys."

"Which do you like better?"

Dr. Odd scratched his head. "Little boys, usually. But little girls can be fun, too."

"I have a brother," Sydney said.

"You do?"

"Yes. He wants to make some money, too. He's back in our motel room. Would you like to meet him?"

"Is he as pretty as you?"

Sydney smiled and nodded. "He's beautiful."

Dr. Odd's smile grew even wider. "Well, in that case, I would *love* to meet him. My car's right over there. Come on. Let's go."

They got in his car, and Dr. Odd drove them away.

On their way to the motel, Sydney said, "Can we stop at a store? I need to get some candy and some trash bags."

"Of course. I need to get more booze, anyway."

He stopped at a grocery store that sold liquor, and they both went inside. Sydney purchased candy and trash bags. Dr. Odd bought two bottles of whiskey.

Then they went to the nearby motel and carried their bags into the room. Dr. Odd closed the door behind them.

"Will you lock it, please?" Sydney said.

"Of course." Dr. Odd locked the door.

Sydney sat down at the dinette table. She set her trash bags on the floor and began eating some candy.

Dr. Odd sat down on the edge of the bed. He opened one of his bottles and took a drink of whiskey. "Nice place. Very relaxing."

Sydney nodded. They could hear the sound of water running in the bathroom.

Dr. Odd took another drink. "Is your brother taking a shower?"

"Yes. He wants to be clean for you. Do you like your little boys to be clean?"

Dr. Odd shrugged. "Sometimes." Then he flashed her a grin. "And sometimes I like them to be dirty."

He got up, started walking around the room, and then stopped in front of a yellow raincoat folded atop the dresser. Next to the raincoat sat a wide-brim fishing hat. He picked the raincoat up and let it unfurl to the floor: it was as long as he was tall. "Is this your father's?"

Sydney shook her head. "No. Our parents are dead."

"Your brother's?"

"Yes."

Dr. Odd's eyes shot to the bathroom door. "Your brother is tall."

"Yes."

Dr. Odd smiled. "I like them tall."

He folded the raincoat and set it back down on the dresser. Then he sat on the edge of the bed again and took another drink. "Mind if I take my shoes off?"

"Not at all. Go right ahead."

Dr. Odd took his shoes off.

"Nice socks," Sydney said.

"Thanks." Dr. Odd's black socks had white skulls and crossbones on them. "They were a gift from a friend of mine who no longer walks the planet."

Time passed. Sydney ate candy while Dr. Odd drank whiskey. The water in the bathroom continued to run.

Dr. Odd said, "Your brother likes long showers."

"Yes. He's probably waiting for you to join him."

"You think so?"

"Yes."

Dr. Odd took a drink. Then he got up and headed toward the bathroom.

"Wait," Sydney said.

Dr. Odd turned around.

"Take your clothes off," she said. "I want to see you naked."

Dr. Odd stripped naked. "Do you like what you see?"

"Yes. And I'm sure my brother will like what he sees, too."

Dr. Odd smiled. Then he opened the bathroom door and stepped inside.

"Close the door," Sydney said. "My brother likes his privacy."

Dr. Odd closed the bathroom door.

Sydney heard the water shut off, followed by the shower curtain swishing open. Then she heard Dr. Odd yell: "Jesus Christ!

What the—"

She heard a brief struggle, a choked scream, some gurgling sounds, and then there was silence.

Sydney resumed eating her candy. Over the next several minutes, she heard breaking, grinding, ripping, and slurping noises coming from the bathroom.

Then she heard the shower start again.

Sydney got up, took the money out of Dr. Odd's wallet, and put it in her pocket. She put his car keys in her pocket too. She put his clothes and his bottles in a trash bag.

Then she stretched out on the bed and finished her candy.

They emerged from the motel room around four o'clock in the morning, holding each other's hand. Carl towered above Sydney in his raincoat and wide-brim fishing hat. He carried the trash bag. Sydney carried the two pillows she had stolen from the motel room.

Carl put the trash bag in the back of Dr. Odd's car and got in on the passenger's side. Sydney put the two pillows on the driver's seat and sat down behind the steering wheel.

"The road." Carl said. "Our favorite place to be."

Sydney started the car and drove them away.

About the Author

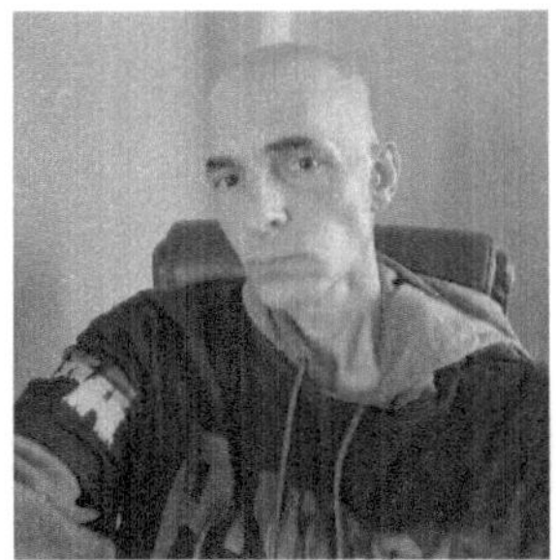

Splatterpunk Award-nominated and Godless Award-winning author Brian Bowyer has been writing stories and music for most of his life. He has lived throughout the United States. He has worked as a janitor, a banker, a bartender, a bouncer, and a bomb maker for a coal-testing laboratory. He currently lives and writes in Ohio. You can contact him at brian.bowyer@hotmail.com.

PRAISE FOR STINA LINDENBLATT

"Be warned dear reader, this book will have you giggling and blushing as you devour it."—Subclub Books (*Decidedly with Love*)

"I laughed with this book, but also cried a lot."—Blog on the Run (*Decidedly with Love*)

"...I was captivated by the shenanigans of this duo. Not to mention laughing out loud and blushing. Boy do these two turn up the heat."—The Subclub Books (*Decidedly off Limits*)

"A feel good, sensual, intoxicating and sexy love story; if you love contemporary romance you do not want to miss Decidedly Off Limits."—Slick, Guilty Pleasures (*Decidedly off Limits*)

"Sweet, sexy and invigorating, Decidedly off Limits is a friends to lovers story that is truly a breath of fresh air!"—Read & Share Book Reviews (*Decidedly off Limits*)

"So many laugh out loud moments that you do not want to be reading it in public or be ready for some weird looks. I speak from experience here."—The Subclub Books (*Decidedly with Baby*)

"There are steamy moments but you are just left with feel good melty moments more."—Books Are Love (*Decidedly with Baby*)

"...a truly unique and utterly swoon-worthy romance." — Mary Dubé at Frolic/USA Today's HEA (*Decidedly by Chance*)

"Decidedly By Chance is a well written emotional story that will tug on your heart strings."—MI Bookshelf (*Decidedly by Chance*)

"...it's an opposites-attract romance that will evoke all the feels."—Mary at USA Today HEA/Frolic (*Fix Me Up, Cowboy*)

"I just love this book!...add in some tense situations and five (YES FIVE!) hot, sexy, alpha, ex-navy SEALS and you got me!"—A Book Lover's Emporium Book Blog (*While You Were Spying*)

"While You Were Spying is a heart pumping sexy read! You've got action, intrigue and suspense and then on the other hand you have sexual tension, swoony romance, and sassy banter." —Julia Red Hatter Book Blog (*While You Were Spying*)

"Everything – the plot, the characters and the dialogue – made this story captivating"—Harlequin Junkie (5 star Top Pick review for *My Song For You*)

"A well-written story that kept me entertained from start to finish."—Harlequin Junkie (4.5 star Recommends review for *This One Moment*)

"I love that Stina Lindenblatt was able to layer this book with so much depth, mystery, hurt, friendship, and of course love." —Four Chicks Flipping Pages (*This One Moment*)

ALSO BY STINA LINDENBLATT

DECIDEDLY WITH LOVE

SPECIAL EDITION

STINA LINDENBLATT

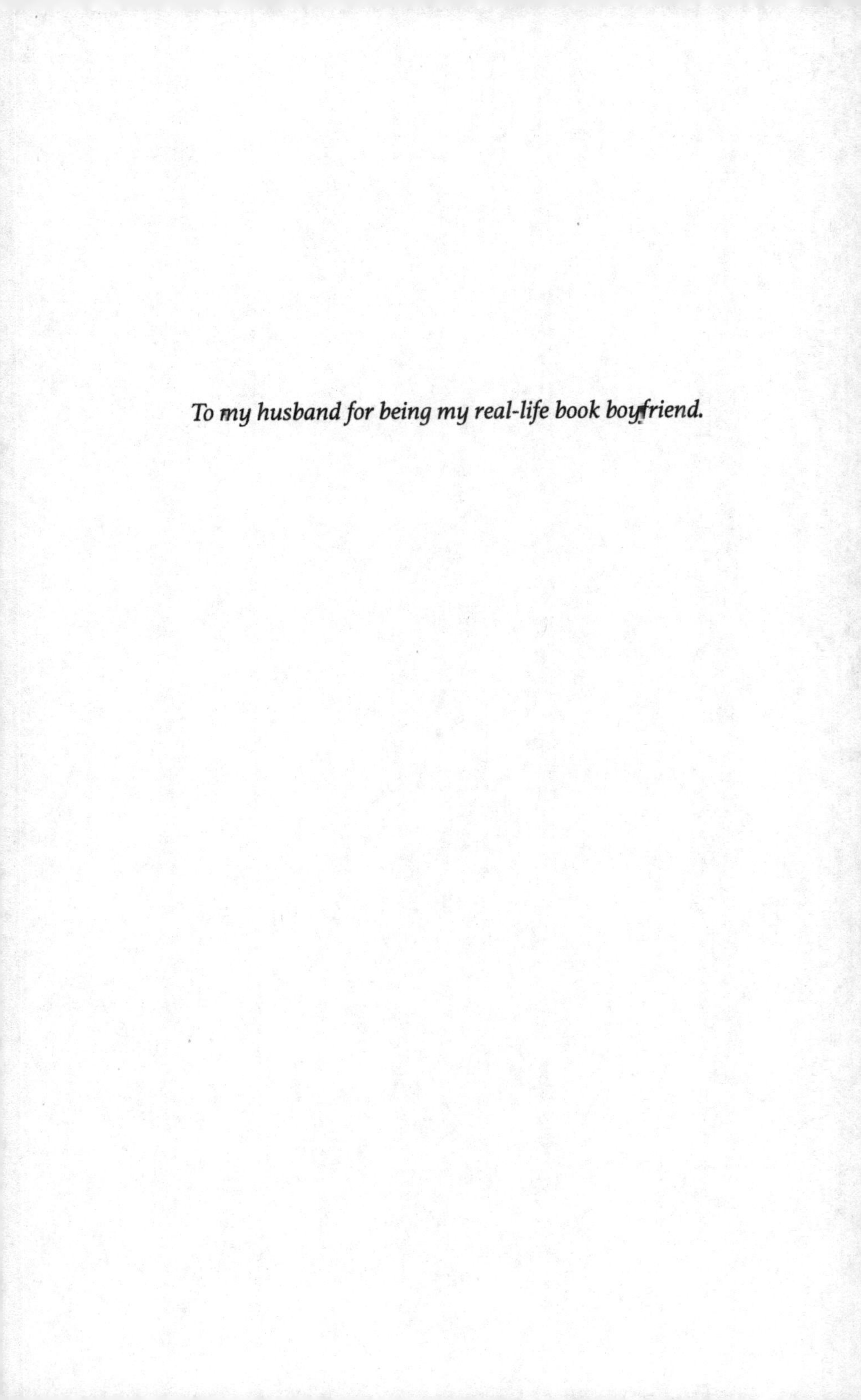

To my husband for being my real-life book boyfriend.

DECIDEDLY WITH LOVE

PART I

DECIDEDLY WITH LOVE

1

EMMA

Dear Dr. Lovejoy,

I'm a huge fan of the Harry Potter series. My
bedroom is even decorated in a Harry Potter theme. But
my new boyfriend told me that the books are for kids,
and I should get rid of it all. What should I do?

"As if there's any question. Dump him," I said under
my breath as the bell above the door jingled. A
moment later, Kate entered Aphrodite's Boutique.
Glowing.

I slipped the independent newspaper under the counter.
Did I have a Harry-Potter-themed bedroom? No...although
that would be cool, especially since the series had been my
favorite as a kid. Why? Because I could relate to Harry. No, I
didn't have any magical powers—which was too bad.

Like Harry, I had no parents or family. But unlike Harry's
mother, mine didn't fling herself in front of evil himself
because she loved me more than anything.

Not even close.

Kate strolled past the display of sensual bath products, massage oils, and scented candles near the front of the store. Her gaze paused briefly on the section farther back with the sexy lingerie.

As she walked to the counter, I pretended to straighten the heart-shaped cookies in the basket near the till.

Correction—as she practically *floated* to the counter. Her expression held the look of love. I hadn't personally experienced it. I thought I had in college....I was wrong. *Silly me.*

How did I know it was the look of love? Hazard of my job —love all around me—in case you missed it from the store's name.

Aphrodite was the ancient Greek goddess of love, beauty, procreation, and pleasure. Just not the self-induced pleasure I was more familiar with.

Still glowing, Kate placed a large paper coffee cup on the counter and held her left hand out in front of me. Unlike the last time I'd seen it, her ring finger now sported a diamond capable of making all other gemstones jealous.

I squealed. "Ohmigod, Jamie proposed?" I rushed from behind the counter and hugged her. "I'm so happy for you both."

The tears in my eyes? Dust. Must have entered the store at the same time as Kate.

Right—it was raining. My point? The tears had nothing to do with Kate finding the most amazing guy in the world. And it had nothing to do with how at seventeen minutes past six that morning, I had officially become a twenty-eight-year-old spinster.

A spinster who didn't even have a cat.

Maybe I needed to get a cat.

"Thank you," Kate said, hugging me back. "You were so right in your Dr. Lovejoy column. He would never have settled down if he thought I'd be around for him no matter what. When I moved out of our apartment last week, he finally realized he couldn't live without me."

"I figured he'd come around sooner or later."

Dr. Lovejoy? Yeah, there might be a slight chance that I wrote the weekly column in The SF Metro, one of the city's independent papers. Was I a doctor? Not exactly. Lovejoy was my last name...but I didn't have a PhD or anything like that. I had a business degree with a minor in psychology. I did take a human sexuality course in my undergrad years, but the professor who taught it had been as exciting as a wet towel left in the rain.

Kate hugged me again. Was I jealous that she was now engaged? Not at all. Everyone deserved to find love.

"But remember," I said, "no one is supposed to know I'm Dr. Lovejoy." It was a fluke that Kate had figured it out. My bio didn't proclaim I was also the owner of what most people referred to as the "love store." And very few people had figured out that I was the same Lovejoy who wrote the column. Heck, very few people were aware that my last name was Lovejoy.

"Don't worry, I haven't told anyone. Like I promised. Anyway, I need to get back to work." Kate owned the coffee shop next door. "I just had to tell you the good news and drop off a little thank-you present." She indicated at the paper coffee cup. "It's your favorite. Skinny butterscotch latte."

"Oh, God, I love you!" I said, a step away from squealing.

"I know you do," she said over her shoulder, chuckling, and left the store.

"Come to Mama," I said to the coffee and took a deep, satisfying whiff of the butterscotch richness. My coffee mug with, "You're my sunshine on a rainy day" on it sat empty and alone by the cash register.

"Sorry," I said to my mug, "I'm not risking any of this

amazing coffee by pouring it into you. I was up late last night baking cookies for the store. I need this happy dose of caffeine."

Yes, it was official. I was losing it. I was reasoning with a mug. Next up? I'd be asking it advice on my lack of a love life.

And no, the irony wasn't lost on me. I wrote an advice column and owned a store that specialized in love and romance, but when it came to myself, I had yet to find Mr. Right.

Or even Mr. Close Enough.

As I sipped my precious beverage, the bell above the door jingled, and three women in their late seventies entered. They took in the store—the fountain, lingerie, bath and massage supplies, books, housewares—with eager grins on their faces. It didn't matter if you were looking for a touch of romance or the whimsical or full-out sexiness, you could find it here. Although if you were looking for something featured in *Fifty Shades of Grey*, you'd be sorely disappointed. Leather and whips were not on the agenda.

I drank another quick sip of my coffee and placed it on the counter behind me. The three women shuffled farther into the store until they came to the fountain.

That's right. I have a fountain in the store. And yes, the goddess of love is perched in the middle. Nice touch, huh?

"Wow," the woman in the light blue trench coat said, examining the fountain. Her expression was one of awe...and mischief. "It reminds me of the *Fontana di Trevi* in Rome." She turned to me as I approached. "Are you familiar with the Trevi Fountain?"

Was I ever. "Legend claims that if you throw a coin into the Trevi Fountain, it guarantees your return to Rome. The second coin will ensure a new romance. A third coin guarantees marriage."

Do I believe in the legend? Well, I've already thrown in about fifty dollars' worth of coins over the past two years, and I'm as single as the day I was born.

I know. I know. The legend only applies to the fountain in Rome. And heck, mine isn't even a replica of it. But it's always nice to dream. Besides, the fountain is there for another reason....

"That's right," the woman said.

"And just like with that fountain," I explained, "all the coins thrown into this one go to charity."

The woman in a trench coat covered with large, bright pink flowers glanced at me and smiled. "What charity?"

"The James Bell Youth Center. I've been donating the money to them for the past few years. I'm currently saving to have a mural painted on their wall. You know, to brighten the place and to give the kids hope."

And I was almost there. At least I was there when it came to the supplies. I wasn't close to the amount needed when I factored in the cost of the artist.

The women fished through their purses and removed some coins. The woman in the blue trench coat, who had asked me about the Trevi Fountain, turned around so her back was facing it. "You need to throw the coins over your left shoulder with your right hand."

The other two women followed suit and turned around.

"Are we supposed to make a wish first or just throw in the coins?" the shorter woman asked. Her white trench coat hung below her knees.

"If this was the real Trevi Fountain, no wishing would be necessary," the woman in blue said. "But it wouldn't hurt to clarify things, just in case."

The woman in white nodded as if this made sense.

The woman in blue threw in her coins. *Plop. Plop.*

Guess she wasn't interested in returning to Rome.

The woman in white threw her coins next. *Plop. Plop. Plop.*

The first woman peered over at her, eyebrow raised. "You want to get married?"

"Why wouldn't I wish to get married? I loved being married to Frank. Best years of my life."

"Is there anyone you have in mind?" The woman in the flowery trench coat asked.

"Possibly."

"Would it *possibly* have to do with the handsome gentleman in apartment thirty-four?" The woman in flowers then said to me, "He's been a widow for five years now. There isn't a senior in our building who hasn't been lusting over him."

The woman in white giggled. "Including poor Mathew in apartment forty-eight. But I'm pretty sure he's barking up the wrong redwood tree. He's gay," she added, in case I hadn't figured that out myself, I guess.

"So is that a yes?" the woman in flowers asked.

"Possibly."

"I'll take that as a yes," the woman in blue said, grinning. "Okay, Fanny, your turn."

The woman in the flowery trench coat got into position and threw the coins over her shoulder. *Plop. Plop.*

Ah, she was looking for a new romance.

She switched the coins from her left hand to her right and tossed them over her shoulder. *Plop. Plop. Plop.*

"Wait!" The woman in blue said. "You're hoping to get married *and* have an affair?"

Fanny laughed. "I'm almost eighty. How much energy do you think I have?"

"Then why did you throw in five coins?" I asked. Maybe she knew something I didn't when it came to the fountain's lovemaking abilities.

And no, I don't mean its abilities to fuck. I mean its abilities to help me find love.

Maybe I had been doing it all wrong.

"The first two were for me. It's been twenty years since my dear Robert passed away, and I'm finally ready to climb back on that horse again."

"Except now you're too old to ride the horse—if you get what I mean." The woman in white snickered.

Ohmigod, was I seriously listening to eighty-year-old women talking about sex?

"What about the other three coins?" I asked, almost afraid to hear the answer.

"Those are for my grandson. He's twenty-eight years old and still single. I want him to hurry up and get married and give me some great-grandkids *before* I end up next to my poor Robert in the ground."

Okaaay. "I'm not sure the fountain works quite that way." Oh, who was I kidding? The only magical powers the fountain had were to add to my energy bill and provide money to the youth center.

"Well, I'll take whatever it's willing to give me. A person who never made a mistake never tried anything new. Albert Einstein said that."

I had no idea what it had to do with the fountain or her grandson—and figured I was better off not knowing.

A musical tune played from her purse. She removed her phone and answered it. "No, I didn't forget my appointment, dear....I'm at Aphrodite's Boutique....You know, the love shop." She gave whoever was on the other end the address. "Alrighty. I'll see you soon."

Fanny ended the call and dropped the phone back into her purse. "Speak of the handsome devil himself. That would be my grandson. Apparently I forgot about my doctor's appointment." She flashed an *oops-what-can-you-do?* grimace.

The woman in blue laughed. "What did I tell you about setting up reminders on your phone?"

Fanny shrugged. "I keep forgetting to do it. What can I say? I'm still an old-fashioned-paper-calendar type girl."

"So why didn't you write it on your calendar?" the woman in white asked.

Fanny shrugged again. "I forgot to."

"Or more like you don't want to go to the doctor, so you intentionally didn't write it down."

Fanny winked at me. "It might have been something like that."

Her friends laughed.

"I guess we'd better get cracking before my dear grandson arrives to drive me to the appointment I'd rather not go to. Anyone interested in checking out the vibrators?" Fanny asked with a chuckle. "You do have vibrators, don't you, dear?" she asked me.

The woman in blue threw her head back, laughing. "It's not vibrators we need."

"True," Fanny said, then to me asked, "I don't suppose you have any magic potions to help my grandson fall in love with a woman?"

"Is that your way of saying you don't believe in the fountain's magic?" the woman in white asked.

"No, it's my way of saying my grandson is too goddamn stubborn for his own good and needs all the help he can get in that department."

Fighting back a grin, I shook my head. "Sorry, the only magic in this store belongs to the fountain."

"Darn. That's too bad."

While Fanny waited for her grandson to show up, the three of them wandered around the store.

Five minutes later the bell above the door jingled again. I

glanced up from the display of romantic cards I was organizing near the front counter.

Holy. Shit. What was he doing here?

Who was *he*? Travis Hamilton. The guy I'd had a thing for during our junior year of high school.

The guy who broke my heart.

2

TRAVIS

Ten bucks says you can guess the last place I ever expected to be...but there I was.

And what was with the stone woman wrapped in a sheet and standing in the middle of the fountain? Although upon closer inspection, she did look freshly fucked. The best look, if you asked me, for a sex store.

Don't think it's an adult store? That's where you're wrong.

Except it wasn't an adult store designed for men. It was for women who wanted to get their men off. A number of my team-mates' wives had been known to shop there, and let's just say we had some very satisfied players show up for practice the next day.

So the real question wasn't so much what I was doing there—it was what the hell Granny was doing in the store.

And don't you dare suggest it was to improve her sex life. The woman's almost eighty, for Christ's sake.

I scanned the store for the three troublemakers. My grandmother, Abigail, and Hazel were giggling like a couple of schoolgirls.

Yep, they were up to no good.

And if I was lucky, whatever they were up to had nothing to do with me.

What do I mean?

In the past two weeks, Granny had tried to set me up with the granddaughters of two of her friends. Both times I said I wasn't interested. If they had only been interested in commitment-free sex—then sign me up.

But try telling that to my grandmother.

Why wasn't I interested?

My track record when it came to women wasn't too hot. Nope, I didn't mean in bed. No woman had ever been unsatisfied in that department. I wasn't a jack-off who only took care of himself.

So what was the problem?

The life of a hockey player revolved around road trips. Lots of them. We were gone more times than we were home. And then there was the issue of being traded to another team. If you were married, the wife had to give up everything to be with you. If you had a girlfriend, it came down to if you wanted her to move to the new city and if she was interested in joining you.

What happened if you didn't want her joining you and she had already planned her happily-ever-after...with you in it?

Long story short—the fallout was never fun.

But it wasn't the trials of being a hockey player you had to worry about most. It was the people you loved. The people who meant the world to you...and then died.

Unfortunately, that was something I was very familiar with. First with my parents. And then my best friend in college.

So, to sum things up.

No. Girlfriends. For. Me. *Ever.*

One-night stands were so much easier, thank you very much. No emotions involved. No hearts at risk.

No chance of losing someone you loved.

But also, try telling *that* to my grandmother.

As if sensing my presence, Granny turned and waved. Then she and her posse ambled over to where I was standing near the entrance.

Or rather, they ambled to the counter where a redhead stood that I hadn't noticed until now. And how I hadn't noticed her before was beyond me. Her long hair was a mass of loose curls, which made her look as sexy as all freaking hell. Her dark green T-shirt skimmed her mouthwatering curves.

For a second, the image of her straddling me and riding my cock hard flashed in my head. But before said vital organ had a chance to react, the girl glanced at me. And let's just say the images of her riding my cock were *not* parading through her mind.

From the way she was scowling at me, it would seem that she was thinking of removing my cock with a cleaver. *Well, that would be a first.*

Granny and Co. paused at the fountain. Behind me, the annoying sound of a bell jingled. I turned in time to see a brunette sail into the store as if she owned the place. Her hair was pulled back in a high ponytail and she was wearing scrubs, the top covered with cartoon cats.

Unlike the redhead, she didn't shoot flaming daggers at me with her gaze. Instead, it appraisingly slid over me. She gave a brief nod of approval, then moved on.

For some reason, I felt compelled to walk to the counter where she and the redhead were standing. I tried telling myself it was because I was interested in flirting with the brunette.

Sounds like a reasonable explanation, right?

I thought so. My cock didn't. The poor wayward idiot didn't so much as twitch at the memory of her. He was still hung up on the redhead. He and I really needed to have a heart-to-heart.

I waited near the counter for Granny to join me. My gaze drifted to the redhead's T-shirt. "Love does not need to be perfect. It just needs to be true."

I'd have to take its word for that. Couldn't say I'd ever been in love. Not in the way the T-shirt was referring to.

"I just need to pay for this," Granny told me holding up what looked like a bottle of bubble bath.

I nodded.

She removed a plastic-wrapped, heart-shaped chocolate chip cookie from the wicker basket on the counter. "I've heard these are to die for." She parked it next to her other purchase.

"Emma bakes them," the brunette said. She smiled at her friend as if the redhead had solved world hunger.

"Your boyfriend is a lucky man to have a girlfriend who bakes treats," Granny said.

The brunette laughed. "Emma is as single as they come."

The woman in question just shrugged it off. "I can't help that I don't have time for a boyfriend."

"True. Between the store, volunteering at the youth center, and writing the Dr—" The brunette's words stopped faster than a Ferrari at a red light at the glare Emma leveled at her. "And you've clearly been dating the wrong men." She exaggerated a yawn, complete with covering her mouth, that had the redhead rolling her eyes.

"Well, that's a shame, dear," Granny said. "Remember, you fall in love with the most unexpected person at the most unexpected time."

Think she made that up? Nope. One of Granny's favorite hobbies was finding random quotes off the internet and spouting them at the oddest moments. Sometimes they worked—sometimes they left you scratching your head.

She glanced back at me and it took everything in my power not to roll *my* eyes. Granny could be as subtle as a stampede of bulls in a china shop.

"You almost ready?" I asked her.

That sigh of hers? She loved going to the doctor as much as I loved getting a penalty during the final minutes of a game when the teams were tied.

It was a sigh I'd frequently heard from her, but it didn't change anything.

"I don't suppose I can bribe you with this?" She removed another cookie from the basket and offered it to me. "How about you enjoy this delicious cookie and forget the appointment?"

"Sorry, no can do. But nice try." I'd almost lost her back in high school. Given that she was the only grandparent or parent I had left, I wasn't ready to lose her.

And yes, I would do anything for her, especially after she'd put up with my bullshit following my parents' unexpected deaths. It had fucked me up big-time. My parents had meant everything to me. They'd showered me with love and respect and support—and the feeling had been mutual.

After their deaths, Granny was the one who helped me eventually move on and glue my broken pieces back together. So like I said, I would do anything for her—other than have a girlfriend.

And other than let her talk me out of driving her to her medical appointment.

She finished paying, then hugged her friends good-bye.

At my car, I helped Granny into the passenger seat and climbed behind the steering wheel. We were pulling away from the curb when she said, "Did I tell you that Abigail's grandson had a baby boy the other day?" She gave me the same theatrical I-wish-I-had-a-great-grandchild sigh I'd already heard a million times.

Did I know his wife was pregnant? You better believe it. But not because I knew them personally. Granny had told me the news at least once a month—as if telling me would make me magically desire a child.

Or a wife.

The last I'd seen, I had testicles and not ovaries, so her plan had fallen flat on its face.

"No, you didn't," I said.

She didn't say anything for a full minute. *Hmmm.* I got off pretty easy this time. "You're still coming for dinner tonight, right?" she asked.

"Yes, but I'm getting together with some friends afterward, so I can't stay long."

Granny smiled knowingly—which was never a good thing half the time. Only I had no idea which half-the-time this was and what it meant.

And that made me slightly nervous.

3

EMMA

"**S**o what was that all about?" Hannah asked a second after the door shut behind Fanny's two friends. Did they buy the sexy teddies they had been eyeing at one point? No, they both settled on bubble bath from the romance line—a sweet blend of vanilla and roses.

I liked the bubble bath, but my favorite was the one that should've said, "Warning: one sniff of this and you'll be jumping your man's bones," on the label.

Which was great if you had a man for bone jumping. Not so great if it was just you and Alejandro.

Alejandro? What did you expect me to call the one thing capable of giving me regular orgasms?

Alejandro and I went way back. He was the ultimate boyfriend. He never broke my heart. He was always there for me—unless his batteries died.

Reminder to self: buy new batteries on the way home.

"Earth to Emma," Hannah said, waving her hand in front of my face.

"Huh?"

"You wanna explain why you were scowling at that hot guy with the old women?"

"He wasn't with them. He came to pick up his grandmother." And yes—I did think it was incredibly sweet that he was taking Fanny to her medical appointment when it was clear she didn't want to go.

He loved his grandmother, and that's what you did for people you loved.

What you didn't do was walk away from them because you couldn't be bothered to care.

Too bad my parents hadn't figured that one out on their own.

"And you felt the need to scowl at that, why?" Hannah asked.

Hmmm. This counter sure is messy. Maybe I could polish it or something.

"I wasn't scowling," I said, concentrating on the invisible mess and doing an awesome job of not looking at Hannah.

"Right. And I'm engaged to the Prince of England," she deadpanned.

I grinned. "Congratulations! Do I get to be a bridesmaid? I mean, unless you're planning to select a dress in some hideous color that will clash with my hair." That was a disadvantage of being a redhead. Blondes and brunettes didn't know how lucky they had it.

Hannah rolled her eyes. "Ha, ha. Very funny. But switching the topic won't change anything."

"Honestly, there's nothing to tell."

"You're a terrible liar, Emma."

I slapped my hand against my chest, doing my best not to giggle. "That seriously hurt."

"Okay, so you're not going to tell me. I guess that means I'll just have to eat your birthday cupcake myself." With a devious grin, she lifted the small white box I hadn't noticed she was holding. "Maggie's Bakery" was embossed in gold on the side.

I squealed—because we were talking about a cupcake from San Francisco's finest bakery.

Hannah set the box on the counter and opened the lid.

"Is that...?" I asked.

She nodded. "Chocolate raspberry lava. I placed an order for it last week." You had to either do that or camp out overnight just to be the first person in the store when it opened. Sleep in—your loss.

She glanced at the ceiling. "I guess the sprinklers will go off if I light the candle."

I looked up. "That's my guess, too."

"All right, you can pretend to blow it out. I'm pretty sure your birthday wish will still come true." She pushed the red candle into the thick chocolate frosting and waited for me to make a wish.

I wish...I wish that a guy would become my sunshine on a rainy day. Yes, my coffee mug might've been the inspiration behind it. But I figured I might have better luck with a more poetic wish than a straightforward, "I wish I could find Mr. Right."

Because dating a string of Mr. Wrongs had quickly grown old.

Which was why I was currently on a vacation from dating.

"Okay, I'm ready," I told Hannah.

She removed the two plastic forks taped to the box lid and handed one to me. "Happy birthday to the *bestest* best friend a girl could ever want."

It was the same thing we said every year on each other's birthday, starting from the time we met in foster care during our final year in the system. I had just been transferred yet again to a new home. The same home Hannah had been in for the past year. Whereas some girls became territorial when a newbie was dumped into their space, Hannah and I had instantly bonded.

Best friends forever.

Which was how I knew she craved the same thing as me: to be loved.

Because when you grew up in the foster care system, love was in short supply. What wasn't in short supply? Rejection. Abandonment. The I-don't-give-a-damn-about-you-so-get-out-of-my-fucking-way attitude.

Hannah and I devoured the cupcake in record time. You know what they say about chocolate? It's a replacement for sex. And given that neither of us had fucked a guy in a while (two years to be exact for me), the cupcake never stood a chance.

"Sorry I have to work tonight," Hannah said. She was a nurse at the children's hospital.

"That's okay. I'm looking forward to a *Sex and the City* TV marathon. Plus I need to write next week's column."

Maybe my *Sex and the City* marathon would help me with the article. One could always hope.

"Well, have fun with that." Hannah waved good-bye and left the store.

Like most days, the afternoon was a combination of slow and busy. I spent the next few hours setting up several new displays, accompanied by the soothing sounds of the fountain and the upbeat music in the background. I played all kinds of music in the store. Rock. Pop. Country. Anything romantic that had nothing to do with being dumped.

I used to play music from the local radio stations, but it must have been a bad year for the major recording artists. I swear most of them had been singing about broken hearts. Not exactly the ideal music to play in a store that was all about romance.

Just before Lisa was scheduled to arrive for the evening shift, a couple entered the store, holding hands.

For me, the handholding was a sign of love. He wasn't afraid of showing the world that she was his. No, I don't mean in the caveman, asshole way. That would involve tossing her over his shoulder and grunting. The handholding was sweet and swoony.

I released a dreamy sigh—fortunately too quiet for them to hear me. They walked past the fountain and headed for the section in the back where I kept the sex toys. This was the one place in the store where kids weren't permitted. Did I get a lot of kids in here? Only the young ones with their moms— who were looking to spice up their sex life. The moms, that is.

Lisa showed up a few minutes later. "Anything exciting happen today?" she asked after stowing her coat and purse in the staff room.

"Not really." I brought her up to speed on what I'd like her to do if things got slow, which usually wasn't the case in the evenings. Thanks to the store ads near my weekly column, business was good. The paper had been nice enough to run the store ads whenever I had the column.

By nice, I meant they paid me less than the other weekly columnists, but who was I to complain? Hello, increased business.

After grabbing the paperwork I needed to do that night, I headed back to my apartment building, which was an easy twenty-minute walk from the store.

I unlocked my door and called out, "I'm home," as I entered. Like I did every time I came home. Deep down, I kept hoping that one day someone would answer and tell me how much he'd missed me.

That he would come out of the kitchen, hug me, and give me the most passionate kiss known to womankind. Then we would head to the bedroom and have the most amazing sex.

Of course, this was based on the assumption that sex really was as amazing as the romance novels claimed, especially when you were in love. Or maybe that was just a myth—like Santa and the Easter Bunny.

That's right. Those times I'd had sex were hardly what I'd call spectacular. And this included the one time with my old college boyfriend, the guy who claimed to love me, then walked out the door after taking my virginity and never called again.

I know. I should've seen it coming. *Oh, well. Live and learn.*

While dinner simmered on the stove, I caught up on my bills. Once the food was ready, I ate it and watched *Sex and the City*. But by the end of the third episode, my deadline called to me.

How did I get the job of writing the Dear Dr. Lovejoy column? Simple. An editor from The SF Metro paper came into the store one day. After I talked to her for a bit, she suggested I write a guest column. So I did—as a joke.

I never expected the joke to become a regular gig.

I booted up my laptop and stared at the blank page.

And stared.

And stared.

Usually I answered questions the paper sent me. But when there weren't any that week or my editor hadn't forwarded them yet, I made up my own.

Dear Dr. Lovejoy,

Always a good start.

I've been friends with this one guy for five years now. Recently I've begun fantasizing about him as something more than a friend. What should I do?

Sincerely,

Falling For My Best Friend

Hmmm. Too boring. I deleted it and started again.

Dear Dr. Lovejoy,

I've been going out with my boyfriend for a year now. Sex is good, but I would love it if he would go down on me. What should I do?

Sincerely,

Need A Little More Sexy Fun

This fell within the independent paper's guidelines. Just.

Dear Need A Little More Sexy Fun,

The most important thing in any relationship is communication. If you aren't able to tell him that you would love for him to go down on you, how will you be able to talk to him about more difficult topics? The first question I have for you is, are you going down on him? Because if you aren't, this would be a good time to start and see if he reciprocates.

If you are and he hasn't been doing the same for you, then you need to give him some not-so-subtle hints of what you want. Men aren't so great when it comes to subtle. But do it in a way that makes him think he's the one in control—not you. While you're moaning and writhing at his touch, tell him how you would love it if he went down on you.

If he balks at the idea, don't say anything then, but

casually bring it up at another time. There might be a reason he doesn't like to go down on women—something to do with his past. Be gentle. Again, let him feel like he's in control. If he doesn't give you an answer or still isn't willing to go down on you, then you have two options. The first one is to accept him as he is. Him not going down on you isn't the end of the world...or your sex life. But if this is really important to you and he just won't bend, maybe it's time to end the relationship and find someone new.

I edited the column and emailed it to my editor. Then I retired to my bedroom for a good book and another satisfying night with Alejandro.

Except he wasn't performing his magic this time. Without meaning to, I let my thoughts drift to someone else. The someone I shouldn't have given a moment's consideration to, the someone I hadn't thought about in years—but that didn't stop the sudden image of Travis's fingers against my clit from sneaking into my mind.

With my eyes closed, I pushed away the thought of Travis's imaginary fingers and let Alejandro guide me to the edge of euphoria. Warmth filled my lower belly, then an orgasm rocketed through me, and I cried out.

But as good as it had been, something about it felt lacking.

I mean, other than a real man taking me to happy land.

Fortunately, this was just a momentary glitch when it came to my love affair with Alejandro.

The laughing? Ignore it. That's just the voice in the back of my head completely disagreeing with me.

But what the hell did it know?

4

TRAVIS

"I'll raise you two," I said, putting my chips on the table. We were at Wes's fancy-ass condo after I'd escaped from Granny's apartment an hour ago. *We* being myself, Wes, Trent, Josh, and Liam.

Liam had recently left the Navy SEALs and was in the process of setting up his security business in San Francisco. He had no doubt moved here to keep an eye on his little sister Kelsey and her fiancé, Trent. Trent was Liam's best friend—the guy who had once been off-limits when it came to Liam's sister.

"I'll see your two. How was dinner with your grandmother?" Wes casually asked.

I groaned. Wes laughed. "That bad, huh?"

"That depends on whether you think your grandmother trying to set you up with a puck bunny is a bad thing or not."

You heard me correctly. Turned out dinner wasn't just my grandmother and me. She had invited guests—as in the woman from the apartment down the hallway and her granddaughter. The granddaughter who had puck bunny vibes pouring off her.

To top it off, she had disappeared at one point to use the bathroom and came out braless—her nipples pressed against the tight fabric of her top.

I wasn't the only one who had noticed, if Granny's "Oh, my," was any indication.

The guys burst out laughing after I told them what had happened. "Did she know the girl was a puck bunny?" Josh asked. He didn't have to inquire how I knew what she was. As a former NHL player, he was more than familiar with those types of "fans."

"I doubt it. She just thought she had found me the future Mrs. Hamilton."

This caused the guys to laugh even harder. Glad they were so supportive.

"She's still trying to set you up?" Wes asked.

"Apparently so. It's not so much that she tried to set me up with a puck bunny that's the problem." I mean, hello, easy lay. "It's just that after two failed attempts to set me up with girls in the past two weeks, you'd think by now she would've gotten the hint I'm not interested."

"So tell her you aren't the marrying type."

"Already tried that. She figures I just haven't found the right girl yet."

"Maybe you haven't," Trent said. "Maybe you'd feel differently if you met the right woman."

Of course he would believe that. From what Josh had told me, until Trent and Kelsey had hooked up, Trent had been a confirmed bachelor like the rest of us.

And whatever had been in the water that caused Trent to change his mind about his bachelor status had infected Josh as well. The only difference was that Josh had married his girlfriend—the mother of his child.

"I'll pass, thanks," I said. "Or are you forgetting about my ex-girlfriend from hell?" They all cringed, familiar with the story.

"You know what you need?" Wes asked me.

"Psycho-girlfriend repellent?" You had to admit that would be super helpful—because knowing my luck, the next woman Granny tried to set me up with would be psycho ex-girlfriend's evil twin.

"No, a fake girlfriend."

"How's that going to help me?" I gulped back some beer. I had a feeling I would need it.

"If you have a fake girlfriend who your grandma believes is the real deal, she won't bother setting you up anymore."

True—me plus one fake girlfriend would equal one very happy Granny. "Sounds like a great idea. But where exactly do I find a woman who's willing to be in a fake long-term relationship?"

"One thing's for sure," Josh said, "you need to find a woman who won't fall in love with you and expect the fake girlfriend part to turn real." He spoke as if he knew exactly what he was talking about. But I guess in a way he did. At one point he had pretended to be engaged to the woman who was now his wife. But the chemistry between Josh and Holly had been off the charts even before he faked being her fiancé. Only they hadn't realized it at the time.

"No problem. I just need to find someone who hates me and ask her." Think I piled on enough sarcasm?

Okay, maybe not hate me. But I definitely needed someone who wouldn't want the relationship to become real.

"That might be a start," Liam said, chuckling. "And by the way, I'll see your six dollars and raise you two." He placed the chips on the table, reminding us that we were here to play poker and not yap like schoolgirls.

The guys quickly returned to the task at hand...while I

mentally went through all the girls I could possibly ask to help me out.

It took awhile but I eventually came up with a good possibility.

Tomorrow I would ask Lydia, my old semi-regular hookup partner.

She owed me one. And she was the perfect option because her career was more important to her than having a boyfriend.

Or so I thought.

5

TRAVIS

Typically I'm a spontaneous guy—except for when it comes to hockey. Planning is for the stick-up-their-asses type A personalities.

And that's definitely not me.

Spontaneous people don't have a Plan A and Plan B. They go with the flow—and hope the flow goes their way.

Why am I telling you this?

You'll see in a moment.

When I'd contacted Lydia this morning, I didn't tell her what I needed to ask her. We had hooked up numerous times before, so I assumed she would guess this was another booty call. A long overdue booty call. Was I surprised when she arranged to meet me at the coffee shop instead of her place?

A little.

But not just any coffee shop. This one was in the same building as the love shop—the same brick building where Liam's and Wes's offices were.

No, Liam and Wes didn't work for the same company. Among other interests, Wes ran a successful computer soft-

30

ware company. In other words, he had made a shitload of money designing games.

But not just any computer games.

These were used for training purposes for all kinds of situations.

Anyway, back to Lydia. I was sitting at a table near the window, my coffee in front of me. For some reason, my gaze kept shifting to the love store. Which would explain why I hadn't noticed Lydia enter the coffee shop.

"Hi, Travis," the familiar female voice said next to me.

I swiveled around and my gaze fell to her stomach. Her very pregnant stomach.

Holy fucking shit.

That wasn't the only new thing about her. She now wore a diamond ring on her left hand.

Well, that explained why she had suggested this place instead of her apartment.

Lydia sat in the seat across from me where her coffee was waiting.

"I got your favorite," I said, "but I guess you're probably not allowed to drink coffee anymore." Not that I was an expert on the topic.

"Screw that." She grinned at the cup and picked it up. "Come to Momma. I've been dreaming all day about you."

I assumed she was referring to the coffee and not me.

She took a long sip of the drink, then put it down. "So, as you can tell, there are no more booty calls for me." She held up her left hand in case I hadn't noticed the massive diamond.

"Congratulations. When did this all happen?" And more importantly, why couldn't she have waited another few years before getting hitched and knocked up?

"Well, I'm six months pregnant, and Robert proposed this weekend."

Six months? Then definitely not mine. Now that I did the mental math, the last time Lydia and I had hooked up was more like eight months ago.

And I guess we all knew what this meant. I was screwed. Fucking. Royally. Screwed. There was no way I would be passing Lydia off as my girlfriend.

"So what did you want to talk to me about?" she asked.

I gave her the abbreviated version.

She stared at me for a heartbeat, letting the final words sink in.

Then she laughed.

I swear she was laughing so hard, I thought she would go into labor.

"I'm sorry, Travis," she said, once she'd stopped laughing long enough to speak. "I really am. I would've helped you if I was still the woman you used to hook up with."

Yeah—I already missed that woman. And no, it had nothing to do with the sex.

Well, not much anyway.

"I don't suppose you know anyone who would be willing to help me?" I asked.

She laughed again and shook her head. "Sorry. I'm the last of my friends who wasn't married or in a serious relationship. And everyone else I know would probably fall madly in love with your sexy hazel eyes and hot bod, which isn't what you need."

Well, doesn't that just fuck all?

The last thing I wanted was to go through the hell of breaking up with someone else. I'd rather have my eyeballs plucked out of my head and used as hockey pucks than break up with a chick.

Call me a coward if you must. But seriously, breaking up with a woman was hell. Don't believe me? Ask any guy.

The only guys who enjoyed it were masochists. And trust me, you were better off without them anyway.

Now that Lydia and I had gotten that out of the way, we caught up with what had been happening since we last saw each other. Eventually she had to leave. As I was about to walk out with her, my phone rang and Granny's number flashed on the screen.

Lydia waved bye and kept going as I answered my phone.

"So what did you think of Candace?" Granny immediately asked. "Isn't she um...friendly?"

That noise? It was me choking back a laugh. Yes, Candace was very friendly—as my cock could attest. Somehow she had managed to reach under the table during dinner last night and casually stroke my package. I wouldn't have been surprised if she had accidentally dropped her fork on the floor, climbed under the table to retrieve it, and given me a blowjob while she was down there.

Normally I was a huge fan of blowjobs. Huge, *huge* fan. But getting one while sitting at the same table as Granny did not a turn-on make.

So, how did one explain to Granny that Candace was a puck bunny?

One didn't.

Granny didn't need to know that her friend's granddaughter was only interested in fucking me.

"Sorry, she's not my type."

The sound of a disappointed sigh vibrated through the phone. "No one ever seems to be your type, Travis."

Not true.

"Are you...are you gay?" she asked. Good thing she hadn't said it while I was drinking my coffee.

"Because there's nothing wrong with that if you are," she hurriedly added. "This is San Francisco after all."

I know what you're thinking. Since I didn't have anyone

lined up for the role of fake girlfriend, maybe I should go with the "yes, I'm gay" theory.

Except that idea wouldn't work either. The last thing I needed was to round up a guy to pretend to be my gay boyfriend. But if I didn't, Granny would be searching to find me a boyfriend instead of a girlfriend. And I wouldn't put it past her to then hunt for a surrogate mother to help fake boyfriend and me give Granny her much-desired great-grandchild.

Which left me back at square one: in need of a fake girlfriend.

"I'm as straight as they come, Granny. Look, I've got to get going. I'm meeting up with Wes. I'll talk to you soon."

"Say hi to him for me. Say, he's not still single, is he?"

Now, did I throw my friend under the bus, so to speak, or cut him a break?

"No, he's still single." And the bus it was. Maybe she would give up on me and decide to find him a girlfriend instead.

Good point. Even if she could find him a girlfriend and they had lots of cute babies, it wouldn't be good enough for Granny. Then she would be even more determined to get me hitched.

I ended the call as I strolled out the door...and right into the woman who had haunted my dreams last night.

Don't get excited. I didn't mean it the way it sounded. We had sex. Lots of it.

But unlike in my dreams, the curly redhead wasn't smiling seductively at me while riding my cock.

Her gaze dropped to my lips for a heartbeat, and her teeth momentarily dug into *her* lower lip. The lower lip I wouldn't have minded sucking on.

Remember what I said about me being spontaneous? Good. Because hopefully what I said next will make sense.

I gave her my best charming smile. "Just the person I need to talk to."

Yes, I was aware that some of the scariest serial killers of all time had charming smiles. If I was lucky, that wouldn't be the first or second thought to cross her mind at the sight of mine. "My grandmother came into your store yesterday."

She nodded. "I remember her. She seems like a sweet woman."

"She is. But she's determined that I find a woman and fall in love."

"And you're too good for that?"

I snorted. "Not too good at all. But the last thing I have time for is a girlfriend. I don't want to break my grandmother's heart. I just want her to be happy." I know, low blow—because what girl wishes to break the heart of an old woman? But low blow or not, it was all true. "I thought if I had a fake girlfriend, I could spare my sweet grandmother from wishing for something that will never happen."

Emma shrugged. "So what does that have to do with me?"

"I thought you could be my fake girlfriend."

The corners of her mouth twitched as she fought back a smile.

"Does that mean you'll do it?" I asked.

"No, it just means you're insane. I'm not interested in being someone's fake girlfriend." She pushed past me and walked to the counter.

And being the desperate idiot that I was, I joined her at the end of the line. "Is there any particular reason why not?" I asked.

"Because unlike you, I don't have commitment issues."

"You don't even know me. What makes you think I have commitment issues? And what does that have to do with anything?"

She laughed what had to be the sexiest sound I'd heard in a while. My cock twitched in agreement.

"I know your type," she said, facing forward.

I felt my mouth shift into a smirk. "And what type is that?"

"You're a good-looking guy who doesn't care whose heart you break. I bet you've hooked up with girls who would be amazing girlfriends, but you're too chicken to commit. And I bet you've broken some hearts because of that."

What was I supposed to say to that?

Other than, "I'll pay you."

She didn't bother to turn around. "Trust me, there's nothing you can give me that will change my mind."

"Really, nothing?"

This time she did turn to face me. "That's right. Nothing. Now run along. I've got more important things to do than stand here talking to you." She waved me off, but her hand accidentally brushed against my chest—and a warm sensation zinged through me from the spot. *Weird.* That was new.

But new or not, it was obvious I was getting nowhere with her. I would've had better luck asking a nun to help me out.

"Next," the blonde behind the counter said, smiling at her. "Hey, Emma, the usual?"

I didn't stick around to hear if she wanted her regular or not. I left the store and headed up the courtyard stairs to the second level.

Shit. Where the hell am I going to find a fake girlfriend?

But more importantly, how was I going to stop wishing that Emma would agree to take on the role? And why the heck did I even care that she thought I was good-looking?

6

———

EMMA

"**W**ho was that guy?" Kate asked.

I glanced over my shoulder. Travis had already vanished.

I let out a relieved breath—which was accompanied by a resounding "Boooo" from my girlie parts. For some reason, when my hand had accidentally brushed against his chest, they got excited. They might have also threatened to stage a coup if I didn't recant on my decision to not pretend to be his girlfriend.

Or at least if I didn't start dating again, preferably with a guy who was interested in a long-term relationship.

A guy who was interested in falling in love.

A guy who was talented between the sheets. All right— that would be an additional perk.

I could only come up with two reasonable explanations for my body's reaction to Travis: First, it was experiencing rejection-induced amnesia when it came to what happened back in high school. Second, it had voted that I should agree to be his fake girlfriend—that way he and I could have sex.

37

But if he was just looking for a fake girlfriend, I doubted this included benefits from the Department of Orgasms.

Yes—I did believe that Travis was synonymous with orgasms. The short dark hair. The mesmerizing hazel eyes, which were more playful than serious. The mouthwatering muscles. He was sex on a stick and then some.

A voice in the back of my head reminded me that good looks didn't necessarily mean good in bed—as experience had taught me.

"He's no one," I told Kate, answering her question.

"Well, *no one* is very good-looking."

I smirked. "Aren't you engaged?"

"I'm engaged, not dead. And I'm just thinking about you. When was the last time you went on a date, Emma?"

"You know, Hannah never gives me a hard time about my current lack of dating life."

Kate rolled her eyes. "That's because hers is as pathetic as yours. But she doesn't write a column on sex and romance. How can you write about something you know nothing about?"

"Easy," I said, grabbing my cup that the coffee dude had just set on the counter. "I live vicariously through you." I winked at her and headed back to my store.

Did I agree with Kate? A little.

All right—more than a little. But you had to admit, dating was tough. It didn't matter how great the guy might seem when you first met him, the interest in him quickly waned as soon as you got to know him. Or maybe that was just me. And since I had a three-date policy (three dates with a guy before I had sex with him), it didn't usually bode well for me when it came to making my girlie parts happy.

Hence the reason Alejandro and I were intimately acquainted.

Lisa was busy helping a woman in the Home Style

department when I entered. I walked over to check on the couple searching through our selection of books on sexual positions. Always a popular favorite.

And yes, I might have studied a few of them at one time or another.

Purely for research, of course.

"Which book do you recommend?" the woman in her thirties asked—as if I had personally tested each one.

I wish.

I pulled a book from the shelf. "This is our most popular one." I took that to mean it was an excellent book.

After they thanked me and paid for it, I headed to my office. Lisa had things under control, which meant I could catch up on some paperwork. That unfortunately never seemed to end.

I'd been placing an order when my office door opened.

Thinking it was Lisa wanting me to cover for her during her break, I started to stand, my attention still on the computer screen. "Should I order more pink vibrators or try the purple ones this time?"

Only then did I glance up.

Have you ever met that one person who, no matter what you say or do, makes you feel like you're the dog shit he stepped in?

Meet the owner of the building: Donald Shrivener.

Or Old Shriveled Ass as Hannah and I called him—just not to his face. Hannah was positive the last time he'd had sex was sometime during World War II. I had to agree with her there.

Every time he came into the store, his gaze narrowed as if I was selling dark magic. I kept expecting him to show up one day with a priest and have the store exorcised.

Fortunately, he didn't come here very often since the rent

was automatically withdrawn from my bank account. Which was why I was confused by his presence in the store.

"Is there something you need?" I asked in the voice usually saved for my customers.

He grinned—his teeth stained and crooked. Unlike most people when they smiled, it didn't make him seem friendly. Creepy was more like it.

"I came to remind you that your lease expires in two months," he said.

"I know—and I told you I'll be renewing it for another year."

Wow. I didn't think his grin could grow any creepier. I was wrong. "I came to tell you the building is going to be converted into a condo complex, and your store will no longer be considered appropriate for the retail space. Consider this your notice."

"But you can't do that."

"Sure, I can. You're perfectly welcome to stay...if you change the nature of your business. A sex shop is considered highly unsuitable." His voice was I-know-you-have-sex-slaves-here smug. I fought the urge to roll my eyes. Barely. "Maybe you could open a bakery instead. I hear your cookies are popular."

So were my scented candles and bath products and everything else. I itched to point that out but didn't. It wouldn't have changed his mind if I had.

"So the construction for the condos starts as soon as my lease expires? And why is this the first I'm hearing about the plans to turn the building into condos?"

"Because details haven't been finalized yet," he said, looking down his long skinny nose at me. "But since your lease is about to expire, no point delaying the inevitable."

I guess not.

With the smug look still on his face, he walked out of my

office. Well, more like skipped from my office like a giddy schoolgirl.

Shit.

I slumped back in my chair and dropped my face into my hands. What the hell was I going to do? This store was like my second home. Heck, with the amount of time I spent here lately, it was more like my first home.

But this wasn't the end of the world, right? I had survived tougher. Being a foster kid had taught me to be resilient.

I just needed to find a new location.

No need to pull out the pity party decorations.

I am woman. Hear me roar!

Would that have been more convincing if I hadn't been clutching the desk?

"Are you okay?" a woman's voice asked from the doorway. I looked up to find Fanny standing there, her two sidekicks behind her.

All three of them appeared concerned like I would expect grandmothers to look when their grandchild had fallen off her bike and scraped her knees.

You know the look? The one where cookies are involved.

Or at least that was the look that had starred in my childhood fantasies—when I used to dream about fairytale princes and having a grandmother who loved me as much as I loved her.

Did my own grandmothers love me? I wouldn't know. I had never met either of them. My father's identity was a mystery to me. He had never wanted me, plain and simple.

And my mom's parents? From what I understood, they'd kicked her out of the house when she got pregnant with me. Nice, huh?

Yes, even before I was born, my family had rejected me. And when I ended up abandoned and alone, no one came rushing forward to claim me. For me, life hadn't been a Hall-mark movie.

So as you could imagine, having Travis's grandmother and her friends look at me with concern caused a warmth to fill me.

Yeah, ignore the tears. How about we just blame them on PMS—even if it isn't technically that time of the month?

I sniffed. "I'm fine, thanks."

It might have been more believable if another tear hadn't slid down my face. I needed to get these three out of my office before their concern did me in. Full-out sobbing would be really embarrassing.

But of course, instead of leaving my office, they entered it.

"Is there anything we can help you with?" Fanny asked.

I laughed. All right, it wasn't a ha-ha type laugh. More like an I'm-in-serious-trouble-but-thank-you-for-asking laugh. At least it didn't sound like someone was dying—so bonus points for me.

"Unless you know of a great place where I can relocate the store," I said, my smile weak, "then probably not." I totally blamed their grandmotherly pheromones for my blurting that out. Clearly they were a dangerous thing.

Forget interrogating the bad guys—send in these three women and the men would be confessing their crimes in no time.

"I think I can help you there," Fanny said with a grin.

7

Dear Dr. Lovejoy,

I know they say leopards don't change their spots, but is it possible for a guy to change? Can someone who was a jerk before suddenly become Prince Charming?

Sincerely,

Hoping for a Miracle

Dear Hoping for a Miracle,

There's a reason that wise saying exists. Heed its warning. No one can change for the better that quickly. If someone does change, it's probably because deep down, he already was an amazing person. You just failed to see it because you didn't know him as well as you thought.

As for the Prince Charming part...you do realize he is nothing more than a cartoon man, right? You can do a lot better than that!

8

EMMA

Why was I sitting in the front seat of Travis's SUV while Fanny sat in the back?

Good question.

I wasn't exactly sure how it happened, either. One minute I was waiting outside my apartment for Fanny to arrive. The next she was ushering me into the front seat of the SUV, and officially introducing me to her grandson.

And judging from the surprised expression on Travis's face when he saw me, he had been just as clueless about me joining them as I had been.

"This is the place," Fanny said as I was considering if I should ask Travis what he did for a living. Or maybe it was better if I didn't ask. Maybe he had some super boring job that he hated.

That was the case for the last guy I'd dated. He spent the entire evening explaining in great detail why his job sucked.

Even the waiter had felt bad for me. He'd kept flashing me pitying looks.

Fanny pointed to the brick low-rise building with stores

on the lower level. It was a quaint building in a quaint part of San Francisco.

Travis parked the vehicle, then he and I followed Fanny to the front entrance. He and I hadn't said much to each other the entire trip there. Fanny had been doing all the talking while I was doing my best not to notice how great Travis smelled. I had no idea what soap or aftershave he used, but the woodsy scent definitely worked for him.

"Did you give any more thought to being my fake girlfriend?" he casually asked, voice low.

"It's still no," I said, my voice equally low. "And in case you're wondering, it will be no tomorrow, too."

"You have a boyfriend?"

"No. But that's because I haven't found the right man yet." *Not even close.*

"So you're available?"

"Available to date or available to be your fake girlfriend?"

"Both."

Why did I have a sudden craving to kiss the cocky smirk off his face?

That was new. Or was it?

I mentally went through the Rolodex of past dates and tried to remember if any had possessed sexy smirks. I came up blank.

Maybe I could add that to the list of requirements for the next guy I went out with.

It couldn't hurt.

"I'm available to date," I said as Fanny waved at us then opened the store door. "I'm not available to be your fake girlfriend." Or even his real girlfriend if he had asked.

And not just because of what happened in high school. His no commitment policy also ruled him out as a potential date.

Inside the empty store, I began imagining how it would

look set up like my current location. The space was smaller than Aphrodite's. And where would I put the sex toys so kids didn't accidentally find them?

"Hi, I'm Janet Featherbridge," the woman said. She must be the realtor Fanny had mentioned.

"It's a nice place," I said, shaking her hand.

"And a great location. The clientele who come to this shopping area are in the upper-income bracket. What kind of retail store are you looking at setting up?"

"It's called Aphrodite's Boutique. It caters to the inner romantic in all of us."

Behind me, Travis snickered—too soft for Janet and Fanny to hear.

But what did you expect from a guy who no doubt believed jerking off in the shower was the same thing as romance?

An unwanted image popped in my head of Travis standing in the shower, his muscular body glistening with water. His erection proud and ready to pound into me.

I seriously didn't just moan, did I?

I shook the image from my head and moved away from Travis and his delusion-inducing masculine scent

But what did I expect? I was no different than someone who had been wandering aimlessly in a desert for several days and had just spotted a lush oasis. It wasn't Travis I was responding to. It was just a symptom of the dry spell known as my sex life.

"I'm familiar with the store," Janet said. "I haven't visited it, but I see the ads for it whenever I check out Dr. Lovejoy's weekly column. Do you read it?"

I could feel Travis's gaze directed at me, which was enough to cause my face to heat up. Why did I react that way? I have no idea. I doubt he remembered my last name from the short time we were in the same high school together. He certainly hadn't stuck around long enough as my project partner to learn it.

Which was a good thing—even if it hadn't felt that way at the time. It meant he had no idea I was Dr. Lovejoy.

Not that I expected him to bombard me with dating and sex questions even if he did piece things together.

"I've read it from time to time," I said, not willing to admit that I was the one who wrote the column. And since Fanny had set up this meeting, Janet had no idea my last name was the same as the person who wrote it. "How much is the lease for a year?"

"Rent is eighty-seven dollars per square foot a year, and at seventeen hundred square feet"—she glanced at the page in her hand—"that would be just under one hundred and forty-eight thousand dollars per year."

Ouch. Double what I was currently paying but for a lot less space.

"That's higher than I've budgeted for. And I'll really need another eight hundred square feet." Or else I would have to get rid of the fountain.

She considered it for a moment. "All right, I have some other properties that might be more suited to what you're looking for."

She gave Travis the address for the next location and got into her BMW.

Travis, Fanny, and I returned to the SUV and followed her.

"Do your parents live in San Francisco?" Fanny asked me.

How was I supposed to answer without explaining my sob story? Sure, if I wished for people to feel sorry for me, then it was an awesome tale to tell.

But I was familiar with Travis's opinion when it came to foster kids who had been tossed away by their parents. I had experienced that pain in high school when he bailed on being my history project partner. According to his ex-girl-friend, he hadn't wanted to work with me because I was a foster kid. No point going there again.

Besides, that was over ten years ago. People changed. So far he seemed nice. He didn't have to help me look for a new location. I mean, sure, Fanny had set this up, but he could have said no and driven away.

"They're dead," I said. Simple enough explanation. For all I knew, my parents could have been dead.

"Oh, I'm so sorry," Fanny said. "Well, it looks like you and Travis have that in common."

We do?

Travis didn't say anything, his attention on the road.

"I'm sorry," I told him and meant it because I was positive his parents had loved him. He'd lost that and I'd never had it to begin with. It was hard to mourn something you'd never had.

It just made you long to experience it that much more.

"So why are you moving your business?" Travis asked.

I guess Fanny never told him. Bonus—because it also meant he didn't know about those pseudo-PMS tears.

"My lease is expiring in two months, and the owner isn't renewing it because he's turning the building into a condo complex. He feels the store will no longer be suitable for the location once the condo is finished."

Did I go to the local bar after work the day Old Shriveled Ass told me the news and throw darts at his imaginary picture? I might have. I might have also scored a couple of bull's-eyes.

"That's news to me about the renovations," Travis said.

"Me too. I can't figure out why the owner wants to change it. The current design fits the area perfectly and it already has apartments." But I guess since the owner was a man, he was going with the belief that bigger was always better.

Janet turned down a street and a bad feeling rolled through me.

"Well, um, this is an interesting neighborhood," Fanny said as we took in the low-income area.

Both Travis and I kept quiet as we drove past a cop car, the officer assisting a man into the back seat. *Oh, boy.*

We still didn't say anything as we parked on the side street near the building we were going to check out. But really, what was there to say?

Other than I'd be having a *menage-á-trois* with Cupid himself and his best buddy before I moved my store here.

"Stay right here," Travis said before climbing out of the SUV. He shut the door, and with his key fob, locked the vehicle.

He walked to Janet's car as I undid my seat belt and reached for the passenger door.

"You should probably stay put, dear," Fanny said.

"It's going to be a little hard to check out the store if I'm still in the vehicle."

"I know, but Travis told us to stay here...and you can't tell me you're honestly considering moving the store here." She peered out the window again and shuddered.

"No...but—" I didn't get to finish the sentence. Travis returned to the vehicle, climbed back into the driver's seat, and turned the ignition.

"Why aren't we going into the store?" I asked.

He flashed me an *are-you-fucking-kidding-me?* expression. I was positive he would have verbalized it instead if not for his sweet old grandma in the back. "We're going to the next place."

Janet's brake lights came on and she pulled away from the curb.

And so continued our day of checking out potential retail spaces for Aphrodite's Boutique. How did it go?

Fifteen locations.

Five were too small.

Seven were too expensive.

Three were in a part of the city that would put me out of business in no time because no one would go there.

The grand total of potential locations?

A big fat pathetic zero.

Now, you're probably thinking, "Hey, but that's only fifteen locations. There's got to be more than that in San Francisco and The Bay Area."

You would think, right?

Wrong—because based on my needs and my price tag and the fact that I didn't wish to be shot or attacked, there were no suitable rental properties.

So unless I was willing to compromise, I was up-the-creek-in-a-leaky-canoe screwed.

Screwed—and with a body that thought lusting over Travis was a brilliant idea.

Oh, nuts.

It couldn't have at least lusted over a guy who actually wanted a girlfriend, now could it?

9

TRAVIS

> Me to Wes: Are we still on for lunch?

> Wes: Yes. An hour?

> Me: Can we make that an hour and a half? At doctor's with Granny to discuss her test results.

> Wes: Sounds good. Meet you there. Hope things are okay.

The "there" that Wes was referring to was The Unicorn, the pub in the building he owned. The same building where Emma's store was located.

"How was your workout this morning?" Granny asked after she had stopped watching two kids playing in the corner of the waiting room.

"It was good. I met up with some of the guys from the team at the gym." Even though August was off-season when it came to hockey, that didn't mean I got to take the summer off.

And with only six weeks until the start of hockey season, my training had increased in intensity.

"And that's why you have the body young ladies drool over," Granny said with a wink.

Okaaay. Didn't need to hear that from my grandmother—even if it was true.

"Have you figured out who you're bringing to my birthday party?" she asked.

"Me and myself." Although if I could drag Josh there, I'd gladly do it. Spending an evening alone with my grandmother and her crazy friends wasn't up there on my list of fun ways to spend a Thursday night.

Why was I going? Because I loved my grandmother and owed her the world for putting up with my bullshit after my parents had died. Their unexpected deaths had screwed me up to the point where I was skipping classes and had come close to being cut from my midget hockey team.

Granny was the reason I hadn't been. I don't know exactly what she did, but I got the general gist that she marched into the head coach's office and scared the crap out of him.

And Coach Kaufman was not the type to scare easily.

Granny smiled in the way that always got me nervous. It was the smile associated with her plotting to set me up with a female.

Shit.

Before I could say anything, a nurse called out Granny's name. We both followed her into the exam room, sat on the plastic chairs, and waited for her to finish typing on the laptop before she left and we could resume our conversation.

"Don't even think of setting me up with another of your friend's granddaughters for your party," I told Granny mere seconds after the door clicked shut. "I'm perfectly capable of finding my own date if you really want me to bring one."

She eyed me for a moment. "You're not bringing one of

your teammates, right?" Her eyes took on a mischievous glint. "Not that my friends would complain, especially if your teammates showed up shirtless like Chippendale dancers."

"My teammates enjoy body checking the opposition. They aren't dancers." At least not professional dancers. I'd witnessed a few of them on the dance floor at the clubs we'd been known to frequent from time to time.

Granny let out a long, disappointed sigh. "That's too bad."

I groaned. "You're almost eighty years old!"

"That's right, Travis. I'm almost eighty. I'm not dead. I don't have much time left on this planet, and in case Heaven isn't filled with hot men like I would prefer, then I'd appreciate getting to ogle them while I still can."

I thought about this for a second. "If I got my teammates to dance like Chippendale dancers for your birthday, would you stop pushing for me to find a girl, get married, and give you great-grandkids?"

Hey, it was worth asking. He who didn't ask would never know.

Laughing, Granny patted my hand. "I'd pay to see your teammates do that. But no, I still want to see you happy. But if you have a girlfriend, then I'll stop trying to set you up. Your teammates dancing for my birthday party would be an added bonus. But if I'm on my deathbed and there are no adorable great-grandchildren to say good-bye to me, then I'll come back and haunt you worse than Abigail's shrimp casserole."

I grimaced at the memory of the only time I'd eaten it. It took me three days to recover—and the Rock lost the game against Anaheim that I missed. Was it my fault? No—but it felt like it was at the time.

"Point taken," I said.

The door opened and Granny's doctor entered. Whereas Granny was almost eighty, I had pubic hairs older than this guy. Heck, I wouldn't be too surprised if he didn't even have any yet.

Not that I was about to ask him.

After he got through the normal niceties, he sat on the padded stool.

"So how long do I have left?" Granny asked.

"Left?" He turned to me as though I knew what the heck she was talking about.

"You know, before I join my maker?"

The look she flashed me? It was to remind me time was ticking on giving her a great-grandchild.

Maybe Josh and Holly would let me borrow their daughter and I could pretend she was mine. Of course then I'd have to explain to Granny in nine months why my new baby was already two years old.

So strike that idea.

"You're not dying if that's what you're asking," the kid said. "But I am concerned with your cholesterol levels especially given your history of having a stroke. I would like to switch your meds to help manage it better."

"So I'm not dying anytime soon?"

"Well, I can't say with any certainty if that's true or not. I'd be a psychic if I could predict that."

Good to know. About the dying—not the psychic part. Which meant I didn't have to rush out and find a fake great-grandchild. Yet.

After we finished talking to the doctor, I drove Granny to her pharmacy to pick up the new prescription, then dropped her off at her apartment.

Wes was seated at a corner table in The Unicorn when I arrived. We didn't have to sit for long before the waitress approached to take our order.

"So what's this about you turning your building into a condo complex?" I asked after she'd walked away. I hadn't had a chance to ask him since finding out about it from Emma. Wes had been away at a gaming design conference.

"What are you talking about?"

"One of your tenants said her lease isn't being renewed because you're converting the building into a condo complex, and her store doesn't fit the new image."

Confused? Let me get you up to speed. His grandfather used to own the building. When he died, instead of passing it to his daughter, he'd willed it to Wes. Only a few people knew this. Everyone else just assumed he was a tenant in the building like they were, and he preferred it that way. But while he might have had someone else manage the building, he was still very much involved in the decisions surrounding it.

"That's news to me," he said. "Which store?"

I told him.

"That would explain it," he said, his tone betraying that inwardly he was rolling his eyes. "Donald believes the store is the work of the devil—or something along those lines."

"So he lied to the owner and told her she had to move when her lease expires?"

"It would seem so. But thanks for letting me know. I'll make sure my dear sweet uncle tells her the truth."

"So the building is staying as is?"

"I'm planning to do some long-needed renovations to it, but nothing beyond that. And no one is being evicted."

Nice to know I wasted all that time driving Emma and my grandmother around for nothing.

Or not.

"Look, could you do me a favor?" I asked.

"What kind of favor?"

"The kind of favor where you hold off telling Emma—the store's owner—the truth for a while."

Wes looked as though he was going to say something but

then clamped his mouth shut. I found out a moment later why when the waitress placed our drinks in front of us.

She told us our food would be ready soon and left. Wes drew a long sip of his soda—keeping me in suspense.

"Care to explain why you don't want Donald to tell her that she isn't being evicted once her lease expires?" he asked, lowering his glass to the table.

"Not really."

He raised an eyebrow but didn't say anything.

If you think I got off that easily, you obviously don't know Wes.

"You remember how you told me to get a fake girlfriend to get Granny off my back?"

He nodded. "I remember."

"Remember how Josh recommended I find someone who won't fall in love with me? Someone who pretty much hates my guts?"

"I do—although I'm not sure your acting skills are good enough to pull off dating a girl who doesn't like you."

He had a point there. "I'm sure it won't be an issue. It's not like I'm auditioning for a Broadway show." And Emma ran the love shop, which meant she could probably do a decent job of faking things, too.

"True....So what does Donald not telling her about the lease have to do with anything?"

"Because she pretty much hates my guts." Okay, that might be an overstatement. The dislike she had leveled my way when I first entered her store wasn't there when I drove her to all those retail spaces over the past couple of days. But she already knew I was anti-commitment, so she would still be a good choice. "I already asked her if she would be my fake girlfriend...."

"And she said no," Wes guessed.

"That's right."

"So what are you planning to do? Tell her you'll convince the building owner not to evict her if she helps you out?" He chuckled a you-really-are-an-idiot laugh.

"Wow, and they say you aren't smart," I said with a smirk. No one could claim the MIT grad lacked intelligence.

Me, on the other hand? Yes—given my idea, my level of intelligence might be questionable.

"You really think it will work?"

I shrugged. "I have no idea, but right now I'm running out of options."

"Okay, I won't say anything to Donald for now. But if you can't convince her to be your girlfriend in the next three days, then I'll have to tell her the truth about her lease. And you will owe me big-time for this."

That was a given.

"Anything else I should know?" He picked up his glass and started drinking.

"My grandmother wants my teammates to reenact a scene from *Magic Mike* for her eightieth birthday party."

I probably should have waited until he'd finished his soda before springing that on him.

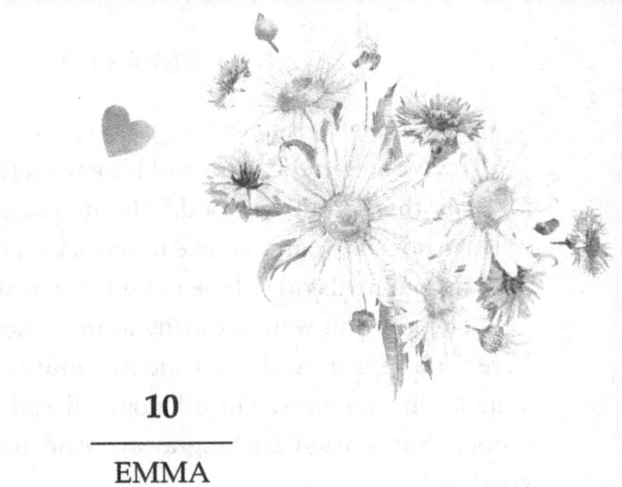

10

EMMA

Sitting on the fountain's ledge, I pulled on my rubber boots. Why the boots?

You didn't expect me to climb into the fountain in my heels or go barefooted, did you?

"Wow, that looks like so much fun," Hannah said, laughing. "If I didn't have to go to work in a few minutes, I would've volunteered to help you. But alas..." She snickered. "Why are you doing this when there are no birds in the store to crap on the statue?"

"Just because there are no birds doesn't mean Aphrodite doesn't get dusty." I had no idea if the woman in the toga really was supposed to be the Greek goddess of love, but she looked similar enough. "Plus I need to remove the coins, and it's a lot easier to do that by climbing in the water to retrieve them."

"If you say so." The laughter in her voice was still there.

The bell above the door jingled and I glanced up to see if I was about to be busy—or if Lisa could handle things. Several people already were milling around, checking out the merchandise or trying on the lingerie in the fitting room.

59

Oh, God. Not him again.

Travis entered the store and his gaze settled on me.

"Oh, this should be good," Hannah said. "Too bad I have to leave now if I want to make it to work on time."

I turned my head to look at her. "What should be good?"

"The guy you were scowling at the other day is obviously here for a repeat. And this time he's minus the senior citizen squad. On that note, I'm off now. I'll call you later for the scoop." She started backing away. "And have fun with your goddess."

Before I could respond, she was out the door, pausing only long enough to give Travis a quick once-over and wave good-bye to me.

He wasn't the only one to be given a once-over. Except in my case, his gaze slowly traveled up my body as if he were undressing me—removing my ever-so-sexy rubber boots; my whimsical blue floral sundress that brushed against my knees; my white lacy bra and underwear, which he couldn't see but I was sure he was imagining on me. That, or he was imagining me in a thong.

Once his gaze was on my face, his mouth slid up to one side. "The boots are definitely a nice touch. But I must admit I'm more a fan of stilettos." He leaned in closer, his breath brushing against my ear...and my body decided to go rogue and ignore my brain telling it to take a step back.

"Especially when the legs they're attached to are wrapped around my waist," he added. No—the girlie part between my legs did not release a longing sigh. Not. At. All.

Note to self: add dirty talk to list of requirements for next boyfriend.

I stepped away from him, the back of my calves hitting the low fountain wall. "What are you doing here? I thought we weren't checking out any more retail spaces until next weekend."

"I came to talk to you."

"I figured that, but now's not a good time."

"Why's that?"

I indicated the fountain. "I have to clean it and remove the money. So unless whatever you need to tell me can be done while I'm working, you'll have to come back later." Or preferably never.

"I can wait."

Of course he could.

"Don't you have to be at work or something?" I had no idea what he did for a living, but it probably didn't involve hanging around my store.

He opened his mouth to answer but didn't get that far.

"Ohmigod, aren't you, like, Travis Hamilton?" A tall teenage girl asked him. She was pretty, with an athletic body and long dark hair spilling down her back.

She didn't wait for him to reply. "I also play defense. You're like my idol."

I felt my eyebrows climb north. Idol? Why would she idolize him?

And how did she even know him?

Maybe I should have Googled him...like I had with some of my past dates.

Not that I was going out with him.

He offered her a friendly smile—not like the smiles that threw me off kilter. "Nice to meet you."

Her friend was looking at Travis as though she also had no idea why the girl was excited seeing him here.

"This is Travis Hamilton," the dark-haired girl explained. "He plays defense for the San Francisco Rock. The NHL team."

He does?

She kept chatting to him, mostly about hockey. Since I still had work to do, I grabbed the cloth on the ledge and climbed in. I'd already turned the water off before putting my boots on.

Have you ever tried walking through a fountain while wearing rubber boots? It's not easy. And I don't care how graceful you normally are, this sucks all the gracefulness from you in one easy swoop.

But I figured the sacrifice was worth it. For Aphrodite's sake…which could only help benefit the store.

Now if only Aphrodite could help me with my lease problem.

Splosh. Splosh. Splosh.

"Ready for a little spa treatment?" I asked the statue in almost a whisper. No need for the customers to believe I was crazy.

I dipped the cloth in the water and began cleaning her.

"What are you doing?" Travis asked.

"What does it look like?" I spared him a glance over my shoulder. The girls he had been talking to were no longer with him.

"It looks like you're giving her a sponge bath. Very kinky, by the way."

I rolled my eyes. "I'm cleaning her and then I have to remove the money."

"What do you do with the money?"

"It goes to charity," I said, my attention on my task.

"What charity?"

"A youth center for underprivileged kids where I volunteer."

"Why a local youth center for underprivileged kids?"

I shifted around and glanced at him from over Aphrodite's shoulder. "Why *not* there?"

The corner of his mouth twitched up to one side. "I asked you first." At my silence, he continued, "The Rock encourages its players to be active in the community. Some players donate large amounts of money to a charity of their choice. Some participate in various events at the children's hospital, which are always popular with the kids. For some players, they do it simply because publicity recommended they give back to those less fortunate—because it makes the player look good. Others do it because their charity has special meaning to them. So which is it for you?"

"Which type of player are you?" I replied. Or maybe he donated neither time nor money.

"I donate money to a charity that provides sports equipment to kids. Because of the cost, they might not otherwise be able to play hockey. And I participate in the annual wheelchair hockey game at the kids' hospital."

Did I have "selfless" on my list of requirements for potential boyfriends? No—but it was a given. I'd written off a few individuals in the past because they didn't believe in donating either time or money to a worthy cause.

So, yes, my heart had warmed up a little bit more toward Travis. Not that it mattered. He wasn't looking for a girlfriend, and I wasn't looking to be a fake one.

"How come that charity and event?" I asked.

The smirk was back on his face. "Uh, uh. You first. Why the youth center?"

The coins in the water shimmered under the bright store light overhead, almost as if encouraging me to tell him.

"Because I understand what it feels like to be underprivileged. I grew up in foster care."

Which he would know if he remembered me from school. But he didn't—so what was a girl to do?

Apparently Aphrodite had an answer for that. The pump that I had turned off before climbing into the fountain suddenly turned on. Water burst up from the jets hitting me full on—and I shrieked. *Ugh!*

Then the fountain turned off as quickly as it had turned

on, leaving me standing there with water dripping from my hair and down my body. My now-wet dress clung to me, leaving not much to the imagination, including my white lacy bra and underwear.

"Sorry," Lisa called out, returning from the back. "I accidentally hit the switch to the fountain." Her gaze landed on me, soaked and still standing in the water, and her hand flew to her mouth. Not from shock. She was attempting to hold back a giggle.

Nice.

I stepped over the fountain's low wall. *Squish. Squish.*

"I'm so sorry," she said, her hand still covering her mouth. The corners of her eyes crinkled with barely held back laughter.

Travis wasn't doing much better.

I tried to yank off a rubber boot—which wasn't easy when your foot was wet and you were standing. Swaying on one foot, I grabbed the closest thing available to hold on to: Travis's arm.

And wow, the man worked out.

Don't think about his muscular body. Don't think about his hot, muscular body....

I would've removed my hand from his arm, but it was either touch him or risk falling over.

The boot eventually slipped free of my foot. I tilted it, pouring the water back into the fountain. Once it was empty, I placed the boot on the ledge and proceeded to do the same with the other one while still holding on to Travis.

With what dignity I had left—which was pretty much zero—I walked toward the back where my office was located. With my body shivering, thanks to the air conditioning, I tossed an "I'll be back in a moment" over my shoulder to Lisa.

In my office, I scanned the area for something to dry off with.

The door clicked shut behind me. I startled and spun around. Travis was standing in front of the closed door, his eyes dark and focused on my breasts. Or more specifically, my perky nipples pressing against the wet fabric of my thin bra and dress.

I crossed my arms in front of me, doing my best to hide the view. Doing my best to warm my girls up.

"Is this a good time to ask you again about being my fake girlfriend?" In his hand was a soft wool throw from the store. Red on one side and white on the other, it was covered in hearts of the opposite color.

"So what's the deal? You'll give me the throw if I agree to be your fake girlfriend?" There might have been some teeth chattering when I said it. "And just so you know, that's not going to work. For one, I can't sell the blanket if it's dirty."

"And what's the second?"

"It will take a lot more than a blanket for me to agree to be your fake girlfriend." A deliciously warm blanket.

"So does that mean you're considering it?"

I shook my head. "There's nothing you can offer me that will make me change my mind."

"How about you not being forced to relocate? Would that cause you to change your mind?"

I snorted a laugh. "How exactly do you expect to do that? The owner doesn't want my store in the building anymore because it won't fit with the new image."

"I might be able to change his mind."

"Right. *Might.* So what you're really saying is I help you and at the end of the day I'm still screwed?"

"No. That's not it at all." He stepped closer. "The blanket's now mine. And I don't care if it gets dirty." When I didn't say anything, he wrapped it around my shoulders. His finger accidentally brushed against my bare arm. And this time when I shivered, it was for an entirely different reason.

"Thank you."

"You're welcome. Now back to you being my fake girlfriend."

I shook my head again. "Not happening."

"How about if I can't get the owner to change his mind about your store by October first, I'll help you find another location that fits your needs."

"That's not enough. If I'm pretending to be your girlfriend, I won't be able to date a real man."

"The last I looked, I *am* a real man." He gestured at his shorts...and the noticeable bulge there. A bulge that wasn't so noticeable earlier.

A laugh burst free. "Sorry. I wasn't laughing at your manhood," I quickly said, doing my best to not start giggling.

He raised an eyebrow and my attempt to curtail my giggle failed.

"Are you doubting that I'm a real man?" His tone mocked but didn't condemn.

I wrapped the throw tighter around me and reined in my laugh. "Not at all. And that's not what I meant when I said I won't be able to date a real man. It means I can't date anyone else." Not that there was anyone else, but that was beside the point.

"Why not?"

I gave him my best *well-duh* expression. "I'm more of an exclusive dater. It doesn't matter if you're my fake boyfriend or real boyfriend, I can't date someone else at the same time. It wouldn't be fair to the other guy."

Travis chuckled—and the rich, hearty sound did nothing for my already taut nipples. "All right. What would it take for you to agree to be my fake girlfriend until hockey season begins, and to make up for not being able to date anyone else during that time? My helping you with your lease and what else...?"

I frowned. "When does hockey season begin?"

"October eighth."

Six weeks? That's doable, I guess. "I've been thinking of a way to promote the store. I would love to host a special evening event, possibly a fundraiser with the money going to the youth center. It would bring people into the store and benefit both the store and the kids at the center."

"You mean like my teammates dancing around onstage and removing their clothes stripper style?" His eyes widened as if he hadn't meant to say that but for some reason just blurted it out.

"Ohmigod, that would be perfect. I agree to those terms," I said in a rush. "You convince the owner of the building to let me stay *and* I'll host a special fundraiser event with your teammates going *Magic Mike*. They don't have to do the full monty. In fact, I'd prefer they didn't. But they do have to come pretty close to it."

I knew he would never agree to it—which was too bad, actually. It would've been fun watching a bunch of professional hockey players dancing onstage for an audience of lust-filled, screaming women. And more importantly, the money raised would have been great for the youth center.

"Okay," he said.

I blinked. I must have gotten water in my ears, because there was no way he would've agreed to all of that. "Wait— are you saying you'll do all of that if I pretend to be your girlfriend for six weeks?"

"I'm saying exactly that."

No—my mouth didn't flop open.

11

TRAVIS

What the hell was I thinking?

That thought echoed through my head like the bells of Notre Dame—repeating itself again and again until the words were too soft to hear.

There might have also been a few fucks thrown in for luck.

Somehow Granny joking about my teammates dancing half-naked at her birthday party and then me blurting it to Wes at lunch had gotten the thought lodged in my brain. So when Emma mentioned the fundraiser for the youth center, the words about my teammates going *Magic Mike* just tumbled from my mouth.

Why did I agree to her terms?

Because otherwise she would have helped me for the wrong reason. She wasn't being evicted like she'd been led to believe. So deceiving her that way felt as appealing as being knocked out of commission with diarrhea during a playoff game.

No, I hadn't missed the irony. I had no issue with

deceiving Granny when it came to having a girlfriend—but I couldn't do the same to Emma.

Maybe it had something to do with her growing up in the system.

Maybe it had something to do with her helping underprivileged kids.

Either way, she deserved more than me lying to her.

Did that mean I planned to come clean about Wes and the building?

Hell, no. I didn't want to risk her not helping me out. All she had to do was be my fake girlfriend, then Granny would be happy.

So there you had it—except for one minor issue.

Right. One I'm-so-totally-fucking-screwed major issue.

Now I had to convince some of my teammates that stripping in front of a group of screaming women was a brilliant idea. Correction. Make that stripping and *dancing* in front of a group of screaming women was a brilliant idea.

But this wasn't like dancing at a nightclub. It needed to be choreographed. And what did a bunch of hockey players know about that?

Emma's grin faded. "What if your grandmother doesn't believe I'm your girlfriend?"

"Why wouldn't she believe it?"

"I'm not a very good actress...mostly because I'm not good at lying." She lifted her shoulders in a *what-can-you-do?* shrug.

"Didn't you used to play make-believe as a kid?" I asked.

"Sure I did, but that was different."

"How so?"

"Well, I don't know about you, but I never kissed anyone when I was playing make-believe."

I laughed. "Good point. So you don't think you'll be convincing if you have to kiss me?"

Her face grew flushed and she shrugged again.

A drop of water dripped from her hair and trickled down her cheek. I brushed it away with my thumb. She gasped softly, the pulse in her neck beating fast. I pressed a light kiss against her lips.

She didn't pull away—always a positive sign.

With my mouth still tingling from the simple touch of my lips against hers, I kissed her again, this time a little harder. Unable to stop myself, I traced the tip of my tongue along her lower lip. She released a stuttering sigh.

In the back of my head, I was vaguely aware of a door clicking open. "Sorry to interrupt," a girl's voice said.

While I might have been a little dazed by the kiss, Emma wasn't. The way she leaped back and banged into the desk, you'd have thought she had been poked with a branding iron.

"Yes?" Emma asked, holding the blanket tightly around her, her wet dress clinging to her legs. Unfortunately, with the way she was gripping the blanket, I could no longer see her bra and pebbled nipples—the cause of my hard-on.

"Any idea when we're getting more Sensual Sunburst massage oil?" the girl in the doorway asked.

"I put in an order for it not long ago. Let me just look through the shipment that came in this morning. It might be there."

"Okay. I'll tell the customer you'll be right out."

The girl gave me a quick, curious glance, then left.

Emma turned around, scanning the office. It was only then that I noticed various sized shipping boxes stacked against the wall.

She walked to one pile, shifted a few boxes around, and placed one on the floor. She opened it and searched through the contents.

I guess whatever she was looking for wasn't there. She moved the box to the side and grabbed another one.

I crouched beside her. "You want any help?"

She studied me for a moment before finally nodding. "If the massage oils were included in this shipment, they'll be in one of these boxes." She removed another one from the pile and handed it to me. "Thanks."

While I opened it, she grabbed a third box and pulled the top open. We both searched through our respective boxes.

"What's the oil called again?" I asked, holding a bottle of vanilla sugar massage oil. According to the label the oil was self-heating and enhanced stimulation during intimate and erotic massages.

Not surprisingly, my cock thought this was a good idea, and hinted I should pick up a bottle.

Or two.

"Sensual Sunburst massage oil." Emma leaned over to see what I had in my hand. "Nope, not that one. Are there any other massage oils in the box?"

One by one, I pulled each of them out far enough to check the labels. "Yes, but none of these are what you're looking for."

I reached for another box similar to the ones we had been opening. "What made you decide to open the woman's version of an adult store?"

Emma huffed, then grumbled, "It's not an adult store."

"You sell sex toys and porn, right? That makes this an adult store."

She glared at me. Clearly I'd hit a sore spot. "But unlike an adult store, the sex toys and porn sold here aren't the hard-core ones designed for men. Plus they're in a separate part of the store. The majority of the merchandise here supports the concept of love and romance. It's not just about sex. It's about finding the right person and being an equal with them. It's about acceptance and being comfortable with who you are."

"So why this business instead of a bakery or a clothing store?"

She laughed. "As much as I like baking, I'm not a morning person. So that was a definite no when it came to opening a bakery. I'd rather be in bed at four a.m. than making bread and other baked treats."

"So why the love store?"

She shrugged, her attention on the closed box in front of her. "I guess that's because I grew up in the foster care system. It's not a very loving environment. I mean there are some good homes out there, but there are a lot of bad ones, too. The good news is you don't stay long in the bad ones. The bad news is you don't stay in the good homes for long either. Maybe I was just hoping the store would bring me luck when it came to finding someone to love me no matter what."

"Has it?"

"Not yet. But in the meantime, I get to watch people in love. I get to see mothers with their young kids, and I get to see how much they love them." Something about her voice on the last part gave me pause.

The sadness.

The emptiness.

The pain.

But that came as no surprise. Her parents had died and she was dumped in foster care. The same place I would have ended up if not for Granny.

"How old were you when your parents died?" I asked. I had a feeling she was a lot younger than I had been when mine died.

She chewed on her lip for a second, then opened the box. "My parents aren't dead. Or maybe they are now and I'm not aware of it."

"What do you mean?" And why did I have a feeling that

whatever had happened left her more damaged than she let on?

She shrugged again and searched through the box. "It's no big deal. They're no longer in my life, and I've long since moved on." She pulled out a bottle of massage oil. "Here it is."

Before I could say anything, she scrambled to her feet and disappeared out the office door.

When she didn't return after a few minutes, I left the room to search for her. The girl who had come looking for the massage oil was ringing it in, but Emma was nowhere to be seen. While I paid for the heart blanket, I asked her where Emma had disappeared to.

"She went home to change into dry clothes. I doubt she'll be long if you want to wait."

"That's okay. I'll catch up with her later."

First things first.

I needed to convince my teammates to help me out with the second part of my deal with Emma—the part that involved our clothes coming off in front of a live audience.

And for that, I needed all the luck I could get.

12

EMMA

By the time I returned to the store, after changing into dry clothes, Travis had already left. Fortunately. Yes, there might have been a good chance I regretted what I'd told him about my parents. Why couldn't I have left it at, "Why yes, Travis, my parents are dead."?

What was so wrong about him believing that? It sure was better than him knowing that I wasn't lovable and the people who counted the most had just given up on me.

Not that it mattered what he thought...because it wasn't like he cared. He wasn't looking to settle down with a woman and have a happily ever after. He just wanted to make his grandmother happy.

Had I expected him to give me the freaking brilliant idea for the fundraiser? Heck no. That alone made pretending to be his girlfriend worth it. Did I believe he would be able to convince the building owner to let my store stay? No. Not really. But at least some good would come from it when it came to the youth center.

I mean, hello, who wouldn't want to see a bunch of hockey players go *Magic Mike*?

After dinner, I turned on my laptop. I was due at the center soon but wanted to work on next week's column before I left.

Dear Dr. Lovejoy,

Instead of contemplating next week's question, my thoughts drifted to the one place they shouldn't have gone—to the kiss in my office.

I could have strangled Lisa when she walked into the room—or hugged her. I wasn't sure yet which was better. The kiss had been nothing more than a teaser of what I could expect if I'd let things go further.

Did I wish for them to go further? The correct answer was no...except that would be a lie. The way my body reacted to the tease of a kiss meant I was in deep trouble. Yes, I had kissed a lot of guys before. Okay, maybe not a lot, but enough to recognize the difference between those kisses and the one with Travis. His were in a whole other universe.

The problem? I hungered for more than that kiss. A whole lot more than Travis Hamilton was capable of giving. I longed to fall in love with a guy and for him to return the sentiment. That wasn't asking too much, right? I also longed for a guy who would prove to me that he would never give up on me—the opposite of everyone else in my life.

But maybe this deal with Travis wouldn't be so bad. I wasn't just talking about the fundraiser and the chance to keep my store where it was. If he was amenable to it, maybe the deal would include us kissing.

With all those perks rolled into one tidy package, what could go wrong?

Right—back to my column.

I've been seeing a guy for a few weeks and really like

him. But now I have to do the unthinkable...introduce him to my friends. My past boyfriends were jerks and because of that, my friends are insanely overly protective of me. What should I do?

Sincerely,

Finally Found A Good Guy

I mean, who hadn't dealt with overly protective friends when it came to boyfriends?

Had Hannah ever been that way? You'd better believe it. But that probably had more to do with the abuse I'd suffered in foster care than anything else. She never wanted to see me get hurt again. Which meant a guy had a better chance of surviving a face-to-face meeting with a Siberian tiger than if he pissed Hannah off.

Dear Finally Found A Good Guy,

The first thing you need to ask yourself is if this boyfriend is everything you think he is. Given your track record, there is a chance you've fallen into your regular pattern of being attracted to the wrong guy. If you are positive this guy is different, then you'll need to give it time before you introduce him to your friends. Make sure he is ready to stand by your side no matter what. A guy who is strong enough to survive whatever your friends throw at him is more likely to stick around for the long haul. In time, he will win your friends' trust. But if you throw him to the tigers too quickly, your relation-ship might not have a chance.

At least I didn't have a pattern. I mean, sure, most guys didn't make it to date #3, but some had. Hannah had a pattern—a pattern of not giving guys a chance beyond the first date.

Yes, the two of us were quite the pair.

"Will you play foosball with me?" was the first thing Nikki said when I entered the game room at the youth center. The foosball, ping-pong, and hockey tables awaited eagerly to witness my defeat.

I sucked at them all—but at least I was slightly better at foosball.

Nikki and I got into position. "How was school today?" I asked her. Nikki was seven years old and lived with her single mother.

"It was okay. We had a spelling test." She made a face, her eyes crossing comically.

I laughed. "Went that well, huh?"

"I hate spelling tests. They're sooo boring."

"I'll agree with you there." Fortunately, God created a life-changing invention called spell check that saved my ass more times than I cared to admit.

I pushed the ball through the hole in the table and the game began. It was only a minute before Nikki scored on me. As much as I would've liked to pretend I had let the ball slip past my goalie, it just wasn't the case.

"Do you have a boyfriend?" Nikki asked.

I shook my head. "No, I'm single."

She contemplated that for a moment. "Do you want a boyfriend?"

"You don't need one to be happy." How was that for a non-answer?

Those early Disney animated princess movies had it all wrong. They had little girls believing you could only be happy if Prince Charming came along and swept you off your feet. But who needed Prince Charming when you were a smart and independent woman? And it was my generation's job to teach girls that.

Yes, I took my responsibility very seriously.

"What about a girlfriend? Would that make you happy?"

The corners of my mouth twitched up. "No, I'm definitely into guys. But what I mean is that I run a successful store. *That* makes me happy."

"Momma's got a new boyfriend."

"Does he make her happy?"

Nikki and I could have almost been sisters. Only difference was that while her father wasn't part of her life, her mother loved Nikki. She willingly sacrificed everything to ensure her daughter felt loved.

Nikki grinned. "Very happy. Maybe he has a brother for you."

I pressed my lips together to keep from laughing out loud. "Don't worry, I'm doing fine without you checking if he has a brother." Or a cousin.

"You sure? Because I really don't mind." She said it so seriously, I couldn't help the laugh that burst free.

"I'm sure." Of course the memory of Travis kissing me picked that moment to flash in my brain.

He's probably not even that good a kisser, the reasonable voice in my head said. My lips sighed dreamily—or maybe that was me—and I asked the voice how it enjoyed living in delusional land. The kiss in my office might have been brief, but it had been knock-my-socks-off amazing.

Which left the one burning question I was afraid to ask: would a deeper, fuller kiss be the equivalent of rip-off-my-panties earth-shattering?

I guess I'd be finding out soon enough.

Only I would keep my panties firmly in place.

Which wouldn't be too hard—I just had to remember the humiliation I'd experienced back in high school.

What happened?

It was Travis's and my junior year. Our teacher had paired us together for our history project. Yes—there was a good chance I'd been slightly crushing on Travis since transferring to the school two months before that. He had been dating one of the popular girls until their recent breakup.

I was positive he wouldn't be interested in me. Unlike his ex-girlfriend, my clothes weren't fashionable or trendy. According to her, I wasn't good enough to walk the same planet she inhabited.

Nice, huh?

Another awesome lesson I had learned back then was that I was pretty much an open book. She had seen me staring at her ex-boyfriend and decided I was nothing but a creepy stalker. She even threatened to tell the school if I didn't keep away from him.

Anyway, back to the history project. The day I showed up to work on the project with Travis, my heart was beating something fierce—thanks to Kendra's threat and my crush on him.

And then I got the update. Travis wasn't going to be my partner. I had to do the project myself. How did I find this out? His ex-girlfriend had been more than delighted to share that with me. She always was a generous person. She also told me that Travis hadn't been interested in working with a reject like me. A reject who was part of the foster-care system.

The good news in all of this? I got top marks on the project.

The second piece of good news? I whipped his ex-girlfriend's ass on it. Of course, she took this like the spoiled brat that she was and accused me of cheating. The teacher ignored her. Apparently he wasn't her #1 fan, either.

So there you had it—the reason for why I shouldn't have liked Travis. Or at least why teenage me had been destroyed by Kendra's comments. But after spending time with him during the past few days, I was starting to question the truth of what she had told me.

Now that I thought about it, I didn't remember seeing Travis much during that final month of school. He had been there, but not as much as before. He'd barely been in our history class. But because of my teenage insecurities, I had been easy prey for Kendra and her cruelty.

Now satisfied that she didn't have to help me find a boyfriend, Nikki got down to business—which involved beating my ass for the next two games.

And while this was happening, I tried not to think about pretending to be Travis's girlfriend, tried not to think about the kiss he and I had shared. And I also tried not to think about how much I craved kissing him again.

Right—I would've had better success swimming across the Atlantic...to England.

13

TRAVIS

"Have you seen the movie *Magic Mike*?" I asked Mark Milone and Sean Burrows, two forwards from the Rock, along with Josh. We were in the gym where we trained during the off-season.

"Isn't that the stripper movie?" Josh asked.

"That's the one." I removed the clip from the bench press bar.

His mouth quirked up to one side. "Then that would be a definite no. Not my scene."

"Bridget dragged me to see it when we started dating," Mark said, his voice low, as though admitting this would be a major blow to his manhood.

Had I seen the movie? I might have watched a clip from it on YouTube. I might have also seen the climactic dance scene from *The Full Monty*.

Completely for research purposes, mind you.

"Never seen it," Mark said as I slid the twenty-pound metal plate onto the end of the bar. "Fortunately, Becca went to see it with her friends."

After securing the clip at the end of the bar, I lay on the

bench and positioned my hands shoulder-width apart. I had already loaded the other side of the bar with another twenty-pound plate.

"Why do you want to know?" Josh asked from behind my head.

"Because I thought we could do something like that to raise money for the James Bell Youth Center." I glanced up at Josh. It had nothing to do with him being the one who was spotting for me. It was because Josh and I were similar when it came to our grandparents raising us—or grandmother in my case. Except instead of Josh's parents dying in a car accident, his asshole father had played in the NHL and had been more interested in puck bunnies than his own wife and son. He abandoned them when Josh was a kid. A few years later, his mother did the same thing.

So if there was one thing Josh could appreciate, it was what a lot of those kids at the youth center were dealing with.

How did I know what they were dealing with? I had done research on the center after I made the agreement with Emma. It helped kids who were at risk because of their home environments.

"We?" Josh asked, amusement in his tone and the quirk of his mouth. "You expect us—as in you and me—to dance around onstage in our skivvies?"

Still lying down, I said, "No, not just you and me. Us—as in the four of us, and anyone else from the team who wants in."

Sean laughed. "You've got to be shitting us, right?"

"Do I look like I'm shitting you?"

"Not exactly," Mark said, looking like he was doing his best to not laugh, "but where the hell did you get the idea? I mean, what did you do—wake up this morning and think that stripping in front of a bunch of horny women would be a brilliant idea?"

"Trust me," I told him, "you don't want to know."

Mark glanced at both Josh and Sean. "What do you say, guys? Do we want to know where he got the idea from?"

Both guys nodded. "Yep, I'd be interested in finding out," Sean said.

"Me too," Josh added.

I sat up. This conversation wasn't one I wished to have while lying on the bench. "Well, if you have to know, it was my grandmother."

All three guys stared at me for a second, then burst out laughing.

"Are you seriously telling us your eighty-year-old grand-mother said she wants to see members of the team dance onstage in our underwear?" Mark said, the first one to get his laughter under control—if you could call it under control.

"Technically, she said shirtless, but I figured if we did something like on *Magic Mike*, we would raise more money for the center. Women go nuts for crap like that."

"And you think the team won't have an issue with us showing off our junk to a group of screaming women?" Sean asked, eyebrow raised.

"Well, Becca definitely will have an issue with it," Mark said.

"Yeah, I can't see Holly being too impressed, either," Josh piped in.

"We're not completely stripping," I said. "Our underwear stays on."

Sean frowned. "You're not making us wear a thong though, right? Those things look damn uncomfortable."

"Yet I bet you have no issue if your woman wears one."

The corner of Sean's mouth tugged up to one side. "Damn straight."

"No thongs." Because as hot as they looked on women,

there was no way I was wearing anything stuck between my ass cheeks.

"All right, so we've cleared that up," Josh said. "Except what do you know about choreographing a stripper act? Or do you have other skills beyond playing hockey and painting murals we're not aware of?"

Sean and Mark both looked at Josh. "He paints murals?" Sean asked.

Josh nodded. "He painted one in Lily's bedroom when Holly was pregnant. But painting and dancing aren't the same thing."

No shit.

"How hard can it be?" I asked.

Right—I didn't believe it was all that easy either. But it wasn't like we needed to dance like professionals. I mean, have you seen *The Full Monty*? Those guys definitely weren't professional dancers.

Of course they had something I didn't have—a choreographer. But I didn't mean the old guy in the movie who supposedly came up with the dance routine. They had someone behind the scenes. Someone who knew what the fuck they were doing.

"I don't suppose any of your wives have ever taken dance?" I looked at all three men.

Mark and Sean both gave a hell-if-I-know shrug. Josh looked like he would be more than happy to hightail it from the gym.

"Holly can dance?" I asked him.

He nodded. "She took lessons when she was a kid."

"Do you think she'd be interested in helping us? For charity?"

If Holly helped, how could Josh say no?

He shrugged, but unlike with the other two guys, I wasn't letting him off the hook. Not that I was letting any of them off the hook for long. "Can you call her and ask?"

A few minutes later, I had my answer.

"You owe me big-time for this," Josh said after getting off the phone with his wife.

"Does this mean she's in?"

"Yes, she's in. I believe her exact words once she stopped laughing were, 'I can't wait.' So I guess that means I'm in too?"

The grin on my face? I hadn't expected it to be so easy to find someone who could help with the actual dance.

But while that might have been the easy part, I knew the rest wouldn't be.

Christ, my plan to get Granny off my case about having a girlfriend had better work after all of this.

I looked at Mark and Sean. "So what do you say? Are you two in?"

They exchanged glances. "Yeah, I guess I'm in," Mark said at the same time as Sean's "Looks like it."

"So it's only going to be the four of us?" Josh asked.

"I'm hoping to convince a few more guys on the team to join us," I said.

SEVERAL HOURS AND A BUNCH OF PHONE CALLS LATER, I HAD recruited a total of eight teammates—including Josh— willing to join me onstage for the fundraiser. Unfortunately, not everyone on the team lived in San Francisco during the off-season, or else I might have gotten a few more yeses.

Now I just had to figure out the other details...like when and where we would be rehearsing.

At the thought of the planning involved in the event, a shudder rolled through me.

It was late afternoon by the time I returned to Emma's

store. She was at the back, where the boner-inducing, sexy underwear was kept.

"Are you planning to wear that on our first date?" I asked as she hung the black lacy number on the rack. The black lacy number that left nothing to the imagination—other than me visualizing what she looked like in it.

She rolled her eyes. "Since we're not actually dating, that would be a no."

Too bad. Although I guess it didn't matter—not unless I could convince her that a good fuck or two while we were "dating" would be worthwhile...for the sake of appearing authentic.

Would Granny find out about it? Hell no. And I was sure she wouldn't want to know all the details—unless it meant she would be getting a great-grandchild.

Did I see kids in my future one day? It wasn't on the agenda—nor was a wife. I just wanted to focus on what was important: my career.

But that didn't mean I wasn't a fan of kids. Far from it.

A woman walked to the fountain. Her lips moved but I couldn't hear what she was saying. Then she tossed money into the water. *Plop. Plop.*

She turned away from the fountain and walked over to the shelf containing mugs.

"People actually believe their wishes will come true just by throwing coins in the fountain?" I asked Emma. If only it was that easy. I'd do that in a heartbeat if it meant winning the Stanley Cup.

"It's not about wishing for something. It's about the possibility of finding love. Most people realize it's not as easy as simply tossing the coins into the water—but it's nice that they want to believe it. And thanks to them, I've raised enough money to buy paints for a mural at the youth center. Now I'm working on raising money to pay for an artist who can paint it. I would do it myself, but a monkey can draw a better stick man than me—which doesn't bode well when it comes to creating a mural."

"What kind of mural are you looking at doing?"

"Something bright and colorful, with rainbows and butterflies and dolphins."

"Why those?"

"They make me think of hope, especially the rainbow and butterflies. And the dolphin symbolizes protection and joy and inner strength and cooperation. I figure with everything some of those kids have gone through, that's all important to them."

Without giving her a clue of what I was thinking, I switched topics. "I rounded up volunteers for the *Magic Mike* part of the fundraiser."

Her eyes widened. "You found hockey players willing to dance on stage shirtless?"

"What—you didn't believe I could do it? I even found someone willing to help choreograph the routine."

Wow, Emma's eyes really could go wider. Time for me to make the most of this.

"And since I went beyond what you were expecting, it's no longer enough that you pretend to date me." I leaned in closer, my words warm against her ear. "I think we should also have sex." Hey, it was worth a try.

She gasped in a soft breath. "You do, do you? And why do you think that?"

Was it my imagination or did anyone else notice how she shifted closer to me so our bodies almost touched?

"Because nothing says, 'I'm happy in my relationship' like a satisfied look on your face. Then my grandmother will have no doubts that we're dating."

Emma turned her head to me. "Are your acting skills that bad? Is that really the only way she'll be convinced?"

"No, but it will help."

"And what if we can't convince her?"

"You sure ask a lot of questions," I said, fighting the urge to knot my fingers in her curls and kiss her senseless.

She smirked. "Yes, I do. And I can't help but notice you didn't answer the last one. What happens if we can't convince your grandmother that we're dating?" She stepped back and removed another hanger with sexy lingerie on it from the plastic crate on the floor.

Good question. "I won't talk to the building owner about your store."

"What about the fundraiser?"

"No, that's still happening. Which brings me to why I'm here. Where are you going to hold the event and when?"

"To be honest, I have no idea. I didn't believe you'd actually pull it off. I thought you were kidding."

I shortened the distance between us. "Sweetheart, I'm never kidding when I promise something."

I glanced around the store. "We'll need somewhere with a stage. I might have an idea. Give me a few days, and I'll see what I can come up with." I started to walk away but then tossed over my shoulder, "Our first date will be on Sunday. At Granny's apartment for dinner."

Then I walked out the door—to see Wes.

14

Dear Dr. Lovejoy,

I've just started seeing this girl. When is a good time to introduce her to my family?

Sincerely,

Am I Moving Too Fast

Dear Am I Moving Too Fast,

There are two things you should ask yourself: One—do your parents have any embarrassing childhood photos of you on the wall? Two—if they do, what are the chances you'll die of mortification if the girl sees them?

And let's not forget those equally embarrassing stories that moms can't wait to share with their child's new love interest.

When is a good time to introduce her to your family? When none of the aforementioned things matter to you. When you would gladly submit yourself to it all just so your family can finally meet your girlfriend.

15

EMMA

That Sunday, I was waiting outside my building when Travis pulled up in his SUV. As I clicked the seat belt into place, he handed me some papers. I took them and flipped through the pages.

Each one contained a different design with butterflies, rainbows, and dolphins. They were exactly what I had envisioned for the mural. "Where did you get these?"

"I drew them."

"You draw?"

"Apparently." He steered onto the street. "I can paint, too. At least I can paint murals. They aren't all that hard."

"You've painted murals?"

"Well, technically I've painted *a* mural. I did it for a friend of mine—for his daughter's bedroom."

Anyone else impressed?

Was I aware that he was an artist? Not at all. Not once in high school had I seen him draw or paint. But then it wasn't like I had spent any time with him. All I knew about him back then was that he played hockey and was popular at school.

"What do you charge?" I asked.

"Are you asking if I'll paint the mural at the youth center?"

I glanced back at the drawings. "In my convoluted way, yes—that's exactly what I'm asking." Before he could respond, I added, "These are great, by the way. I especially love the one with the butterflies flying across the sky, each trailing a different color behind them." Together they created the rainbow that reached halfway across the page. Underneath it, two dolphins were jumping out of the ocean as if excited by the sight of the rainbow.

"I could be persuaded to do it." His teasing tone was ripe with innuendo.

"And what exactly do I need to do to persuade you?" My body had a few suggestions of its own.

Nice try, body! Just because the heroes in romance novels knew how to make a woman's toes curl during an orgasm, didn't mean that mere mortal men had the same skill.

As most of the guys I'd been with had proven.

Naturally, the ache between my legs disagreed—pointing out that not all men were hopeless—and became that much more achy.

Hot date with Alejandro tonight? That sounded about right.

The ache pouted, wondering when it would ever get to experience a man's touch again.

"I'm sure you can figure something out," Travis said, his voice low, husky, and pure sensual male.

He really wasn't playing fair.

"I've got enough money for the paint," I said, "but what would something like this cost when it comes to your time?" From the looks of it, it would take quite a few hours or days to do it.

"I'll do it for free. For the kids. But I need your help."

"My help? Did you forget the part where I can't draw?"

"You don't need to draw. I'll do that. You can paint between the lines, right?"

"Yeah, I guess."

"Good. And I've got a place that can host the fundraiser."

"You do? Where?"

"The Unicorn."

The pub in my building. It had a stage where bands played several nights a week. "How did you swing that?"

"I have my ways, but I'd have to kill you if I told you." He smiled what had to be the sexiest smirk on the planet. I had no doubt whatsoever that he used it often to get into women's beds. Too bad he couldn't use it for a greater good...like solving world hunger or creating everlasting peace.

"So this is really happening?"

"Yes, it's really happening."

Now it was *my* turn to smirk. "I could kiss you for that."

He chuckled. "I'm all for that. But how about we save it for my grandmother's benefit?"

My heart rate picked up at his suggestion. I had no idea why. "I have to kiss you in front of your grandmother?" That squeaky voice? Completely your imagination.

"Yep, in front of Granny. But to be convincing, we have to make it look like we sneaked off somewhere to kiss and got caught."

A laugh burst from between my lips. "Put a lot of thought into this, did you? Or have you had that many fake girlfriends that you speak from experience?"

The corner of his mouth twitched. "No, you're definitely the first. I'm a virgin at this."

"That makes two of us." And because that didn't quite sound the way it had in my head, I hastily added. "I mean at being a fake girlfriend."

The voice in my head barked a laugh. No, I hadn't

sounded ridiculous at all, especially since it didn't matter whether I was a virgin when it came to sex. He and I weren't going there.

I ignored the booing from my girlie parts.

Forty minutes later, Travis parked his car in the visitors' parking lot of a low-rise apartment building.

"This is where Fanny lives?" The golden stucco, Mediterranean-style balconies, and well cared for garden all gave the place a welcoming feel.

"Yes, her and the other two troublemakers."

"Troublemakers?"

"Her two friends who you've already met. Hazel and Abigail" He glanced up at the building, a slight frown on his face.

I snickered. Yeah, I could almost see them being labeled as troublemakers. But if I had a grandmother, those three were exactly what I'd wish for her to be like.

"I swear they're convinced that they're twentysomething college students," Travis said. "In fact, I'd hate to see what they'd be like if they were." He faked a considerable shudder and I laughed.

We exited the car and headed toward the building. Travis reached for my hand. My sweaty hand. *How nice!*

"Can your grandmother see us out here?" I asked—because that was the only explanation I had for why Travis would want to hold my hand.

"No—but her eyes can. Their apartment is on this side of the building."

I laughed again. "Ah, she has spies."

"Pretty much."

From the way Fanny was beaming at us when she opened her door a few minutes later, it was clear her underground spy network had alerted her to our arrival.

"I'm so excited to see you again, Emma," she said, waving

us in. "When Travis told me you two were dating, I couldn't have been happier." She winked at me.

Yeah—I had no idea what that was about either.

I found out a moment later when she added, "That fountain of yours clearly is magical."

Right. Her wish. The one where she had asked for Travis to hurry up and get married and give her great-grandkids before she died.

I smiled at her while feeling about two inches tall, then glanced at Travis to see if he felt as guilty about his lie as I did. My gaze met his confused one. Well, at least he had no idea about her wish—not that he believed in the fountain's magical powers.

"Travis," she said, "why don't you show Emma the view from the balcony?"

"Okay," he replied and started walking down the short hallway. I followed after him, stealing quick glances at the photos covering the walls.

"Are you in any of those?" I pointed at them as we strolled past.

"A few. Mostly when I was a kid."

I stopped abruptly. "Show me."

Fanny didn't give him a chance to respond and pointed out some of his photos. "...and there he is when he was five years old," she said. Behind me, Travis groaned.

Five-year-old Travis was standing on the beach, searching for something in the sand. The wind was blowing his brown hair about, and grains of sand peppered his skin.

"Ohmigod, you're adorable."

"All right, enough of the family photos," he said, nudging me forward. "Time for me to show you the view."

Grinning at his obvious embarrassment, I entered the living room.

It was small and filled with an eclectic mix of modern

furniture and antiques. The brown leather sofa and recliner were facing the large-screen TV. Everything else—the side cabinets with glass covered bookcases, the coffee table, the end table—was a combination of dark rustic wood, lacy doilies, and decorative plates with hand-painted landscapes and cities on them.

Travis opened the sliding glass door and stepped onto the balcony with me trailing behind him. The fresh ocean breeze kissed my face as I appreciated the spectacular view.

"Wow," was all I could say. I hadn't paid much attention when Travis had driven us here, so I didn't realize until now how close we were to the ocean. It stretched out on the horizon, with houses and trees partly blocking the view. But even then, you could still see the water glimmering from the low angle of the sun.

I placed my hands on the metal railing. Without looking, I could feel Travis close behind me. He wrapped his arms around me in a loose yet intimate embrace.

There was a slight chance my body might have melted against him. All for Fanny's benefit—or so I told myself.

"Impressed, huh?" he murmured in my ear.

Heat rushed to my core, getting the situation all wrong. My body and I really needed to have a heart-to-heart.

"Very impressed," I whispered.

Travis brushed my hair aside, exposing my neck, and traced his lips along my skin. The stubble on his jaw caressed me and I sucked in a soft breath.

His mouth moved to my earlobe and he nibbled the shell of my ear.

That moan, "Oh, God"? It might have been me.

Purely on instinct, I turned around in his arms. Before I could say anything, his mouth caught mine in a kiss.

And not just any kiss. He tugged on my lower lip with his

teeth, teasing me. How could I not open up? Then the next thing I knew, our tongues were getting acquainted.

As they slid together, exploring, dancing, my hands moved to Travis's hair. I knotted my fingers in his soft strands and a desperate moan slipped from my lips.

I couldn't remember a kiss being this heart-stoppingly delicious—and I was just his fake girlfriend. What would it be like if we were really dating?

I was afraid to ask.

Travis's hand moved to my lower back and he pressed me closer. The movement caused my head to tilt back, allowing him to deepen the kiss.

We kept kissing...until the loud noise of a seagull's shriek jerked me back to the present. Startled, I pulled away, slightly dazed from the kiss, and stared at Travis.

"Wow," I said, echoing my earlier sentiment.

The corner of his mouth slid up to one side. "Impressed, huh?"

I blinked myself out of my Travis-induced trance. "Not at all."

Mischief gleamed in his eyes. "I think you're lying."

"And I think someone has an overinflated ego. You might want to get a doctor to check it out."

Travis laughed. "Something tells me I'll live."

A movement from the balcony door caught my attention, and I turned in time to see Fanny moving away, trying to be inconspicuous.

"You think she bought the kiss?" I asked, keeping my voice low so she couldn't hear me. If she hadn't believed that the kiss was genuine, I was royally screwed—especially since I couldn't be any more convincing than that.

Even my body was fooled.

Except now it craved more—a helluva lot more.

"There's one way to find out." He grabbed my hand and

led me back into the living room. Fanny was busy pretending to set the dinner table, which looked exactly the same as when we had first entered the room.

"You have a lovely view," I said.

The grin on her face from earlier? That had nothing on this one. "Yes, it's a very lovely view."

Why did I have a feeling we weren't talking about the same view?

"Dinner is ready. Emma, why don't you sit there." She pointed at a chair. "Travis can sit in his usual spot."

Travis pulled my chair out for me and I sat. He took the one next to mine.

"Would you like red wine?" Fanny asked me.

"That would be nice, thank you."

But instead of Fanny pouring the wine, Travis did the deed. He left Fanny's glass empty while giving her a long look. Fanny let out a suffering sigh that was more on the humorous side of things.

"How is it that you two started dating?" she asked us after she'd finished serving us the meat loaf, roasted potatoes, and vegetables.

And pickles. Apparently Fanny really liked pickles.

I flashed Travis a devious grin, wrapped up neatly with a bow. "Why don't you tell her, sweetheart? You always tell the story best."

Yes, I might have thrown him under a bus, but it was so worth it. Neither of us had thought to come up with a story about how we started dating.

"Not a problem, pumpkin." He gave a strand of my hair a slight tug. That smirk? No, it wasn't sexy. It was even more devious than the smile I had just given him. And for the record, my hair wasn't pumpkin orange. It was more like a bright auburn.

He turned back to Fanny. "After we spent the third day

driving around the city, looking at possible new locations for the store, Emma invited me out for a drink. Well, turns out she can't hold her alcohol very well. She'd had only one drink, but when I returned from the bathroom, I found her on the table, declaring to the pub why she liked me."

I took a sip of wine.

"Apparently, she really likes my ass."

The wine went the wrong way and I began coughing.

"Are you okay, pumpkin?" Travis asked, his smile even more devious than before.

I nodded, still coughing. "Sorry. The wine went the wrong way," I managed to say weakly before grabbing my glass of water.

"You know who has a really nice backside?" Fanny asked, not fazed at all by what Travis had told her. 'That Chris Hemsworth boy." She said it so matter-of-factly, you would've thought she and her friends discussed the topic on a regular basis.

"Ryan Gosling isn't too bad either," she added, and Travis groaned.

Flashing him an amused grin, I slipped in my vote. "While I have to agree with you on both choices, Ryan Reynolds's as—butt is mighty fine, too." And then, because I couldn't resist it, I patted Travis's cheek. "But not as fine as yours, sweetheart."

Truth? I did like his ass—more than I should. Second truth? It was hotter than the asses of the other three men combined.

But I wasn't about to admit that to Travis.

"Anyway," he said, clearly pretending the current conversation wasn't happening, "after Emma's declaration to the entire pub, how could I not ask her out? And the rest, as they say, is history. She and I are now dating exclusively."

Did it sound like he almost choked on those last two words? That alone made the charade all the more fun.

"Well, I think this deserves a toast." Fanny picked up her water and waited for us to pick up ours. "To the happy couple. May your days and nights together be blissful and plenty."

My girlie parts sang out, "Here, here," in chorus. *Traitors.*

And then Fanny added, "Difficult roads often lead to beautiful destinations."

Yeah—I had no idea what she was talking about, either. It just came out of nowhere. Travis gave her a *that's-nice* smile and went back to eating as though she hadn't said anything—which was pretty much what Fanny did, too.

The rest of the dinner went well. Fanny was funny and highly entertaining. Or maybe the way she constantly embarrassed Travis was highly entertaining. She also said a few more random phrases like, "Choose kindness and laugh often," and "I'm not what has happened to me. I am what I choose to become." Apparently the last one was from Carl Jung. Unlike the other ones, that quote hit close to home.

The only thing that wasn't entertaining was the level of guilt clogging my insides like day-old constipation. The more I got to know Fanny, the worse I felt about Travis's and my deception.

Was the guilt enough for me to tell her the truth? Hell, no. I couldn't afford to lose my store. It meant everything to me. Plus, she was happy. That was what Travis wanted. That was what I wanted. For Fanny to be happy.

Was it too late to become Catholic, go to confession, and say a hundred Hail Marys (or whatever it was that Catholics said after they'd sinned)?

Okay—how about I call that Plan B?

On the way back to my apartment, Travis and I discussed the mural some more.

"I'll talk to Amelia tomorrow and finalize the details," I said.

We had already discussed how we needed to use two coats of blue paint on the wall, to represent the sky. That would be our first project.

"So, why does your grandmother say all those random comments? You know, the positive affirmation ones?"

He shrugged. "I have no idea. She started doing it a few years ago. She likes to write them in a notebook every time she sees one. Abigail gave her positive affirmation toilet paper for Christmas one year. After that, Granny kept saying them out loud. But because the sayings never fit what she was talking about, she got into the habit of blurting them just because she could."

I barked a laugh. "That is the funniest and most adorable thing I've ever heard."

Travis pulled up in front of my building.

"Thanks for offering to help me with the mural," I said, and leaned in to give him a quick peck on the cheek. But at the last second, he turned his head and my lips—the heat seeking missiles that they were—landed on his mouth.

And apparently that wasn't enough for them. They parted and my tongue welcomed Travis's. A hunger for him consumed me and I deepened the kiss. The ache between my legs begged me to straddle his hips and rub it against his length. It ignored the part about the steering wheel being in the way.

I reminded it of our hot date with Alejandro.

All right—maybe I was crazy thinking that would be enough to appease it.

Silly me.

I pulled slightly back, breath ragged.

"You're welcome," he said. The amusement in his tone? I

had a feeling he was talking about the kiss and not why I had really been thanking him.

I quickly escaped his car and didn't even give him a second glance as I headed to the building. But while I might have been acting nonchalant about the kiss in the car and the one back at Fanny's apartment, the thoughts powering through my brain were the furthest from nonchalant as you could get.

Somehow I managed not to stumble as I walked up the pathway to the entrance.

Once inside the building, I hightailed it up the stairs to the third floor and entered my apartment.

"Hi, I'm home," I called out to the emptiness.

I really needed to get a pet. Like a fish. Or a snail.

I made a beeline to my bedroom.

The plan? Happy time with Alejandro.

But the ache between my legs wouldn't cooperate and gave me the silent treatment—as in no orgasms for me. They didn't even materialize when I thought back to when Travis kissed me on the balcony. That alone should have been enough—but the mutinous ache refused to budge even an inch.

Eventually giving up, I returned a dejected Alejandro to my bedside drawer.

Now what was I supposed to do?

I ignored the whispered suggestions about Travis the ache threw my way.

16

TRAVIS

What's the worst thing about musicals? They're unrealistic. I mean seriously, how many people do you know who would be strolling down the street with their friend one minute and dancing the next? In the real world, life isn't like how it's portrayed in musicals. Why? Because behind those movies are a choreographer, talented dancers, and a shitload of practicing. That is how they make everything look so effortless.

Which was the exact opposite of how Josh my seven teammates, and I looked as we tried to do the simple—in Holly's opinion, not mine—dance routine.

We hadn't even made it past the first few steps before we were crashing into each other.

"It's turn to the left on the third step," Holly said, her Aussie accent still as strong as it was when I met her two years ago. She smiled in a way that was supposed to be encouraging. And it might have worked—if we were five-year-olds.

We knew we sucked.

Holly didn't have to tell us that.

The difference between Holly and Coach Fusco? Fusco would have been yelling at us to get our act together.

Fortunately, skating without landing on your ass, even with the other team body checking us, was a lot easier than dancing.

We were in the dance studio that Holly had lined up for us so we could practice during the next few weeks. The friend of one of her colleagues owned the place and was happy to let us rent the space before the evening classes began.

"All right, let's try that again," Holly said and demonstrated the steps once more.

By the third time, we didn't come off quite as incompetent as we had in the beginning. But it was still close.

"Hopefully by the time we tear off our shirts," Mark said, "the audience will forget how bad we are."

"Someone care to remind me again why we're torturing ourselves this way?" Sean asked.

"Christ, you sound like a bunch of fucking old ladies." That was Josh.

"At least then we would know what the heck we're doing," Sean pointed out.

Holly wrapped her arms around Josh's waist. "Honestly, you guys are doing great. And like Mark said, the women won't care if you aren't perfect onstage. You're just there to fulfill their sexual fantasies."

"Don't tell that to Bridget," Sean said. Mark nodded in agreement as did the two other married players.

The rest of us thanked God we were single. Or at least I was positive the other three single players were thinking that. The show was scheduled prior to the beginning of hockey season, which meant Emma and I would still be pretending we were an item. And since Granny and her cronies were planning to attend the event, it meant I wouldn't get to appreciate the benefits of being single when it came to some of the horny women in the audience.

What did the Rock organization think about what we were doing? Yes, I did have a meeting with several members, including the general manager. Because the proceeds were going to charity, they were on board with it—as long as we followed a lengthy list of rules.

The #1 rule? Keep it family friendly.

No lap dancing.

No grinding.

No bare asses.

No removal of our pants—unless we were wearing family friendly shorts underneath.

Even though the guys and I were still a long way from nailing the first part of the dance, Holly taught us what came next. An hour later, we were dripping with sweat and looked like we had just finished playing the third period of a playoff game.

The door opened and in walked Emma, followed by a woman who I recognized as Josh and Holly's nanny.

Yes—the woman who resembled a fifty-year-old male boxer. And equally as attractive.

But as scary looking as she was, she was amazing with their eighteen-month-old daughter. Lily adored her. Holly adored her. So all was great.

Josh walked to the woman, grinning in the way I'd only seen him do with his daughter, and scooped Lily out of her nanny's arms.

"How's my big girl doing?" he asked her in the singsong voice he saved for his daughter. But it worked for him—and I didn't just mean with Lily.

Apparently babies and cute toddlers were babe magnets. I kid you not. If a woman walks around with a baby strapped to her chest, guys take a wide berth around her—as if afraid the baby will turn into a repulsive two-headed monster.

Not so when a man has a baby strapped to his chest. Then every baby-craving female in a ten-mile radius will hone in on the pair. Although in most cases, the man isn't looking for a baby mama. He already has one.

But hanging out with your friend while he's carrying around a babe magnet doesn't mean you'll get lucky once the girls realize he isn't single. It doesn't matter if most times you have no trouble getting laid, hanging out with your friend and his child is an instant babe repellent for all us kid-free men.

I know—completely unfair.

Emma joined me and I introduced her around—including to Holly, Josh, and Lily.

Yes, I noticed the similarities between Holly and Emma too, with the bright auburn hair. But as hot as Holly was, she didn't incite the same reaction in me that Emma did.

Emma had a sexy, adventurous look about her, thanks to her mess of curls. It made me believe that she'd be a wildcat in bed.

My cock twitched, seconding that assessment.

"How's it going?" Emma asked us.

"Not bad at all." Could she tell I was lying? Hopefully not.

Although from the way the guys squirmed at the question, she might have guessed I was being less than truthful.

"Can I see?"

"See what?" Yes, I knew exactly what she was asking.

"The routine."

A smirk grew on my face. "Impatient much? Hate to see what you're like at Christmas."

"Santa and I have an understanding that he never lets me wait."

"Sorry, sweetheart, but I'm going to have to disappoint

you this one time. But I promise you, this will be the only time I'll disappoint." No hidden innuendos there at all.

No siree.

Her gaze dropped momentarily to my package. "I'll have to take your word for it."

"You do that." I winked.

"So," Mark said in his okaaay-moving-right-along voice, "are we done here?" He looked at Holly, his expression hopeful.

"Yes, we'll resume tomorrow where we left off.'

With that, the guys grabbed their stuff and bailed.

"Aren't you just adorable?" Emma said to Lily, who was now in her mother's arms while Josh toweled the sweat from his body.

Lily giggled her agreement.

Emma grinned at her, but that wasn't the only emotion on her face. I recognized the yearning in her eyes. She longed for what Holly had—a man and a child.

Fortunately, it wasn't the same expression she leveled at me. Did I feel bad that our deal kept her from finding a man in the meantime?

Not at all. For some strange reason, satisfaction paraded through me. Besides, it wasn't like she would be my fake girl-friend forever. It was only for four and a half more weeks. Surely that wouldn't make a difference in her long-term plans.

After she finished gushing over Lily, I asked her if we were still on for tomorrow. We'd planned to paint the wall blue where the mural would be located at the youth center.

"I'll be there," she said, smiling.

For a second, I thought she was going to kiss me like she had in the car the other day, but instead, she and Holly started talking.

I'd be lying if I said I wasn't disappointed that she didn't even try.

And I'd be lying if I said I wasn't contemplating what it would feel like to be burrowed deep inside her. Unfortunately for my cock and me, Emma was the one who had the final say in that.

And from the way things were currently going, it looked like my cock and I would continue to be disappointed...for a very long time.

17

___

EMMA

After leaving Travis and his friends at the dance studio, I met Hannah at the hardware store so I could buy the paints for the mural.

"You know," she said as I pushed the shopping cart up the aisle, "first comes love, then comes marriage, then comes Emma with a baby carriage. But nowhere in the song does it say, 'First comes the guy stripping off his clothes in public.' "

"What the heck are you talking about? I'm not in love." Lust, maybe.

Definitely lust.

She laughed. "Didn't say you were. *Yet.* But hello, I've seen the guy. How can you not be interested?"

"Looks don't mean everything," I said, stopping in front of the paint I was searching for. "A guy might look hot but end up being a jerk."

"So true." Hannah was more than familiar with this type of man. She was the epitome of a jerk magnet. I was just the magnet for boring. "But let's examine for a moment what we know about Travis. First—he didn't have to but he's helping you paint the mural at the youth center, *and* he's doing it for free. Doesn't sound like a jerk to me."

"True, but—"

"Second—even though he didn't have to, he and his teammates will be stripping in front of a bunch of horny women to raise money for charity."

"Well, they're not exactly stripping all the way. Their hockey team won't allow it."

She flicked her hand in the air as though batting away an annoying housefly. "That's neither here nor there. He's still doing it."

"Also true."

"And let's not forget he could've just told his grandmother to bugger off about his love life. But instead of hurting her feelings, he's pretending to date you so she's happy for the time being. And he has to sacrifice sex for the next four and half weeks because of this."

I snickered. "Yes—the poor baby. The mayor should erect a statue in Travis's honor because of his sacrifice." Yep, the pun had been intentional.

Hannah burst out laughing. "You know what you need?"

"Paints. And some paintbrushes." I grabbed a paintbrush from the shelf. "Plus the rollers."

"You need to get laid." Of course she said this as a woman who looked to be a day short of one hundred years old approached us.

I flinched. "I don't need to get laid," I said, practically hissing the words, but low enough so the woman wouldn't hear me.

Only I suspected I wasn't all that successful. She turned to us with the same impish gleam in her eyes that I had seen with Fanny. "Everyone needs to get laid, young lady. Some of us just aren't so lucky to get it anymore."

"And there you have it," Hannah said, the corners of her

mouth twitching. "It's official—you need to get laid. While you still can."

"What do you mean while I still can? I've got plenty of time."

"You got four and half weeks left with Travis. That will be gone before you know it, and then you'll regret you waited so long."

"Oh, please, there'll be other guys after him."

Hannah raised an eyebrow. "Really? Because I can't remember the last time you actually went out with a guy."

"That doesn't mean I won't go out with anyone after Travis and I end things."

The woman listened avidly to our conversation, her head moving back and forth between us as we spoke. "Is your boyfriend moving away?" she asked.

"No," I replied without thinking how that sounded. "It's only a temporary thing." Yes—because that had sounded so much better. I mentally groaned.

"Temporary? Is he not a very nice young man?"

Hannah chuckled. "No, I'd say he is a nice young man. At least so far he seems that way."

"It's complicated," I added.

"What relationship isn't complicated?" the elderly woman said. "And sometimes those are the best ones."

"Not in this case." And because the woman must've had magical powers, the words I'd never even told Hannah broke free. "I was in the same high school as him for a few months. He was supposed to be my project partner for one of our classes, but because he didn't want to work with me, he got out of it and I had to do all the work myself."

Was that cathartic—laying it all out to a stranger? Nope, not at all.

I wasn't sure why I'd even said it. I had already made peace with what had happened.

"Why do you believe he didn't wish to work with you?" the woman asked.

"Because I was living in foster care. And not a great one at that. I didn't have fashionable or new clothes. Not like his friends at the time had. My clothes were falling apart and out of date. His girlfriend used to make fun of me and call me a homeless street bum." *And she still called me that after they broke up.*

Did I need a violin to play along as I explained it to the woman and Hannah? No, it was all good. Kendra couldn't hurt me anymore.

And really, when I thought about it, it all came down to Kendra, not Travis. Her words still cut deep. For years after, I'd felt undeserving...unworthy.

"Oh, honey," the woman said, "I doubt he didn't want to do the project with you because you were in foster care."

"And I bet if that were the case now," Hannah said, eyes glistening, "he wouldn't still feel that way. Not with everything he's doing to help you when it comes to the youth center."

I smiled softly. "I know." And I did.

"Can I ask how you ended up in the system?" the woman asked.

"My mother got bored of being my mom. She walked away one day and never came back."

"And your father?"

I shrugged. "Never knew him. Other than his accidental sperm donation, he wasn't in the picture and my mom never talked about him. It was like he never really existed."

I glanced behind me, almost expecting to find a comfy leather couch. *Attention ladies and gentlemen. We have free psychotherapy in aisle five.*

Did I want to run and hide from the truth? Yes—but somehow telling a complete stranger my dark secrets felt good. I had never shared them with anyone before, not even with Hannah.

"How many foster homes did you live in?"

"Seven."

"Boyfriends? Other than your current one, how many have you had?"

I glanced at Hannah and almost laughed at her please-don't-let-her-ask-me-these-questions expression.

"A serious one back in college. Since then, I've been dating guys but I haven't met the right one yet."

"And how did it end with the boy back in college?"

That's right, everyone—Dr. Lovejoy was a fraud.

Fortunately, the elderly woman had no idea about my alter ego. What did Hannah think about it, given both our love lives sucked? She got a huge kick out of it.

"I gave him my V-card...I mean my virginity. He couldn't get away quick enough after that." Even Olympic sprinters couldn't move that fast.

The woman's eyes were free of sympathy—always a bonus. Instead, understanding lit them from within. Only I had no clue what she understood.

"You said you've dated other men. Is it usually just one date or more than one?"

"Depends on the guy."

"They rarely last more than three dates," Hannah piped in. Her expression then morphed into an Oops-didn't-mean-to-do-that look.

I nodded at the woman's questioning gaze. *Yes, it's true.*

"Friends? Other than..." She indicated to Hannah.

"Hannah's my best friend. We lived in foster care together when we were seventeen. And I have a few other friends." Like Kate.

"Are you close or are they friendly acquaintances you hang out with from time to time?"

"I guess more like the latter. We're all busy, so we don't get together as much as we would like." That was one of the joys of owning your own business. No time.

"Seems to me that you have a fear of being abandoned again like your father and mother did to you. Like your ex-boyfriend did to you. Which means you tend to avoid long-term relationships. Other than with Hannah, you don't let yourself get too close to people."

I shook my head. "That's not true. I don't fear being abandoned, I don't avoid getting close to people, and I do want a long-term relationship."

Hannah's expression said the opposite. She agreed with the woman.

And here you've been judging Travis and his fear of commitment when you're no better than he is, a know-it-all voice in my head pointed out.

Denial twisted inside me. I pushed it aside.

"Are you telling me I'll never have a boyfriend again?" Wow, talk about depressing. Maybe it was time to do a little research. I had always longed for a big chubby cat. Could you be a crazy cat lady with only one cat? Or did you need an army of them to qualify for the title?

"But you already have a boyfriend, dear," the woman said.

"Only for four and half more weeks."

"Because it's complicated?"

I nodded. "Very complicated." I didn't want to imagine what she would think if she found out I was just Travis's fake girlfriend. "So what can I do to fix me? I don't suppose I'll get lucky and there's a pill I can take?" Or maybe my fairy godmother would finally pay me a visit and make everything better.

No, I didn't believe that would happen either.

Or maybe this woman *was* my fairy godmother. But

instead of saying, "Bibbity bobbity boo," the modern-day version just doled out advice.

"You might consider therapy."

My heart sank in my chest, knowing I would never do that. For one, I didn't have time.

And what if someone found out Dr. Lovejoy yearned to fall in love but was afraid of being dumped again? Because with my track record, it was bound to happen. It wasn't like there was a twelve-step program for people like me.

"You'll have to learn to trust that people who care about you won't hurt you like you've been hurt in the past," the woman said. "And that will take a very special young man to earn that trust—because it won't be easy."

Which meant after Travis was no longer in my life, there would be no more chances to get laid.

Yeah, yeah—I know. That wasn't exactly what she meant. But the reality? I didn't do one-night stands. And given how my body was currently on strike when it came to orgasms and Alejandro, I was seriously screwed—and not in the good way.

I thanked the woman for her advice. After she left us, Hannah and I found the paint and supplies I needed. Neither of us spoke much—both deep in thought about what the woman had told us.

At least that's what I assumed Hannah was dwelling on, due to her sudden subdued self.

What else was I thinking about?

Travis. This afternoon. Shirtless.

18

EMMA

The following evening, Travis and I were busy preparing the wall at the youth center that we would be painting. Normally the room would've been filled with kids, but their activities had been temporarily relocated so Travis and I could work.

Or at least try to work. All I could think about was the elderly woman's psychoanalysis of me in the hardware store.

Okay, truthfully? I was still dwelling on how Travis might be my only opportunity to ever get laid again.

I mean, sure there was always a chance I would meet a guy and trust he wouldn't hurt me like so many others had. But there was also a chance a plane would land on me while I crossed the street. And let's just say the odds were looking more favorable when it came to the plane squishing me.

"How did you get the scar on your chin?" Travis asked.

The scar in question? It was a small scar that one of my foster mothers had given me. I was fourteen at the time and she accused me of seducing her husband. No idea why she had believed that. The guy made a sumo wrestler look anorexic.

"You know the superstition about how stepping on a crack will break your mother's back? Turns out, tripping on a crack will cause you to cut your chin."

Well, more like having someone jab you with a broken beer bottle, but close enough.

"Do you have any scars?" I asked. At least he couldn't see the ones on my chest.

He laughed. "I'm a hockey player. Scars are part of the game. Mine aren't too bad. Not like some of my teammates."

"And at least you still have all your teeth,' I said as I dipped the roller into the paint. I glanced at him, doing my best to ignore how hot he looked in his shorts and the T-shirt stretching nicely across his chest. "You do have all your teeth, right?"

I hadn't noticed any missing when I kissed him—not that I'd done a thorough inspection with my tongue the other day.

"Yep—definitely still have them all." He was quiet for another few minutes as we continued painting. "Can I ask why you ended up in foster care if your parents didn't die? But if you don't want to tell me, that's fine, too."

"There's not much to tell. Never met my father and my mom wasn't cut out to be a mother. She abandoned me when I was eight."

"Shit," he muttered.

I laughed, the sound filled more with humor than the bitterness that had once kicked me hard in the ass. "Shit's about right."

Time to lighten things up. "How about we play a game?"

"What kind of game?"

"Kind of like Truth or Dare." Although I had no idea what dares I would make Travis do.

"All right. You go first."

"What's your favorite ice cream?"

"Christ, Emma, you really know how to ask the scary

questions." The sexy smirk, which the ache between my legs greatly appreciated, slid back on his face.

"Just answer the question, sir, or you'll have to do the dare."

"Oooh, now you really have me scared."

I lifted my chin. "You should be scared. And you do realize there's a time limit, right? Sounds to me like you're stalling. Is this your way of saying you don't like ice cream? Because if that's true, I'll need to rethink this whole fake girl-friend arrangement."

"Chocolate."

I expected him to ask me a similar question. Did he? No—he went in for the kill. "The first time you had sex?"

"Are you talking about how old I was?"

"How about the who and the where?"

"That's two questions."

"Which I combined into one. You didn't specify in the rules I couldn't do that."

"That's because it's a given you can't." *Roll. Roll. Roll.*

Travis chuckled. "You might want to put some paint on your roller."

Slight technicality.

I dipped it into the paint, taking the time to ensure it didn't have too much on it.

"You're stalling," Travis said. "Is this your way of saying you're still a virgin?" He sounded like he believed that as much as he believed in the Easter Bunny.

"I'm not stalling." I straightened and returned to the wall. "It was my college boyfriend and we were in the apartment Hannah and I shared."

"Sounds like fun." Nope—he clearly didn't believe that either. "Your turn."

"What's the most exciting place you've had sex?" *Oh crap!* Did I really just ask him that? What the hell was I thinking?

Oh, right—apparently I wasn't.

He actually had to contemplate it for a moment. Either he was trying to remember such an event, or there were so many to choose from.

My bet was on the latter.

"That would have to be several years ago. A group of us were hiking in the woods near where we were camping. One of the girls we had met the previous night and I slipped away." The wistful smirk on his face made me wonder if there was more to it than that. Maybe they'd had hot sex while swinging from a tree. Like Tarzan.

What—Tarzan didn't have sex with Jane while they swung from tree to tree? Sure, he did.

"What about you?" Travis asked, breaking me from my thoughts about sex with Tarzan.

"What about me?"

"What's the most exciting place you've had sex?"

Double crap! "You can't ask the same question I just asked," said the woman who had been fine if he asked me the question about my favorite ice cream flavor.

"Says who?"

"It's in the rules?"

His eyes sparked with amusement and challenge. "Prove it to me."

"Fine," I said with a huff. "I'll answer your question."

Now here lay the problem. The only place I'd ever had sex was in bed.

No, that didn't sound lame at all.

I strained to remember an exciting place mentioned in the romances I'd read over the past few years. Some had been erotic romances. Nothing got a girl in the mood for a night with their own Alejandro than a steamy erotic romance. Read one of those sexy scenes before turning on your orgasm buddy, and you were bound to come hard and fast.

Anyway, I digress. Back to the exciting place dilemma. In one book I'd read, the hero and heroine met up in a bar and he caused her to come while they were sitting at the table. Then they hooked up in a bathroom stall.

"That tough to come up with an answer, huh?" Travis asked.

"I'm thinking. Give me a second."

He chuckled again. "Except you don't have the look of someone who's reminiscing about some hot fuck sessions. You have more of a constipated look."

"I don't look like that." *Do I?*

"Yes, you do. Which means you can't remember any exciting places where you've done it."

I moved my shoulders in a *whatever* shrug. "Hot sex can happen in bed. It doesn't need to be somewhere exciting for it to be hot."

"True. But counter and shower sex are fantastic, too." He winked at me and my girlie parts gave a dreamy sigh.

Paint. I need more paint on my roller!

I fussed around for a minute with the paint pan, making sure the roller was adequately coated. The entire time, my girlie parts worked hard to remind me of yesterday's conversation in the hardware store. No, not the one about my fear of abandonment. The one about me getting laid. By Travis.

Naturally, my brain thought it was a bad idea. My body told it not to be so hasty—maybe they could come to some sort of compromise. A compromise that involved my body getting its way.

Given my newfound revelation that I was commitment phobic, maybe my body had a good point. What was wrong with having some fun? Didn't I deserve it?

"Okay, my turn to ask a question," I said. "Do you have any hobbies?"

"Don't really have time for hobbies during hockey season.

And even off-season, I don't really have any hobbies that I regularly do. I don't even sketch as much as I used to. I'm more of a do-whatever-I-feel-like-doing-at-the-time guy. Mostly training. Hanging out with the guys. Stuff like that."

"Fair enough. Your turn." I continued painting the wall.

"How long has it been since you last fucked a guy?"

Seriously? That was the question he was going with?

And what was it with all the sex-related questions?

He's a guy, the logical voice in my head reminded me. *What did you expect?*

Good point!

Since lying wasn't my thing, I blurted, "Two years ago." Not once did I stop painting or look at him when I said it.

I could feel him staring at me as though I had announced I was running away to join a convent. Considering I was practically a born again virgin, it was always a possibility...if you ignored the part that I wasn't Catholic.

"You're shitting me, right?"

"Why would you think that? Not everyone does one-night stands. Some of us prefer to go out with the guy a few times first." The indignant tone? Totally justified.

"So you're telling me you haven't dated in two years—or you just haven't had sex for two years?"

"More like both." I shrugged. "I've been busy."

It wasn't like single men normally came into the store. Usually if a guy came in, he was with his wife or girlfriend or boyfriend. So that didn't leave me with many opportunities for meeting guys these days.

Travis went back to painting. "So how many boyfriends have you had?" His tone was casual, non-judgmental—nothing but pure curiosity.

And because I was beginning to view Travis as something more than a fake boyfriend—a friend—I went with the truth. "One serious boyfriend in college. Nothing since then."

His eyes widened as if I had confessed to loving chocolate covered ants. "Why did you guys break up?"

"The guy was a prick. He convinced me that he loved me" —*Keep rolling on the paint. Don't look at Travis whatever you do*— "and he convinced me to have sex with him. Then right after he came, he was out the door. Never heard from him again after that."

I kept on painting, still not looking at Travis. The air was silent other than the wet sound of my roller moving against the wall.

"Are you fucking kidding me?"

"Wish I were," I said. "But that's okay. Lesson learned."

"So why no more boyfriends after that?"

"Hey, isn't it my turn to ask *you* a question?"

"Sure, if we were still playing the game. But we're not."

I guess that also meant I couldn't take a dare instead of answering him. "I don't know. Maybe I've increased my standards and no one has met them yet."

If the woman from the paint store was here, she would no doubt claim I'd increased my standards to make it impossible to meet Mr. Right—which might be true given the recent additions to my requirement list: sexy smirk and dirty talk.

I mean, really, what was I planning to do? Audition guys to see if they could talk dirty?

I mentally laughed at that—doing my best to ignore how Travis already met those two requirements.

19

—————

TRAVIS

All I could do was stare at Emma for what had to be several seconds. The woman owned a store that sold all things dealing with love and romance, and she'd only had one boyfriend—six fucking years ago.

She had even admitted to wanting to find love one day. She wasn't afraid of it. But if that was true, then why was she still single? The Emma I'd gotten to know during the past week was not only gorgeous, she was sweet and smart and funny. Any guy would be lucky to be with her. Hell, if I wasn't so anti-commitment, she would be exactly the type of woman I'd go for.

Anger burned in my veins at how her shithead ex-boyfriend had treated her. It had scarred her—that much I could tell. You didn't need to be a shrink to figure out that between what her parents had done to her and how her ex had treated her, she was equally as messed up as I was.

Lucky us.

Ever since I'd kissed Emma the other day at Granny's, I'd been craving to taste her again. Maybe it was time to renegotiate the terms of our relationship.

I parked my roller in the pan and walked to where Emma was furiously painting the same spot she'd been working on for the past few seconds.

A quick glance at the door told me we were safe from prying eyes. Everyone else was in the gym.

"I think we need to reconsider the terms of our fake girlfriend-boyfriend arrangement," I murmured in her ear. My lips brushed against her jaw. That sharp inhalation, too soft to be heard by anyone but me? I was definitely affecting her.

"What terms are you thinking about?" she whispered.

"That we can kiss each other anytime we want. We don't have to just save it for my grandmother's benefit."

"Oh, you think so, do you?"

See the way her pulse was rapidly beating in her neck? I lightly ran the tip of my tongue against it.

She released a subtle moan. *Christ.* I wanted her. Badly.

"I bet you're hot and wet for me," I said against her ear. "Tell me, sweetheart. If I slip my fingers in your pussy, will I discover that I'm right?" My voice was pure sex and lust—the kind I knew from experience turned girls on.

But in this moment, I only craved to turn on the woman who just whimpered at my words.

I grinned against her neck. "That's what I thought."

"Maybe we should get back to painting," Emma said. If my voice was pure sex and lust, hers was let's-get-it-on husky —a complete opposite to her words.

"Sure, but you need to kiss me first."

"Why's that?"

I didn't answer with words. Instead, I showed her exactly why she needed to kiss me—why we should take this further once we were done there for the night.

My mouth and tongue danced a slow and hungry waltz with hers. I savored the taste of her as satisfaction hummed deep in my bones. I couldn't remember the last time kissing had felt this way.

Damn, I had been missing out. Thank God, I still had four more weeks to enjoy this.

I wrapped my arms around her and pulled her close. My brain vaguely registered something cool and wet against my leg, but I was otherwise too preoccupied to figure out what the heck it was.

Somewhere in the recess of my mind, I heard a door click open. This was followed a moment later by the singsong voice of a young girl. "Emma and her boyfriend sitting in a tree. K.I.S.S.I.N.G."

Emma pulled away as though lightning had hit her. We both turned to the door. The little intruder continued singing, "First comes love—"

"Hey, Nikki," a now red-faced Emma said, and I chuckled at how adorable she looked when embarrassed. "Is there something we can help you with?"

"I came to see if you need an assistant." Nikki looked like a mini version of Emma. But instead of Emma's flaming curls, the young girl had long, curly black hair that looked like it had gotten caught in a windstorm and came out the loser. Her skin was pale with a spattering of freckles across her nose.

With wide, curious eyes, she gave me the once-over. "Are you a nice man?"

"I'd like to believe that I am," I replied, although I was positive whatever team I played against felt differently whenever I kept them from scoring. Several players had tossed a few names my way—"nice" never being one of them.

Her curious gaze switched to Emma. "I thought you don't need a boyfriend."

"That's right, I don't. Not to make me happy."

Emma might've said that, but from the way she had been

responding in my arms a moment ago, she seemed happy to me. Happy and sexually frustrated. I took full credit for the latter—but I'd be lying if I didn't admit that I itched to be responsible for the first part, too.

"Travis," she said, "this is my friend Nikki."

Nikki held her hand out for me to shake. "Nice to meet you, Travis," she said as she enthusiastically shook it.

"Nice to meet you, too."

Nodding, she let go of my hand. Her gaze dropped to my leg. "Why do you have blue paint on your leg?"

I peered down to see what she was talking about. Well, that explained the wet sensation I'd felt while Emma and I were kissing. She still held the roller in her hand.

Emma laughed. "Oops."

I bit back what I wanted to say—words involving a shower, Emma, and expanding her list of exciting locations she'd had sex in. Words that weren't appropriate to say in front of a seven-year-old.

"What do you think?" I asked Nikki. "Is blue my color? Or maybe I should go with something greener?"

She giggled. "I like you."

"Well, thank you. I like you, too."

The door opened and the director of the center entered, smiling softly at the girl. "There you are, Nikki. Remember what I told you? This room is off-limits for now."

Nikki stuck out her lower lip. "I wanted to help."

"I know, sweetie. But I bet if you ask nicely, you might get to watch Emma and Travis when they paint the mural."

The little girl's face lit up when Emma and I nodded in agreement at the suggestion.

"Sorry about the paint on your leg," Emma said after Nikki and Amelia had left the room to go to craft time. "I guess I got a little distracted while you were kissing me. I forgot I was holding the roller. But blue is definitely a good color on you." She laughed the sweetest, sexiest sound.

"I'll keep that in mind for the next time I paint my apartment. In the meantime, how about we go back to our previous conversation?"

"You mean the one where you were trying to convince me our fake relationship should come with all the perks of a regular one?" she asked with another laugh.

Regular perks? If she was also talking about sex, then hell yes to that.

She caught her lower lip between her teeth, deliberating. "I was thinking you might have a point about us kissing each other anytime we want like a regular couple. And..." She chewed on her lip again.

"And?"

"And I think we should take things to the next base. I mean more like a home run."

I might have mentally fist-pumped the air.

"So let me get this straight so there's no confusion..." I said. "You want to have sex with me?"

Unlike before, she no longer looked uncertain. Her mouth curled up to one side. "I'm interested if you are."

Double fist-pump.

"But remember," she said, "it's been a long time since I last had sex. I'm not sure if I remember how to do it anymore." The impish spark I'd previously seen in her eyes was back. And shit, did my cock ever appreciate it.

"Sweetheart, it's like riding a bike...you never forget." I traced my tongue around the shell of her ear.

She whimpered at my touch and a slight tremor traveled through her.

Hell, yes!

20

EMMA

As soon as I'd agreed to have sex with Travis, that was all the motivation either of us needed to finish painting the wall.

Flash-forward to over an hour later, to my bedroom where we were standing fully clothed and kissing. Needing to feel the warmth of Travis's skin, I slipped my fingertips past the hem of his T-shirt and explored the valleys and ridges of his abs.

I wasn't the only one hungry to explore. Travis's hand skimmed up my side and cupped a breast. Even with the fabric of my bra and T-shirt between us, I could feel the heat of his palm soak through.

His thumb brushed against my nipple. It sighed in satisfaction. Satisfaction and the desperate need for more. Fortunately, Travis seemed perfectly happy to give it just that. He slipped his hand under the hem of my T-shirt, and a moment later my girls were free of the confining bra. *Impressive.*

He palmed the flesh, his hand hot against my skin. But it wasn't enough. I leaned into him, thirsty for more of this, more of him, more of everything. I was rewarded with a pinch to my nipple. Hot need rushed to my core and I moaned.

But his teasing still wasn't enough. I craved to feel his skin against mine. I pushed his T-shirt up, exposing his abs. Yes—they were as glorious as I had imagined.

I didn't have to waste a moment wondering what his chest looked like. His T-shirt was on the floor faster than you could say *Magic Mike*. Was the fundraiser audience in for a treat? You had better believe it—especially if the other guys looked half as good as this.

But only *I* would know how it felt to touch him—thanks to the rules his team had imposed. Luckily for me, those rules didn't extend to girlfriends—fake or otherwise.

Travis had stopped kissing me long enough to remove our T-shirts and take in the sight of me. For a second I longed to cover my breasts with my hands—but not out of modesty.

His eyes were dark with lust and a thrill trembled through me. "Christ, I want you so bad," he murmured, voice matching the need in his hazel eyes. His hands moved to the waistband of my shorts, and with the same deft skill he had exercised with my bra, he slipped the button through the hole.

He slowly unzipped them, giving me time to change my mind—as if that was even a consideration. Was I nervous, especially because it had been awhile since the last time I'd had sex? I'd be lying if I said I wasn't. But I wasn't nervous enough to want him to stop. Just the opposite. I was nervous that he would stop before I was ready.

I mentally shoved the fear aside—which wasn't too hard given what his fingers were now doing. He slipped my shorts down past my hips, and his fingers shifted to between my legs. He brushed a digit against my aching core. A whimper escaped my lips.

The ache thanked its lucky stars that I had finally come to

my senses and retired Alejandro for the time being. As fine as my dear friend was, nothing came close to having Travis touch me there.

"You're so fucking wet for me," he said. "Just like I figured you'd be." It looked like he was about to say something else, but then his gaze settled on the one thing I had hoped he wouldn't notice on my right boob. The three small, round puckered scars—burn marks. "What's this?"

"It's nothing, really. Cupid's tiny dragon created them. Okay, let's get back to the part where I'm wet for you...." I reached up on my tiptoes and nibbled on his earlobe.

Was it enough to distract him?

I wish.

Frowning, he pulled away. "What happened?"

"It's not a big deal, Travis." No—at this particular moment, sex with him was a much bigger deal.

"Did someone do this to you?"

I heaved a put-out sigh—echoed by the ache between my legs. "If I promise to talk about it afterward, can we get back to the part where we're about to have sex?" Because if I had to wait any longer, I was likely to explode—and not in a good way.

He gave the scars another long look, then nodded. "Fine. But you're not getting out of telling me."

Once I'd nodded my agreement, he returned to his goal of removing the rest of my clothes. Although from the way I was feeling, I would have agreed to anything just to have Travis go back to touching me the way my body craved.

Impatient to get going, I shimmied my shorts and panties down my legs before he could stop me. *That* was enough to distract him.

Okay—that, along with me cupping my hand against his crotch was enough to distract him from my old owies.

And oh my, may I point out he had quite the package?

With a heated look in his eyes, Travis practically ripped off his shorts. He then stood there in his almost naked glory, his firm cock straining against the cotton of his boxer briefs. I took a mental picture so I would have something to remember when it was back to just Alejandro and me.

Travis removed his underwear. "See anything you like?" His voice held an edge of a smirk. I had no idea if there was a smirk on his face—that wasn't where my eyes were focused.

All I could do was nod—and wonder what it would feel like to take him into my mouth.

"Sit on the edge of the bed," he directed, his tone commanding, and my body went all tingly.

Curiosity spiked in me as to what he planned to do. It was answered a second later when he moved one of my feet and then the other onto the mattress, opening me up for him to see.

His heated look burned even brighter as he studied me. Not just my girlie parts laid out for him to clearly see. But also the rest of me, leaning back on my elbows. Seeing him like this pushed away any and all nervousness that I'd had up till now. It gave me confidence.

Wow, he was good.

"You okay?" he asked with a tone opposite the one he had just used.

I flashed him a genuine smile. "Definitely."

He bent down and removed a square wrapper from his shorts, but instead of opening it and sliding the condom on, he set it on the bed.

He then ran his fingers along the inside of my thighs. Fortunately, they were scar-free. No need for him to stop again because he felt compelled to know where I'd gotten them.

Sex—the only thing that was on my agenda for the next while.

Travis knelt between my legs. "You don't know how long I've waited to do this."

Oh, I could guarantee nowhere near as long as I had... considering he didn't even remember me from high school.

Before I realized what he was going to do, his mouth was on the ache between my legs, making it very *very* happy. I might have let out a moan to that effect.

Clueless what I was supposed to do with my hands, I grabbed the bedding. Except as I got closer to the peak, I wasn't sure if that would be enough. Even with Alejandro, it had never been like this.

The ache between my legs would have said, "Told you so," but it was otherwise preoccupied.

"I'm going to come very soon," I said, in case Travis hadn't guessed it from all the withering and moaning.

"Good." He went back to what he was doing with his extremely talented tongue.

"I mean, if you want to be inside me, you should do that now."

He chuckled against my clit, eliciting a louder moan from me. "Don't worry about me. After I get you off, I'll sink deep inside you." The way he said the last part was like pushing the detonation button. *Kaboom*.

An orgasm to rival any that poor Alejandro had ever given blasted off inside me. I wouldn't be half-surprised if I went up in flames.

By the time I returned to earth, Travis had the condom on and was standing.

After checking if I was still alive—very considerate, if you ask me—he lifted my legs onto his shoulders, positioned himself against my entrance, and pushed inside. He didn't thrust into me right away. He just stood still, with only his tip inside me, allowing my heat to adjust to his width. Then he slowly entered me until he was fully seated.

And holy fuck, did it ever feel good.

But that was nothing compared to what came a moment later. He started moving his hips in circles, hitting places inside me I wasn't aware existed.

"Oh. God. Oh. God. *Oh, God.*" That was as far as I got before another orgasm hit, equally intense as the last one.

Yes—it was official. I had died and gone to heaven.

It wasn't long before Travis joined me in sated land with a final grunt and thrust of his hips. He leaned down, gave me a long, satisfying kiss, then removed himself and disposed of the condom.

I had no idea what to expect next. While I didn't have any personal experience with one-night stands, I knew there tended not to be sleepovers. Not unless you enjoyed the awkwardness of getting rid of the person the next day.

What about the guys who had made it to date #3? All right, I'll admit it—I usually gave them an excuse why I couldn't stay the night and they never tried to persuade me to stay. There was never a date #4 after that—my choice.

And thanks to the woman in the paint store, I now understood why.

To be honest, I expected Travis to do the same thing.

Which was why you could've knocked me over with a chocolate bar when he walked past his clothes and joined me on the bed.

He climbed under the covers and turned to face me. His fingers traced over the round scars on my chest. "So, you gonna tell me how you got these?"

"Is that your way of saying you don't believe Cupid has a tiny dragon friend?" I asked. "You've hurt his little dragon feelings. Hope you're proud of yourself."

"I'm sure both he and I will live. Now spill it. Did this happen in foster care?"

I glanced away.

"The reason I don't want a girlfriend," Travis said after a beat, "is because I had one while I was playing in Dallas. We weren't serious. At least I didn't think we were. I play professional hockey, which means I can easily be traded at any time. So I figured we'd have fun while we were together, and if I was traded then there'd be no expectations.

"Only she didn't feel the same way. When I got traded to the Rock, she thought she was coming with me. It didn't go down too well when I told her I didn't want that."

"What happened?" I asked, awed that he was opening up a bit of himself, even if it was to get the truth out of me about the scars.

"She started telling everyone we were engaged. Then she showed up here, somehow managed to track down where I lived, and broke into my apartment. In a wedding gown."

The giggle? It just kind of popped out. "Sorry, I had an image of a woman in a white gown and tons of tulle, trying to scale your building. Was she arrested?"

The corner of his mouth tilted up to one side. "Now that would have been more entertaining. She would've had a harder time explaining her way out of that. Yes, she was arrested for breaking and entering, and I got a restraining order."

I sat up and removed the small Cupid statue from my nightstand. In my best announcer voice I said, "And the nominees for being in the worst possible relationship are... Emma Lovejoy and Travis Hamilton." I pretended to open an envelope. "And the winner of the dubious award is...Travis." That got a laugh out of him.

With a faked fanfare, I handed him the statue. "Congratulations, Travis. Do you have any parting remarks for the audience?"

He threw his head back in laughter. "I guess we do make

quite the pair." He traced his fingers over the scars on my chest again.

I swallowed and pulled up my lacy big-girl panties. "They're cigarette burns. It happened when I was fifteen. I made the mistake of getting mad at my foster father at the time and told him he smelled like a flatulent cow. Needless to say, he didn't have a great sense of humor and punished me with the burning end of his cigarette."

"Did you report him?"

I choked back a laugh. "Right. That wasn't how it worked. And other than the one time, the family wasn't all that bad. I could have ended up with someone worse." Which I did—the home where I'd gotten the scar on my chin.

He ran his fingertip across said scar. "Did you really get this one from tripping on a crack in the sidewalk?'

I shook my head. "It was a gift from one of my foster mothers. She falsely accused me of seducing her husband." I screwed up my nose to show what I thought of that preposterous idea. "She jabbed me in the face with a broken beer bottle....Anyway, don't scars build character?"

Anger flickered on his face, quickly replaced by tenderness. He cupped my cheek with his hand and his thumb traced my lower lip. "You're something, you know that?"

I grinned. "Is that a good thing or a bad thing?"

"Definitely a good thing." He leaned in and showed me how much of a good thing it was with a gentle kiss.

Which progressed to a deeper, all-consuming kiss—because life was just that good.

Eventually he pulled away, allowing us to regain our breaths. He rolled onto his back and dragged me against him. I rested my head against his heart. The steady *thump-thump-thump* was soothing. Another point for the real deal versus poor Alejandro.

"When I first came into your store the day I had to pick up

my grandmother," he said after a few minutes, "you acted like you would rather have your eyeballs dunked in hot sauce and barbecued in a fire pit than have me there. At first I thought it was because I had fucked you at some point and couldn't remember you, so you were pissed."

"What made you realize it wasn't that?"

"Because I knew I could never fuck you and not remember you."

Only he didn't remember. At all.

Maybe if you'd had sex with him in high school, the practical voice said, *he would remember you from back then.*

I shifted off him and rested my head on my hand, my elbow bent on the bed. "You really don't remember me from our junior year in high school, do you?"

21

TRAVIS

ere's the thing about teenage boys...they never forget a hot girl. They can forget everything else—where they put their iPhone, where they put their car keys or bus pass, what time curfew is—but thanks to their out-of-control hormones, they never forget a great pair of tits.

And they certainly never forget a girl when her great tits are paired with the rest of a boner-inducing package.

So it didn't make sense that I couldn't remember Emma from high school.

"Are you sure we went to the same school?"

Social media was always showing one celebrity or another's doppelgänger—that mystery regular person who could easily be mistaken as the celebrity in question. Maybe my doppelgänger had gone to Emma's high school.

Sounded feasible.

"You went to Parkdale High School, am I right?" she asked.

Okay—so much for my theory.

"Yes, but I honestly don't remember you."

The pain in her eyes? Not a good thing.

"We were in the same history class."

I cringed and tried to remember my classmates from twelve years ago. I vaguely remembered a cute redhead with curly hair. She had started late in the term and had been in one of my classes, but don't quiz me on which one. It had been a rough year for me—what with Granny's stroke. Most of it had been a blur.

"So that's why you were mad at me in your store—because I don't remember you from high school?"

"No—and I wasn't mad at you. I guess the old feelings from what happened after class one day resurfaced when you came into the store."

"What exactly happened?"

"We had been assigned to be project partners, but Kendra, your ex-girlfriend, told me you dumped me for being a foster kid. According to her, I wasn't good enough for you to work with."

"Why would you believe that?" And why did I have no idea what she was talking about? Maybe I had very early onset Alzheimer's.

"Because our teacher told me you could no longer work on the project with me. He didn't tell me why—he just told me I had to do it on my own."

"When was this?" I asked, frowning. I had known back then that Kendra could be a bitch, but she was hot and I was your typical shallow, horny teenage boy. It was during our junior year that I'd had enough of her games and dumped her.

Several weeks later, she'd hooked up with the school's quarterback.

"I don't remember exactly. Sometime early spring."

Christ—now that did sound familiar. "My grandmother had suffered a stroke and because she was all I had, the school made allowances so I could be there for her."

Emma's eyes widened, her mouth a perfect C. "Oh, God. I'm so sorry. I had no idea."

Her words were a hard kick to the nuts. Her parents had dumped her when she was a kid, she had been tossed from foster home to foster home, and her asswipe ex-boyfriend had also walked out on her. And what did I do—even if it hadn't been intentional? Exactly the same.

Shit.

"Believe me, I would never have dumped you as a project partner. If Granny hadn't had a stroke, we would've still been partners—no matter what Kendra said."

As if to erase the pain I had inadvertently caused her, I kissed Emma. Lightly at first—but it quickly escalated into something more intense. And before long, I was thrusting inside her to choruses of "Oh, God," and my name.

Afterward, once I'd disposed of the condom and returned to the bed, I pulled her against me and wrapped my arms around her. I couldn't remember the last time I'd done this with a woman. Usually I'd fuck them, leaving them satisfied, and bail.

I kissed her shoulder, and an odd feeling brushed against me—one that was comforting but at the same time unnerving.

"Is Fanny's stroke the reason you're so protective of her?" Emma asked. "And the reason you're pretending to date me instead of putting your foot down about your dating life?" Her tone was both sweet and non-judgmental like a welcomed hug.

"That, and because she took me in after my parents died. I wasn't easy on her—being the grieving teen that I was. But no matter what I did—how stupid I was—she was patient and always there for me...until she almost wasn't."

"She's an amazing woman," Emma said, softly.

"She is."

"And you're an amazing grandson."

I wasn't so sure about that. If you looked up "amazing grandson" in the dictionary, I could guarantee my photo wouldn't be there.

The tension in Emma's muscles melted away as I continued holding her. A moment later, her breathing evened out.

And I was left contemplating if I was making a big mistake when it came to both Granny and Emma.

But at least Emma knew what she had signed up for. When she and I went our separate ways, this time she wouldn't feel like I had dumped her. I wouldn't be yet another asshole who had abandoned her like trash on garbage day.

22

Dear Dr. Lovejoy,

I've been pretending to be this guy's boyfriend (don't ask), but I'm starting to develop real feelings for him. How do I make him see we have real potential?

Sincerely,

Why Fake It When It Can Be Real

Dear Why Fake It When It Can Be Real,

Simple. Make sure he sees what he will be missing out on once you're no longer in his life. No, no, I don't necessarily mean have sex with him. Although that won't hurt if it's memorable—in a good way. I'm talking about the kisses. Make sure they shake the earth under his feet.

I'm talking about those small moments where you show him just how special he is. Show him in a way only you can do.

23

EMMA

Five days later, I was in the store, organizing the shipment of sexual bathroom products that arrived that morning. Had I seen Travis since we had sex?

Nope. He had slipped out during the night—as I'd expected he would.

Now, some girls might feel offended if a guy they'd fucked did that. For me? The complete opposite. My ex couldn't have escaped my apartment faster unless the building had been about to explode—I had learned from the best in that regard.

Travis had at least waited until I fell asleep.

He had held me in his arms—allowing me to pretend I meant something to him.

Don't worry. Like everything else, I realized that night with Travis hadn't been real. I mean the sex was real. Poor Alejandro had gotten a complex because it had been so freaking real—as in the no-longer-working kind of complex.

I mentally added, "Buy replacement Alejandro" to my To-Do list, although the new one had a lot to live up to. With Alejandro the First, there hadn't been any expectations on my behalf. But after last week, I now knew how wrong I had been.

But while I might not have seen Travis since that night, the same couldn't be said about hearing from him. He'd sent me daily texts to check up on me, and to update me on the rehearsals and the mural.

Even though I'd promised to help him with it, things hadn't gone as planned. The first night he'd worked on the mural, I couldn't make it because Lisa called in sick. Since my weekend girls weren't able to cover her shift, I had to. By the time I got home, I was only capable of doing a face-plant on my bed and not moving until morning.

Tonight I could finally help him.

"Well, if it isn't my favorite future granddaughter-in-law," Fanny said from behind me.

I spun around to find her, Abigail, and Hazel beaming at me.

"I'm just dating Travis," I reminded them. "It's definitely too early to be considering marriage." Especially since it would never happen. Not when Travis was commitment phobic.

"Ah, but I've seen how he looks at you," Fanny said, still grinning.

Right—he's been looking at me like a guy who wishes to get laid.

"I've seen how he looks at me too," I said, "and it has nothing to do with marriage."

In spite of my words, Fanny continued grinning as if she knew a secret.

Well, that made two of us—and my secret was one she wouldn't like.

Okay, two secrets she wouldn't like—not unless she was pro commitment-free sex.

"Am I too late for those mouthwatering cookies of yours?" Abigail asked.

"I haven't been able to make them. My oven stopped working on the weekend."

Just like Alejandro. Maybe it was a conspiracy. I finally get laid and my appliances quit working.

The way the three women gasped, you'd have thought I had announced I was joining a sex cult.

"You're welcome to come over and use mine," Fanny said. "In fact, I insist on it."

I opened my mouth to graciously decline the offer, except Hazel cut me off before I could say anything. "You can't say no. It's your duty, Emma, to ensure your customers are happy. And those cookies make us *very* happy."

"That's right, dear," Abigail said. "We're three old women who haven't had sex in an extremely long time, and with no prospects of getting any in the near future. So it's your duty to provide us with an alternative in the chocolate department."

Fanny and Hazel laughed while I mentally cringed at the image now residing in my head.

"I'm not—" I began.

"Uh, uh," Fanny said. "No excuses. Plus, Travis is dropping by later to check on me. And I know he'll be happy to see you there. Maybe you can even distract him with another of your hot kisses."

"Distract him from what?"

"From keeping me from living my life."

That was what she got for having an alpha male for a grandson. He was overly protective to the core. Especially since he had already lost his parents, and almost lost his grandmother when she had a stroke.

"He only does that because he loves you," I said.

She smiled. It wasn't as bright as when she'd called me her future granddaughter-in-law, but it was still just as warm.

"I know. And because of that, you can't say no about coming over to bake those cookies. I'll even help you if you'd like. Life is way too short to spend another day at war with yourself."

"Did you make that last part up?" Abigail asked, chuckling.

Fanny's smile widened. "Nope—I found it on Google images this morning. But I thought it was perfect for this discussion."

"Are you sure about me coming over?" I asked, fighting back a grin.

"Of course I'm sure. Especially if I get to sneak one."

"And Abigail and I can pop in to make sure they're acceptable to sell here." Hazel winked at me and I laughed.

"Okay, I'll come over after work."

The bell above the door jingled, and my mouth dropped open at the sight of the five people who entered the store.

Three of them I had already met...including the adorable toddler. The man and woman with them I didn't know. She was pretty and blonde with shoulder-length hair. He was dark-haired and definitely hot. And it didn't take much to see that she was the center of his universe.

Normally when I saw two people very much in love, a dreamy sigh would escape me. Not this time. This time panic charged through me like a participant during the running of the bulls. Were Holly and Josh aware that Travis and I were in a fake relationship? Nope—not at all.

As far as they knew, Travis and I were just friends and he had offered to help with the fundraiser. They had no idea he was also trying to save my store.

How was that going?

Let's just say I was wishing on every shooting star that I spotted. Or at least I would be if I could find any. Apparently they were in short supply these days. And maybe that was why Travis still hadn't found me a suitable location to move to and he hadn't yet convinced the building owner to let me stay.

The foursome ambled over to us, with Josh carrying Lily.

When some women see a cute baby or toddler, their ovaries send *I-want* messages to their brains. Well, apparently the same thing happened to old women, too. Except instead of the I-want-a-baby message being sent, it was more along the lines of I-need-my-grandchild-to-give-me-one-of-those. STAT.

The longing in Fanny's eyes was enough to knock me on my ass. Hard.

"Hey, Fanny." Josh gave her a one-armed hug, taking care not to squish his daughter between them.

"Hi," Lily said to her with the cutest smile and waved.

"Oh, aren't you the sweetest thing alive?" Fanny said.

"Hi!" Lily repeated, which I took to mean she agreed with her.

"Have you met my future granddaughter-in-law yet?" Fanny asked Josh and winked at me. I rolled my eyes. Then cringed at what she had just told Josh and his friends.

The confusion on Josh's face? Definitely not good.

"No, Travis isn't engaged," I said, doing my best to keep everything from blowing up in his face and mine.

"Not yet," Fanny said. "But give it time. I know you two have just started dating, but like I said before, I've seen how he looks at you."

"This is perfect," the blonde said. "The four of us are spending this weekend in Napa Valley in a house we're renting. It's a couples' weekend type thing. Trent's sister and husband were going to join us but had to cancel. You and Travis should come. It'll be a lot of fun."

"My mum's visiting from Australia and will be looking after Lily," Holly added with her cute Aussie accent. "So it will also be an adult-only weekend."

"Emma and Travis would love to join you," Fanny said before I had a chance to decline.

"I'm sure Travis is busy then," I hurriedly said. "He has a... a thing."

The earlier confusion on Josh's face? It was contagious. Now Fanny shared the same look. "What kind of thing?" she asked.

A sudden understanding lit the dark-haired man's face and he smiled, a mischievous gleam in his eyes. "I'm sure Travis will be more than happy to cancel his *thing*. In fact"— he looked at Josh—"wasn't he saying at poker night a few weeks ago how he wasn't too sure what to do about it?"

Josh smirked. Why did I have a feeling I was missing something? "That's right. He did say that." Josh leveled his grin at me. "So it's settled. You and Travis are joining us. I'll send him the info."

"I can't believe how much she's grown," Fanny said, her gaze back on Lily.

Josh patted his daughter's head. "I swear her nanny is feeding her Miracle-Gro for toddlers."

"Hi," Lily said to me and waved again.

"By the way, Emma," Holly said as the three older women fussed over her daughter. "This is Kelsey and Trent. We've been dying to visit your store ever since you told me about it."

Trent laughed. "You and Kelsey are the ones who've been dying to come here. Josh and I are just here as the supportive husband and fiancé."

"Because you know the two of you will benefit from this as much as Kelsey and I will—especially this weekend."

Kelsey gave her fiancé a shy smile that practically left him drooling.

While Fanny and her friends continued to fuss over the great-granddaughter she wished she had, I showed Holly and Kelsey around the store.

"So that's how you persuaded Travis to do the *Magic Mike* routine for the fundraiser," Holly said. "It's because you're dating him. Pure genius."

I blinked. "I had nothing to do with that. It was all his idea." I only encouraged him to go for it—mostly because I figured he was kidding.

"That was Travis's idea?" Holly asked, eyes wide in surprise, but she was also clearly trying not to laugh. "I guess he didn't realize how tough it would be. Those guys are amazing skaters, but put them on stage and everything falls apart."

"So you're warning me not to expect much?" She wasn't the only one doing her best not to laugh—and barely succeeding. The image in my head of the nine hockey players attempting to dance onstage was amusing—and absolutely adorable.

"Fortunately, they're all good-looking and rock hot bods," she said, "so the women in the audience will be more forgiving. Plus it's the thought that counts, and we still have two more weeks to go."

"Well, if it wasn't for you, there would be no show. I'm not sure they could've come up with something themselves."

Holly's ability to hold back her laugh failed this time. "You're probably right, but it would have still been fun watching them."

"I can't wait to see it," Kelsey said. "Trent once participated in a bachelor auction to raise money for charity, and it was the sweetest thing I've ever seen."

"I'm still disappointed I missed it," Holly said. "I would have paid a lot of money just to watch my colleague make a fool of himself."

"An adorable fool of himself," Kelsey amended, grinning.

Twenty minutes later, the girls left with their husband

and fiancé. Both men strode out with huge grins, thanks to what Holly and Kelsey had bought.

Fanny and her cohorts had left a while ago.

Five minutes before I was due to go home, a text from Travis popped up on my phone screen.

Travis: You okay for this weekend in Napa Valley?

Me: As long as you are. Sounds like fun. I like your friends.

Travis: I am. It should be. I do too.

I had to laugh at that.

FANNY WAS EAGERLY WAITING FOR ME WHEN I ARRIVED AT HER apartment. She wasn't the only one. All three women practically drooled at the sight of me—like Pavlov's dogs.

They made themselves comfortable on the tall chairs on the other side of the kitchen counter overlooking the living room. And while I mixed the cookie dough, Fanny shared more stories of Travis growing up.

No—they weren't the kind that would leave him blushing, which was too bad. Who wouldn't have loved to hear them? And yes, I was positive Fanny had tons of those stories to share.

These were the sweeter stories that melted your heart. Like the time he was ten and found some abandoned kittens. When he couldn't convince his parents to let him keep them, he worked hard at finding them good homes.

They were the kind of stories that were supposed to cause me to fall in love with him.

Was I? No—but I could definitely see myself heading in that direction if it weren't for the ticking clock on our fake relationship.

My heart pinched—not quite agreeing with me. Maybe that could be my next column for the paper.

Dr. Lovejoy,

I'm falling for my fake boyfriend—the guy who doesn't commit to relationships. What should I do?

Except I had no answer—other than "Run!"

Sounded like good advice to me, although I was positive the paper would require something longer.

Run fast and far, a voice in my head not-so-helpfully suggested.

My heart pouted, clearly not on board with that advice either.

I'm not falling in love with him, I told myself.

I'm not falling in love with him.

I'm not falling...

My heart, being as stubborn as it was, laughed at me.

I guess the woman at the paint store had been wrong after all. I wasn't scared of commitment.

Or maybe you're falling for Travis because there is a ticking clock on the relationship, the know-it-all voice in my head said. *You know exactly when it's going to end.*

"Mmm, the cookies smell sooo good," Hazel said, eyeing the oven where a batch was currently baking. She was right though. The rich, chocolaty smell filled the air, setting our stomachs grumbling.

A few minutes later, as I was removing the cookie sheet from the oven, the apartment door clicked open. Travis entered the living room soon after.

He stopped short, his face betraying his surprise at seeing me there—which quickly morphed into something more heated.

"Hi," I said as an unexpected awkwardness settled on my shoulders. I swallowed. "My oven's broken, so your grandmother invited me over to make the cookies here."

"And we're the official taste-testers," Abigail added, not noticing the tension that had sprung up between him and me like the electrical current just prior to a lightning storm...the prelude to something spectacular.

In three long strides, Travis was in front of me, his eyes dark. He grabbed the cloth from the counter and used it to remove the baking sheet from my hand, which he relocated onto the cooling rack.

Then his mouth was on mine.

And instantly the world around us was forgotten.

The dreamy sigh? No idea if it came from me or someone else, though the whimper was definitely mine.

Like a hungry man who hadn't eaten in several days, Travis continued to consume me. Wow, who knew the smell of chocolate chip cookies could be such a powerful aphrodisiac? Maybe I could bottle the smell and scent the store's air with it—to increase sales.

Hopefully, it wouldn't result in strangers suddenly kissing each other. I mean, if that were the case, bakeries would be the new singles club.

"The way those two are going at it," Abigail said in a loud whisper. "I wouldn't be surprised if you're a great-grandmother in nine months."

Someone laughed, but I was too preoccupied with Travis's lips to figure out who.

"If you believe you can get pregnant from just kissing," Hazel said, "it's a wonder you had any kids at all."

"I don't know about that. Look at those two go."

"Maybe if we leave," Fanny said, "they'll just do it on the kitchen counter. I've heard that's big with kids their age these days."

"Where did you hear that?" Abigail asked. Her eyes were wide if her tone was any indication.

"I've read it in a romance novel or two."

"No one ever has sex on the kitchen counter in the books I read," Hazel grumbled.

"That's because you read thrillers," Fanny said. "I'd be surprised if anyone has sex in those."

"Maybe we should hose them down," Hazel said. The other two women laughed.

That was when Travis finally pulled away. The mischievous gleam in his eyes? He'd also heard every bit of their conversation.

"I'd rather not be hosed down, thanks." His hand slid to my butt and he gave it a quick squeeze. Thanks to the counter blocking the view, none of the women witnessed it.

"I didn't realize you were coming over to bake cookies," he said to me. He removed one from the baking sheet and took a bite of it.

The gazes of the women followed the cookie's movement from the baking sheet to his lips as if it had been the only cookie there.

"Mmm that's amazing," he said around the mouthful.

Fanny's smile filled her entire face. If there had been angels hanging around, they would have broken out into joyful chorus. But I suspected it had nothing to do with how great the cookie tasted and everything to do with Travis's reaction. Maybe when she was younger, that was how you landed a husband, which would explain how the saying, "The way to a man's heart was through his stomach," came about.

Travis's declaration was all Abigail and Hazel needed to hear. They each grabbed a cookie.

Not wishing to miss out, Fanny also bit into one. "Oh, gosh. I thought they were good before, but they're like little bits of heaven when eaten right out of the oven."

Abigail and Hazel hmm'd their agreement while still munching their cookies.

"Gosh, no wonder Travis is dating you," Hazel said.

I glanced up at Travis in time to catch amusement and lust in his eyes.

Hot damn.

24

TRAVIS

Emma and I stayed at Granny's for dinner before heading to the youth center. Was I surprised to see Emma there when I'd shown up? Yes.

I also hadn't expected to find her making cookies.

Another item to add to my list of things I hadn't expected? The strange feeling I got seeing her in the kitchen with the freshly baked cookies in her hand. But it had nothing to do with the cookies...and everything to do with the intense craving to kiss her.

Right—that wasn't the only urge I'd had. The other one I'd managed to keep from being obvious to everyone in the room by reciting my hockey stats from last season in my head.

Had I ever gone a week without sex or kissing a girl? Yes, lots of times. I enjoyed sex whenever it was available, but I wasn't a manwhore. It wasn't like I needed to fuck some chick on a daily basis.

Which was why I couldn't explain the reason I had craved the feel of Emma's lips against mine the moment I saw her.

"So you're really okay about this weekend in Napa

155

Valley?" Emma asked while painting the rainbow's yellow stripe. I was crouched on the floor, working on a dolphin.

"Why wouldn't I be?"

"Well, for one, your friends don't know that we're not *really* dating. Or did you explain things to Josh?"

"Josh and Trent already knew. Josh was the one who made me think of you as a potential fake girlfriend."

Her paintbrush paused on the spot. "What do you mean?"

"Josh figured the last thing I needed was for my fake girlfriend to fall in love with me."

"Because that would be an awful thing to happen?" Her voice sounded a little strained but since there was no reason for that, I shrugged it off. Her gaze was still on the spot she'd been painting, her hand paused midair.

"Of course," I said. "I mean the reason for having a fake girlfriend is to avoid having a real one."

"Right. Guess I forgot that part." Her voice was still slightly off, but she went back to painting the rainbow without sparing me a second glance.

"Do Kelsey and Holly know I'm not the real deal?" she asked after a few minutes.

I dipped my brush in the blue-gray paint. "I have no idea." It wasn't something I had discussed with the guys. Part of that was because I hadn't originally expected the two women to actually meet Emma.

Suffice it to say, there were a lot of things I hadn't expected to happen in the past four weeks.

I continued painting the dolphin.

"Did Josh or Trent tell you it's a couples' weekend?" Emma asked. "And since we're not a real couple, maybe we shouldn't go. It could get awkward."

"Why would it get awkward?"

You know that look mothers get whenever they're explaining something and the kid just isn't getting it? Now you can appreciate Emma's expression. "Are they expecting us to share a bed?"

"Aren't we?"

She rolled her eyes. "Just because we're pretending to be boyfriend and girlfriend doesn't mean I'm automatically sleeping with you."

"Let me clarify something here. Are we talking about actual sleeping together or fucking? Because in case you've forgotten, we've already done the latter."

Her lower lip disappeared between her teeth for a moment. "Both, I guess."

"So you're saying you don't want to sleep or have sex with me?"

She shrugged. "It's not that. It's just I don't know if we're only going as friends, or if we're keeping with the fake-couple act while we're there."

I straightened to my feet and stepped closer to her. "I don't know about you," I said hotly against her ear, "but I'd be more than happy to keep the act going while we're there. For practice." I ran the tip of my tongue against the shell of her ear. She shuddered as a soft whimper fell from between her lips.

And a smug smile slid onto my face. Score one for me.

I stepped away. "But there's an extra bedroom, so you don't have to sleep with me if you don't want to." And given that I wasn't one for actually sleeping with a woman, that arrangement was even better.

"All right. Both the sleeping arrangement and practicing kissing work for me." Her voice dropped for the next part, taking on a husky tone my cock highly approved of. "I can definitely use more practice."

No—I was pretty sure she was already perfect when it came to kissing. But who was I to turn down the opportunity to do more of it if the occasion should arise?

We returned to painting the mural.

We'd been working on it for an hour when the door clicked open. Wes and Liam entered the room. "Hey, guys, what are you doing here?" I asked.

Emma glanced at them with no hint of recognition on her face.

"We came to check on you." Wes inspected the mural. "Nice job. Looks like you have quite the career ahead of you once you leave hockey...between this"—he gestured at the wall, his mouth tugging up to one side—"and your stripping career."

"Not all of us can be a brilliant-assed game designer," was my *not*-so-witty retort. But he did have a point. I had no idea what I would do once I retired. For now, it wasn't something I had to worry about. Much. "Emma, this is Wes"—I gestured at him—"and Liam, Kelsey's brother. They both have offices in the same building as your store."

A sudden understanding lit Liam's face. "You're the owner of that sex store?"

"It's not a sex store. It's a boutique that focuses on romance," Emma explained. She did a great job of not rolling her eyes. She didn't do such a great job keeping the same exasperation from her tone.

"But it does sell sex toys and adult movies, right?"

This time Emma wasn't quite so successful at not rolling her eyes. "We have some, but I doubt they're what you're looking for. The store caters specifically to females."

The disappointment on Liam's face? Definitely genuine.

"Here's an idea," Wes said to Liam. "Find a girl—because, *Christ*, when was the last time you got laid?—and get her to watch girlie porn with you."

"Ha, ha. You're a real Dr. Lovejoy," Liam said, shaking his head.

Emma stiffened next to me.

"Dr. who?" Wes asked, frowning.

Why did the name sound familiar?

"That's the author of the weekly sex advice column in The SF Metro paper," Liam said, paying more attention to Wes than to Emma.

"And the nominees for being in the worst possible relationship are Emma Lovejoy and Travis Hamilton." Her words from last week reminded me exactly where I'd heard the name before. I swiveled my head at lightning speed to the side, checking her reaction to his words.

Wes laughed out loud. "If you're reading a weekly sex advice column, you're more hard up than I realized."

"And when exactly was the last time *you've* been with a woman?" I asked Wes. "Of the three of us, I'm the only one who hasn't been dealing with a dry spell."

"Point taken," Wes said, still smirking at Liam.

"If you two actually left your offices every now and then," I said, "you might meet some women to hook up with."

Liam folded his arms across his chest. "I leave my office all the time."

"Right, but how many of your security missions have ended with you getting laid?"

At Liam's silence, I added, "That's what I thought. And you..." My gaze swung to Wes. "You spend your days and nights locked in your office, working on your games. Other than your computer-generated women, when have you actually hung out with a real one?"

All right—what I really meant was when was the last time he'd had a good fuck? But for Emma's sake, I edited what I was going to say. She looked traumatized enough at the mention of Dr. Lovejoy.

He shrugged.

"Right, that's what I thought."

"There is one woman I might be interested in," Wes casually said as though merely discussing the weather. But I knew Wes. What might have sounded casual was the complete opposite.

"What woman?" Liam asked, eyebrow raised. "When have you been out of your cave long enough to see a woman?" He glanced at Emma. "Present company excluded."

With a small smile, she nodded at him. A noticeable sense of relief washed over her.

"I've seen her around the building a number of times," Wes said. "She doesn't work there though."

"You know everyone who works in the building?" Emma asked, her tone taken aback. She might not have felt that way if she knew he was the owner.

Realizing he'd almost revealed too much, Wes just shrugged. His shoulders were getting quite the workout with this conversation. "She's often wearing scrubs, which tells me she doesn't work in the building." *Nice save, dumbass.* His building didn't have a medical or dental office in it. "You know, white pants. Colorful tops with cartoon characters. That kind of stuff."

"Slim brunette with straight, shoulder length hair, right?" Emma asked.

Wes's eyebrows rose up his forehead. "That's right. You know her?"

"You could say that. We both grew up in foster care and lived in the same hellhole for our final year in the system. But she doesn't exactly trust men. And while she might come off as the kind of girl who's only interested in having a good time and not settling down, that's just her front.

"So if all you're interested in is having sex with her, I suggest you find another woman to sniff around." Emma stood a little straighter, doing her best to come off as intimidating, a protector of her friend's virtue. Except with the streak of yellow paint smeared on her face, she sat more on the adorable side of the fence than the intimidating side.

Seeing her ready to take on any guy who dared hurt her friend—no matter how big he was—gave me a whole new level of respect for her.

And it gave me another snapshot of what her life had been like growing up.

Without thinking about what I was doing, I wrapped my arm around her waist and kissed her temple.

Naturally, this amused my two friends. *Dumbasses.*

"Thanks for the warning," Wes said with a slight nod of his head. "I'll definitely take that into consideration."

"You guys almost finished here?" Liam asked, examining the mural.

"You mean in general or for tonight?" I asked.

"For tonight. We're heading to The Unicorn. Trent and Kelsey are going to be there, too. Thought you guys might be interested in joining us. It's live band night."

I glanced at Emma. "You interested?"

"I could be convinced."

And the challenge was on....

I murmured in her ear so the two dumbasses couldn't hear me, "They have dancing. Which means lots of opportunities for dry humping. And maybe I could even reveal a few of my *Magic Mike* moves."

She laughed. "Well, when you put it that way.."

# 25

EMMA

Hannah had the evening off from work, so I called her after leaving the youth center to see if she wanted to join us. Did she know about the little conversation I'd had with Wes—about my warning to him? Heck no. I just hoped he wasn't planning to be an asshole like the ones she had been involved with in the past.

Not that she couldn't handle him if he did end up being one. The woman loved her karate and practiced it often. Her goal was to eventually get her black belt.

Was I going to warn Wes about that little tidbit? Nope—figured I'd let him discover that on his own.

The table where everyone in the group was seated had only one empty chair—between Travis and Wes. On the other side of Travis, talking to him, was a gorgeous blonde in a tailored suit. She laughed and tucked her shoulder-length hair behind her ear in full-out flirt mode. Whatever she said must have been funny because Travis also laughed.

And jealousy stomped through me—the sound drowned out by the live band.

You're being ridiculous, I told myself. *He's not really your boyfriend*. Once our farce was over, he could go back to screwing whomever he wished.

Did my little motivational speech help?

Not even a little.

Hannah and I approached the table and I introduced her to everyone. Only then did Travis look up at me. He grinned with a relieved expression—not the stamp of annoyance I'd expected from my intruding on his flirting with the blonde.

"Babe, what are you doing here?" a guy said behind me. I spun around to find the last creep Hannah had gone out with.

He was wearing a T-shirt for a band I'd never heard of and had a sleeve of tattoos on one arm. He wasn't bad looking, but all the guys at the table were much hotter. I couldn't remember his name....So how about I call him "the idiot" to make things easier?

"I'm not your babe," Hannah said with a sneer. He was lucky. At least she hadn't practiced one of her karate moves on him.

Yet.

Oh, just a little warning—unless you know what you're doing, never offer to help Hannah practice her karate. But don't worry, my ankle was fine after a few days. And the bruise on my hip wasn't all that noticeable—under my clothes.

Wes stood up. He easily towered the idiot by a few inches. "I like this song. You wanna dance?" he asked Hannah.

She glanced between the two men. She wasn't the kind of woman who enjoyed playing damsel in distress—which was why she practiced karate. But Wes was a better alternative than taking down the idiot in the pub. The owners might not have appreciated it.

And since this was the location of the fundraiser—and

Hannah knew this—she fortunately decided to take Wes up on his offer of an easy escape.

The idiot glared at their backs as they walked away, then returned to whatever hole he had slithered from.

Before I had a chance to go back to contemplating the seating issue, Travis's hands were around my waist and he pulled me onto his lap. I fought back the urge to scan the pub for Fanny or her friends—or anyone else who could possibly report back to her about our true dating status.

"Figured you'd be comfier on my lap," Travis said as if reading my mind.

The blonde he was talking to eyed me with interest—but not the kind that involved pulling my hair out because I was after her man.

"Jennifer, this is my girlfriend, Emma." Travis's thumb brushed against my lower back. "Jennifer is Abigail's granddaughter."

It took a second for his meaning to sink in. *Oh.*

"I was surprised when my grandmother told me that Travis had finally settled down," she said.

"Travis and I aren't—"

"We aren't ready to announce anything just yet, are we pumpkin?" Travis's arm moved to around my waist and he gave me a brief squeeze.

Again I didn't have a chance to say anything. The band began playing a ballad, and Travis almost dropped me on my ass as he scrambled to his feet. Luckily for me, his hands were on my hips, which prevented me from making nice with the floor. "Oh, look, it's our song," he said even though I'd never heard it before. "Let's dance."

He grabbed my hand and led me to the dance floor. Hannah and Wes were heading back to our table.

Travis pulled me close and my arms automatically went around his neck. And like a magnet, my gaze was drawn to his lips. It had been a long time since I'd last kissed him. The craving to feel his mouth on me was overwhelming. Was this what a drug addiction was like?

It would certainly explain why my brain turned to mush every time I kissed him. His kisses were a drug. A wonderful, the-earth-is-shaking-under-my-feet drug.

"You can kiss me if you want," Travis said, smirking. "In fact, I highly recommend it."

My smile now mirrored his. "You do, do you? And why is that?"

"Because you know what they say about a kiss a day?"

"What's that…it keeps the doctor away?" More like it made you incredibly horny.

"Something like that," he said, his voice I-want-to-toss-you-on-the-table-and-fuck-you-long-and-hard sexy.

The soft moan? Your imagination.

We continued to sway in time to the music. He brought his mouth to mine—and then we were kissing.

Yes—his kisses were exactly like a drug. A drug I never wished to give up. Going cold turkey would be tough. But like a dieter who ate as much junk food and chocolate as possible before giving it all up, I continued to devour him.

After a few minutes, we eventually came up for air.

"You think Jennifer will tell Abigail that she saw us making out on the dance floor?" I asked after I'd regained my breath.

"Hopefully it was enough to convince her."

I frowned. "Convince her? She needs to be convinced?"

"She was hitting on me before you showed up."

"And you don't like it when beautiful women hit on you?" Not that I was complaining when it came to that particular beautiful woman.

"Not when they're testing me," he said.

"Why would she be testing you? Is she interested in you?"

Because that wouldn't surprise me. What woman wouldn't be interested in him? Unless they had something against hockey players.

"I have no idea if she's interested in me...although Granny did try to set me up with her a few months ago."

Of course she did.

"I just don't think she bought into our act," he said.

I moved my hand from around his neck and cupped his face—all for Jennifer's benefit. Okay—for mine, too. "Why wouldn't she?"

He turned his head to kiss the palm of my hand. I had to fight back the urge to check her reaction. "Because after Abigail tried to set us up, Jennifer confronted me and told me once a manwhore, always a manwhore. Apparently she's a defense lawyer and a very good one. If we can't convince her that we're an item, she'll expose us to Granny."

This time my frown wasn't one of confusion. "Why would she do that?"

He shrugged. "It might have something to do with her ex-husband cheating on her."

"Ouch."

"Ouch is right." Travis dipped me, then pulled me up so suddenly, I practically stumbled into him.

"A new move you learned for the fundraiser?" I asked.

He laughed. "Not unless I'm planning to use it on Josh, and I have a feeling he'll have something to say about that."

I grinned. "Then I'm impressed. Was that by any chance for Jennifer's benefit?"

"Maybe it was. Or maybe it was so I can do this again...." His mouth crashed against mine in a not-so-gentle kiss—and I definitely wasn't complaining.

Nor were my girlie parts—especially if the kiss led to something that would make them extremely happy.

Sorry to disappoint, girls, but that's not on the agenda.

Naturally, they weren't too impressed with this and threatened to ignore Alejandro the Second once I introduced him to them.

I inwardly sighed.

The song ended and we returned to the table. Jennifer was no longer there. She was sitting at another table not far from ours, with four other men and women, all chatting animatedly.

She peered over at us, her expression not giving anything away.

Oh, boy.

"For a moment there," Liam said, "I thought we'd have to grab a fire extinguisher before you two burst into flames."

Trent and Kelsey had that look people got when they suddenly understood something. Only I had no idea what they understood. Liam and Wes were staring at us like we were a jigsaw puzzle they were attempting to figure out—and they didn't have a picture on the box to go by.

Hannah's expression was the one that had me worried. *She knows.* Somehow she'd added two and two together, and realized my feelings had gotten things all screwed up when it came to the simple task. The simple task that involved me pretending to be Travis's girlfriend—and in return, he helped save my store and helped with the fundraiser.

Why both? The logical side of my brain prompted. *Why not just help me with the store?*

Because he understands how important it is that I help the kids at the youth center, I pointed out. It was why he was also helping me with the mural.

And because if in the end he couldn't help me save my store, at least it wouldn't feel as though I had pretended to be his girlfriend for nothing. He had already given me so much more than I'd expected.

Now if only Jennifer could read me as well as Hannah

could, then she'd have no doubts that my growing feelings for Travis were real. But that wasn't the problem. The issue was that Travis would never feel the same way about me. This was all a charade for him—nothing more.

I excused myself to use the bathroom. Hannah and Kelsey joined me. Fortunately neither of them said what was really on their minds when it came to Travis and me.

After we were finished, we wove through the crowd back to our table. The band was on a break and recorded music played in the background.

The first thing I noticed was the way Jennifer was watching our table with great interest. Like you would expect a defense lawyer to eye the victim just prior to interrogating them on the witness stand.

My gaze shifted to her target—Travis and the brunette now sitting in my seat. But unlike Jennifer, this woman wasn't wearing a suit. And her low-cut top didn't leave much to anyone's imagination. It was also clear that she was shamelessly flirting with Travis.

Was he flirting back? Not at all. If anything, he had a slight frown on his face—possibly because he knew Jennifer was mentally writing up a report for her grandmother.

Needing to save both our asses, I squeezed past the pair and sat on Travis's lap. There was a good chance I might have "accidentally" bumped my hip against the brunette's head. *Oops.* Well, that was what she got for leaning so close to him.

"Who are you?" she asked, clearly taken aback that I had plonked myself on his lap—and disappointed she hadn't thought of it first.

"His girlfriend. You are...?" I asked.

Her gaze switched back and forth between us—the confusion still there on her face. "But since when did you start seeing anyone?"

Was I the only one who felt that was kind of stalkerish?

Was there a website that updated women on NHL players' dating status?

"Well, he is." I thought my voice was sweetly polite, given that she was still sitting there. In my mind I said, "Now run along." What she actually heard was, "Can I help you with something?"

Travis tenderly kissed my neck, which was exposed thanks to my messy ponytail. My skin shivered at the delightful sensation of his lips against it.

The woman never answered my question. She pushed herself off the seat and sashayed away without so much as a good-bye. I mentally waved adios.

"Does that happen often?" I asked Travis as he kissed my neck again.

"What's that?"

"Women hitting on you. I mean, it wasn't like I was in the bathroom long." I didn't give him a chance to answer before the next words tumbled out. "I bet you'll be happy once hockey season begins and you can go back to screwing around with other women." Pretty impressive how I managed to keep jealousy from my tone, huh?

He shrugged and my neck instantly missed his lips. "Wouldn't matter. I'm not into puck bunnies or women who are only interested in me because of my salary."

"Puck bunnies? Is that as bad as it sounds?"

"Depends on your point of view. If you just want an easy lay, and you don't mind that the puck bunny might have slept with your teammates, then they're great. But you need to take precautions."

"I can see that," I said, cupping his face and giving him a tender kiss—all for Jennifer's benefit like earlier. "You don't exactly want an STD or unexpected pregnancy to knock you on your ass."

Right—not quite the conversation you'd expect while I was giving him sweet kisses. But Jennifer didn't know that.

"Well, that too," he said. "But you also don't want to find your naked ass doing the rounds on social media."

I could have sworn my eyebrows jumped up my forehead. "That actually happens? Did it happen to you?"

"No—one of my teammates."

"Ouch."

"Ouch indeed."

"So she's a puck bunny?" I nodded toward where the brunette had disappeared.

"No, she's the one hoping to snare a rich husband."

"You can tell the difference?" It wasn't like she had a warning label stuck across her chest—although that wouldn't have been a bad idea.

"After a while you can pretty much figure it out."

"Is that why you've been avoiding having a girlfriend?" I asked. "Because you're worried they'll turn into gold diggers or crazies?" Because that made a lot of sense. It would be enough to make most smart men leery.

He nodded—but that look in his eyes? I hadn't nailed the whole truth. There was more to why relationships scared him.

But as much as I wished to find out what it was, this wasn't the time and place to ask him. So I whispered in his ear, "Do you think Jennifer bought that we're happily dating each other?"

"I guess we'll know soon enough—once she reports back to her grandmother."

26

EMMA

The house where we were staying in Napa Valley two days later was nothing like I had imagined. It was a two-story freaking mansion. A gorgeous, freaking mansion built from stone with lots of archways and a generous curving driveway. Even the clay roof shingles were curved. Everything about the place made me think of the Mediterranean.

This was the kind of location where you expected celebrities to live.

"And out back is the heated pool and hot tub," Kelsey explained as she showed us around the house. She and Trent had already been there for two hours. Josh, Holly and Travis had been practicing the dance routine this morning for the upcoming fundraiser, so we had only arrived ten minutes ago.

Had I seen the routine yet?

No—it was still top secret.

And according to Travis, I wouldn't get to see it until the day of the big fundraiser.

And yes, we had begun selling tickets for it. Despite The

Unicorn being a decent size, the tickets were almost sold out. The pub had even offered to donate half the profits that night to the youth center.

Several businesses in the building had also stepped up to donate prizes for the silent auction.

Everyone was excited—but no more than I was.

And yes, Fanny and her friends had bought tickets. I just hoped they didn't have heart attacks from seeing so many hot half-naked guys in one night. As far as Travis and I could tell, we had passed Jennifer's report with flying colors. Fanny and her cohorts still believed he and I were dating.

"This place is amazing," I said to Kelsey. "Have you stayed here before?"

"No, not in this house. But we rented another one two years ago that was almost as nice."

On the second floor, we stopped in front of two closed doors opposite the hallway from each other. Kelsey opened one of them. "This is your room, Emma. Travis is across the hallway."

I entered it. "Wow," was all I was capable of saying.

"I know," Kelsey said. "All the bedrooms are gorgeous. And they each have their own private bathrooms."

I was vaguely aware of Kelsey and Holly taking Travis to his room as I continued staring at the furnishings in mine. If there was one word to describe it that would be romantic— but not in an overly girlie way. It was a mix of modern and antique, with dark wood furniture and a four-poster bed. The walls were a soft moss green.

Welcome to my dream bedroom...if I ever lived in a place like this.

I opened the balcony door and stepped out. The balcony, with its wicker patio furniture, stretched between my room and the neighboring one. I paused at the black metal railing and took in the incredible view: the peaceful, well-maintained gardens leading up to the house, the vineyards, and the gentle rolling hills in the distance.

In all the years I'd lived in foster care, not once had I imagined being in a location like this. Of course, I also never imagined pretending to be Travis's girlfriend back then either, so clearly I was on a roll.

"So what do you think?" Travis asked behind me.

I glanced over my shoulder, smiled at him, then went back to appreciating the scenery. "It's breathtaking. Could you imagine living out here all the time?"

"Probably not. I'm used to living in the city."

"Me, too." But I was also used to living in foster care and I got over that soon enough.

A bird chirped from the nearby tree. Another one answered it. Travis placed his hands on the railing, caging me in. A combination of his man scent and aftershave wrapped around me, and I leaned back against him. *Oops.* Hadn't meant to do that.

Not at all.

We stood still for a few minutes, looking at the surrounding grounds. You'd never guess the battle waging inside me at his close proximity. Part of me wished to see if Travis would open up to me some more. The horny part just craved to drag him to bed and have wild sex with him.

Was Travis facing the same battle? If he was, the horny side of him was winning. Big surprise there. He was a man after all.

His hand covered mine and drifted up my arm, slowly igniting each and every nerve.

At my elbow, his hand moved to my ribs. My girls, their nipples now perky, silently begged for his hand to move up slightly. As if heeding their needy pleas, Travis caressed my side for a moment with his fingertips, then shifted one hand to cup my breast.

Oh, God, I whispered in my head. At least I hoped it was in my head.

"Christ, I want to be inside you so badly, Emma," he murmured in my ear, the sound so low it was almost a growl.

My body screamed out, *Give the man what he wants.*

I turned around in his arms and gazed into his beautiful hazel eyes for a heartbeat. "I want that too," I whispered.

And with that, his mouth was on mine, and we began savoring each other with our eager tongues. At some point, Travis dipped down, grabbed the backs of my thighs, and lifted me up. My legs instantly wrapped around his hips. My dress bunched up around *my* hips. The only things between his thickening length and my throbbing core were his jeans and my panties.

If he hadn't been stepping into my room, I would've been dry humping him.

Oh, what the heck. I did it anyway.

He swallowed my moan and placed me on the bed so I was sitting.

Our lips still attached, I started unfastening his shirt buttons. His shirt was already untucked from his jeans, and I slid my hand through the newly created opening and trace my fingers along the ridges of his abs.

Not wishing to miss out on the fun, Travis trailed his fingertip along the pink lace edging of my demi-bra. The cream satin material with small pink roses pushed up my breasts, giving him quite the view. "I swear this is my new all-time favorite bra." His finger slipped under the lace and shoved the fabric down, revealing the taut nipple. "Definitely my new favorite bra."

His teasing finger brushed against it and I whimpered.

Wetness rushed to my core. I squirmed on the bed, my clit pleading for his finger to brush against it next.

He bent down and took the greedy bud into his mouth. My fingers knotted in his hair. I might have even gently yanked the soft strands.

A moment later, his skilled fingers had removed the bra, and the other breast was appreciating his lavish attention. My hands slipped between his collar and the skin of his neck. I needed to touch him all over, and I needed to do it now.

Luckily for me, Travis could read my mind—or so it seemed. He quickly removed the offending shirt and tossed it to the side.

Ooh, that was more like it.

I stood up and let my dress fall to the floor, leaving me in nothing but matching panties.

Travis's eyes adopted a heated look. A volcano couldn't have gotten any hotter than the way his gaze was taking me in. A level of confidence I'd never had before with men glowed inside me, and suddenly I wanted to be the one calling the shots.

"Remove your jeans," I said, my voice rough and sexy and demanding.

At least I hoped it was all of that.

Travis's mouth curled up to one side. "As you wish." He removed a condom wrapper from his back pocket and set it on the bedside table. Then he slowly unzipped his jeans and pushed them down his legs. His cock strained against the fabric of his boxer briefs and I licked my lips in anticipation.

"Now the underwear."

He did as I said, and then to tease me further, he took his cock in his hand and pumped his fist along the length.

And I'd be lying if I said it didn't make me wetter.

I shimmied my panties down my legs and kicked them to

the side. Then I knelt in front of him and wrapped my fingers around his hard length. Pre-cum leaked from the opening, and I licked him like he was a lollipop.

That primal growl? Definitely him.

Which only made me feel more confident. Nothing said you were driving a man crazy in a good way than when he made that sound.

I slipped his cock into my mouth and gently grabbed his balls. I'd read somewhere that men loved it when you did that. Might as well see if it was true.

And...it was.

"Christ, Emma. You're going to be the death of me."

Did it sound like I would be the death of him?

Maybe if death and orgasm were the same.

Let me point out here that I'd never gone down on a guy before...not even with my ex-boyfriend. Couldn't say with him I'd even been curious or interested. But it was different with Travis.

The way I felt with Travis was different—even though he didn't feel the same way about me.

Taking him as far as I could, I cupped myself and brushed my finger against my clit. I released a strangled sound that was a cross between a hum and *Oh, God*.

Needing to see his reaction to what I was doing to him, I peered up. What I hadn't expected was to find him looking at me. If I was to rate the level of heat and lust and want in his eyes from one to a hundred, it would be a definite one thousand.

Hello, girl power!

"Keep touching yourself like that, Emma," he said, voice rough. "Keep touching yourself and let me know how much you enjoy it."

The low growl of his voice caused a new rush of moisture

to my core. I'd never realized before this just how much of a turn-on dirty talk could be.

With my gaze still on Travis, I let his noises guide me as I moved my mouth along his length. Well, as far as I could go. I hadn't yet mastered the fine art of taking him deeper without annoying my gag reflex.

"I'm going to come," he said after a few minutes, voice strained.

I slipped his cock out of my mouth. "Thought that was the general idea."

"It is...if I didn't want to come inside you. But I do—more than you could possibly know." His gaze dropped to my hand still pleasuring myself. Or rather that had been pleasuring myself. I had to stop a moment ago because I'd been so close to coming, I was afraid of biting Travis's cock off.

I pushed myself to my feet and climbed onto the bed. Travis followed.

"Bring your knees to your chest and open yourself up to me, Emma."

I did as he asked. Instead of feeling vulnerable and exposed as I would have expected, I was even more turned on.

Travis touched my sex and I came close to launching off the bed. That smug, satisfied smile of his grew, and he grabbed the condom wrapper from the bedside table. After he slipped the condom on, he positioned himself against my entrance, and with a quick thrust, buried himself inside me.

It didn't take long for us to fall off the edge of ecstasy together and letting everyone in the mansion know exactly what we were doing.

Oops.

That hadn't exactly been on my agenda for this trip, especially since Josh and Trent were aware that our relationship was fake. But since we were two consenting, horny adults, what else did they expect?

After he had dealt with the condom, Travis returned to the bed and kissed me. But unlike the hungry kisses of a few minutes ago, this kiss was tender and sweet.

This was the kiss of happily ever after—if I had been living in a different fairy tale.

27

TRAVIS

What's the golden rule of flings and one-night stands?

Don't stick around—because the girl will always want more than you are willing to give. If not now, then soon enough.

But somehow that rule with Emma never seemed to apply. Why? Because it was *me* who longed for more than I was willing to give. But in the end, love only resulted in pain.

Too melodramatic for you?

Let me explain. My parents were the greatest. When most teens were rebelling against their parents' rules, I worshiped Mom and Dad. They respected me and I respected them. They had sacrificed everything for me and my hockey. They came to every game. They took turns driving me to my super early morning practices without complaint...which was more than I could say about myself.

Was Dad one of those scary hockey fathers who yelled at everyone—the coaches, the other players, the refs, and even his own kid? A few of my old childhood teammates had fathers like that. The men had aspirations for their kids. Aspi-

179

rations that involved not only playing in the NHL but also winning the Stanley Cup. Aspirations that involved hefty several-million-dollars-a-year salaries. Aspirations that involved the father's own failed ambitions. They drove their kids hard—preventing the kid from truly loving the sport.

But hockey dads weren't the only ones who were terrifying. Hockey moms could be just as bad, if not worse.

My parents had been the complete opposite. They always had a kind word to say about my games, even if I had screwed up and accidentally scored on my own goal. Yes, it sucked the big one whenever the puck bounced off your body or skate and landed in your own net. Some dads would've chewed their kid a new one. My parents always had milk and cookies and a warm smile no matter what happened. They always dwelled on the positives.

They made me feel like there was nothing I couldn't do. They made me feel proud to be their son. So when I lost them, it had almost killed me.

You know the story about Granny and how she had helped me get through my parents' deaths—even when I was acting like a piece of shit. She never gave up on me. And like my parents, she sacrificed everything to make sure I could keep playing the sport I loved, the sport that helped me get through my loss.

And I almost lost her because of the stroke.

And then a few years later, I did lose my best friend and teammate in college. He always had my back like I always had his...until I was no longer able to watch his back and he died of cancer.

So, to sum it all up—loving someone came with risks. The kind of risks that involved you losing the person—and subsequently, a piece of your soul.

Why am I telling you this?

Because I was starting to feel things for Emma that I shouldn't.

Things that scared me.

And what did guys who were afraid of falling in love excel at? That's right—running.

I knew what Emma really wanted to happen next. It was what ninety percent of girls desired after a good fuck—to cuddle.

But I couldn't do that. Not this time.

"I should go and get changed so we can join everyone by the pool." I scrambled from the bed as if I had been lying with a rattlesnake instead of the freshly fucked, hot redhead who was staring at me in confusion. "I'll see you downstairs."

I didn't bother to wait around to witness the hurt on her face. I shoved on my jeans, grabbed the rest of my clothes from the floor, and bailed the room, shutting the door behind me.

Naturally, I couldn't have a smooth escape, with no one witnessing my assholiness. I bumped into Holly and Josh in the hallway. Well, more like plowed into them.

If they were surprised to see me practically naked and escaping from Emma's room, they didn't show it. But given how noisy she and I had just been, I'd be surprised if even the neighbors hadn't heard us.

"I'll be down in a minute," I said to the pair, then pretty much hurled myself into my bedroom.

I didn't exactly rush to join everyone downstairs. I cleaned up and changed into my swim trunks.

Josh and Holly were sitting on a pair of recliners, watching Trent and Kelsey in the pool, when I walked out the patio door. Trent grabbed Kelsey around the waist from behind. She gave a little shriek, then giggled as she squirmed to get away...just not very hard. Her blonde hair had been pulled into a high ponytail, which Trent was making the most of. He nibbled on her exposed neck.

I might have been watching Trent and Kelsey, but that didn't mean I failed to notice the moment Emma stepped from the house to join us. I turned around—and I wouldn't be surprised if my jaw hit the ground.

She was wearing a black one-piece swimsuit. The front scooped down to an inch above her belly button, revealing her cleavage. What kept her breasts from falling out? The ties that zigzagged from the bottom of the opening to just below the top of the tempting mounds of flesh.

Sure—it was sexy as all hell. But that wasn't what completely did me in and caused my dick to react. Her curls were loosely piled on her head, with strands framing her face. She reminded me of the fountain in her store. If I was asked to describe the goddess of love, this woman in front of me would be it.

"I love your swimsuit, Emma," Holly said as I continued staring at her, my heart thumping harder in my chest than it had been while we'd been having sex.

She smiled at Holly, either oblivious to how I was looking at her or choosing to ignore me after I'd pulled the fuck-and-dash a few minutes ago. "Thanks. How's the water?"

"I haven't been in yet," Holly said, "but those two"—she indicated Trent and Kelsey—"claim it's warm."

That was too bad because the way my cock was responding to Emma, I needed to jump in a freezing pool to deal with my dilemma.

As if privy to my thoughts, Emma's gaze dropped to my swim trunks and her eyes widened. She then tore her gaze away and walked toward the steps leading into the pool.

And like a puppy eager to play with his owner, I followed after her. The only difference between me and a puppy was that I didn't bound after her and I didn't nip at her heels—but I only came within an inch of not doing that.

She tested the water's temperature with her toes and continued down the steps until her body was submerged enough to cover her tits.

I entered the water after her. Kelsey laughed and squirmed out of Trent's reach. She managed to run a yard or two before Trent easily caught up with her. She splashed him, but it wasn't enough to deter him—not that it looked like she wanted to deter him. He grabbed around her waist and pulled her to him.

Kelsey wrapped her arms around his neck and kissed him in a way that I was surprised didn't heat the pool another ten degrees.

Okaaay. I knew from experience they'd be busy for a while. Holly and Josh were also preoccupied. Josh had abandoned his recliner and had joined his wife on hers. From the way they were leaning toward each other, it was clear they would be making out shortly.

And the prize for the most awkward couples weekend went to...

But it wasn't awkward because Emma and I weren't a real couple. It just felt that way because of how I'd acted after she and I had fucked.

I approached her the same way you would a live wire—very cautiously. But like a kid who was tempted to stick a fork in an electrical socket after being told not to, I couldn't control myself. And yes—I would swear that till my dying day.

Emma watched me walk closer to her but didn't move. The same heat I'd seen in her eyes before, along with a dose of self-preservation, glared back at me.

I slowly reached out to her. When she didn't flinch or

scowl at me, I caressed the soft skin of her shoulder. "I'm sorry about earlier. I didn't mean to leave like that."

She shrugged and for the first time I noticed the smattering of freckles on her shoulder.

"I don't really expect much else from you," she said. Or at least I think that's what she'd said. I was too mesmerized by her freckles.

I ran the pad of my thumb across them. "You know, if you joined these with a sharpie, you'd get a heart shape." I traced the pattern with my fingertip.

She turned her head to see. "Guess I've never noticed. Must mean I was always fated to have a career in romance. My calling was in my freckles." She smiled but it never made it to her eyes.

It didn't take a fucking genius to figure out why. "Someday a man's gonna fall in love with you, Emma, and he won't want to let you go. He'll never let you down." *Not like you've been let down in the past.*

My words were supposed to reassure her, but they had the opposite effect.

Instead of the smile I'd expected, she looked away.

But not before I noticed how her eyes glistened with unshed tears.

Unshed tears that almost gutted me.

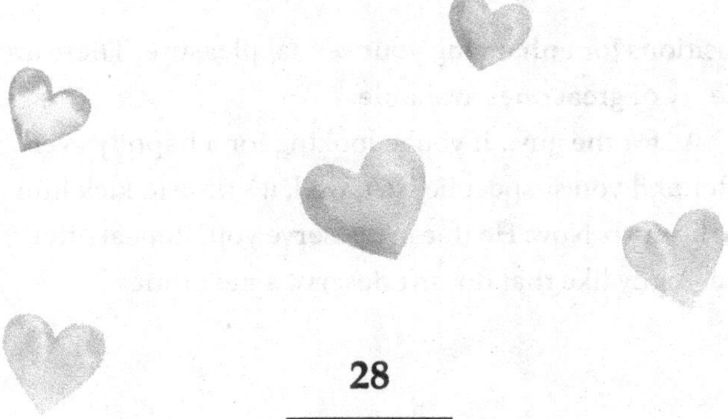

28

___

Dear Dr. Lovejoy,

The guy I'm seeing couldn't get out of the room fast enough the last time we had sex. Do you think he has commitment issues or was the sex really that bad?

Sincerely,

What Did I Do Wrong?

Dear What Did I Do Wrong,

The first thing you need to ask yourself is, what did you think of the sex? The fact that you are asking makes me think it wasn't all fireworks for you, either. My recommendation is to at least read some erotic romances. You'll get some great ideas there for spicing up your sex life. And don't forget the guides on different positions for enhancing your sexual pleasure. There are plenty of great ones available.

As for the guy...if you're looking for a happily ever after and you suspect he isn't, well, it's time to kick him to the curb. Now. He doesn't deserve you. Repeat after me. A guy like that doesn't deserve a next time.

29

EMMA

What's the one thing you never wish to hear the man you're falling in love with say to you?

Yep—Travis pretty much nailed it when he told me that someday a man would fall in love with me and never let me down.

What he meant was he wasn't the man who was capable of falling in love with me and loving me unconditionally.

It was official: I was cursed. Like Sleeping Beauty. She was born to a king and queen who forgot to invite the evil fairy to her christening. The fairy was ill-tempered and got pissed off. She cursed the poor child so that when the princess turned sixteen years old, she would prick her finger on a spinning wheel and die. Luckily for Sleeping Beauty, a good fairy was able to change the curse so the princess wouldn't die, but would sleep for a hundred years...or until her prince kissed her. True love's kiss ended the curse and they lived happily ever after.

Great story, except in my case there was no super long nap to contend with—no true love's kiss to help me. I was cursed forevermore to never find and experience love.

I was just the poor sap who doled out advice on the topic.

Those tears in my eyes? Must be the chlorine in the pool.

"You're right," I said, avoiding Travis's gaze. "I'm sure one day I'll find an incredible guy who will love me."

It was a good thing the readers of my column didn't know the truth about me, or else they'd be storming the paper with pitchforks in hand, declaring I was a fake.

Which I was. A fake everything—including a fake girlfriend.

Hmm. Maybe the paper would be interested in changing things up. I could have a weekly column on how to be a fake girlfriend. Because so far—if you ignored the part about falling in love with Travis—I was rocking that.

"I know you will," Travis said. "And he'll be lucky to have you," he continued, because apparently unwittingly stabbing me in the heart wasn't enough.

Right. "Well, now that we've had that heart-to-heart," I said, working hard to keep the hurt from my voice, "I think I'll read now."

What was I reading? The first Harry Potter book. Again. Why? Because it was a nice reminder that some parents did love their kids. And not only did they love their kids, they were willing to die for them.

I climbed out of the pool, grabbed my towel from where I had folded it on the recliner, and dried myself. Holly and Josh were in their own little world, so I picked up my well-read book, made myself comfortable on the seat, and began reading.

I had read a couple of paragraphs when a shadow fell over me. "Isn't that a kids' book?" Travis asked.

"And there's a problem with that?"

"Not at all. I just pegged you as someone who only reads romances."

Normally I was—but Harry Potter was one of those few exceptions. "There's nothing wrong with variety."

Truth? I thought guys should read at least one romance—preferably erotic romance—to know what women liked. It should be mandatory reading in high school, like Shakespeare. That would save us all a lot of grief.

"True." He sat on the seat next to mine.

"And what do you read?" All right, my tone might have implied I didn't believe he read at all. Or at least not novels.

"This and that."

"So stuff with a lot of car chases in it?"

He chuckled. "My mom got me hooked on the Harry Potter books. She read them first and got a little geeky about them."

"You've actually read the series?" I somehow couldn't see him being into them, but he would've been about ten when the first book came out, so it was possible.

"Did you have any aspirations to go to Hogwarts?" Like I had.

He shifted to the end of my recliner. I moved my feet up to give him more space. "They didn't play hockey there, so that would be a no. And flying around on a broom while chasing a tiny gold ball with wings wasn't my thing."

"Afraid of heights, are you?"

"I'm not a big fan of them. What about you? Were you waiting for your letter?"

I laughed. "You got me. But alas, no such luck."

He looked away—and I knew not to push him anymore on the topic. It only reminded him of the mother he'd lost.

I opened my book again and disappeared into the story I'd read so many times growing up. But back then, I had borrowed the books from the library because I didn't have any money to buy my own copies—and there was no way any of my foster parents would have bought them for me.

"You write that newspaper column, don't you? The Dr. Lovejoy one." Fortunately, he kept his voice low so that no one else heard him.

But that didn't stop me from glancing over at the others to double-check.

For a heartbeat, I thought of lying, pretending I had no idea what he was talking about. But the way he was expectantly regarding me caused the wall around that secret to crumble. He already knew so much about me, what was one more thing?

"Yes, I do. But I prefer no one knows it's me." *Hint. Hint.*

"So how come you write it?"

"Because someone asked me to. And because I enjoy it. It's fun pretending I know what the heck I'm talking about when half the time I probably don't." I had meant that last part as a joke, but from the way Travis was staring at me, I got the impression he hadn't interpreted it the same way.

"I've read a few of them," he said. "Sounds to me like you know what you're talking about."

"Says the guy who doesn't know the first thing about romance." I looked down at my open book, hoping he'd get the message.

"Hey, I know lots about romance. I just choose not to be romantic. Romance is for guys who want to settle down."

"Which, as you've already established, isn't you," I said, my gaze still locked on the words in front of me and doing my best to ignore the tightening in my chest.

Travis didn't say anything after that, remaining quiet the entire time I read. Eventually, the girls and I started dinner while the men got ready to barbecue the steaks. After our meal, we hit the hot tub.

Before I had a chance to climb in, I spotted a lavender plant nearby. I rubbed a stalk of the fragrant flower between my fingers and inhaled its perfume. "Hmm. I love lavender," I said to no one in particular. "It was once believed to be the herb of love. Cleopatra was thought to have used it when she seduced men."

"Maybe you could grow some in your store," Travis said, "and sell it as a love potion." He laughed.

"Hey, don't laugh," I said, climbing into the hot tub. "Why do you think my lavender scented bath products are so popular?"

He shrugged. "Because girls like the smell of it."

"Maybe it's because they're aware of its magic powers." I winked at him, knowing his opinion of my so-called magical fountain.

"This is so nice," Holly said a few minutes later, leaning back against her husband. Above us, the night sky looked like a kid's art project, with silver glitter sprinkled over black paper.

"It's gorgeous." I was sitting next to Travis, a few inches separating us.

Just straddle him and kiss him, a persistent voice said. I swear the voice and my body were in cahoots.

My brain, fortunately, was the voice of reason, so to speak, and pointed out that doing such things would be a big mistake. My heart was bruised enough from everything that had happened in the past.

My heart said fiddlesticks—it was a big girl and could handle so much more.

Fiddlesticks? Clearly Fanny had quite the influence over my heart. It was beginning to sound and think like her.

One thing was for certain though—it wasn't just Travis I was falling in love with. The more I got to know them, the more I fell in love with Fanny and Travis's friends. Just not in the same way I was falling hard for him.

And what was I going to do once this masquerade was over? Yes, Josh and Trent were aware our relationship was fake. Only Holly and Kelsey thought it was real. But would they still wish to hang out with me after our time together had ticked to an end? And would I even want to spend time with them, knowing I could never be with Travis the way I longed to be? Knowing that every time I saw them, my mind would torture me with wistful memories of him?

Yes, I was aware of the irony that I'd finally truly let a man into my heart, had finally quit running because of my fear of being abandoned, and it was all for naught.

After we were finished in the hot tub, I headed to my room for a shower and then bed. It was late and I was slightly buzzed from the wine we'd been drinking.

In the bathroom, I stripped off my clothes and climbed into the large shower. With the lavender scented shower gel, I caressed my body, pretending my hands were Travis's, giving my breasts extra attention—like he would.

My eyes closed, I slipped my fingers between my legs and brushed them against my clit. It had been begging me since Travis's and my little tryst earlier to let him give me an encore. "You'd better get used to this," I muttered. "Only three more weeks and then it will be over."

I imagined Travis's fingers touching me, but as close to coming as I was, I just couldn't quite get there. "Traitor," I muttered to my aching core. It had only gotten achier since I climbed into the shower, but it still refused to let me visit happy land.

Giving up, I turned off the water and pushed open the glass door. I stepped onto the bath mat—and that's when I saw it, on the floor, next to my clothes.

A big-ass fucking spider.

I stared at it for a heartbeat while the logical voice in my head tried to reason with me, telling me it was just a harmless spider. Unfortunately, the rest of my brain didn't care if that was true or not. I did what any red-blooded American who valued their life would do—I screamed.

And this wasn't just any scream. It could be heard even in Australia.

A moment later the bathroom door flung open, with me standing there completely naked.

Startled by Travis's abrupt entrance, I stopped screaming.

He took a moment to eye-fuck me—or to check that no one had actually attacked me in the shower. It could have gone either way.

I looked down at the spider...but it was gone.

"What happened?" Travis asked. He was wearing only his jeans, but even the sight of him shirtless didn't distract me from scanning the room for the evil beast.

"Spider," I managed to get out. "Big spider!" Where the fuck had it gone?

Two possibilities existed—neither pleasant. Well, three, but I didn't think I was lucky enough that it had spontaneously combusted.

It had either snuck into my clothes—in which case I would have to burn them. Or it had crawled out the bathroom and was currently plotting to attack me while I slept.

I shuddered at the possibility.

Travis handed me the towel from the rack. With my gaze still searching for signs of the spider, I took it from him and clutched it to my body. A little too late at this point when it came to Travis, but I didn't need the spider to see me any more naked than it already had. Plus there was always a chance someone else in the house would come to check if I was all right.

"I don't see it," Travis helpfully pointed out.

"It's here somewhere. Please get it out of here." Yes, that might have been near panic in my voice. Oh, who was I kidding? That was it's-going-to-kill-me-while-I-sleep full-out panic.

"You're not afraid of spiders, are you?"

I threw him a *what-do-you-think?* look. "No, I just thought I could invite him to sleep with me tonight." I shuddered once more.

"It won't hurt you. It's only a harmless spider."

"How do you know? You never even saw it." It could have been a black widow for all he knew.

I glanced at my clothes lying innocently on the floor and pointed to them. "Maybe it's in there."

Travis picked up each piece of clothing and shook them. Nothing fell out.

Which meant one thing...

The freaking creature was planning to sleep with me tonight.

"I can't sleep in there," I said, gesturing wildly at my bedroom. My arm shook as did the rest of me. "It's in there somewhere, waiting for me."

Travis looked in the direction I was pointing. "If it makes you feel better, you can sleep with me tonight."

I eyed him for a moment. What were the chances of the spider crawling into his room while we slept? Probably not as high as it staying in my room and terrorizing me.

"Maybe you could try catching it." Then I wouldn't have to sleep with Travis and I wouldn't have to worry about it tracking me down.

Travis let out an it's-just-a-harmless-spider sigh and turned to leave.

"Where are you going?" I asked, my voice back to its previous state of panic.

"To look for it while you get dressed."

"Oh. Okay."

He left the room and I quickly toweled myself off. Two

minutes later I was standing in the middle of my room, wearing only a skimpy pair of sleep shorts covered in hearts and a plain white tank top. Both were well-worn, the fabric thin. Which meant there was no hiding the fact that I didn't have a bra on.

Under any other circumstance, I would have been slightly mortified, but a big spider loose in my room trumped all.

Travis looked behind the chair by the window, then walked to the dresser and looked under it.

"Any sign of it yet?" I inwardly groaned. Of course he hadn't found anything. If he had, he wouldn't still be searching for it.

"It could be anywhere—and if it doesn't wish to be found, it won't be."

I glared at him. "You're really not making me feel better."

That goddamn sexy smirk on his face? It almost made me forget about the spider. *Almost.* "I know what I can do to make you feel better."

"Kill the spider?"

He leaned in. "Fuck you so hard you'll see stars and forget about it."

That was definitely tempting. "Did you mean it when you said I can sleep with you tonight?" I asked, scanning the room in case the spider had crawled out of hiding.

"Yes."

"Even though you hate sleeping with women?"

"Define sleeping."

I rolled my eyes. "You know what I mean. When was the last time you actually slept through the night with one?"

"Not for a few years, I guess."

Why didn't I suggest we switch rooms? Because if the spider did sneak into his room and I saw it, I needed Travis there to get rid of it.

"Well, you'll be happy to learn that I don't bite," I said.

"Maybe I do," he said in the voice that always got my girlie parts excited.

Yes—that was my moan...combined with a yawn.

Having a spider scare you to death sure took a lot out of you. The wine and hot tub didn't help either. But thanks to the monster now inhabiting my room, the happy buzz had long since vanished.

Travis parked his hand on my lower back and nudged me toward the bedroom door. "C'mon, sleepyhead."

"I have to brush my teeth first. Guard me while I do that, okay?" I didn't wait for his reply. I trudged back to the bathroom and quickly got ready for bed.

He stood in the bathroom doorway, looking breathtaking. Like my own sexy bodyguard—ready to take down all scary spiders that approached me.

In his bedroom, I considered for a second placing pillows between us on the bed but quickly discarded the idea. We'd already had sex—twice. Creating a barricade between us wasn't much of a deterrent. If Travis desired sex, my traitorous body was hardly going to say no. If anything, he was more at risk of me jumping *him*. Spider or no spider, my girlie parts still ached from my unfulfilling shower.

"Which side of the bed do you want?" I asked.

"The left side."

I slipped under the cover, curled up on my side, and closed my eyes. "Goodnight, Travis. And thanks."

"For what?"

I felt his side of the bed dip slightly. "For letting me stay in your room."

"You're welcome. Now go to sleep."

Easier said than done. I might have been tired a few minutes ago, but between Travis's delicious scent now invading my space and my still aroused body, sleep evaded me.

I shifted position, but it didn't make a difference. I turned onto my back and stared at the ceiling.

"Can't sleep, huh?" he asked.

"No, I'm good." At least I would be once my girlie parts settled down for the night.

I shifted again. Nope—still not happening.

"I can help you fall asleep."

Even without looking at him, I could tell he was smiling. "How?"

Yes—I had my suspicions too about what he had in mind. The smile in his voice gave it away.

He didn't answer. Well, not with words anyway. He rolled over and his lips were on mine. And because I had no intention of saying no or playing hard to get, I let him in.

That wasn't the only part of him that got busy. His cock hardened against my hip and his palm cupped my breast. So I did the only thing I was capable of—I groaned.

He pinched my nipple and I groaned even louder.

"Like that?" he asked against my lips.

"Very much."

"Hmmm. Wonder what else you would enjoy." And he proceeded to find out.

My clothes were off in record time. His too. Not that it took much to remove his boxer briefs.

"I've missed the taste of you," he said, bending my knees and moving my legs apart. He nipped his way down my inner thigh, rubbing his stubble against my skin. I squirmed at the erotic sensation and bit my lip so no one else could hear what we were up to.

But then decided I didn't give a damn what anyone thought. They were probably too preoccupied to care anyway.

No sooner had I thought that, then Travis licked my clit

with enough pressure to cause me to see stars. "Oh, God," I groaned, my eyes squeezing tightly.

"I can guarantee God had nothing to do with that."

Giggling, I opened my eyes. "Don't worry, in my mind you get full credit."

"That's good to know. Now, no more closing your eyes. I want you to watch me make you come."

"Yes, sir." I propped myself on my elbows.

His mouth curled up to one side. "Yes, master, will work, too."

My mouth copied his. "Are you going to fuck me, *master*, or just talk?"

"Definitely fuck you." He ran the tip of his tongue against my sex. "I missed you, pussy. Did you miss me?"

"Oh, she missed you all right. You don't have to worry about that."

"Who's worried?" He flicked his tongue against my clit, and I had to fight to keep my eyes open.

It didn't take much in terms of his lavish attention before a rush of heat powered through my lower belly and lit me up like a truckload of fireworks.

July 4th celebrations had nothing on this.

Travis reached for a condom from his nightstand.

"Wow, were you a boy scout?" I asked. "Because you definitely come prepared."

"More like I'm prepared to make you come again." He winked at me and my body went all tingly.

"Sounds good, but..." I sat up. "But I want to ride you this time."

The gleam in his eyes? I translated that as a yes.

He sat back on the bed, a pile of pillows behind him. I shifted my body to straddle his hips and took the condom wrapper from him. But instead of rolling it onto him, I leaned forward and flicked my tongue against his nipple.

He groaned; I grinned. Then I closed my lips around it and sucked. That too was rewarded with a moan. Not wanting the other nipple to feel ignored, I adjusted my body and lavished nipple #2 with the same attention as the first.

The ache between my legs was resting against his hard length. He rocked his body, pressing himself against me in a way that nearly had me coming once more.

I chuckled. "Hint received." I ripped open the condom and removed it from the wrapper. "I've only put one on a banana before." And they weren't exactly the same thing.

I peered down at his cock. His was much wider than a banana. Yep—not the same thing.

He laughed. "A banana?"

"Yes, it was Hannah's idea in high school...just in case." The just in case I never had to worry about until now.

"I'm sure you'll do fine." He parked his hands behind his head and nodded for me to continue.

Once I had it on him, with relatively little trouble, I got into position, his tip against my entrance, and lowered myself until he was deeply seated inside me.

I leaned back and thrust my hips forward. My already sensitive clit promised me an orgasm to break all records if I kept that up. So naturally I did it again. "Oh, God."

"I think this is my new favorite position," Travis said, his eyes on my breasts. He leaned forward and took an eager nipple in his mouth—and I had to second his opinion.

While he teased my happy nipples with his mouth and fingers, I continued the slow yet deep thrusting movements of my hips. But once he'd finished feasting on my breasts, he grabbed my hips and switched the pace to something faster and harder.

My heat clenched around him as another orgasm rocketed my body into the stratosphere—where Travis joined me a moment later.

Once we had returned to the planet, spent and satisfied, Travis removed himself from me and disposed of the condom. He then climbed back in bed.

Lying next to me, our legs tangled together, he traced his thumb against my lower lip. I would have given anything to know what he was thinking—or not. He was a guy, which meant he could be contemplating a million different things—and none of it to do with us.

"You must think I'm silly being scared of spiders," I said.

"It's no big deal. Everyone is scared of something."

"Right. Are you saying that big bad alpha you is scared of something?" I believed that as much as I believed I would wake up tomorrow a million dollars richer.

"I lost my parents and then I lost my best friend in college to cancer. And I almost lost my grandmother when I was a teen..."

He didn't finish the sentence but he didn't have to.

"You're afraid of losing someone you love?"

It all made sense now. He didn't keep girls at a distance because of his crazy ex-girlfriend or because he was worried he'd get screwed over by someone only interested in his bank account. It was because he was protecting his heart.

"I don't exactly have a great track record." He shrugged as if it were no big deal.

Except it was a very big deal.

Only I had no idea what to say to it. It wasn't as if I had lost anyone I loved. Not in the same sense as Travis. No one had cared enough about me to stick around—with the exception of Hannah.

"But you can't give up on love because of that," I said. "Everyone loses someone they love at one time or another. We're humans, not immortal."

Did he look convinced? Not at all. He had spent half his

life feeling this way, and nothing I could say would change his opinion.

"Doesn't matter either way. I'm a hockey player, Emma. We get traded all the time."

"That doesn't mean you can't love someone. Are your teammates all single?"

"No, but—"

"There are no buts. If the girl loves you, she'll be willing to move with you. Or the two of you will work something out so you're together during the off-season. But either way, you can't give up on love because you're scared of losing the person like you lost your parents and best friend.'

I cupped his face and studied his beautiful hazel eyes. But it was clear that no matter what I said, he wasn't convinced. Not that it mattered when it came to my heart. He didn't love me. I was just someone to keep his grandmother happy until hockey season commenced.

I gave him a small smile, keeping him from guessing the truth, and kissed his jaw. "Good night. And thanks again for protecting me from the vicious spider."

Too bad he couldn't have protected me from my own foolish heart.

30

EMMA

What's the best way to deal with a broken heart? Hang out with the guy's grandmother and break your heart some more.

Right—that wasn't the best advice, but it was exactly what I was doing.

Travis and I had returned from Napa Valley three days ago. Neither of us had talked about what happened the night the spider decided to be an unwelcome intruder. We had continued as if we hadn't discussed Travis's fear of losing someone he loved. And yes, that included having more incredible sex.

Why weren't we currently working on the mural? Because we had finished it last night.

And since I hadn't gotten my oven fixed...

"Have you thought of making sugar cookies and decorating them with little love sayings?" Fanny asked as I added chocolate chips to the cookie batter.

"You mean like those little candies?"

"Yes—but with longer sayings. Like 'I just want to be yours,' 'Forever yours,' and 'You're my new favorite feeling.'

You can cover the cookies with icing and then pipe the sayings on. My hands aren't steady enough, but I bet you could easily do it."

"Even though I know nothing about doing something like that?" I asked.

"Sweetheart, I'm sure you've heard of these little things called Google and YouTube. Great inventions. I've found all kinds of information on them."

"It's not a bad idea," I said, and I meant it. "I could at least try it out and see how things go."

Grinning, Fanny patted my hand. "That's the attitude. Difficult roads often lead to beautiful destinations. You know, you really are something special, Emma."

Right—that was kind of random. I didn't mean the difficult roads part. That was just Fanny being Fanny. I meant the second part. She thought I was special because I'd agreed to make cookies with messages on them?

"I'll be back in a moment," she said and walked to her bedroom. She returned a minute later carrying a small box covered in blue velvet. "For years, I've wondered if Travis would find a woman who would make him happy. A woman who I'd be thrilled to call family. And I'll admit I was getting worried when that wasn't happening. Until you..."

Oh, no. Can't we go back to discussing cookies?

"You've made Travis happy, Emma. And because of that, you've made me happy." She opened the box to reveal a twisted gold pendant about an inch in length, with six small red gems and a bunch of smaller clear ones. "Those are diamonds and rubies," Fanny said. "My sweet Robert gave it to me on our thirtieth wedding anniversary, even though it wasn't our ruby anniversary. He didn't believe in following tradition. He believed in following your heart.

"And since Travis has finally followed his heart, I'm giving you this for being the one willing to cherish it." She handed me the box. Pesky tears clouded my vision.

How many people had ever given me a gift—if you didn't count Hannah?

None—that was how many. Maybe there had been some when I was born but I didn't remember any of those. I only remembered seeing kids at school showing off their birthday or Christmas or just-because presents. They were always so happy. And each time, for a brief moment, I had allowed myself to pretend it was me. That I was the one getting to show off my gifts.

And when I was younger and the teacher announced our birthdays to the class? I would lie about my presents because it was better to do that than to admit no one cared about me enough to remember my birthday.

Not even my foster homes had bothered to acknowledge it. Yes—I had won the lottery jackpot when it came to foster care parents. Not all were like that. Hannah had gotten lucky in some of her homes.

"I didn't mean to make you cry," Fanny said, looking concerned.

I gave her a weak smile. "I'm sorry. It's just I grew up in foster care. I'm not used to getting gifts."

Fanny's hand flew to her mouth, her eyes wide. "I had no idea," she said at the same time I said, "But I can't accept it."

Why couldn't I? Because it would be wrong. She was giving it to me because she wanted so much to believe that Travis was in love with me. But he wasn't—and would never be.

Lines creased on her forehead. "Why not? You're like a granddaughter to me. I love you like a granddaughter."

The tears came harder at that—because Fanny was the grandmother I'd never had. Or if I had a grandmother, she hadn't bothered to track me down.

"Why do I have a feeling those aren't happy tears?" Fanny said, looking even more confused. She stepped forward, her arms wide as if to hug me.

But I couldn't let her hug me—not with all the lies Travis and I had told her about us being a couple. I didn't deserve a gift or a hug.

What did I deserve? To sit on the platform in a dunk tank and have people toss baseballs at the target. At least the money could go to charity, so it wouldn't be a complete loss.

"I'm not Travis's girlfriend," I said.

Her frown deepened. "What do you mean?" Then her eyes widened again. "You two broke up? When?" The compassion in her voice almost did me in.

I could lie and pretend that Travis and I broke up the other day, after our weekend in Napa. But I'd fibbed enough and couldn't do it anymore...even if I was throwing Travis under a train. Maybe I could toss him a puck bunny or two to keep him company while I was at it.

"We were never together. We told you we were because Travis knew it would make you happy. All he wanted was for you to be happy."

And yes, Travis was going to be beyond pissed at my telling her this. My brain pointed out this was a good thing, then after he'd finished yelling at me, he'd never want to see me again. And in time, I would be able to move on with my life.

My heart wished me luck with that; it had no intention of making things that easy for me.

"But he loves you, Emma. I've seen the way he looks at you."

What do you know? Once his hockey career was over, he had a bright future ahead of him as an actor. He had to be good to have convinced his grandmother that he was in love.

Shaking my head, I lowered the box onto the counter. "Travis isn't interested in falling in love."

"It's not about whether or not you want to fall in love. We don't always have a say in the matter. It just happens because the heart knows what the heart knows. And there's no arguing otherwise."

Except in Travis's case, even his heart didn't want to fall in love. It didn't wish to risk being damaged more than it already was.

I could relate.

"That doesn't matter," I told her. "He's not interested."

She studied me for a moment. "Are you interested in falling in love with someone?"

Falling? Try fallen—bruised butt and all.

Despite my deep-down fear of commitment—my way of protecting my heart from more pain—I had screwed up. I had let Travis in when I shouldn't have. But was I willing to do that again with another man?

I nodded, even though I wasn't sure if I wanted to fall in love again. There was only so much being kicked around that my heart could take.

I grabbed the spoon on the counter and scooped cookie dough from the bowl. "No," I said as I dropped it onto the cookie sheet.

"Hmm."

I dug the spoon back into the bowl, giving the task one hundred percent of my attention. *Shit, why did I come here?* At least if I hadn't been baking cookies, I could have bailed.

Hello, awkwardness, my old friend.

What would make this more awkward? That's right—Travis showing up.

I slapped my palm against my forehead. "Oh, I can't believe I forgot. I have a meeting with my realtor." I backed toward the hallway. "Do you...can you finish the cookies for me?"

Now that I had broken my part of the agreement with Travis, I would need to contact the realtor anyway. Fair was fair. I didn't expect him to still help me now that Fanny knew the truth.

I grabbed my purse from the kitchen chair. Fanny followed me into the hallway.

"I can't believe I'm so forgetful," I said, hurrying toward the door. "I'm really sorry about that, but I'm sure Hazel and Abigail will be happy to eat them."

"You don't want us to bring them to the store tomorrow?"

More than anything I longed for her to do that, but it would be wrong. She wasn't my grandmother and I had to stop wishing she were.

Maybe I could find a place that rented out grandmothers for the day, to help me move on.

Or maybe once I was kicked out of my store and had to begin all over again, I could create my own "grandmothers for hire" business for people like me.

"Or Travis can drop them off?" she suggested.

Right—because that was so much better. While he was at it, maybe he could bring his next fake girlfriend with him.

"That's okay. They're for Hazel and Abigail and you. And I'm really sorry about everything."

Luckily for me, I was quicker than Fanny. I was out the door and racing down the stairwell faster than you could say, "Bingo night."

At my car, I sent Travis a text.

> Me: Your grandmother knows I'm not your girlfriend. I'm sorry. But you're off the hook to find me a new store location.

Now if only we weren't still working together on the fundraiser.

But after I screwed things up for him, maybe he would avoid me anyway.

Hello, my new awkward. Pull up a chair and grab some popcorn.

31

***

TRAVIS

Holly turned off the music. "That's looking much better. Mark, remember to relax. And Sean, nice wink at the end. You caused the women in the corner to swoon."

Sean gave the rest of us a smug smirk.

"Great job, Sean." I slapped him on the back. "You made a group of make-believe women faint. I bet Bridget would be proud." Bridget was his wife.

What was going on? Next week was the fundraiser and we were rehearsing. Those women Holly had referred to? They didn't exist. We were just pretending the room was filled with a group of overly excited women.

"I'm picking up the costumes tomorrow so we can start dress rehearsals on Friday," I told my teammates. The granddaughter of one of Granny's friends from the senior center had offered to sew them. Granny had already hinted that the woman was single. Not for my benefit, but for the benefit of my single teammates.

There was a good chance I failed to mention it to them. Like me, they weren't the settling down type.

The guys began packing up. I checked my phone and discovered a text.

> Emma: Your grandmother knows I'm not your girlfriend. I'm sorry. But you're off the hook to find me a new store location.

Shit.

How the hell did Granny figure out the truth? I thought we had been very convincing and our kisses looked real. They had sure as hell felt real.

As it was, I hadn't kissed Emma since Sunday night, when I dropped her off at her place. I missed her kisses. I missed the way it felt to be inside her and to hold her in my arms.

While the temptation to go see her and discover what had happened was strong, I needed to check on Granny first.

A short while later, I knocked on Granny's apartment door. The entire way over, I'd gone through several scenarios in my head as to what had happened. None of them were good.

The deadbolt clicked and the door opened.

I'd never seen my grandmother pissed before, so the look of utter disappointment leveled at me just about kneed me in the nuts. Even when I had been a pain-in-the-ass teen, she had never looked at me that way.

Definitely not good.

Forget being up a creek without a paddle. I was going over a deadly waterfall backward without said paddle.

She stepped away from the doorway to let me in.

Maybe I should've come bearing gifts. Was it too late for me to draw a picture for her refrigerator—like I had done when I was a kid?

"Emma made cookies before she left," Granny said. "You might as well come and have some with us."

"Us?" Like I needed to ask.

As I suspected, Abigail and Hazel were sitting at the kitchen table, a plate of chocolate chip cookies in the middle. Each woman had a glass of milk in front of her and a scowl on her face directed at me.

Inwardly, I sighed. Thank God they loved Emma's cookies—or else I was at risk of being stoned by them.

Abigail gestured at the seat opposite them. I sat, a bad feeling churning in the pit of my gut. Even though I wasn't hungry, I grabbed a cookie. The three women weren't the only ones who loved Emma's baking.

Granny didn't sit next to me. She pulled her chair from under the table and moved it to join her friends, like a senior-citizen-style firing squad. Once seated, she took a cookie from the plate and bit into it.

Her scowl softened. "Mmm. These are so good," she said around the mouthful.

Hazel elbowed her, and the scowl returned in all its I'm-still-pissed-at-you glory.

"So I understand you felt you had to lie to me about Emma being your girlfriend." Granny's tone was cold enough to freeze the milk in the glasses.

Busted.

"How did you find out?"

"Emma was over earlier and told me."

Anger should've coursed through me at Emma ratting on us, but instead, I squirmed in my seat. It didn't matter that I was a six-foot-three, one-hundred-and-ninety-pound hockey player, these three knew how to make me feel five years old again. A five-year-old who was at risk of not getting ice cream for dessert. "I'm sorry I lied. I just wanted you to be happy and for you to stop trying to set me up with any more women."

Granny slowly shook her head and I had to fight off the

urge to sink lower in my chair. "So instead of making me happy, you broke Emma's heart?"

I shook my head in denial. "She and I are friends—nothing more." Friends who'd had sex—which Granny didn't need to know about.

Abigail removed a cookie from the pile, nodded at me, and with her gaze burning into me, she broke the cookie in half.

Message received.

I really couldn't figure out why they were acting like this. Yes, I had lied, but weren't they getting a little carried away with their pissed off attitude? I had done it for Granny's benefit and not my own.

All right—it had been for my benefit, too.

"Look, I'm really sorry I pretended that Emma and I were dating. But it's not like I hurt anyone."

All three rolled their eyes like disbelieving teenage girls. "Only a man would think that," Hazel said.

"A man without any balls." That came from Abigail. I guess I should've been happy that Granny hadn't been the one to say it.

Granny nodded in agreement with her friends. "But you did hurt someone. And I'm not referring to me, Travis. You hurt Emma in a way you can't even begin to imagine." She pushed a small velvet box across the table to me.

"What's that?" I asked.

"Open it."

I did. Inside was a necklace I'd never seen before, with a bunch of red gemstones.

"Your grandfather gave it to me for our thirtieth anniversary. Those are rubies and diamonds."

"It's nice, but what does it have to do with Emma?"

"Because I tried to give it to her. I've seen how you two are together, and I didn't want to risk not being around later to give it to her."

Somehow I managed not to roll my eyes. "You're turning eighty next week. You're not dying."

She grunted a you're-missing-the-point noise.

"Why would you give her something so valuable anyway?" I asked. "Just because we were dating doesn't mean we were getting married."

This time all three women grunted. Clearly they all thought I was an idiot. Maybe I was—an idiot for having no idea where this was all going.

"As you can see, she didn't take it. She said she couldn't because you two weren't really dating. You were just faking it for my benefit."

"And you have a problem with her not taking it?" I asked, frowning. Wasn't that a good thing she hadn't accepted the necklace, considering there wasn't really a "her and me"?

An odd sensation stirred in my chest at that thought. I shoved it away.

"No, it was her reaction when I gave her the gift that's the problem. It was like I had given her the world. Then she started crying because it was one of the few gifts anyone had ever given her, and she couldn't take it because your relationship was a lie."

The odd sensation in my chest? It turned into a ten-ton weight—and dropped to my stomach.

It had never crossed my mind that she had been so deprived as a kid. She should have grown up feeling loved, but that had never been her reality. It was no wonder she was so eager for love. Eager for anything that said it was out there for her one day.

"Do you still believe no one was hurt with your lie?" Granny asked.

"I never meant to hurt her."

Granny gave me the first smile I'd seen from her since I arrived at the apartment. But it still wasn't at full capacity. "I know. But the truth is there's a woman out there"—she pointed toward the living room window—"who cares a lot about you, possibly even loves your sorry backside—"

"I believe in this situation," Hazel said, " 'your sorry ass' works even better."

One side of Granny's mouth jerked up. "Right. Who possibly even loves your sorry ass, and you've made it quite clear to her that you aren't interested in falling in love."

All right—it was now official. Granny was senile. "Emma doesn't love me. We're just friends."

"You keep telling yourself that if you think it'll make you feel better," Abigail said. "But it won't change anything. That girl loves you and you threw away the best thing that's ever happened to you."

Clearly Abigail and Granny had picked up a two-for-one special on going crazy if they really believed that.

"I'm telling you, she doesn't love me." Because if she loved me, she wouldn't have ended things with me. That wasn't her M.O. She was the one people usually abandoned. She wasn't the one who walked away.

Or maybe Granny is right—and Emma left you because she does love you and is afraid you'll abandon her like everyone else, the logical side of my brain suggested.

I turned my back on it...because it was wrong.

EMMA

And here I was again.

Well, not the same place I was last time...but the same idea.

Sorry, let me rewind and start from the beginning. Yesterday, after I'd come clean to Fanny about Travis's and my fake relationship, I contacted the realtor who was helping me find a new store location. Or at least she had been prior to Travis taking over the job.

So here I was, driving to the first address on the list. The difference? Hannah was with me instead of Travis and Fanny.

Had I heard from Travis since I spilled the beans to his grandmother?

Yes, several times. First to make sure I was okay. And then to update me on details about the fundraiser next week. Even though I was organizing the event, he was the one contacting the owner of The Unicorn with details about the performance.

I'd also heard from Fanny, telling me the cookies were to die for, and no matter what happened between Travis and me, I would always be like a granddaughter to her.

Did I tear up when I read the text?

Maybe a little.

Okay—a lot.

"You know what you need?" Hannah said in the voice people always used whenever they knew damn well their answer wouldn't match your own.

"What?"

"To go out on a date."

Yes—well, about that. The way my heart was slumped in my chest, I didn't believe going on a date would work for me. "Great idea. But since no one's asked me out, looks like that won't be happening any time soon."

A word to the wise...when your best friend mentions you need to go out on a date, it's usually because she already has one lined up for you.

Was Hannah aware of what had happened between Travis and me? Yep—every juicy I'm-such-an-idiot detail.

Her reaction? You mean after she said she would love to meet him down a dark alley and practice karate on him? She declared he was the king of douchebags.

Did she believe that? No—but that was what best friends did. They tried to make you feel better by pointing out all your ex-boyfriend's—or in my case ex-fake-boyfriend's—flaws.

"Not a problem," she said, confirming what I had suspected. "I've got a date tomorrow night with the hot resident I was telling you about."

"And let me guess...he has a friend."

Hannah laughed. "You might wish to contain your excitement. Wouldn't want you hurting yourself doing cartwheels or something crazy like that."

"Yes, because I'm known for doing cartwheels at exciting news like that," I said dryly.

She grinned at me in the way that always had me

agreeing to her plans. It was more lethal than if she had attempted puppy dog eyes. "It will be fun. I promise you. We'll see a movie and grab some pizza to eat afterward."

It will be fun. Famous last words.

"What movie?"

"A total man flick."

"No kissing?" I turned down the street where the realtor had disappeared.

"You mean in the movie or with your date?"

I slid her a look. "In the movie. But if you wish to kiss your date, it's totally up to you."

"Please, Emma. You'll be doing me a huge favor. I like Tony, but it's one thing to flirt with the guy at the hospital and another to actually go on a date with him. What happens if he's a complete dud? At least you'll save me from the agony of being stuck alone with him if he is. And his friend is cute and nice."

"All right. But only to help you out. I'm not there because I want to go out with your date's friend."

"Understood."

"Good—as long as we've got that straight." I parked my car next to the realtor's and released a long God-I-hate-this sigh.

"You know, you could have broken up with Travis *after* he found you a new place for the store."

"We didn't break up. To break up, you have to be dating the person first." I opened my door and slid out of my seat.

Hannah leaned over, peering out my open door. "Looked like you guys were dating to me. You even spent a couples' weekend together with his friends. If that's not dating, I don't know what is."

Not waiting for a response, she opened her door and climbed out with what could only be described as a victorious expression on her face.

"That wasn't dating," I said. "That was because one couple had canceled and Travis's friends invited us to join them."

Hannah snorted a laugh. "But they invited you because you two were a couple." The I'm-right-and-you-know-it expression was back.

I did the only thing I could do. I rolled my eyes and made sure she saw it.

Her response was another snorted laugh.

The remainder of the evening was spent with the realtor showing us around the different retail spaces for rent.

"This is the best one we've seen so far," Janet said. "The location is good, the price is within your range, and while it's a little smaller than your current location, it's still doable."

Standing in the middle of the space, I turned around, envisioning how I would lay out the store.

She was right. It was doable. The price was at the higher end of my range. Higher than where I was currently located. And I would have to drive to work because it wasn't within walking distance to my apartment like I was now. But given I would be forced to relocate soon, I didn't have much choice.

"I'm definitely interested," I told her. "But could I have a day or two to think about it?"

She narrowed the distance between us, her high heels clicking against the tile floor. "I wouldn't wait too long if I were you. I wouldn't be surprised if it's quickly snapped up."

I smiled at her, a nervous feeling taking up residence in my stomach. "I'll let you know tomorrow."

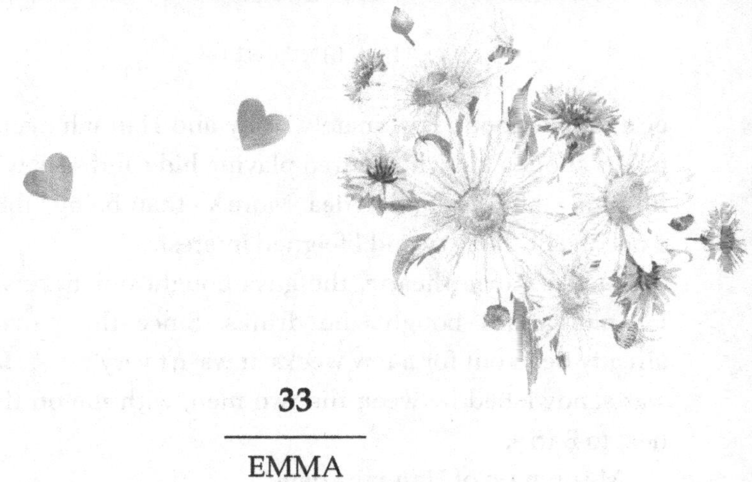

33

EMMA

The following evening, Hannah, Tony the resident, and Barry the blind date picked me up at my apartment in Tony's beat-up truck.

"Do you work at the hospital too?" I asked Barry as we drove to the theater. We were both sitting in the back seat.

What did he look like?

He reminded me of a blond teddy bear—but not in a bad way. He was stocky and worked out, but he had more stuffing on him than hard muscles. I guess you could say he looked cuddly.

And cuddly could be good.

If your heart wasn't somewhere else.

"No," he said. "I work in the legal department for an accounting firm. Tony said you work in a clothing store. Do you enjoy it?"

"I own a boutique that caters to the romantic in all of us. And yes, I love owning my own business."

And that, ladies and gentlemen, was the end of that conversation.

We both sat there, struggling to come up with something

else to talk about. Fortunately, Tony and Hannah decided to tell us about a kid who figured playing hide and seek with the hospital staff was a great idea. More so than being jabbed by a needle. Both Barry and I feigned interest.

At the movie theatre, the guys bought our tickets while Hannah and I bought the drinks. Since the movie had already been out for a few weeks, it wasn't very busy. Hannah was sandwiched between the two men, with me on the seat next to Barry.

My opinion of Hannah's date?

He was good-looking. I'd give him that. And he seemed nice enough—not that it was easy to tell with all the small talk the four of us had done so far.

The movie began, and I settled in for a show that had nothing to do with romance...yet I couldn't stop thinking about Travis and about my store.

I hadn't signed the lease for the new location, but I had phoned Janet after deciding to go for it. She was dropping by my store tomorrow. I couldn't explain why, but it just felt wrong moving to another location—not that I had a choice.

Don't quiz me on what the movie was about. It was a blur of mindless action and pointless banter that had Barry and Tony laughing. Oh, well. At least *they* were enjoying themselves.

Things didn't improve much once we got to the restaurant.

"Naturally, I'm disappointed that Chelsea was appointed head of the committee," Tony told us. "I was obviously a much better choice."

No—I had no idea what committee he was talking about. I'd kind of tuned him out about three minutes ago. Hannah, on the other hand, was listening to him, with rapt interest, as if he was explaining how he had found the cure for the common cold.

Shortly after the waitress took our order, Hannah's phone pinged. She glanced at the screen and typed what I guessed to be a reply to whoever had sent her the text.

"Hannah mentioned you work in retail," Tony said, feigning the same level of interest as I had just done to him.

"That's right." I gave him a wide grin. "I own a store that is about love and romance and hot sex."

Nothing spiced up a conversation faster than the mention of hot sex.

Tony's gaze slid to Hannah in the most appreciative, sleazy way. It was much the same look Barry gave me. Not that I cared. It wasn't like I was ever seeing him again.

"Who doesn't like hot sex?" Tony said. "What kind of things are we talking about?"

"Porn, sex toys, lingerie," I said, doing my best not to laugh. The poor idiot had no idea he had stepped into a trap.

Hannah, on the other hand, was watching me with her eyebrows raised in surprise. Normally, I wouldn't mention hot sex when talking about my store—and she knew it.

She also knew I was up to something.

The tip of Tony's tongue slid along his lower lip. "Whips and leather?"

The worried look in Hannah's eyes? Yeah—I'd be worried if I were her, too.

Funny, he didn't look like the BDSM type. But what did I know?

Hannah's worried expression changed and she looked… relieved? Her gaze was focused on something over my shoulder. Around us, the typical restaurant chatter increased to a new level of excitement.

"Hey, what are you two doing here?" Travis asked behind me—and just like that, my heart rate picked up speed and my traitorous body cheered.

Inwardly groaning, I spun around in my seat. Travis

wasn't alone. Wes and Liam were with him, both appearing amused.

Travis held out his hand to my date. "Hi, I'm Travis, and you would be...?"

Barry shook Travis's hand with such vigor, I was surprised it didn't fall off. "Hey, man, I know exactly who you are. Travis Hamilton. Defense for the San Francisco Rock. I'm Barry—Emma's date."

"What are you doing here?" I asked Travis, repeating his original question. Of all the restaurants in San Francisco, why this one?

"They have great pizza."

True. "What—you don't have any great pizza places near your apartment?"

"Sure, but this one's the best."

Liam and Wes nodded in agreement, still looking amused.

The hostess who had seated us approached the three men. "Your table's ready now."

Barry scanned the nearby tables. "Is it possible to bring that table"—he pointed to the one in question—"over here so our friends can join us?"

Our friends? Since when did introducing yourself to a stranger suddenly turn you into buddies?

I expected Travis to turn down the suggestion. I mean, surely they had better things to do than crash Hannah's and my date.

"That's a great idea," Travis said, and I barely kept my mouth from flopping open. But considering it was my date's idea, there wasn't anything I could do...other than suck it up.

The hostess indicated to the nearby busboy. Together with Travis's help, they moved the empty table and chairs to join us. Wes sat next to Hannah. Liam sat at the end of the table, leaving only one other spot available.

Next to me.

And if I'd thought I was a lost cause at the sound of Travis's voice, that was nothing compared to his familiar scent and pheromones being so close to me. Even in the two days since I'd last seen him, my reaction to them hadn't weakened. Quite the opposite.

Travis leaned in close to me—a little bit too close.

Just ask my heart. It was now beating like a crazed fangirl on caffeine.

Encouraged by my girlie parts, of course.

Damn them all.

"So how long have you two known each other?" Travis asked me and Barry.

"Barry's a friend of Tony," I said, pointing to Hannah's date.

Wes leaned in front of Hannah and extended his hand to Tony. His chest pressed against her shoulder and she flinched. "Hey. Wes."

Tony shook the proffered hand. "Good to meet you." His tone implied the opposite.

Wes straightened and parked his arm partly on the back of Hannah's chair. "So how do you know each other?" he asked the happy couple.

Hannah gave him a blank look and glanced at Travis.

Travis shrugged at her unspoken question. Why did I feel like I was missing something here?

"I'm a resident at the hospital where Hannah works," Tony said.

"Did you hear the great news?" Hannah asked Travis even though she sounded far from excited. "Emma found a new location for Aphrodite's. She's signing the lease tomorrow."

Wes's questioning gaze shot to Travis.

Travis shifted in his seat, his leg brushing against mine. I gasped softly at the electrical current zinging through me and jerked my leg away.

"When did you start looking for a new location?" he asked me, frowning.

"Yesterday. Like I told you the other day, since our little arrangement's over, I didn't expect you to help me anymore."

"But what about the part where I said I would talk to the owner of the building and convince him to let you stay where you are?"

"And what if you can't do that? I couldn't take the risk. I need to advertise the move and I was running out of time. Now I can announce it at the fundraiser next week."

Wes cleared his throat.

"Do you want to move?" Travis asked me.

"Of course not. I mean the new place is nice and all, but I'm happier where I am. But this isn't about me being happier there. It's about my lease not being renewed. It's about me losing everything I care about." I gave him a pointed look I knew he couldn't translate. He had no way of knowing how I felt about him.

And I wasn't about to tell him now—especially not in front of my date.

Either deciding that our conversation was over or he just wasn't interested in it, Barry jumped in with a barrage of questions about the Rock and about playing in the NHL.

Not once during their conversation did he acknowledge my existence. I could have gone to the bathroom and he wouldn't have noticed.

Ooh. That was a good idea.

I excused myself.

Hannah pushed her chair away from the table, forcing Wes to drop his arm from the back of her seat. "I'll come with you." She threw Wes an exasperated look and scrambled after me.

"I can't believe he showed up here," I muttered on the way to the bathroom.

The comment was intended for myself, but I guess I said it loud enough for Hannah to overhear. "Why wouldn't he show up?" she asked.

Her response caused me to stop and I spun around to face her. "What do you mean why wouldn't he show up? He had no idea I was going to be here."

The best thing about Hannah? She wasn't good at poker—which meant she hadn't developed a poker face.

"You *told him* I'd be here?"

"I might have hinted it when I saw him in your building yesterday."

"But why would you do that?" I asked.

"Because maybe I was hoping he would show up, get jealous at seeing you with another man, and realize he loves you."

"Clearly your plan backfired. He's not in love with me and he knows it. But Wes definitely seems intent on sabotaging *your* date."

Hannah rolled her eyes. "He's just acting like an alpha jerk."

"An alpha jerk who obviously likes you."

That earned me another eye roll.

The bathroom was empty when we entered. We quickly did our business and left.

A word of advice. It's always a good idea when you leave the bathroom to look where you're going. Eyes in front. Because Murphy's Law clearly states that if you aren't looking in front of you, this is when you're guaranteed to walk into someone.

I slammed into the poor unfortunate soul I wasn't paying attention to. "Sorry," I said as I glanced up...and groaned. Travis.

But I guess I shouldn't have been too surprised. The tingling that I'd experienced when he'd accidentally brushed his leg against mine at the table? It had zinged through me once again when I bumped into him.

"Do you make it a habit of lurking outside ladies' bathrooms?" I asked.

Hannah slipped out from behind me and walked away without a word to us.

"I want to talk to you," he said.

"Kind of guessed that. But I should get back to my date. He's waiting for me." Unless the gods of bad blind dates had decided to give me a break and Barry had already bailed.

Travis parked his hand on the wall above my head. "Are you interested in him?"

"Weren't you the one who said that someday a man's gonna fall in love with me and never want to let me go? Maybe he's the one." Did I believe that was the case with Barry? Not in a million and one years.

"You never answered my question," Travis said. "Are you interested in him?"

I shook my head as my heart demanded I tell him that I loved him—because what was the worst he could do?

Laugh in my face.

Remind me that he'll never risk loving anyone.

Run.

Most likely run.

If I wasn't Dr. Lovejoy, I'd write to her to get some advice. But since I was, that wasn't an option. It was always easy to give advice when it wasn't *your* heart at stake.

"Are you interested in me?" His voice was rough and raw sensual man that set my body tingling again.

My gaze dropped to his mouth. My body screamed, *Of course I'm interested in you.*

Some people claim that when you're in a life or death

situation, your life flashes before your eyes. My life wasn't in jeopardy, so instead I witnessed a montage of those people who had given up on me. My father. My mother. My ex-boyfriend.

And what were odds that Travis would be no different than everyone else?

"No—I'm not interested in you either." It might have been more convincing if I hadn't still been staring at his lips.

With all the willpower I had inside me, I turned to walk away.

I didn't get far. He blocked my escape route.

Then his lips were on mine and my traitorous legs decided to stick around.

They weren't the only mutinous parts. Even though the kiss was nothing more than the light questioning of lips, it wasn't enough for me. I let him in.

Needing to taste him, I stroked my tongue against his and softly moaned. If this was heaven—I never wanted to leave.

Travis knotted his fingers in my hair and tugged the curls, pulling my head back and deepening the kiss.

It only lasted for several heartbeats before Travis moved away. "That's what I thought."

And with that he walked away, leaving me standing there dazed.

Still in a daze, I returned to the table. Everyone there was laughing when I approached. Not at me but at something one of them had said.

Pretending nothing had just happened between Travis and me, I sat. Then I spent the rest of the meal wondering how I would survive once he was no longer in my life—beginning next week, after the fundraiser.

Lucky me.

34

EMMA

"I'm running a little late," Janet said on the phone Sunday afternoon. "But I've got the papers for you to sign."

"Not a problem," I said. "I'll be here."

She ended the call and I continued straightening the cushions on the shelf, making sure their romantic sayings faced out for the customers to see.

That stupid smile I get whenever my thoughts are filled with you.

You are every reason, every hope, and every dream I've ever had.

You're the smile to my face and the beat to my heart.

Each one was a pain-in-the-ass reminder of the lack of romance in my life.

Maybe I shouldn't sign the lease for the new location. Maybe it was time for a career change.

I could be a lion trainer.

Dangerous? Perhaps. But at least I would be so busy trying *not* to be eaten, I'd be too preoccupied to dwell on how

228

I was never going to find the love in my life I was so sorely missing.

What about my date from last night? Well, that ship had sailed and I made sure I wasn't on it. When he asked for my number, I sweetly smiled and told him I didn't think it would be necessary. Then I bailed the truck faster than you could say, "Blind dates suck."

The store door opened—and like it did every time the bell jingled since I spoke to Fanny, my heart rate jumped up. Why? Because the damn thing kept believing that Travis would walk through the door at any moment and tell me he loved me.

My heart always was the romantic.

Much more so than my girlie parts. They just wished to get laid.

Preferably by Travis.

But it wasn't Travis who stepped into the store. It was Old Shriveled Ass, the building's owner. What the heck was he doing here? On a Sunday?

I hadn't seen him since the day he told me the lease wouldn't be renewed.

I guess it had been too much to hope that he would never step into the store again.

As usual, he scanned the area as if imagining the contents burning in hell. He wasn't Catholic. That much I could tell. He wasn't holding up a cross and damning everything to the fiery pits of you-know-where.

Guess he wasn't here to buy a cookie—the ones with romantic sayings on them that Fanny had suggested I make and sell in the store.

He approached me, the sneer still on his face. "After much consideration, the owner of the building has decided to renew your lease."

"The owner?" Wasn't *he* the owner?

"That's right." He handed me a thick document with "Lease Agreement" typed at the top of the first page. I stared at it, confused.

"I thought you said the store didn't fit the image of the new condo development."

"He decided not to go through with those plans and that your establishment can stay." The way he said "establishment," you'd have figured it was a whorehouse from back in the day.

When I didn't take the papers, he tried to shove them at me. I just continued staring at them, unsure what to do.

"What's wrong?" Shriveled Ass asked. Well, more liked grumbled. There might have also been an edge of panic in his voice, but I couldn't be certain.

"You told me I was being kicked out, so I found a new place."

"Have you signed the lease for it yet?"

I shook my head. "But the realtor is on her way now."

"Then that don't mean anything. As long as you haven't signed that lease, you're free to sign this one." He waved the papers under my nose.

The bell over the store door tinkled again. This time Wes entered. Old Shriveled Ass scowled. Wes ignored him and approached us.

A wave of panic surged through me. You know how many times Wes had been in the store, despite working in the same building as me?

Zero. Zippo. Nil. And since he didn't have a girlfriend, I couldn't see him needing to come in here...unless something was wrong with Travis.

"Is everything okay?" I hurriedly asked him. "Did something happen to Travis?"

He smiled, clearly amused at my question. "Travis is fine.

I wanted to make sure nothing went wrong with you signing the lease." He gave Old Shriveled Ass a pointed look.

The pain-in-my-ass shrugged. "She said she's signing the lease for another place."

"Do you mind if we continue this in your office?" Wes asked me.

The store was busy, like it normally was on the weekend, but the two girls working the shift could handle it. I was just here for the distraction anyway.

"Why would you care if I sign the lease for here?" I asked Wes once we, along with Shriveled Ass, were in my office. "It's not like you actually shop here."

"I have my reasons."

Shriveled Ass rolled his eyes like I was an idiot. "Because he's the owner and for some ridiculous reason he feels that saving this place of sin is a good idea."

"For God's sake," I blurted out. "It's not a brothel."

Because I was so pissed at his attitude, it took a moment for the first part to sink in. "Wait—you're the owner?" I asked Wes. He couldn't be.

Because if he was that meant Travis was aware of it, too.

Nodding, he glared at Shriveled Ass. In turn, the old man cringed. At least that part was satisfying.

"How come I didn't know this?" Not once had Travis mentioned it or had Wes given any indication he owned the building.

"Because everyone thinks I'm just another tenant, and I prefer it that way."

"Does Travis know?" I asked even though I was pretty sure I knew the answer.

"He does. So does Liam. But that's it."

"Fair enough. Your secret's safe with me." He had his reasons for not telling anyone and I respected that.

I opened my mouth to say something, but then glanced at Shriveled Ass and changed my mind.

As if sensing my reluctance to talk in front of the man, Wes took the unsigned contract from him and dismissed him.

Shriveled Ass huffed like the big bad wolf preparing to blow the place down. Wes indicated to the closed door with the jerk of his head and the older man left, muttering something I was positive I didn't wish to hear.

Once the door clicked shut, Wes nodded for me to go ahead and say whatever I needed to ask.

"When did Travis talk to you about my lease?"

"A couple of weeks ago."

Was that before or after I had agreed to be his fake girl-friend? "And he convinced you not to shut down my store?"

That would explain why Travis hadn't been too worried about finding me a new location. He knew he had a good chance of convincing his friend to let me stay.

"He's going to kill me for telling you this...but your store was never in jeopardy. I didn't even know you were operating under the belief you had to find a new location. Travis told me."

I frowned. "Then why did Old...I mean, why was I told my lease wasn't being renewed?"

"That would be my uncle's doing."

"Your uncle? Who's your uncle?"

"Donald Shrivener. The building manager."

Oh. That would explain everything. So the old bastard had lied to me.

"But why would he tell me it wasn't being renewed?" I had my suspicions but I wanted to hear it from Wes.

"Because he doesn't agree with anything to do with romance. Let's just say if Cupid really did exist, my uncle would track him down like he was a deer during hunting season."

I cringed on poor Cupid's behalf. "And Travis knew this about the lease?"

Wes didn't answer—which pretty much was my answer.

"So I pretended to be his girlfriend all for nothing."

Right—that wasn't entirely true. I got to fall in love with someone who couldn't love me in return. Added bonus for me.

Wes held out the contract to me. Reluctantly I took it and stared at the blasted thing.

Someone knocked on the door. At my "Come in," the door opened and in walked Janet, damp from the rain.

She smiled at me. "I've got the paperwork for you to sign."

"I have to head out," Wes said. "But let me know what you decide." He turned to leave but then swiveled back to me. "For the record, Travis did what he did because he wanted to help you out. He didn't have to be involved with the fundraiser. He did that because it's important to him—and because he felt he was cheating if he had stuck with the original terms of your deal."

This time, Wes did leave.

"Should we get going with this?" Janet asked as I stared numbly at the closed door.

35

Dear Dr. Lovejoy,

I've finally found The One. But until her, I was commitment phobic—and she knows that. What should I do to prove that I had it all wrong?

Sincerely,

I Was An Idiot

36

TRAVIS

How did I know Emma had lied when she told me last night at the restaurant that she wasn't interested in me? No—it wasn't the way she had been staring at my lips. Although that had been the driving force for what happened next.

It was the kiss itself. None of the kisses I'd experienced over the years had ever felt the way they did with Emma.

Had they affected her too? Damn straight they had. And no, I wasn't saying that because I was a smug bastard who thought highly of his ability to kiss women. Something deep in my soul had told me she needed me as much as I needed her. I'd never felt that way before about anyone.

And it fucking freaked me out.

But you know what else freaked me out?

The thought that I could lose her.

Some sense was finally knocked into me while I was waiting for Emma to return to the table and I remembered her words from Napa:

If the girl loves you, she will be willing to move with you, or you two will work something out so you're together during the off-

season. But either way, you can't give up on love because you're scared of losing the person like you lost your parents and your best friend.

So what was the problem?

She had talked to Wes a few hours ago. I hadn't spoken to her yet, but he let me know what went down when he'd admitted the truth to her.

And it didn't look good for me.

Between the omission of information about Wes owning the building and me lying to Granny, I was fucked. Big-time.

On top of that, she believed I *had* given up on love. So I had to prove to her that she was wrong.

I hadn't given up on love—I loved *her*.

I only hoped Granny and her cronies were right—that Emma loved me. And I hoped that she'd be willing to make things work between us even if I was traded at some point.

The question was: how was I going to prove to her that I loved her?

When girls needed advice about love, they called up their best friends. But guys didn't do that.

So I did the second best thing....

Scanning the restaurant, I spotted the four people I needed to talk to. Well, more like two. Josh and Trent kind of came as part of the package deal.

I joined them in the quiet booth in the corner. The booth had been my idea when I'd booked the reservations. It would make it easier to talk.

What I hadn't counted on was it also gave Josh and Trent the opportunity to snuggle with their wife and fiancée.

Which was the kick-in-the-balls reminder I didn't need that I had royally screwed up with Emma. Because if I hadn't, she would be cuddled up to my side as we checked out the menu.

After we ordered our meal, I got right to it. "I'm in love

with Emma, but I fucked up big-time and need to figure out a way to let her know that I love her. Any ideas?"

Both Trent and Josh gave me the man's version of a sympathetic look. The women were a different story. They exchanged glances then cracked up laughing.

Not very reassuring.

"What's so funny?" I grumbled.

"What they're trying to say," Josh said, "is that we're going to make you figure it out yourself."

"Just like Kelsey and I made Josh figure things out on his own when it came to Holly," Trent said. "We gave him a little nudge in the right direction. That's all."

"A very little nudge," Kelsey said, her expression giving away that she was struggling not to laugh again.

"Hey, I could use that nudge," I said.

Holly shook her head. "You don't need one. You're well ahead of where Josh was." She gave him a quick kiss on the cheek; he kissed the top of her head.

Once upon a time I would have rolled my eyes at their little romantic gestures.

Now, it was the necessary shove for me to realize what I needed to do to show Emma how much I loved her. After everything that had happened to her, it would take more than a grand gesture to get her to trust me in a way she had never trusted anyone before. But it would take time to win her trust, and I needed to do whatever I could to gain that time.

Except I couldn't do it alone.

There was a proverb that said it took a village to raise a child.

I might not be trying to raise a child...but I did have a village to help me win the woman I could see myself, one day, having a child with.

37

EMMA

Monday morning, I walked to work, going through the list of things in my head that I needed to do during the day—and happy that it didn't include preparing to relocate the store.

That's right. Wes had barely stepped out of the store yesterday before I rushed after him to tell him I would be staying where I was. And it wasn't because the lease was cheaper and because I wouldn't have to relocate. With the way all the businesses in the building had pitched in to make Thursday's fundraiser a success, I realized I didn't wish to leave our little community.

A small vase, with a white ribbon tied around it, sat in front of the store door. A couple of sprigs of lavender—the herb of love—were perched inside. There was no card saying who had sent it.

So I did what anyone who received a mysterious bouquet would do...I turned around and scanned the street. A few pedestrians were strolling along the sidewalk while a couple of cars drove past, but that was it. Nothing to hint who had left the vase.

238

Maybe I had a secret admirer.

I sniffed the flowers and smiled. No one had ever given me flowers before.

LATE TUESDAY AFTERNOON, I STEPPED OUT OF MY OFFICE FOR A few minutes to cover for Lisa while she went on her break.

An oversized envelope with my name on it was sitting on the counter. I opened it to find a folded parchment resembling the Marauders Map from Harry Potter. But instead of a drawing of Hogwarts, the building on the front was the one where I worked, including the courtyard in the middle. I laughed at the footsteps drawn on the map. From the looks of it, Hannah was with Wes in his office. No idea what that was about.

Liam, Kelsey, Trent, Holly, and Josh were in The Unicorn.

Fanny and her cohorts were standing by the counter of my store—no doubt having some of my cookies.

I was standing in the middle of my fountain.

And Travis was right behind me.

Even though I knew he wasn't there—because I wasn't standing in the fountain—I spun around.

Nope, just as I thought.

Grinning, I sent him a text.

Me: Thank you for the map. I love it.

It didn't mean anything other than he still wished to be friends. The only problem was I wasn't sure I could be friends.

Not now.

Not until I was over him.

Wednesday morning, I opened my apartment door, ready to go to work, and discovered a small gift bag hanging from the doorknob.

I removed it and opened the bag. Inside was a key chain. But it wasn't the key attached to it that got me excited. It was what was on the gift that had me gasping softly. Under the clear dome was the picture of a glowing, almost ghost-like doe and the word "Always."

It was based on one of my favorite quotes from the final Harry Potter book.

Like with the flowers on Monday, there was nothing to indicate who it was from, but it didn't take a genius to figure it out.

It also didn't take a genius to guess the reason behind it.

> Me: I know your grandmother told you I'm not used to getting gifts, I told Travis via text, but that doesn't mean you have to send me any.

Then I sent him another one.

> Me: I'm a big girl now, not a kid. You can stop sending them.

> Me: Please stop. Because each time you leave one, it breaks my heart some more.

He replied a minute later as I was switching my keys to the new key chain. Because as much as I wanted him to quit sending me gifts, that didn't mean I was tossing this one.

> Travis: I'm happy to send you gifts. You deserve every single one.

Me: How about we leave that for the man
who falls in love with me?

He didn't respond to my text.
The next morning there were no more gifts.
Nor were there any in the afternoon.
I kept telling myself that was a good thing.
Eventually my heart would finally believe it was true.
Hopefully.
Possibly.
Maybe.

38

EMMA

"I can't believe how many people are here," I said to Hannah, surveying the audience of the sold-out show. Ninety-five percent were women.

Over two hundred horny women—if their catcalls were anything to go by.

And that was before they even saw the hockey players, who were backstage with Holly, preparing to go on.

I hadn't even had a chance to talk to Travis. Just as I was about to check on him and the other players earlier, Fanny told me there was an emergency she needed my help with.

The emergency? She needed me to open a jar of pickles she had smuggled in.

And then when I tried to go backstage, Holly told me it was off-limits to everyone except for her and the dancers.

Had I even seen Travis since he crashed my date?

No—he had been too busy preparing for tonight. So other than the occasional text, I hadn't heard from him. And the last one I received was yesterday when I told him he could stop sending me gifts.

But that was okay. My heart needed to start getting used

to the idea of not seeing him anymore. After tonight, I would go cold turkey.

"I didn't doubt it for a second," Hannah said. "Who doesn't love to support a fundraiser for a worthy cause?"

I laughed. "You mean who doesn't want to see nine hot hockey players take off most of their clothes?"

She barked a laugh. "That too."

Was the staff at the youth center happy about how well things were going with the event?

Why don't you ask them? They were sitting at the table next to the one with eight silver and gold helium balloons floating above the guest of Honor's seat. Today was Fanny's eightieth birthday.

Fanny, Abigail, and Hazel weren't the only ones at the table. Several other eighty-year-old women were also helping her celebrate her big day.

And in case you were wondering who was guilty for the loudest catcalls—look no further than their table.

I glanced at the bar where Liam and Wes were sitting, beers in hand.

"There's a smorgasbord of horny women in this room," Hannah said, her gaze also directed at the bar, "and those two are sitting over there. Alone." She shook her head as if trying to fathom why they weren't attempting to score with some of the women.

"They're here to support Travis and Josh, not to get laid."

Hannah shrugged.

"Why? Are you thinking about getting laid by a certain dark-haired male?" I gave a small nod toward Wes.

She snorted. "He isn't my type."

Nor was Tony apparently. That relationship didn't go beyond the one date. Hannah never told me what happened, but I got the impression the decision to remain friends was mutual.

My phone pinged with a message.

Holly: Okay. They're ready.

My heart rate picked up. Not because I was about to see nine oiled up hockey players shaking their asses onstage. And it wasn't because I was seeing Travis for the first time in five days. All right—that might have had something to do with it. The increased heart rate and sweaty palms were mostly because I was the one introducing the show and thanking everyone for coming.

I showed Hannah the text.

She grinned. "Good luck."

Me : Thanks. Here we go. Showtime!

I released a long slow breath and walked onstage to the thundering applause.

"Hi, everyone," I said into the mic, and waited a moment for the audience to settle down enough to hear me. "And thank you for coming to tonight's show." That was met by another round of applause—and women bouncing in their seats, eager for the show to begin. "On behalf of the Bell Youth Center, thank you for your support of the fundraiser and the kids that they help every day. So far with the ticket sales alone, we have raised almost ten thousand dollars. This will go to help the center's programs that assist high-risk kids, giving them a chance to live to their full potential." The cheers and whistles from the audience made me smile.

"The silent auction will be open until nine p.m.," I said once the cheering had quieted a notch, "and then we'll announce the winners." I paused to let that sink in. "And now the moment you've been waiting for. How about we give a big welcome to the men of the San Francisco Rock?"

If I thought the cheers from before had been loud, that was nothing compared to now. And the men hadn't even stepped onstage yet.

The pub lights dimmed, the spotlights kicked on, and the music started playing. A beat later, nine hot men—wearing dark gray suits, white shirts, and different colored ties—strolled onto the stage, moving in time to the music. I was positive the polar bears in the Arctic could hear the applause.

The wives of the five married players were laughing and cheering as loudly as everyone else. And when their husbands blew them kisses, I swear half the women in the room swooned.

The men started strutting around the stage, teasing the women, thrusting their hips. And *sex-on-a-hockey-stick*, those pants fit their asses just right.

All those hours of training had paid off. Watching them, you wouldn't know they weren't professional dancers. Holly had truly been a miracle worker. Although from the way the women responded, it wouldn't have made a difference if the players were only stumbling about on the stage. Their presence in those suits was enough to cause spontaneous orgasms.

Without meaning to, I ran the tip of my tongue along my lower lip at the sight of Travis. If I had to be honest, he was the hottest one up there. All right—I might be slightly biased. Especially since I knew exactly what was under his suit... something the other women in the crowd wouldn't witness tonight.

At least I hoped no one would witness what was under his briefs. My stomach churned at the thought of one of these women getting to do just that. I pushed it aside. Travis wasn't mine and I had no say as to what he did or whom he went out with.

Repeating that in my head a few times, I cheered the guys on, rivaling Fanny and her friends when it came to the noise.

The men slowly removed their jackets while seducing the women with their eyes. I whistled my appreciation—as did quite a few other women. Without missing a beat, the players flung their jackets to the back of the stage.

Next off came the ties, while the men continued to move in near perfect synchronization. The single guys tossed them into the crowd—with the exception of Travis. The five married players strutted to their wives. I was too busy watching what they were doing that I didn't notice Travis had crossed the stage to where I was standing at the side.

He jumped down in front of me, causing me to startle. Then he looped the tie around my neck and slid the silky fabric from side-to-side. His hips also moved the same way in time to the music. It was all very sensual and my girlie parts got hopeful.

"There's something in my left pant pocket for you," he said, loud enough for me to hear over the music and appreciative audience—but not loud enough for said audience to also hear him.

At his nod, I reached in and removed a piece of paper. This, of course, didn't go unnoticed by the nearby women. As Travis hopped back onstage, they hooted and hollered—some no doubt believing I'd taken the moment to cop a feel.

My gaze shot to Holly, who was grinning at me. *Read it*, she mouthed.

While the guys were swaying their hips onstage, unbuttoning their shirts, I unfolded the paper. *You're the best part of my day.*

With my heart stunned into shock, my gaze snapped up to Travis. He winked at me.

The women continued to go wild as the men's smooth, muscular chests were revealed inch-by-inch. Maybe we should've hired the fire department to help us with the event. I had a feeling a few women would be bursting into flames soon at the sight of all those mouthwatering chests and abs.

The shirts were tugged out of the waistbands of the pants. With their hips thrusting to the beat of the music, the men slid their shirts off their shoulders and down their arms.

Once they had them off, they tossed the shirts into the crowd.

All except for Travis.

He aimed it at me.

Laughing, I caught it and folded it over my arm with his tie.

I glanced at Hannah to see if she was enjoying the show—or if she was watching Wes. She grinned at me and mouthed something I couldn't make out. She pointed to her chest and then to the shirt in my arms. She mouthed the mysterious words again.

I looked at the shirt and noticed something was hidden in the pocket. I slipped my fingers in and removed another piece of paper.

You're the best thing that's ever happened to me.

My poor heart didn't stand a chance after that. It melted like ice cream left in the heat.

Travis wasn't looking at me when my gaze returned to the stage. He and the other players were still dancing. Some women were fanning themselves, ready to pass out from all the hot testosterone onstage. Others were laughing and blushing at the guys' antics.

The men moved into a V formation, with Travis at the front. And then in a swift move, they ripped off their trousers and tossed them into the crowd.

Instead of G-strings, they were wearing basketball shorts. But that didn't stop the audience from jumping to their feet while cheering and applauding—me included.

They had done it. Travis and his teammates had nailed their routine.

They waved at everyone in thanks and moved to the back of the stage, waiting for me to make the next announcement.

But before I got as far as the steps, Fanny was up there… with her own mic. I held back, wondering what she was up to. Travis had never told me that Fanny would be addressing the audience.

"Wow, that was quite the performance, wasn't it ladies?" she said, fanning herself. "Thank you, boys, for making me feel twenty again. I believe my ovaries just kick-started themselves after that."

A ripple of laughter spread through the room, the loudest laughs coming from her table.

"But most of all I'd like to thank three very special people who made tonight happen. First, Holly Hoffer. You might be more familiar with her husband, Josh Hoffer." Screams and cheers filled the room—although I had a feeling that was more for Josh than Holly. "Holly was the one who choreographed the dance routine and got these guys in tip-top shape for tonight. And from what I've heard, it wasn't easy. As superb as these men are on the ice, their skills didn't amount to much on the dance floor."

The players laughed and nodded.

"So thank you, Holly, for all you did to get these men ready for tonight." The audience applauded, thoroughly agreeing with Fanny. If it hadn't been for Holly—along with the players—tonight wouldn't have been the success that it was.

"The second special person who made tonight possible is my grandson, Travis Hamilton."

That resulted in the same reaction Josh had gotten. Grinning until my cheeks hurt, I cheered loudly, adding my own appreciation.

"I had joked a month ago that I wanted his teammates to dance shirtless for my eightieth birthday. Well, thanks to my grandson, I got the best birthday present a grandmother could ask for. Okay, second best present. I'm still waiting for those great-grandchildren." The audience laughed as she winked at me.

I didn't have time to react before Fanny was waving for me to join her onstage. I peeked at Travis to find him smiling. My heart thumped loudly in my chest, eager to break free and kiss him.

"I don't have any granddaughters," Fanny said, "but in the short time I've known Emma, she's been like one to me. Only I don't want her to be my granddaughter. I wish for her to be something more."

I mentally cringed, hoping that she wasn't about to announce to everyone that she wanted me to be her grand-daughter-in-law. That was the last thing Travis needed.

Fortunately, she didn't do that. "Okay, boys." She nodded at the nine men.

A new song pounded from the speakers. Huh? Holly and Travis never mentioned anything about a second dance routine.

Not that I was complaining.

I took a step toward the stairs but didn't get farther than that. Fanny grabbed my arm. "You're not going anywhere, sweetie," she said, the mic no longer on. "Sit back and enjoy the show."

Before I could ask her what she meant, Mark Milone and Josh walked up to us. Mark was carrying a chair, which he placed behind me on the stage. Then he and Josh gently grabbed my arms and encouraged me to sit.

Fanny handed me a piece of paper and walked down the steps to rejoin her table.

I love you even on bad days when everyone else annoys me.

It was signed from Travis. I laughed...until the enormity of what it said hit me.

He loved me?

There wasn't enough time to dwell on that as Mark and Josh strutted back to join the other guys, only to be replaced by two other players. The men moved in time to the music, much like they had with the last song. The audience ate it up —laughing and cheering once more. This time instead of handing me a piece of paper, they each handed me a red rose.

Two by two, the rest of the players followed suit, each handing me a sweet smelling rose. Travis was the last player to strut up to me. He handed me his flower, this one with a message attached, then straddled my thighs and lowered himself, almost sitting on my lap. He thrust his hips forward several times—no doubt violating at least one rule his team had laid out for tonight. Heat flooded my face. I giggled.

But the heat in my face was nothing compared to the ache between my legs. Luckily, no one in the pub was aware of that.

I read the message: *Forever yours...*

Then he lowered his lips and brushed them against mine. The crowd went wild.

"How about we go somewhere quiet to talk?" he said against my ear. "We won't be long."

"Okay," I breathed.

"And then after we're done here, I'm taking you back to your apartment and making love to you all night long."

The ache between my legs gave a heartfelt sigh.

"Okay." That was about all I was capable of saying—my brain cells having melted into a sticky goo.

Travis thrust his pelvis a few more times—much to the audience's delight—then straightened himself off my lap.

As the music came to an end, he held out his hand and pulled me to stand. He nodded to Fanny and led me offstage.

In the background, I could hear her say something in the mic, which made the audience laugh. I didn't hear exactly what it was, but I could've sworn I had heard something about great-grandkids.

Travis led me back to what looked like the staff room. No sooner had he closed the door behind us than he was kissing me.

But unlike the kiss onstage, this one was thorough.

Passionate.

Sweet.

Our tongues made up for lost time, reminding us how much we had missed this.

Because Travis was still half-naked, I took the opportunity to run my hands over his hard muscles.

The moan?

It might have been me.

Or him.

Or us both—I couldn't be sure.

Eventually, we had to come up for air. Travis rested his forehead against mine as we regained our ragged breaths.

"I love you, Emma," he said, voice low, rough, tender. "I'm sorry it took me this long to figure it out."

He looked deep into my soul. It was only then that I realized I had yet to tell him my feelings for him. He had opened himself this way—not just to me but to everyone who had helped him tonight.

And he had done it without knowing how much he meant to me.

Except there was still the one major issue...would I turn around one day and find myself alone again? History was a snooty bitch. And this bitch wouldn't let go of that fear.

Travis ran his thumb against my lip, removing it from my teeth. I hadn't realized I'd been chewing it.

"I know you're scared that I'll be like everyone else who

you thought loved you. But I'm not walking away. I'm in this for the long haul—even if I get traded and you can't come with me because of your store. I'll always come back to you." His beautiful hazel eyes told me he was telling the truth. "I realize that tonight, the small tokens of my love that I left you this week, and the key to my apartment aren't enough..." He paused—long enough for his words to sink in.

"Wait a second," I said, positive I had misheard him. "Are you telling me the key on the key chain you gave me yesterday is for your apartment?"

He nodded.

Oh. Wow.

I just figured it was some random key—because guys like Travis didn't usually give their apartment key to girls.

"Sorry," I said, "you were saying?"

"I realize that tonight, the small tokens of my love, and the key to my apartment aren't enough for you to trust me just yet." He stroked his thumb along my cheek. I shivered at his touch—in the best possible way. "But I'm hoping you'll give me a chance to prove myself to you."

"Those gifts were the best," I said. They meant more to me than if he had given me expensive jewelry. "And yes, I will give you a chance," I added, my heart cheering me on. "But that's because I love you too, and because I believe everyone deserves a second chance." I tenderly kissed him. "Especially you."

And then, because I'd barely survived the last few days without him, I went back to kissing him again.

39

TRAVIS

How did the rest of the evening go with the fundraiser?

No idea. Yes—Emma and I did return to it. Fortunately, everyone was having a great time, so they didn't notice we had disappeared for a while. They kept it to themselves that Emma's hair was a mess—thanks to my fingers that had been tangled in it while we were making out in the staff room.

After we re-emerged, my teammates changed back into their street clothes. Beyond that, the night was a blur of events. The silent auction. The socializing. The stolen kisses whenever possible.

But now we were back at her apartment, our hair wet from the rain that had started on our way home.

Emma opened the door. Before she could step into the apartment, I scooped her up in my arms and entered.

"I think you're just supposed to carry the bride over the threshold," she said, laughing. "Not the woman you told a few hours ago that you love her."

"Maybe I'm practicing for that day," I said with a wink.

She didn't say anything. Instead, the tip of her tongue traced along my jaw—reminding me just how much I wanted to taste her again. Christ, it felt like forever since I'd last done that. I had a lot of time to make up for.

I kicked the door shut and gave Emma a moment to lock it before I headed to her bedroom.

In her room, I lowered her to the floor and nodded at the bed—where a gift bag sat in the middle.

The corners of her mouth slid into a wide grin. "Another present?"

I teased her cheek with the stubble on my jaw, knowing how much it turned her on. "Maybe this one is for both of us." My voice was rough and heated.

She trembled slightly in my arms. "I'm beginning to realize just how much I missed out on by not getting gifts for all those years."

"Looks like I'll have to help you make up for lost time," I said as she removed the bag from the bed and peered in.

She blinked at the contents, then removed the pillar candle and sniffed it. Sandalwood. She had once told me the scent turned her on—not that she seemed to need it. I liked to think I was one hundred percent responsible for that.

She set it on the nightstand and removed the next item. Sensual Sunburst massage oil. "Wow, when did you get this stuff?"

I took the bottle from her and placed it next to the candle. "One of my teammate's wives picked it up from your store for me yesterday."

"Very sneaky of you," she said, grinning.

"Wasn't it?" I settled my hands on her shoulders and turned her around.

I slowly unzipped the back of her dress, my fingertips trailing down her soft skin. A tremor rushed through me. "And now for the next part of your gift."

With a flick of my fingers, her black lacy bra loosened its hold on her luscious breasts. Then I peeled her sleeveless black dress and bra straps down her arms.

"Your present is stripping me?" she asked, smirking.

I laughed. "That would be more like a present for *me*. And no, that's not part of your gift. That's coming next."

The fabric pooled around her feet, still in the black stilettoes, and she nudged it to the side with her foot.

For a moment, I imagined her legs over my shoulders, with me pounding into her while she was wearing those shoes.

But this wasn't about me getting off on that fantasy. This was all about Emma.

I removed a matchbook from my jeans pocket and lit the candle. Then I turned off the bedroom light and indicated to the bed. "Lie on your stomach."

While she removed the stilettos and did as I'd asked, I grabbed the bottle of oil.

She closed her eyes, her head resting on her folded arms. I opened the flip cap with a soft click, releasing the oil's sensual scent.

After pouring some oil onto my palm and lightly rubbing my hands together, I positioned them on her shoulders. With firm strokes, I massaged her upper body...and then her lower back. At the sound of her erotic groans, I barely held back my own primal grunts.

Touching her like this was a mix of torture and satisfaction. Satisfaction knowing she was as affected by this as I was.

My hands slipped under the waistband of her panties and I massaged her ass. My fingers greedily cried out, *Don't forget her pussy!*

I ignored their pleas. You didn't rush dining on fine food and you didn't rush this.

I peeled her panties off, gently parted her legs, and

massaged each one in turn. I made sure my fingers went close enough to her core to tease but not close enough to touch.

She looked back at me. "Where did you learn to be a master—" The rest of the sentence was lost as my fingers finally brushed against her clit.

She moaned; I chuckled. "The master of you?"

"I was going for the master of massage." She might have said that, but her eyes said that I was right. I was as close to being the master of her as I could get.

"I get massages all the time," I said, "as part of my training."

"I'm assuming they aren't quite as intimate as this."

I pressed a kiss on her lower back. "Definitely not. And for the record, you're the first woman I've ever given a massage to."

She lowered her head back on her arms. "For the record, you're the only person who's ever massaged me."

I kissed her back again, a little higher this time. "Well, this won't be the only one I give you. I plan to make up for all those massages you missed out on." This time when my mouth touched her body, my teeth gave her shoulder a little nip.

A needy whimper slipped from between her lips and I smiled. I wasn't the only one being tortured by this.

"Now roll over so I can do your front," I said.

"Ooh. That sounds promising." She flipped over—but then looked me over, her head tilted slightly to the side. "As my personal masseuse, it's your duty to remove your clothes."

That sounded fair.

She sat up and bunched the bottom of my T-shirt up my torso, her fingertips taking the opportunity to explore the muscles on my abs.

Before she reached my chest, I yanked my T-shirt over my head and tossed it onto the floor.

Apparently that wasn't enough for Emma. Her fingers had the button of my jeans undone and the zipper pulled down faster than you could say, "Make love to me."

She pushed my jeans and briefs to my knees. My cock greeted her, proud and ready to appreciate her fine heat.

I shucked off the rest of my clothing. She licked her lip, and just the sight of the need in her eyes almost had me over the edge in record time. Before I could warn her, she wrapped her hand around my near painful length. Pre-cum leaked from the tip and she spread it around the head of my cock with her thumb.

My balls tightened. *Holy. Christ.*

"Uh, uh. Not yet," I said, stilling her hand with mine. "I haven't finished your massage." I gently pushed her hand away from me. The same heat boiling inside of me was reflected back in her eyes.

I brushed my thumb against her nipple. It puckered at my touch. Pride coursed through me at the effect I was having on her body. "I've missed these beauties." I took the nipple into my mouth and sucked on it.

"They've missed you too," she said in a part moan. "But do you think we can skip the rest of the massage for now? I *really* need you inside me."

I hummed a response, her nipple still in my mouth, my fingers caressing her clit and pussy. Then I sat back on my haunches, reached for a foil square in Emma's bedside drawer, and opened it.

She patted the mattress next to her. "I want to ride you."

"Whatever the lady wishes…" I winked at her again and joined her on the bed, a pile of pillows behind me. She rolled the condom onto my length. That whimper? Definitely me.

"Hope you aren't looking for hard and fast right now," I said. "Because I plan to savor this." I wanted something to remember once I was back on the road again with my team.

Something to jerk off to in the shower when she couldn't be with me.

She smiled sweetly at me. "Savor away." She straddled me and eased herself onto my thick length. My balls tightened some more. I wasn't going to last much longer at this rate.

But I needed to last—for Emma.

"Fuck, I forgot how amazing it feels to be inside you," I groaned.

She moved her hips back and forth, riding me like I was a prize-winning bronco. *Yee haw*.

The rhythm was slow, but that didn't mean it was any less intense than all those times it had been hard and fast. With us gazing into each other's eyes and softly kissing, *this* was so much more.

But as we got closer to the moment we'd been heading for, I took control of the pace with my hands on her hips. Faster. Harder. And it didn't take much before we were rushing headfirst over the edge with a chorus of "Oh, God," "Christ," and Emma's and my names.

I gave Emma one long, lingering kiss, then she climbed off me and waited under the covers while I disposed of the condom.

I rejoined her a moment later and tenderly kissed her. Outside, rain pelted the bedroom window.

"It's true," she said.

"What's true?"

"That when you're in love with someone, they really are your sunshine on a rainy day." She nodded at the window. "Even when it's dark."

I chuckled. "Where did you hear that?"

She stroked my chest. The steady pounding of my heart beneath her touch promised her I was worth taking a chance on. "It's on my mug in the store."

I settled my hand over hers and kissed the end of her

nose. "Well, it does have a point. No matter what the weather or time of day, you're my sunshine, my world...and always will be."

Then a few minutes later, I proved it once more by making love to her again.

And again.

And again.

EPILOGUE

EMMA

Six Months Later

Smiling, I unlocked my apartment door. Why was I smiling? Because even though it was April and almost the NHL playoffs, Travis wasn't away on a road trip and he didn't have a game tonight.

Which meant that once I walked through the door, I'd be able to make love to my amazing boyfriend.

And yes, I might've been fantasizing about that for the past two hours while at work.

I opened the door. "Hi, I'm home," I called out even though he didn't need me to announce it. He could easily hear the door unlock from anywhere in the apartment.

In case you were wondering, Travis moved in with me two months ago. It made sense for us to live together—otherwise, we would never have seen each other because of his hockey schedule.

And let me tell you now that had sucked—especially

since I had permanently retired Alejandro the Second. All right, he wasn't completely in retirement mode. Travis found him one day and got excited at seeing my orgasm buddy. But the only time I was allowed to use Alejandro was for special occasions while I was with Travis.

My hot boyfriend had been very specific about that.

Usually when I called out "I'm home," Travis would walk out of the kitchen, give me the most passionate kiss known to womankind...which always led to the most amazing sex.

But this time only silence greeted me.

Disappointment kicked me in the shins. He hadn't said anything about going out. Was it poker night and I'd forgotten about it? I walked to my bedroom to grab some fresh clothes before showering.

And came to an abrupt halt.

Spread out on my side of the bed was my sleeveless black dress, and my black lacy panties and bra. My strappy black stilettos were on the floor. A note was propped up on the bedding. "Put these on and wait for further instruction." It wasn't signed, but I recognized Travis's handwriting.

Well, this was one for Dr. Lovejoy.

Yes, I was still writing the weekly column—only now I no longer felt like a fraud.

And when I didn't have a question from a reader, Travis helped me dream up one to answer—even when he was on the road.

Let's just say there ended up being some highly amusing questions.

I pulled my hair up in a high, loose ponytail. My goddess hairstyle—as Travis liked to call it. I quickly showered, allowing the steam to perk up the curls. Fifteen minutes later I was ready to go, while breaking a few records in the process.

As I waited for the next instructions, I paced around the apartment. Before Travis became my boyfriend, everything about the place reminded me of how alone I was. Sure, I'd had a few friends and I had Hannah, but that was nothing compared to now. Thanks to the fundraiser, I got to know more people in the building, and now we hung out together once a month at The Unicorn.

Plus, Holly, Kelsey, and I had also become good friends. The three of us, along with Hannah and Kate, got together once a month for girls' night.

Now, my apartment no longer reminded me of how alone I was. Now, it reminded me that I was loved—partly in thanks to the framed photo of Travis, Fanny, and me on the wall.

But that was nothing compared to what adorned Fanny's living room wall.

I giggled at the memory of the large signed photo of the nine shirtless hockey players from the night of the fundraiser. She called it her little taste of heaven.

Just as I was beginning to wonder if my next instructions would ever arrive, someone knocked on my apartment door.

I grabbed my clutch purse and walked to the door. Well, more like ran as fast as I could in my stilettos.

I opened it to find Wes. In a suit?

"Hi?" I said. "Travis isn't home right now."

Wes had a nice smile—a really nice smile. But this was the first time I'd seen it so bright. "I've come to escort you to dinner."

"You're taking me to dinner?" And more importantly, where the heck was Travis? Why wasn't *he* taking me to dinner?

"That's right."

"Where's Travis?" I glanced down the hallway—both ways—to see if he was there. Nope.

Wes flashed me another big grin. "You'll see."

I'd known Wes for several months now, so I was used to

him being cryptic. Didn't mean I liked it, but for now I let it go.

I stepped out of the apartment and locked the door. Wes offered his arm and I took it.

He escorted me to the elevator. While we waited for it, he quickly typed something into his phone. A minute later, the door pinged open.

Outside the building, instead of walking me to his car, Wes led me to my store. Huh?

A soft glow came from inside. Not the usual glow after the store was locked up for the night. This time it came from candles flickering in the dark.

"How come the sprinkler hasn't gone off?" I asked Wes.

"I checked with the fire department. A few candles are fine. The rest aren't the flammable kind."

Meaning they were fake candles—the kind that required battery power instead of real flames.

Wes opened the door and waved me in.

"What's going on?" I asked him. *And where the heck is Travis?*

We were the only ones there.

The candles weren't the only things new to the store since I'd locked it up for the night. In front of the fountain—its lights still glowing—was a table for two covered with a white cloth and two chairs. A small bouquet of white roses and several sprigs of lavender sat in a vase in the middle.

"I'll take it from here," Travis said, walking around the fountain to where we were standing.

I hadn't even noticed him up till then. I'd been too busy absorbing what he had done to the store in the short time I was upstairs. Soft classical music filled the space. It wasn't one of my playlists, but it was romantic all the same.

Wes gave Travis a small nod and winked at me. "Have fun,

kids. Don't do anything I wouldn't do." He chuckled and turned to leave.

Travis and I ignored him. I was too busy staring at my boyfriend, who was standing there in his black suit and purple striped tie. He was also doing his fair share of staring, his gaze full of wonder and love.

It was a look I'd often seen on him—a look I could never get enough of.

"You look beautiful," he said.

"So do you," I whispered, then grinned. "I mean you look handsome." Handsome. Sexy. Mouthwatering. All of them described him perfectly.

He leaned in and kissed me. We had kissed this morning before I'd left for work, but it felt like I hadn't kissed him in days.

Unfortunately, the kiss was brief—a promise of what was to come. A promise that I would hold him to.

He slipped his fingers between mine and led me to the table. He then pulled out a chair and indicated for me to take a seat. "I'll be right back with our dinner."

"You cooked? In my store?" Sure, I had a microwave in my office, but it was really only good for heating up food, not for cooking it from scratch.

Travis planted a quick kiss on my lips. "No, I ordered it from La Vita e Bella."

One of my favorite restaurants.

He disappeared into the back and returned a moment later with a bottle of Chardonnay, which he poured into our wineglasses. He placed the bottle in the ice bucket on the fountain wall. When he returned the second time from my office, he was carrying two plates—each containing lobster ravioli, asparagus, and roasted mushrooms. He placed them on the table and sat down.

"I can't believe you did all of this," I said. It was official—I had the best boyfriend in the entire world.

Travis smiled—and like every time he did that, my insides went all warm and squishy.

He picked up his wineglass. "I'd like to make a toast to the woman who taught me how to fall in love. The woman who taught me that falling in love was worth it—and who made me glad I'd waited because...well, because she's the only one for me."

I could feel the heat in my cheeks intensify, but that didn't stop me from returning his smile. "I'm just glad you waited. You're the only man I want to be with."

We clinked our glasses together and began eating the delicious food.

"I can't believe you did all of this," I said and popped the final piece of ravioli into my mouth. I made another "Mmmm" noise that I knew was driving Travis insane with lust. I could see it in his eyes.

Which was why I did it.

I was more than ready for dessert—and he was on the menu.

"It was worth it," he said. "And who knew your store would be the perfect place for a romantic dinner?"

I laughed. "Just don't tell anyone that, or else I'll start getting requests to rent it out just for that purpose." I turned to the fountain. "Especially because of my magical fountain."

"Do you think it's magical?" he asked as I watched the water spray up from the base of the wall toward Aphrodite. She glowed softly in the fountain's lights.

"I do," I said, turning back in my seat.

Travis unfolded from his chair. "So how do you make a wish?" He peered into the water, his right hand fisted.

"Turn so your back is facing the fountain, and toss the

coins over your left shoulder. According to the legend of the *Fontana di Trevi* in Rome, one coin guarantees your return to Rome. The second coin will ensure a new romance. A third one guarantees marriage. You probably have to toss in a billion dollars' worth of coins if your wish is to win the Stanley Cup. But I wouldn't swear my life on that." At least his team was headed to the playoffs, so he didn't have to wish for that part.

He grinned at me—and the girlie part between my legs heated up like a volcano. If it could fan itself, it would. "I don't think my pockets can handle a billion dollars in coins."

Travis turned around, his back to the fountain, and tossed the contents of his fisted palm into the water.

Plop. Plop. Plop.

I gasped, but could only stare at the fountain. *Three coins guarantees marriage*, the four words that I had voiced a minute ago echoed in my brain.

Travis walked over to where I was sitting and got down on one knee. "Emma, I love you more than anything. I can't imagine anyone who I would rather raise a family with and grow old with than you. Will you marry me and spend the rest of my life as my lover and my best friend?"

He slipped a ring from his pocket and held it out to me. I blinked away the tears as he waited for me to say something. Anything.

Between his thumb and index finger was a gorgeous platinum ring with a large square diamond. It was the most breathtaking ring I'd ever seen.

When I looked up at Travis's eyes, vulnerability shone back at me as bright as the diamond. *Answer him*, the choked voice in my head said. *Don't leave the poor man hanging.*

I felt my lips curve up into a wide smile and I nodded. "I would…more than anything," I whispered, emotion clogging my throat. I cough to clear the lump. Those tears rolling down my cheeks? Totally justified. "I would love to be all of that with you, Travis."

He'd barely slid the ring on my finger before I flung my arms around his neck and kissed him. It wasn't long before what was supposed to be a sweet and tender kiss became full out hungry.

I pulled back slightly, my breath coming in ragged. "Maybe we should go back to our apartment and have dessert now." I winked at him.

"I think that's a great idea." His voice was as rough and hungry as mine. "I'm more than happy to make love to my beautiful, future wife."

I was fully on board with that.

PART II

DECIDEDLY WITH MISTLETOE

A HOLIDAY NOVELLA

1

AVA

The clock was ticking down the final minutes. No, not the final minutes until a bomb exploded.

But close enough.

It was December twenty-third. Two days until Christmas.

Thirty minutes before winter break began and I could leave for my week of fun-in-the-snow at Lake Tahoe.

Maybe I'd meet a hot ski instructor looking for a fling. A fling with earth-shattering sex.

When was the last time I'd had sex like that?

Good question. Unfortunately, it was one I had no answer for—other than it had been a very, very, *very* long time.

No, I didn't mean that I hadn't had sex in an extremely long time...which was technically true. I just meant...well, I think you get the picture.

"Miss Versteeg," Jessica said, bouncing in her seat, her arm stretched up as though she were trying to touch the classroom ceiling. "Will you read us a story?"

A symphony of excited voices filled the room—twenty-one first graders agreeing with Jessica's request.

I smiled at their grinning faces. "All right. We have time for one book. What story would you like to hear?"

Maybe they would like to hear the one about the princess who could do no right by her family. No matter what she did, they were never happy.

She got engaged to the prince they didn't approve of.

She became an elementary school teacher instead of following the family tradition of becoming a lawyer.

And then because her prince—her one true love—didn't love her in return (yes, that was a shocker to her, too)...he dumped her.

She did eventually marry another prince—one her family did approve of. This meant their kingdoms would at last be united.

At least that was the case until he ran off (translation: had an illicit affair) with a witch.

Did her royal family send its knights to bestow vengeance on such wanton disregard of the poor princess's feelings?

"Miss Versteeg," Tommy said, waving a book at me with Jolly Old Saint Nick on the cover, and interrupting my not-so-pleasant stroll down memory lane. "Can you read *'Twas the Night Before Christmas* to us?"

Smiling, I took the book from him. "Of course."

I indicated for everyone to sit in the reading corner. The scraping of chairs against the tiled floor and loud voices clambered over each other in the air. Normally, I'd remind my students to use their indoor voices. This time I didn't bother; I just absorbed their happiness. Everyone deserved to be happy, especially at this time of year.

Less than thirty minutes later, the story was read, everything was tidied away in preparation for the winter holiday, and twenty-two glowing faces were waiting by the classroom door.

"Does everyone have all their coats, mittens, hats, and

boots?" I asked, loud enough to be heard over the chatter. It never failed—each day, at least one item was forgotten in my classroom. "Remember, you won't be able to return for missing items until school starts in January."

I glanced at the clock again. *Ten. Nine. Eight.*

Twenty-two little engines revved, unable to hold back much longer.

Five. Four. Three.

"Have a wonderful holiday break, everyone."

The buzzer hummed loudly through the classroom.

And twenty-two eager students were out the door faster than Santa could say *Ho, Ho, Ho.*

And I was left standing in my empty classroom, with the same sense of emptiness gnawing at my bones.

I pushed the pity party aside. Who had time for that?

In less than twenty-four hours, I would be *swoosh, swoosh, swooshing* down the beginner ski run. While, I might add, looking sexy in my new winter gear.

Or at least I hoped I looked sexy.

Had I ever skied before?

Nope. Not at all. My family preferred to vacation in sunny locations. My ex-husband was allergic to the snow.

Well, not literally.

Metaphorically.

I began straightening up my desk.

"Are you ready for your big trip?" Zoe, my best friend, asked from the classroom door. I looked up. In her hand was a long, flat box wrapped in red paper.

"I just have to finish packing. Then I'm good to go."

She rolled her eyes. "Right, as if you haven't already packed. Hell, I wouldn't be surprised if you were packed two weeks ago."

There might be a chance that she was right.

"I have a few last minute things to add."

"Have I told you I'm jealous?" She might've said it a few times, but I didn't buy it for a second. How could she be jealous of me spending a week on my own in the mountains? She had a loving husband and two adorable kids to spend the holidays with. I would gladly trade in my trip for what she had.

My phone rang on the desk. I picked it up and checked the name on the screen. A shudder rolled through me like when the giant from *Jack and the Beanstalk* stomped around the earth. *Fee-fi-fo-fum.*

"Let me guess," Zoe said, an extra dose of pity in her tone, "the Abominable Snow Monster herself?"

I nodded and answered the phone. Experience had taught me that when it came to my grandmother, it was better to yank off the Band-Aid right away. Because if she had to phone you back...

Another shudder rolled through me.

I pressed my finger against my lips to warn Zoe to be quiet, and I upped the volume, so she could also hear my grandmother. It would save time in the long run. Then I wouldn't have to repeat the entire conversation to Zoe once it was over.

"Hello, Grandmother." I didn't bother to fake that I was happy to hear from her. Which was just as well since I wasn't a good actress. Just ask my high school drama teacher.

"What is this nonsense that you're not coming to the Bahamas for Chris and Gloria's wedding?"

And hi to you too, Grandmother. "Because I don't feel comfortable attending my *ex*-husband's wedding."

"Why on earth would you feel uncomfortable?" My grandmother's go-to tone? Ticked off, with a side order of arrogance. She couldn't look further down her nose at me than if she had been standing on top of the Empire State Building. "Their parents have been friends of our family for decades. And your grandfather and I have known their grandparents..."

Zoe mouthed, *Since the dinosaurs walked the planet*, distracting me from the rest of what Grandmother was saying.

A giggle bubbled deep in my belly, ready to shoot out like soda in a heavily shaken bottle. My hand shot to my mouth in a feeble attempt to contain it.

Zoe winked and mouthed, *You're welcome.*

On a scale of one to ten, how successful was my scowl? Negative one to the power of some infinite number—thanks to my best friend's ability to make me laugh.

Clearly my grandmother's question had been rhetorical. She didn't bother pausing her tirade long enough for me to answer.

I opened and shut my hand in a blah-blah-blah gesture. Zoe wasn't so successful at containing her laughter. A loud giggle tore through the air.

"Young lady," Grandmother said, even though I was thirty-one years old. "This is *not* something to laugh at."

Zoe crossed her eyes and made a face.

I snorted and turned around so I couldn't see her anymore. My Spidey senses warned me I was in for a lecture, and I didn't want Zoe to see the impact it had on me.

This was why I never called my grandmother.

Now if only I was equally successful when it came to hanging up on her. It was just one of those things I'd never mastered—mostly because it had been drilled into me from a young age that you had to respect your elders. Even when you didn't necessarily agree with them.

"You messed up your marriage," Grandmother said, "and you dishonored our family with your behavior."

"My behavior?" I said it slowly as if sounding out each

word. "Chris was the one who cheated while we were married."

"But if you had been a better wife to him, it would never have happened. You could have at least tried to look better for him. It wouldn't have hurt you to lose some weight. That's why he's marrying Gloria."

"He's marrying her because she looks like a stick?" A stick that would easily snap in two if accidentally stepped on. "Maybe I don't want to be a stick."

The pout in my tone? Not a good thing.

It was a sign of weakness.

And my grandmother preyed on weakness. Whereas most people fueled up on food, she regularly sacrificed virgins and devoured their weakness like it was candy.

"I will not have you talking about my best friend's granddaughter that way. I booked you a plane ticket to join us tomorrow, and you *will* be on that flight. You *will* attend the wedding, and you *will* be on your best behavior."

Let me just note here that it wasn't my fault I tripped on the hem of my wedding dress. And it was *not* my fault I stumbled into the table that held my wedding cake. Nor was it my fault I couldn't save said cake and it landed not-so-gracefully on the floor.

Was that a sign that my marriage to Chris had been doomed to fail from the very beginning? Quite possibly.

Although looking back, it wouldn't have been a big enough sign to warn me about the truth when it came to my ex-husband—which was revealed after I discovered him and Gloria in our bed. In leather.

Well, Gloria was in leather and slapping a whip against his bare ass.

What was he wearing?

A studded leather collar and a leash.

And nothing else.

You don't want to know how much vodka I shot back to get *that* image out of my head.

"Sorry, but I have plans." In my mind, I was swooshing down the mountain with my hot ski instructor. *Don't let her get to you.*

"Then you will cancel your plans."

Or what? The unspoken question hung out there like dirty laundry.

When I didn't respond, my grandmother released a hard sigh. "Ava, I do understand that it will be mildly uncomfortable for you. But the women in our family always live up to their responsibilities. And attending the wedding is part of your responsibility."

"Seriously, Grandmother, what are you going to do? Threaten to take away my trust fund if I don't show up? Too late. You already did that when I decided to go into education instead of pursuing a law degree. I turned my back on the money years ago. Or have you forgotten that? Anyway, I need to go now. My..." I turned back to Zoe. "The school principal just stepped into the classroom...to...to talk to me."

Zoe checked over her shoulder. At least I fooled one person.

"You will be on that plane, young lady," my grandmother said.

I hung up and grinned at the phone. "Don't hold your breath."

"What will she do if you're not on the plane?" Zoe asked.

"If I'm lucky, disown me. But so far that hasn't happened." I thought when I filed for divorce I had finally hit that point.

The Versteegs never filed for divorce.

Or so I was told.

It would explain why most of my wealthy relatives were grumpy. They were trapped in loveless marriages.

Only my parents' marriage had been filled with love—

and continued to be that way. They were the reason I still talked to my grandmother. They were the only reason I hadn't completely turned my back on my family—even if my parents did side with them most of the time.

"Why do you put up with that BS?" Zoe asked.

"If I put up with it, do you really think I'd be driving to Lake Tahoe this afternoon? No, I'd be on that plane, contemplating the odds of it falling from the sky and sparing me the agony of attending the wedding."

"I can't believe your family expects you to attend, especially after what that asshole did to you."

I let out a long-suffering sigh—faked, of course. Mostly. "It's not like we get to pick our family." If we could, I would've put in a request to be a member of Zoe's. "And it's not like my parents expect me to be there. They understand my reasons for not going."

Did they know about Chris's penchant for whips and leather and chains? I never told them. Telling them about it would've been mortifying beyond words. So I kept the words to myself. Even Zoe didn't know about it.

"True, but it still doesn't make it right." She held out the gift to me. "Merry Christmas. This is exactly what the doctor ordered for your getaway."

I took it from her. "Didn't we already exchange gifts at your Christmas party last week?"

"Yes, but this is something I couldn't give you in front of the kids."

"Given that you gave me a vibrator for my birthday and it's still in tip-top condition, I'm guessing that's not what this is." Plus it felt lighter.

I opened the box and peeled back the tissue paper. Inside were what looked like scraps of red and black and light pink satin and lace.

And a sprig of mistletoe.

I placed the box on the desk and removed the pink satin.

"I realize it's been awhile since you bought yourself any sexy bras and panties, but I know *this is it*." Zoe's barely contained excitement was hard to miss.

"What do you mean 'this is it'? And what's the mistletoe for?"

"To kiss under, of course. I happen to know that you're going to meet your Forever Love at Lake Tahoe. Because of the mistletoe."

I chuckled. "What does mistletoe have to do with me finding my Mr. Right?"

"Because I believe in the power of it when it comes to love. My grandmother was at a military Christmas dance and kissed a handsome stranger under the mistletoe. A year later, they were married. My mother was at a friend's Christmas party and she kissed a handsome stranger under the mistletoe. A year later, they were married. And then my sister—"

"Let me guess...she kissed a handsome stranger under the mistletoe, and a year later they were married."

Zoe laughed. "No, that's not what happened. Chloe already knew Tony. They were friends in college. But he kissed her under the mistletoe, and she fell in love with him right then and there. Eight months later, they were saying their I dos. And then there's me..."

This story I did know. Evan had proposed to Zoe under the mistletoe.

"So you're saying I should spend my holiday at Lake Tahoe kissing all the available men under the mistletoe, just to find this magical guy?" Yes, because that was exactly what the shy girl inside of me wanted to do. Right along with getting all my teeth pulled without any anesthesia.

"Yes, that's exactly what I'm saying. I swear it, Ava. You're going to find Mr. Right while you're away. And you'll have me and the mistletoe to thank for it."

Mentally shaking my head, I returned the lid to the box.

"Promise me you'll do it, Ava. You owe yourself this. Consider it your birthday present to me."

I rolled my eyes. "Your birthday isn't until June."

"So it will be my early birthday present. Just promise me."

"Okay, I promise." Guess it wouldn't hurt to give it a try. Maybe there was something to her family legend...even if I wasn't a member of her family. Maybe just knowing Zoe was enough for it to work for me.

"And you're also going to promise me that you won't spend your vacation working on your next novel."

My next novel being the third one in my middle-grade Greek mythology series. That's right. By day I was an elementary school teacher. By night, an author. "I promise. This trip is about restoring my creative juices. And with that, I should get going if I want to make it to the resort in good time."

"Especially since it sounds like a storm will be hitting the area later tonight."

"It will?"

She nodded. "Evan called earlier and told me to let you know. He said you should be fine, just as long as you don't get delayed leaving on time." She gave me a big hug. "Remember your promise. Kiss every available man you see."

"I promise." *Not to make a fool of myself.*

Where's your spirit of adventure? the know-it-all voice inside my head asked. *And what's the big deal? It could be a lot of fun. You've always wanted to be an actress.*

I have? I must have missed that memo back in private school.

AS I DROVE CLOSER TO LAKE TAHOE, THICK SNOWFLAKES obscured my vision, even with the windshield wipers on. And the defogger was doing a crappy job defogging the window. But at least my radio hadn't failed me. Cheery Christmas tunes continued to fill the small space.

"You do realize you're supposed to make it easier for me to see, right?" I asked. And no—I wasn't actually expecting the defogger to answer me.

I glanced at the speedometer. My car was traveling forty miles per hour under the speed limit. But no way did I want to play risk-taker and go faster. I could see it now: I'd hit a patch of ice, spin wildly out of control, and end up in a ravine.

Wasn't that what happened to Paul Sheldon, the protagonist in Stephen King's *Misery*? He ended up in a ditch, and that crazed fan happened upon him. She got all uppity because he had killed off her favorite heroine...and then the next thing he knew, the fan turned into a psycho bitch.

Did I mention Paul Sheldon was a bestselling author in the novel?

I might have been a New York Times bestselling author for a middle-grade fantasy series, but at least I didn't have to worry about a kid going psycho on me for killing off his favorite character.

Or maybe instead of a psycho fan finding me in the ditch, the Minotaur—the giant beast from Greek mythology—would come across my wrecked vehicle and make a meal out of me.

To distract myself from thoughts of winding up in a ditch and my remains not being found until spring, I sang along with the Christmas music.

The good news? No one was around to hear me. Yes, I'll admit it—I was gifted with the creative gene when it came to my vivid imagination, but I fell short on the ability to sing in tune.

"Not much longer till we're at the resort," I said to either my car or myself or us both. "And then I can hang out in the hot tub. And maybe I'll get lucky and some sexy, single guy will join me." *And then I can put Zoe's mistletoe to the test.*

A sudden thump was the first warning I got that something was wrong. Followed by vibrations rattling me to the core and the steering wheel pulling to the right. I turned off the music and my worst fear was confirmed as a loud *flap-flap-flap* noise taunted me.

My heart picked up its pace, mirroring the flapping of the flat tire. I tightened my grip on the steering wheel.

And because fate clearly hadn't paid attention to my plans for the holidays, my tires hit ice and my car slid toward—just my luck—a ditch.

"Oh, God. Oh, God. *Oh, God.*"

Sad to say, that really wasn't how I had envisioned using those words while on this trip.

That was my last thought before my front tires skidded off the embankment.

2

LIAM

"Make sure you drive carefully," Kelsey's worried voice said through my SUV's speakers.

"Yes, Mom."

Once upon a time, I wouldn't have been able to joke like that to my little sister. But our parents had died over fourteen years ago. Even though we did miss them the most during the holiday season, she and I had long since learned to cope with the loss.

Which meant I could give her a hard time for worrying about me.

I had survived being shot at by the enemy while serving with the Navy SEALs, so I was pretty certain I could survive the drive home from Lake Tahoe to San Francisco.

"I'm not kidding, Liam. Trent told me a storm is expected to hit Lake Tahoe soon."

Soon? Try now. The snow had been coming down heavier with each passing mile. It had begun shortly after I left the mountainous area where I'd been helping with a search and rescue mission. Fortunately, the little girl had been found safe and sound.

Fortunately, she'd been found before the storm hit.

"Don't worry, Kelsey. I'll be careful. There's no way I'm missing Christmas with you and Trent and his family this year." I'd already missed too many holidays as it was, thanks to my time in the military.

Did I regret my stint with the SEALs? Not at all. I had loved my job. But now that I was retired from it and running my own security and investigation company, I was looking forward to settling down. Settling down and possibly one day having my own family—a family like Trent and Kelsey were hoping to start soon.

That's right. My best friend and Kelsey were married a few months ago. This was the same best friend whom I decided not to kill after I found out he was screwing around with my sister.

"You better be," she said, "because I have a surprise for you."

"What kind of surprise?"

"One I'm positive you'll enjoy."

"Even if I don't like surprises?" Surprises were usually not a good thing when you were on a mission with the military. "You aren't trying to set me up with someone, are you?"

Kelsey laughed. "As much as I would enjoy seeing you fall in love, I'm not setting you up with anyone."

"That's good." I was referring to the part about setting me up. Kelsey knew I had already strolled down the route that involved me falling in love. It had been a path filled with prickles and thorns.

But it wasn't the girl who had been that way. That honor went to her family—most notably, her grandmother. They were the ones who'd been against us getting married.

But that was the past. Ten years in the past.

The snow started coming down heavier. Two headlights shone faintly ahead through the near white-out conditions.

"I'll call you once I'm home," I said, keeping an eye on the lights in case they unexpectedly swerved into my lane. I ended the call.

As I drew closer to them, it became clearer that the car wasn't moving. It was stuck in a ditch.

And standing in the headlights was a woman with long, blonde hair whipping about her shoulders. Which was all I could make out of her, thanks to her woolen hat and winter coat. The wind wrapped around her, attempting to push her over. Possibly into oncoming traffic.

Not that there was any traffic—from either direction.

"Shit. What the hell does she think she's doing?" I pulled to the side of the road and turned on my hazard lights.

I climbed out of the SUV and pushed my way through the wind. The snow hit my face with a not-so-friendly reminder that we were still a long way from summer.

"You shouldn't be out here," I yelled as the wind tried to steal my voice away. "It's too dangerous." A car could lose control and pin her against her vehicle.

Not a pleasant way to go, in anyone's books.

She turned around and her eyes widened at seeing me—familiar eyes and an equally familiar face.

"Ava?" I would recognize my ex-fiancée anywhere, even if it had been ten years since I last saw her. And shit, she was as beautiful as she had been back then. Maybe even more so.

My cock stirred, seconding that opinion.

She didn't respond. Her wide-eyed expression then transformed and she glared at me. Glared at me like she would rather be dipped naked in honey and fed to a bear than be in my presence.

Not that I could blame her. I'd broken off our engagement, but as her grandmother had explained to me, it was the right thing to do. For Ava. If she had married me, she would have lost her trust fund. She would have gone from living her former lifestyle to living on a Navy SEAL's salary. And she wouldn't have had the money she needed to attend a prestigious law school.

But instead of being able to remind Ava of those things, her grandmother also kindly pointed out that Ava would've foolishly picked me over the money and her education. And eventually she would've regretted that and resented me.

Her grandmother's solution? I was to convince Ava that I'd changed my mind about marrying her. That I didn't want her waiting around for me while I served my country... because I might not come back home in one piece.

Her grandmother always was the optimist.

Had I bought the part about Ava foolishly picking me? Not at all. Ava would do anything to make her family happy. Picking me wouldn't have been an option for her.

"Any particular reason why you decided to park in that ditch?" I nodded at the car. It wasn't a BMW or some other high-end model you'd expect someone with her wealth to be driving. It was an older model Honda Civic.

"I didn't park there." She let out a long, God-this-sucks sigh. "The ditch just got in my way when my tire decided to call it quits."

The corner of my mouth twitched up. That was one thing I had always appreciated about Ava: her humor. "Must have been a conspiracy."

I checked the offending tire. Or rather, I would have checked it if the side of the car with the flat wasn't buried in snow. The only way I could change the tire was if the car was out of the snow bank.

And even if I could change the tire, Ava would still have to back out of the ditch, and right now that was questionable since she didn't have chains on her wheels.

"Do you have a spare tire?" I asked.

"I think so."

"You think?"

"Well, it's not like I've gone looking for it. This is the first time I've ever had a flat."

A few minutes later, I had determined there was no spare.

"The only thing you can do at this point is call for a tow truck, and have them take your car to a garage. But I don't think you'll have much luck getting one during this storm. They'll be busy with emergencies."

Ava's face paled—her skin only a shade darker than the falling snow.

"Where are you headed?" I asked. She told me. "That's still over an hour from here in these conditions. I can drop you off at a nearby hotel to spend the night. The tow truck can take you and your car to a garage in the morning to get your tire fixed."

"That's okay. I can wait here."

I shook my head. "No, you can't."

"Sure, I can."

"It's only going to get colder, and staying in your car will be dangerous. Someone might drive past and lose control and hit you."

"I'm sure I'll be fine."

Right. Rule #1 when it came to women: if they said they'd be fine, it usually wasn't true. They were just too goddamn stubborn to admit it.

And when faced with a woman like this, there was only one thing to do. I hoisted Ava over my shoulder and started walking back to my SUV.

The second thing I used to love about Ava? She was a fighter. She was never one to go down without a battle—other than when it came to her family.

And in this case, the battle involved her squirming

against my shoulder and pummeling her fists against my back. "Let me go, you barbaric caveman!"

"Hey, that hurt my caveman feelings." I kept moving forward, squinting against the snow.

"I somehow doubt it." She squirmed some more. "Now put me down."

"Not until you're safely in my vehicle."

"And then what?"

"And then I'm driving you to the nearest hotel. After that, I'll continue driving to San Francisco, where my sister and her husband are waiting for me to come home."

Ava stilled. "Wow, Kelsey's married? Oh God, it's not to that boring guy she was dating back in college, is it? What was his name? Oliver?"

"You mean Owen?"

"That's him. Ohmigod, she did marry him! Well...um...I'm sure he's not so boring anymore. I'll shut up now."

Chuckling, I lowered her to the ground. "No, Kelsey didn't marry him. And yes, you're right, Owen was boring. She was engaged to him for a bit but then called it off."

Ava muttered something that sounded like it might be "Must be a family thing," but I couldn't be certain.

I opened the vehicle door and indicated for her to enter my SUV. "Give me your keys, and I'll get your stuff out of your car."

"I'm perfectly capable of doing that myself."

"I know you are, but as you've already pointed out, I'm a caveman. And this caveman was brought up right by his mom. Which makes me a gentleman caveman." I winked at her and held my hand out for her keys.

"Fine," she huffed.

Once I had her stuff safely stowed in the SUV, I Googled the nearest hotel, inn, or motel, and programmed the inn's address into the GPS.

I started the engine. "Do you remember my best friend, Trent Salway?"

"Dark-haired, incredibly hot guy? Yes, I remember him. Why?"

"That's who Kelsey married."

Silence filled the inside of the vehicle. I glanced at Ava to check her reaction. Definitely shocked.

"Wow, didn't see that one coming," she said.

"Neither did I. But he's a great guy and they're perfect for each other, so who am I to complain?"

After we had driven a mile in an awkward silence, I asked, "So what are you up to these days? Did you join the family business?"

"By family business, do you mean did I become a lawyer?"

"Yes, that's exactly what I mean."

"Being a lawyer was never my dream. It was my parents' dream. It was my grandparents' dream. I just became the family disappointment instead."

She didn't sound too upset by it. I was tempted to look up to see if a spaceship was hovering above us with the real Ava Versteeg. Because the Ava Versteeg I knew would have dived into a pool of fire ants if it meant her family's approval.

"So if you didn't become a lawyer, what did you end up doing?"

"I teach first grade. And let me tell you now—I'm probably the only elementary school teacher who has a degree in international politics, along with an education degree. But it has come in handy when it comes to dealing with peace negotiations with my students." She chuckled.

International politics was what she had been studying when we started dating in college. I'd been studying criminology.

It was official. Aliens had abducted the real Ava. Not

because she hated kids and I could never see her as a teacher. She was great with kids. "That's not exactly the high-power career your family was pushing for."

Ava laughed. The sound was as sexy as I remembered it, maybe even more so now. "You remember them well."

Christ, did I ever. "I take it they finally decided to let you do what *you* wanted?" The disbelief in my tone wasn't that obvious, was it?

"Not exactly. They pretty much disowned me when it came to that. Well, my parents didn't *totally* disown me, but they were disappointed in my career choice. But it wasn't like that was the only time we hadn't seen eye to eye."

I choked back a laugh. They hadn't approved of me either. That had been part of the problem when it had come to Ava's and my relationship. "What else did they disapprove of?"

"My divorce." Her tone had an edge of fierceness to it. Not the I'm-going-to-rip-you-to-pieces kind of fierceness. It was more like, *I am a strong woman. Hear me roar.*

"You were married?" The words came out evenly and alpha-man tough—as though I were merely curious. Which was partly true.

"Yes. For two years."

The GPS instructed me to take the next left. The snow was coming down even heavier now, leaving a thick layer on the road in both directions. And the street I had to turn onto wasn't much better.

I drove slowly, not wanting to risk going too fast and having my vehicle follow the same fate as Ava's car. "The inn shouldn't be much farther....So how come only two years?" I asked.

"What difference does it make?" Her voice was still strong but there was another emotion there. Sadness?

"It doesn't make any difference. I'm just wondering what

kind of idiot he was for the marriage to last only two years." Because I was pretty sure it was all on her ex-husband. The Ava I'd known back when we were engaged was an amazing person.

It was her family who had their heads up their asses.

3

AVA

I'm just wondering what kind of idiot he was for the marriage to last only two years.

I almost burst out laughing as Liam's words echoed in my ears. I wasn't sure who exactly had been the idiot: my ex-husband or me.

I mean really, when did arranged marriages ever result in happily ever afters? Yes, I was aware it had worked wonderfully for Jamie Fraser and Claire Randall. But they were characters from a novel. I wrote about Greek mythology, but that didn't mean preteen Poseidon, Hermes, and Aphrodite were walking around San Francisco. It was make-believe. Fantasy.

So why had I agreed to marry Chris? Let's call it a moment of insanity. Or maybe I thought it was a good idea after I went against family tradition and became a teacher. I thought it would make my family happy.

I thought it would make *me* happy.

I also foolishly believed that I loved him and he loved me.

Yep, the winner of the idiot contest went to yours truly. The prize? A divorce certificate to hang on the living room wall.

"He decided that his lover on the side was a better choice," I finally said. "Once I discovered that, I kicked him out."

"Good for you."

"Good for me...except because of the prenup I had signed, I didn't get to stay in our house for long. He got to keep it. I got to keep the wedding photos." *Go me.*

"Ouch." Liam turned into a small parking lot at the side of a chalet-style building. It was quaint and adorable and nothing like the resort I'd be staying at...once I got there. The vacancy sign glowed red.

"What about you?" I asked as he pulled into the only empty spot available. "Did you ever get married?" He wasn't wearing a ring, but that didn't mean anything.

What the heck are you doing? I belatedly asked myself.

My heart clenched, waiting to hear his reply. *It doesn't matter if he's married or not*, I reminded it. *He didn't want me. End of story.* And as soon as I was checked into the inn for the night, he could go on his merry way, and I'd never have to see him again.

He shook his head. "I was still with the SEALs until recently and figured there was no point settling down and having a family while I was serving my country. It wouldn't be fair to my wife and our kids. I didn't want her always wondering if I would be returning home to them and if I would be returning home the same man."

Those words sounded very familiar. He'd used similar ones when he broke off our engagement—along with telling me that he no longer loved me.

But those weren't the only reasons he'd ended our relationship. My grandmother later admitted to me that she had offered him an obscene amount of money if he'd cut me from his life. An obscene amount of money that he had gladly taken.

Once upon a time, the memory of that had made my heart clench into the size of a Christmas tree ornament. Now it was more like a tiny splinter in the fleshy part of the thumb. An irritation but easy to live with. And with a little more time —maybe in a few more years—it would completely disappear.

We climbed out of Liam's SUV and plodded through the strong wind and thick snow on the ground to the inn's entrance. Liam pulled the door open for me. I stepped inside the building, into a lobby straight from a fairy tale. The walls were creamy white, offset by the dark wooden beams in the cathedral ceiling. The same dark wood that matched the front desk.

The small lobby was decorated with rustic Christmas decorations. The same theme was mirrored on the tall pine tree. It was official. I was in love.

"Wow, this place is gorgeous," I said, following Liam to the front desk.

Several families with young kids were hanging out by the fireplace. A man and a woman, still in their winter coats and with their luggage next to them, were talking to the woman in her sixties who was standing behind the desk. The woman who looked like she belonged in a historic era long since past.

Short strands of her white hair poked out from under a forest-green mop cap. The white, buttonless blouse had puffy sleeves and ruffles at the wrists and was partially covered with a floor-length, green sleeveless dress, which was fitted down to her ample waist. She was also wearing a red-and-white ruffled apron.

Mrs. Claus had apparently abandoned the North Pole and was working at the inn. *Ho, Ho, Ho.*

We didn't have to wait long before the couple in front of us was walking away from the desk, luggage in tow.

The older woman smiled at us as we stepped up to her, a

gleam in her merry blue eyes. "You two are in luck. We happen to have a single room available. Our only room available, owing to the storm and the main roads being closed in all directions."

Liam and I exchanged looks. The part about the roads was news to us.

"The sheriff's department issued the announcement only a few minutes ago," she explained as if reading our minds. "No one is getting through, thanks to several major accidents. The room has a queen-sized bed."

"Sounds perfect. We'll take it," Liam said at the same time as I asked, "Do you have an extra roll-away bed?" Because no way in fruit-cake hell was I sharing a bed with him.

All right—maybe that was a little strong. I happen to like dark fruitcake. With marzipan. It was the light stuff I wasn't fond of.

"I'm sorry," pseudo-Mrs. Claus said, "I just gave away our last one to a family."

Liam put his hand on my shoulder. "That's fine. We'll take the room."

I nodded—because what else could I do? It was too cold to sleep in his truck. "How long do they think the roads will be closed for?" I asked. Would I be *swoosh-swoosh-swooshing* down the slopes this time tomorrow? I had a ski lesson booked for the afternoon.

"It depends on how much snow falls overnight and when they get around to plowing the roads. But don't worry, you can stay in the room until then. If you can't leave because of the snow, the next guests booked for the room won't be able to get here either."

Please, please, please, *Mother Nature, stop snowing. Now.* Wasn't it bad enough I had to stay in the same room with Liam for the night?

Not that I planned to share the bed with him. I'd sleep on the floor if I had to.

I fished through my purse to find my wallet.

"I've got this," Liam said, handing his credit card to Mrs. Claus.

"Thank you." She completed the transaction. "If you need anything, just give me a call. I'm Betsy and my husband is Harold. The dining room is just through there." She pointed toward the open French doors. "We provide dinner service between five and ten thirty p.m." She then listed the rest of the mealtimes. "Do you need help with your luggage?"

"No, we should be fine," Liam said with a smile. And my heart did a happy dance at seeing it. *Stupid heart*—even though I couldn't blame it. Liam had the best smile around. Just seeing it was enough to warm you up better than a raging fire. Chris's smile never had that effect on me.

His smiles were warm enough to melt ice cream...on a hot day.

I just didn't realize it until much later.

I began walking toward the entrance.

Liam grabbed my arm. "Where are you running off to?"

"To get my luggage." There was a slim chance I might have used my *no-duh* voice.

All right, a big chance.

"I can get it."

I rolled my eyes. "Get over yourself, Liam. I'm a big girl. And this big girl can get her own luggage."

He grunted his caveman sound. The poor man didn't like *not* having damsels in distress to rescue.

I stepped outside and immediately regretted it. The wind had picked up since we had entered the cozy inn. And now it wanted to ensure we didn't forget about it.

Don't worry. I'll send you a Christmas card if that makes you feel better.

A big, unexpected gust battered against me, pushing me sideways a step. "Fine, no Christmas card for you," I muttered.

"What did you say?" Liam asked, fortunately unable to hear my comment because of the whining wind.

"I can't wait to hang out in front of the fireplace." Because according to Betsy, our room had one.

He nodded and pushed forward through the storm.

I focused on each step—willing my brain not to venture where it didn't belong. By this, I meant how all my family was in the Bahamas for the wedding. On the hot sand. Getting cocktails with fancy little umbrellas.

Another topic that was best for my brain not to dwell on was how Liam's and my engagement ended ten years ago. It was two days before Christmas, and the last thing I wanted was to rehash the God-awful night he broke my heart, even if my heart was eighty percent recovered.

Thanks to Chris's betrayal, it was still a little tender and bruised.

Our previous footsteps in the snow had already disappeared in the short time we had been at the inn. The snow was now over a foot deep, making it even tougher to walk to the vehicle. By the time we got there, I was exhausted. And I still had to carry everything back to the inn.

This is what I got for not packing lightly...and for not going somewhere tropical.

Once back inside the inn, we trudged up the stairs, carrying our luggage. Well, mostly Liam carried our luggage since his consisted of only one item: a duffle bag.

At our room, I unlocked the door with the key card and pushed it open. The inside of the room was as quaint and cozy as the lobby. The only difference was the lack of Christmas decorations.

My stomach made a sound resembling that of a hibernating bear waking up after a long winter nap.

Liam laughed. *Bastard.* "You want to shower first before we head down? Or maybe you'd rather join me to save time." He smirked.

An image of him naked flashed in my head. And naturally, my face heated at the memory.

Liam laughed again. Note to self: Liam had clearly learned the art of reading minds. Must be a Navy SEAL thing.

"That's okay," I said. "I can shower myself, thanks. But I think we need some ground rules if we're going to make this work."

His eyebrow rose, mostly out of amusement. I recognized the look on him. "What kind of ground rules are you talking about?"

"We don't talk about what happened between us. It's almost Christmas and after tonight, we won't see each other again. There's no point bringing up the past. It's over now. Nothing's going to change that, so I don't see a reason to dwell on it anymore. Deal?" I held out my hand to shake on it.

He shrugged. "Sure, why not?" He shook on it.

With that settled, I riffled through my suitcase and found my black jeans and a cream-colored, lightweight sweater. A short time later, the two of us were showered and heading downstairs.

We walked to the entrance of the dining room.

"*Uh, uh, uh,*" a man in his sixties said. Possibly Harold? Like Santa, his hair was white and he had a long beard. He was wearing a white shirt with wide sleeves that were partially rolled up his forearms and a red velvet vest that was unbuttoned, revealing a stomach that was the opposite of Liam's flat one. He also had on black pants and hiking boots.

If I didn't know better, I'd say Liam and I had stepped into Santa and Mrs. Claus's home.

Harold-Santa pointed to something above my head as Betsy approached us.

I looked up. Mistletoe.

His eyes twinkled with mischief. "You two can't enter the dining room until you've kissed under the mistletoe."

I opened my mouth to protest—or announce that Liam was actually my brother or cousin. Anything to keep from kissing him.

"It's okay, Ava." Liam's tone held the familiar teasing I remembered from back when we were engaged. Teasing but also with an edge of challenge. "It's just one little kiss."

I swallowed past the Christmas-ornament-sized lump in my throat and took a step back. But before I could get much farther than that, Liam wrapped his arms around my waist, stopping me from escaping.

He leaned forward, his breath brushing my ear. "Just go along with this. Okay, Ava? Give them the show they want, and everything will be fine." His tone was the same rough one that used to leave my girlie parts excited.

And apparently still got my girlie parts excited.

Traitors.

I nodded, my heart thumping a quick rhythm in my chest. He lowered his mouth to mine, lingered there for several seconds...then his lips were on mine.

I was expecting a quick kiss. But the moment our mouths touched, it was as if I were transported back in time to when his kisses were as essential to survival as the oxygen in the air.

My lips parted and I let him in. Nothing X-rated. Just the brief brushing of tongues. But that was all it took. The familiar hum I'd last experienced ten years ago vibrated through my body.

Oh. That's not good.

My body thoroughly disagreed with that assessment.

You'll find your Forever Love under the mistletoe....Zoe's prediction echoed in my head. So much for that. My body was broken. It thought everyone was my Forever Love.

All right—it hadn't exactly said that. But if it acted this way with the man who'd broken my heart, then my body was clearly faulty.

For a second, I considered grabbing the next guy who walked under the mistletoe, to test if my body reacted the same to him as it had to Liam's kiss. But we were the only four individuals in the area.

And it didn't look like there were any spare single men in the dining room to help me out.

My phone pinged in my purse. I fished it out as Liam and I walked to the empty table next to the window.

The text was from Zoe.

> Zoe: I heard the roads are closed due to the storm. Did you get to your hotel okay?

> Me: No. Stuck at an inn until the roads reopen.

Probably a good idea not to mention Liam or the kiss.

4

LIAM

If someone had asked me this morning what the two things were that I least expected to happen today, I would have said bumping into my ex-fancée and kissing her.

What did I think of the kiss?

Fucking awesome.

But that came as no surprise.

Ava returned her phone to her purse, and we listened to Harold tell us the specials for the day...which were pretty much the only things on the menu.

We ordered our food and drinks—wine for Ava and beer for me.

"Okay, so we've established that I'm divorced and my ex-husband had a mistress, and I became the family black sheep by becoming a teacher instead of a lawyer," Ava said once Harold had walked away from our table. "And we've established that you were serving with the Navy SEALs, which I already knew because I was engaged to you when you joined them. But you're not with them anymore....So what are you up to these days?"

"I live in San Francisco, and I have my own security and investigation company. Plus I volunteer for search and rescue missions when I'm needed."

Her eyes widened. "What kind of search and rescue missions?"

"It can be anything, really. A seven-year-old girl was walking her dog yesterday afternoon and went missing in the mountains. My team was called in to help find her."

Ava's face paled. "Did you…? Did you find her alive?"

I smiled softly at her concern. That was the Ava I knew. She cared about everyone, including strangers. "Yes. She was cold and scared and scratched up, but other than that she was okay."

Ava's shoulders relaxed, the tension releasing from her like air from a helium balloon. "That's a relief." She smiled back at me. "So, you're a hero."

"I wouldn't go that far. I wasn't the only person involved in the mission, but yes, my crew was the one who located her."

"Well, in my books, that makes you a hero."

I didn't know why, but her words ignited something inside me. A raw emotion I hadn't experienced in more years than I cared to remember.

Was it the first time that someone had told me that I was a hero? Not at all. But it was the first time I'd wanted to kiss someone long and hard for saying those words. What I did was my job. It was something I was good at. But this was the first time being a hero to someone *really* meant something— even if it shouldn't have, given Ava and I hadn't been together in ten years.

Harold brought us our drinks and we spent dinner catching up. But even though Ava seemed willing to talk to me, I sensed she was holding back. That she had erected a wall to protect herself and was making sure not a single brick crumbled.

Was I surprised? Hell, no. First I told her that I no longer loved her when we were engaged, and then her ex-husband cheated on her. I'd be surprised if she wasn't more cautious after that.

I silently cursed myself a thousand times for doing that to her. And then I mentally cursed the jackass she'd been married to.

After dinner, Harold and Betsy encouraged us to join them and the other guests in the great hall for Christmas cheer. The great hall? Yes, that was their fancy term for the lobby.

Several kids sat on the couch, watching Harold and Betsy with great interest. Watching them the way a kid would do if they were positive the pair really were Santa and Mrs. Claus.

One ten-year-old was sitting in an armchair, away from everyone, her attention on the book in her lap.

Ava walked over to her and I followed.

She crouched by the girl. The girl kept reading.

"You look like you're really enjoying that book," Ava said.

The kid finally looked up and nodded so fast, I thought her head might fly off even though it was firmly attached to her body. "It's my favorite series. I've already read the first book six times, and I'm hoping Santa will bring me the second book for Christmas."

She lifted the book to show us the cover: *Max Thunder and the Tides of Poseidon*. A New York Times bestseller by AJ Versteeg.

As in Ava Julianna Versteeg?

My gaze shifted to Ava, whose cheeks were now adorably flushed. Her eyes met mine, and her blush deepened.

The girl's head tilted to the side and she studied Ava. Then she turned to the back flap of the book with Ava's picture on it.

Her gaze shot up to Ava's, and she pointed at the photo. "This is you!"

Smiling, Ava nodded. The girl's eyes grew even wider. I couldn't tell if she was going to pass out or start jumping up and down while screaming with excitement.

"Would you like me to sign your book for you?" Ava asked.

"Oh gosh, would I!" the girl practically squealed. "Mandy's never going to believe I met you. She's my best friend, and she's read the book almost as many times as I have. She's already read *Max Thunder and the Helm of Darkness* because it was her birthday last week and she got the book as a present. She's sooo lucky." The words poured from her mouth in a tsunami-strength rush.

Ava searched through her purse and pulled out a pen. A minute later, the book was signed, and Ava was answering a barrage of questions about the series and the characters. Ava smiled and replied to each one with a level of excitement that matched the girl's.

And damned if a new wave of pride didn't almost knock me on my ass at what Ava had accomplished. She'd always had an active imagination. She used to write short stories, even before we were engaged. But she never showed them to me. She never showed them to anyone.

Eventually, the questions came to an end—mostly thanks to Harold and Betsy. "Santa and I are thankful you could all join us tonight. And since we'll be busy tomorrow night, on Christmas Eve, we thought now would be a good time for Christmas caroling."

Next to me, Ava stiffened and shuffled back a small step as if trying not to be noticed. On instinct, I reached back and knotted my fingers with hers. And like when I kissed her, my body felt as if it had become electrically charged.

I guess some things never change.

Betsy handed out the lyrics, then she and Harold began singing the first song: "O Christmas Tree."

The rest of the guests started singing along with them, including me. I glanced at Ava and smirked. I leaned into her, so only she could hear me. "You're lip-synching, aren't you?"

That's right—Ava's tone deaf.

She smirked back and gave a tiny nod. I squeezed her hand, letting her know her secret was safe with me.

Santa and Mrs. Claus ended the singing after eight songs, with the promise that Santa had something for all the good little boys and girls.

Which gave me an idea. "Why don't you go up to our room?" I told Ava. "I'll be there in a few minutes."

Once she was walking up the stairs, I joined Harold in the dining area. "Is it possible for me to purchase a bottle of red wine to take upstairs?"

He gave a merry chuckle from deep in his belly—exactly how I imagined Santa would do...if he were real. "That sounds like a wonderful idea." He went behind the bar, bent down, and popped up a moment later with a bottle of red. He handed it to me, along with two wine-glasses.

I thanked him and returned to Ava's and my room.

She was gazing out the window at the falling snow when I entered. The gas fireplace had already been turned on.

I let the door click shut behind me and stepped farther inside. That was when I noticed the pillows and blanket on the floor by the wall.

"I figured I could sleep there tonight," Ava said, now facing me.

"You can sleep on the bed with me. I really don't mind. I mean, unless you think you might attack me in my sleep." I winked at her.

"No, it's just...I prefer to sleep on the floor."

"Really? So you don't actually have a bed at home? You sleep on the floor?"

The cute blush from earlier returned to her cheeks. "Well, no. But I figured since we aren't actually dating, I should sleep on the floor."

The laugh that I'd kept under wraps when she first suggested this erupted from my lungs. "We were sleeping together even before we were engaged, Ava. Is this 'no sleeping with a man unless I have a wedding band on my finger' a new rule of yours?"

She scowled. "Well, no. But as you pointed out, we *were* engaged. We aren't now. We're not even dating."

"Okay, if you're so adamant about us not sharing a bed, then I'll take the floor."

The scowl was joined by the crossing of her arms. "Why? Because you're a man and you think I'm too much of a princess to sleep on the floor?"

I laughed again. "Sweetheart, I definitely don't think of you as a princess." Even if her family did think of themselves as royalty more times than not. "But in case you've forgotten, I used to be with the SEALs. I'm used to sleeping in locations and conditions that you fortunately never have to consider. If you're so damn determined that we won't be sharing the bed tonight, then I insist on being the one on the floor."

I walked over to the love seat in front of the fireplace and placed the wine and glasses on the small coffee table. "I thought we could continue catching up on what's been going on in our lives since we last saw each other."

She shrugged. "Sure. Okay."

I picked up a wineglass and filled it. "For starters, all I know is that you were headed for Lake Tahoe, but you haven't told me yet why you were heading there two days before Christmas and alone." She had mentioned during dinner that she was driving to Lake Tahoe when she got the flat, but after that, she changed the direction of our conversation.

I handed her the glass of wine and she sat down.

"Today was the last day of classes, and because it was early dismissal, I decided to book the resort for tonight instead of driving there tomorrow morning. I figured it would give me an extra day there."

My own glass now filled, I sat beside her and turned to her. "Are you meeting your family there?"

She looked away, settling her gaze on the fire, and shook her head. "No. My parents and grandparents chose to spend Christmas in the Bahamas."

I frowned. "And you weren't invited?"

She laughed, but the sound was filled with a sadness that I wasn't used to hearing with her laugh. It had always been filled with love and hope and joy. "No, I was invited. In fact, my grandmother phoned this afternoon, demanding I join them. She had even purchased a ticket for me so that, in her mind, I couldn't say no."

"But considering you were driving to Lake Tahoe instead of San Francisco airport, I'm going out on a limb here and guessing you weren't planning to join your family, despite what your grandmother wants?" Ten years ago, I would never have expected Ava to go against her family's demands. She usually did whatever they asked of her, just to make them happy.

She was *always* trying to make them happy.

That was another reason why I had walked away from her in the end. At the time, I had believed that she would never be her own person. She would always be who her family wanted her to be. And I knew eventually, if we had gotten married, our marriage would have struggled to survive.

"They figured my attendance would go a long way toward

repairing the damage I caused...." She took a long sip of her wine.

"Damage? What did you do...break a family heirloom?"

She smiled...only this time, it sparkled with life and amusement. "Not exactly. You know how in the olden days, kings would marry off their sons or daughters to other princes or princesses, with hopes of aligning the two kingdoms to benefit both?"

"Not really. What does this have to do with you and your family and the damage you supposedly caused?"

"They wanted me to marry Chris to align my family with his, so to speak. Both felt this was a great first step to a partnership between my family's law firm and Chris's family business. Don't ask me to explain. I never understood it. Besides, I was only interested in marrying for love.

"So as you can imagine, when I divorced him, neither family was happy with me."

"Even though he was the one who cheated on you?"

"My grandmother and his mother took me aside and told me I should have looked the other way at his dalliances. Love was just a wasted concept, supported by makers of fine chocolate and greeting card companies. People in my family's position didn't have time for such silliness." She gave another shrug. "Apparently, I was just being silly for wanting to be loved. Apparently, she forgot that my parents were in love and still are."

My heart tightened at the part about wanting to be loved. Before I realized what I was doing, I leaned down and kissed the top of her head. "Not silly at all. You deserve to be loved."

She turned her gaze back to mine and gave me a sad laugh. "Now if only the guys I tend to fall for felt the same way. I'm the girl that men love and then leave...if they really even loved me to begin with." She took a long sip of her wine.

I wanted to point out that what she had said wasn't

entirely true. I'd left her because I *had* loved her. But something warned me that she wouldn't believe me. And why would she? I'd done a great job convincing her that I had no longer loved her.

"So do you still hike?" I asked, just to change topic.

Her face brightened. "I do. Not as much as I used to. Mostly because my best friend has a family now and doesn't have time to hike with me. But I am saving up to one day go down to Machu Picchu in Peru and hike there. Plus, I'm contemplating a new middle-grade series based on Inca mythology, and it would be great to just go there and get a feel for the place."

The words rushed from her mouth so fast, I wasn't sure if she had taken a breath the entire time.

But that wasn't the part that had me frowning. It was the part where she'd said that she was saving up to one day go there that had me confused. The Ava I remembered had plenty of money to go on these adventures—and to travel first class. She never had to save up money to do that.

The image of her older model Honda Civic flashed in my mind. The jeans and sweater she was wearing also didn't resemble what I remembered as her typical style. When we were dating, her outfits had been from high-end designers. "Off-the-rack" was a concept her family abhorred. The outfit she now had on was obviously off-the-rack and not exactly new.

"You have to save to go to Peru?" I asked. "Aren't you allowed to use your trust fund for that?" Which made no sense...pretty much like her clothing. Traveling to exotic locales was also on the agenda back in the days. Maybe Peru wasn't considered exotic enough for her family.

Ava flashed me a soft smile. "I have no idea. But since I walked away from my trust fund back in college, it's not something I've given any thought to."

"You walked away from it? How does that even work?" It wasn't as if I knew anything about trust funds.

She nodded. "That's right. My grandmother gave me a choice. Follow in the family footsteps and become a lawyer, or forfeit the right to my trust fund. I wanted to be a teacher. I didn't want to be a lawyer. Money and power aren't important to me...not like they are for my family, not like they are for some people I know." The pain in her eyes stared back at me, and for once I felt like I was missing something—like pieces of a jigsaw puzzle.

But while she might have been staring at me with pain in her eyes, I was gaping at her, dumbfounded. I'd underestimated Ava. I'd underestimated what had been important to her.

"How come you never told me that you wanted to be a teacher?" I asked. Would I have walked away from her ten years ago if I had known? Never. Especially if I had known that she would've rather turned her back on her trust fund and become a teacher than keep her old lifestyle.

"I don't know. I think for the longest time I was afraid to admit it even to myself, just because I didn't think I had a choice. It had been hammered into my head from a young age that I would become a lawyer...and maybe one day run for office. I didn't realize that I could just walk away from the life that didn't hold much appeal to me and set out on my own path."

I smiled. "I'm glad you finally realized that. Something tells me you're an amazing teacher. And if you ever need someone to go hiking with, you can call me." I genuinely meant it. Back when we were dating, we used to hike whenever we could. I missed it—and not just because hiking sex was pretty damn awesome.

But that wasn't the only reason for my offer. It came with an ulterior motive. Ten years ago, I made the biggest mistake of my life and walked away from the girl I'd loved, because I thought I was doing the right thing. And now? Now I wanted to see if it was possible to have a second chance with her. I wanted to find out if we could be a couple again like before— or if going our separate ways had been the right thing to do after all.

But to do that, I needed to regain Ava's trust....

5

AVA

Later, if someone was to interrogate me and ask me what my goal for tonight was, I would've told them it was to spend the evening with Liam.

Because then I could prove to the mistletoe that he was *not* my Forever Love. He'd already had that chance ten years ago and broke off our engagement instead.

Right—the mistletoe didn't care one way or another about Zoe's family legend when it came to finding true love. But it was the principle of it that mattered. My body was confusing Forever Love with a good fuck.

A *very* good fuck, if I remembered correctly.

One I wouldn't have minded experiencing again. As a one-night stand.

Nothing more.

My gaze dropped to Liam's mouth, and I unconsciously ran the tip of my tongue against my lower lip, remembering the taste of him. Craving to relive it for old times' sake.

Yes, I realized that this was the same guy who had broken my heart when he told me he no longer loved me—and was paid handsomely for doing so.

But that was ten years ago. I had long since moved on. Plus, his actions had given me the strength to walk away from my family's wealth and their desire for power.

Maybe that was why I was considering kissing him again. As a thank-you.

If he was interested.

The added bonus was that we could still keep to our ground rule of not discussing the end of our engagement. That was in the past, and this was just making out.

My eyes moved away from his lips, up to his heated gaze. "I know we're not dating—and after tonight we'll go our separate ways—but if you're okay with it, I'd like to kiss you again."

Right—with pick-up lines like that, it was a good thing I wrote middle-grade stories and not romances.

"Are you sure? I know you don't want to talk about what happened—"

I didn't let him finish that sentence. I placed my finger against his lips. "I haven't kissed a guy in a long time. A *very* long time. I just want to make sure I haven't lost my touch. Or gotten rusty."

Wow. I really sucked at seducing guys.

Clearly I needed more practice.

Starting with Liam.

"I mean, if you're not interested," I said, "you just have to tell me. I'll understand. It's just...I had a crappy day what with my car getting a flat, and I'm not at the resort like I was supposed to be. So I'd really like to—"

This time it was I who didn't get to finish the sentence. He lowered his head, and his lips brushed against mine.

And in that instant, I became drunk on the intoxicating taste of the wine on his breath, from his woodsy scent that always did me in, and from the combination of pheromones and testosterone that were all male, all Liam.

A familiar need buzzed impatiently through my body like a hive of bees waiting for daylight to come. *You know you want it*, the pesky, sex-starved voice in my head said. *Just take what you need, and then you can walk away.*

You know what they say about famous last words, right? Run.

Or at least that was what my head was saying. My body—more specifically, my legs—had a different opinion. *Just one time*, it whispered. *What could it hurt to have sex with Liam just one more time?*

My body had a point. What if I didn't end up having sex with a guy at the resort? It wasn't like I planned to throw myself at every single man I met there. What if I changed my mind because I wasn't exactly into one-night stands? Then I'd be forced to go through an even lengthier dry spell.

What was wrong with grabbing a bottle of water in the desert, even when you knew it could be your last one for a very long time?

And because I was on a roll, selling the benefits of having sex with Liam (assuming he wanted to have sex with me), let's not forget the major point. Sex with Liam wouldn't be disappointing.

I opened my mouth and gently sucked on his lower lip. My fingers knotted in his hair. His wonderfully soft hair that loosely curled around my fingers. The last time I had seen him, his hair had been shaved short.

"I love your hair like this," I said against his lips. "It makes you look even hotter." *Oops. Hadn't meant to say that.*

"It's a good thing, then, that I'm keeping it this way. Especially if it means having your fingers in it." He settled his large hands around my waist and pulled me over to straddle his lap. His hard length pressed against my core. We both moaned.

"Christ, Ava. I want you so badly." He thrust his hips,

driving me closer to the edge that I knew would be rapidly coming once I gave my consent.

"I want you, too," I said on another moan. "Just this one time," I clarified. No point in him thinking that I would be his booty call once I returned to San Francisco.

His light brown eyes studied me, a fiery intensity burning in them. "Are you sure?"

"Very sure."

And then Grandma's words and the image of Gloria's skinny body intruded on my lust-filled moment. I chewed on my lower lip.

Liam ran his thumb along it, freeing my lip from my teeth. "You don't look very sure."

"I am...it's just...I'm not a model. I'm not skinny."

"That's good. I'm not into skinny model types." His thumb shifted down to lightly scrape across a nipple, still hidden under my bra and sweater. It puckered at the sensation, pleading to feel his touch against it, pleading to feel his fingers against my bare skin.

His hand trailed along the side of my breast and down my ribs, finally settling on my waist. "From where I'm sitting, I'd say you're perfect."

Liam pushed the hem of my sweater up, tracing his fingers against my flesh. I shivered at his touch, shivered at the memory of what it could do to me.

Impatient to feel him against me, I practically ripped the sweater off over my head and tossed it to the side.

Liam cupped my bra-covered breasts in his hands. My girlie parts did a happy dance.

He scraped his thumbs against the taut buds. "Love the bra," he said, referring to my plain old white one that was more about being practical than sexy. "But I think I'd prefer it much better off you."

My girls and I thoroughly agreed with him there.

Liam reached behind me and unhooked the clasps. His fingers slid up my back to my shoulders, leaving a trail of goose bumps in their wake. His fingers then completed their mission, dragging the bra straps down my arms, freeing my breasts once and for all.

Liam dropped the bra somewhere on the floor and palmed the pale globes. "Christ, I've been fantasizing all evening about touching and tasting you."

His hands shifted to behind me, one on my neck, the other on the curve of my lower back. He leaned forward, forcing me to bend back like an erotic dancer. My breasts jutted proudly in the air. My core rubbed against his length. The friction of my jeans against my clit had it singing "Joy to the World."

I groaned.

Liam circled the tip of his tongue around one nipple, then sucked it into his mouth while pinching the other one.

My clit said, *That's nice, but a little action down here would be even better.*

I had to agree with it there.

As if sensing my internal debate, Liam released my nipple from his mouth and shifted me off his lap. He parked me on the couch and moved the two wineglasses to the side table. He then pushed himself off the couch and relocated the coffee table out of the way.

"What—you're redecorating the room now?" I said with a laugh. I recognized the look in his eyes. The look that warned me I was about to become one *very* happy woman.

He kneeled in front of me and unzipped my jeans. "Take off your jeans and panties."

Still seated, I did as he asked, then enjoyed the view as he removed his own clothes.

He stood before me, his cock proud and patriotic. I smashed my lips together, suppressing the giggle wanting to break free. Liam had served his country and now he was going to serve me.

"Put your heels on the couch and open yourself up to me, Ava."

A shiver raced through me at the command in his voice. Gloria might have gotten off on Chris being a submissive, but that wasn't for me. I wanted a partner who was all about the give and take.

A warm smile grew on his face—causing an equally warm reaction in my lower belly.

"Now, I want you to touch yourself."

I licked my lip, chasing away the sudden dryness. How many times had I masturbated in front of a man? That would be a big fat zero.

My mouth curled up to one side. "Are you going to touch yourself...or is this a one-woman show?"

"This is about me getting *you* off for now. Now touch yourself." At the hoarse roughness of his tone, wetness rushed to my core. Damn, the man had grown even sexier in the past ten years. Sexier and more demanding.

Remember, this is only a one-time thing, the bossy voice said. *And don't you dare let your heart get involved.*

That got a *Hey, I can hear you*, from my heart, which was met by an *And your point is?*

Before they could start squabbling like my students, I slipped my fingers between the lips of my sex and slid them around the wet surface.

That moan? Definitely me. But the groan was one hundred percent Liam.

Good, wouldn't want to be the only one being affected here.

Not that there was any doubt about how turned-on he was from the way his cock grew thicker.

"That's not where my eyes are," he said, amusement in his tone.

My gaze flicked up to his. "Better?"

"Much better. Is there a reason why you've stopped pleasing yourself?"

The smirk returned to my face. "You distracted me."

He nodded for me to continue. I returned to teasing myself with my fingers, bringing myself closer and closer to the point of no return.

Liam dropped to his knees and placed his hand on mine, stilling its movement. "Let me see if you're almost there." His gaze dropped to my sex. "Hmm. Looks like its time for you to come on my face."

Before I had a chance to respond, he was reverently kissing my clit. Then he sucked it into his mouth, and I almost launched into orbit.

"Like that, do you?" he asked.

"Very much so." My voice was no longer my own. It sounded sexier than I'd ever heard it before. Only this man had that effect on me.

His mouth shifted down, to be replaced by his thumb. It circled my clit once, twice, three times. I writhed around on the couch and groaned.

"Christ, you're so beautiful." He ran his tongue along one lip and down the other....And all coherent thought vanished.

My fingers begged to touch him. I slipped them through his hair. God, he had such soft hair. God, he had such a talented tongue. God...I wanted him inside me.

In every possible way.

"Liam," I panted. "I need you...inside me."

"In time, sweetheart. I've been starved from doing this for a long time, and I have no intention of being deprived again."

I heard the words, but given that I was rushing toward the

abyss—breaking all speed limits—his words were without meaning.

And then I fell down, down, down. I couldn't remember the last time in the past ten years it had felt this way. It hadn't even been like this while touching myself with the image of Liam in my head.

Although it had come pretty damn close. A lot closer than when I had imagined someone else in his place. That's right, not even the image of Chris Hemsworth or Chris Pine or Chris Pratt had the same impact as my memories of Liam.

It really wasn't fair.

I was vaguely away of Liam lowing my heels to the floor.

"How are you doing there?" he asked.

"S'all good," was all I was capable of saying. I flashed him a smile—a happy mix of satisfied and dopey.

He leaned in and gently kissed me. "Glad to hear it."

He slipped one arm behind me and the other one under my legs. He hoisted me up, his intense eyes locked on mine, and carried me to the bed.

He lowered me onto it, and kissed me again, this time more thoroughly. I trailed my hand down his muscled torso, exploring every ridge and valley, until I got to his hard length. I wrapped my fingers around it. It jerked slightly in my grip.

I caressed the velvet head, spreading the pre-cum. Liam moaned against my mouth and I smiled. Nothing was more powerful than knowing your every move, your every touch affected the man you were with.

And I didn't even need a whip or to wear leather to get Liam to that point.

He lay down next to me and gently cupped my cheek with his hand. "I'm going to make love to you now, Ava I'm going to take it nice and slow. And then afterward, I'm going to take you fast and hard. Are you okay with that?"

Naturally, my heart picked up on the "make love to you"

part. I reminded it that his pretty words were just semantics. Not that he had to say them to get laid tonight. I was perfectly happy with this being a one-night stand. Come morning, the roads would be clear, and a tow truck would take my car to the nearest garage...and then my vacation at Lake Tahoe would finally commence.

As would Operation Mistletoe.

"Okay," I said with a smile.

He removed a foil square from his wallet, ripped it open, and rolled the condom onto his length. Then he positioned himself between my legs and slowly entered me—with my body welcoming him home.

By the time the two of us came—first me, and then him a second later—there wasn't a part of me that wasn't rejoicing.

I collapsed on the bed while he disposed of the condom. He rejoined me under the covers a moment later and pulled me against him.

I laid my head on his bare chest, listening to the soothing beat of his heart. Liam's hand caressed my upper back, and I further relaxed into him.

I could get used to this.

Which was a bad thing.

A *very* bad thing.

The sooner I got out of here and was on my way to the resort, the better....

6

———

LIAM

Ava began drawing circles on my abs, her head resting on my bare chest. When was the last time a woman did that after she and I had fucked? Never. Not since Ava and I were engaged. It was intimate—not the behavior for one-night stands.

But shit, it felt good when *she* did it.

"How come I never knew that you're an author?" I asked.

"I'm assuming that's because you don't read children's books."

"You have me there." I brushed a strand of hair behind her ear. Any excuse to touch her.

"Were you surprised?"

"Not really." She'd once confessed to me that she wanted to be an author one day. "You've always been a good story-teller. And I think it's great that you became both a teacher and an author of children's books."

She laughed, the sound sad and a little off. "As you can imagine, my family didn't feel the same way."

"Even though you're a New York Times bestselling author?"

"I'm a New York Times bestselling author of two *children's* books. They don't consider me to be a real author."

I frowned. "Why not? The book the kid was reading looked pretty real to me."

"But it's a book for kids. In *their* minds, that isn't worthy of being on the New York Times list."

"Well, I think it's pretty awesome." I kissed the top of her head. "And your family is a bunch of idiots."

She laughed again. This time there was nothing off about it. It was full and rich and beautiful. "I'll agree with you there."

"So that's the real reason you're not spending Christmas with them in the Bahamas? Because they're idiots?" I chuckled. "Sounds like a good reason to me."

"I wish it was as easy as that." She moved off me, but remained on her side, looking down at me. "I didn't want to join them in the Bahamas because I didn't want to attend my ex-husband's wedding."

Shit. "Is that what you meant by if you joined them in the Bahamas it would go a long way in repairing the damage you caused?"

She nodded. "You ready for the best part?"

"Something tells me given what I know about your family, I'll never be ready. So hold that thought, and I'll be right back." I climbed out of bed and retrieved the wine bottle and our glasses. I refilled the glasses, handed Ava's back to her, and placed the bottle on the bedside table.

I rejoined her under the covers. "All right. Lay it on me."

She took a long sip of her wine. "Chris's bride is the woman I found him with in our bedroom. Wearing leather and whipping his naked ass while telling him that he'd been a very naughty boy." She made a face that resembled someone sucking on a sour lemon, then swigged back a healthier dose of wine. "I almost had to bleach my eyes after seeing that."

Was I into leather and whips? Definitely not. Nor did I fantasize about women dressing up like school-aged girls.

And all bets were off if a woman referred to me as her daddy. I had a one-night stand like that once. The moment she asked me to spank her like I was her daddy and she had been a bad girl, I'd been out the apartment door faster than a sniper's bullet.

"I'm guessing your family has no idea about that little X-rated scene."

She snorted a laugh. "Could you imagine? Although now that I think about it, maybe I should have told them. Then no one would want me to attend the wedding. Imagine the scandal if I happen to let slip during the reception that the only way Chris could get it up was if I whipped his sorry ass." She sipped some more wine.

I stared at her for a long moment...digesting what she'd said. "Are you telling me you didn't have sex the entire time you were married to him?"

Her face reddened and she glanced down, suddenly fascinated with the sheet covering her breasts. She fiddled with it, twirling the fabric between her fingers.

I hooked my finger under her chin and forced her to look at me. "Did he at least try to pleasure you?"

Her eyes held the answer I was looking for—the one I'd hoped wasn't the case. "Shit."

"It's not that we didn't have sex at all. We had sex for the first few months. And then he lost interest in me. I guess I wasn't sexy or pretty or skinny enough for him." She drained her glass and held it out to me. "Is there any more?"

I eyed her for a second, wondering if I should give her more wine. I had every intention of proving to her that she was sexy and gorgeous and perfect. I couldn't do that if she was intoxicated.

Agreeing with me, my cock stirred to life under the sheet, eager to prove to her that her ex was nothing more than a brain-dead asshole.

I removed the glass from her hand and put them both on the bedside table. Then I took her hand, yanked down the sheet, and wrapped her fingers around my hard length. "This is what you do to me, Ava. You're more than enough for me. You're more than enough for any man." Except if any other man went near her, then I'd have to do some severe ass kicking. At least for now. At least until I figured out if a second chance between us was possible. "Don't let that shithead of an ex-husband let you believe otherwise." I caressed her cheek. "Promise me."

She nodded and gave me a shy smile.

One minute I was touching her face, the next I was kissing her. Tenderly. Passionately.

The kisses quickly progressed to something hungrier, something possessive. And before I knew it, I was pounding inside of her again and again and again.

7

AVA

You know that moment when you're positive you are dreaming, but you're also aware that at any second you'll be sucked back into your reality?

I clung to the dream I was still in, refusing to let it go. The dream where Liam's warm body was wrapped around mine and his hard length was pressed against my butt cheek.

I was afraid to move and have it all disappear—leaving me in an empty bed with memories dancing in my head of the promise I'd made Zoe. The promise where I was supposed to kiss all the single men under the mistletoe to find my Forever Love.

My requirements for this mysterious man?

1. He isn't commitment phobic. But that's a given.

2. Money and power aren't important to him.

3. He's exciting in bed but doesn't need to be told he's a naughty boy and spanked in order to get off.

4. He loves me for who I am.

Except, how was I supposed to discover if this all applied to my Forever Love simply by kissing him under the mistletoe? I had kissed Liam under the mistletoe when we were engaged, and there was no indication he would one day violate the second requirement.

Not that it had existed back then.

The warm body behind me stirred and Liam kissed my shoulder. Yes, I knew it was him. It was my dream. Who else would it be?

And because this was a dream to make all dreams jealous, I imagined Liam's hand slipping between my legs.

His finger ran along the seam to my entrance. My girlie parts let out a happy sigh. "You were dreaming about me, weren't you?" Dream Liam said. "You're so fucking wet for me." His voice was a low growl that made me wetter still.

He shifted behind me, his cock wide awake. "You feel that? That's what you do to me, Ava."

I pressed back against him and wiggled my ass. He groaned. I smiled, hoping to get in one more round of sex before I woke up.

I felt the sheet slide off my body. Liam adjusted my top leg, bending my knee. He placed my foot on the bed, opening me up. His magic fingers went back to work, caressing my clit while his teeth nibbled my shoulder.

It was only then that I realized none of this was a dream. I really was in bed. With my ex-fiancé.

"Fuck, I want you so badly," he said against my shoulder. "But I only had two condoms in my wallet. It's not like I was expecting to get laid while on a search and rescue mission."

"I have a box of them in my suitcase." Now that I remembered the sex last night was not a dream, there was no way I was missing out on it this morning.

Even if I was a little sore.

It was well worth the sacrifice.

He climbed out of bed and searched through the suitcase. "It isn't even open."

I looked over my shoulder at him. "That's because I

haven't had sex in a while." A very, *very* long while. "I didn't exactly need them."

"But you brought them on this trip?"

I lowered my leg and rolled onto my back. "I brought them in case I needed them. It's always good to be prepared."

He chuckled. "Well, I for one am happy you live by the Boy Scouts' motto."

I laughed. "That makes two of us....Now get over here. I need to have some more sex, and then I can go downstairs to see if they've plowed the roads yet." If I was lucky, I'd be able to leave soon and make it to the resort in time for my afternoon ski lesson.

It didn't take long before his cock was covered, and he was inside me. It also didn't take long for me to realize that after being with him this way, I wasn't interested in screwing anyone at the resort...if the opportunity should arise.

You know the feeling you get when you crave something, but when you finally get it the real thing fails to meet expectations?

After last night's amazing sex with Liam, I had a feeling this would soon be my reality when it came to other men.

Were Chris and Liam the only two men I'd ever slept with?

If we were talking about sex, then no. There had been a few guys after Liam called it quits on our relationship. Sex with them was...okay. Nothing great. Nothing that would star in an erotic romance. Just okay.

Maybe if I had met them before Liam ten years ago, I would have felt differently. Maybe I would have believed they were good.

See my dilemma? Liam had ruined sex for me.

I knew great sex was out there. The question was, would I ever find it again?

If I wasn't preoccupied with Liam thrusting inside me and

driving me closer and closer to the edge of euphoria, I might have kneed him in the nuts for raising my expectations.

Liam's fingers found my clit and pinched it. That was all it took. My muscles clenched hard around his cock—and the most intense orgasm I'd ever experienced rocketed through me. "Oh, God. Oh, God. *Oh, God!*"

Oops. Hadn't meant to be so loud.

Usually Liam would climb out of bed once he was finished to dispose of the condom. This time he collapsed on me, his head on my shoulder.

"Are you okay?" Laughing, I stroked the firm muscles in his back.

His head remained on my shoulder. "I've just decided that I'm spending the rest of the day right here."

"In bed?"

He lifted his head and grinned. "No, inside you." He leaned down and kissed me. Sweetly at first.

And then possessively.

My body added its vote, siding with Liam one hundred percent.

But the voice of reason reminded me that I had (hopefully) places to go and men to kiss under the mistletoe.

Or there was also option B: lie to Zoe and tell her that her belief in the power of mistletoe was misguided. Tell her that I had kissed every available guy at the resort and never found my Forever Love.

Which would have worked as an option if I didn't suck at lying.

Zoe could see through me every time.

"Don't you want to go back to San Francisco and spend Christmas with Kelsey and her husband?" My mouth twisted up to one side. "Won't that be hard to do when you're still inside me?"

His smirk matched mine. "It might be a little challenging, but I'm sure I can figure it out."

I laughed again. "I'm sure you can. But I really do have to go to Lake Tahoe. I'd rather not lose another day of my reservation, especially since I have to pay for it whether I show up or not at this point. It's too late to cancel."

"Even if you can't get there?"

I shook my head. "That's not an option. I *need* to be there."

Confused wrinkles formed on his forehead. "Funny, I never pegged you as a snow girl. You used to be more about being warm than being cold."

"Well, that was the old me. The pre-*engagement-gone-wrong* and the pre-*marriage-gone-even-worse-than-wrong* me." I pointed to my chest. "This girl is all about being adventurous—and doing things I've never done before. Plus Chris hated anything to do with snow, which is another reason why I'm going to Lake Tahoe instead of the Bahamas."

Liam laughed. "Then I'd say that's a good reason to pick Lake Tahoe over the Bahamas."

With both hands, I gave Liam's shoulders a nudge. "Okay, time to get up. I've got a ski lesson to get to this afternoon."

He removed himself from me and sat up. "You ski?"

"Not yet, but that's part of the plan."

"And does this plan explain why there's mistletoe in your suitcase?"

I shrugged and climbed out of bed. "That was my best friend's plan."

I grabbed my clothes from my suitcase and hurried to the bathroom as he called out, "What plan is that?"

It was the plan I didn't want to explain to him.

Not now.

Not ever.

8

LIAM

"**S**orry," Harold said from behind the front desk. "The last report is that the snow has slowed since last night, but it will still be awhile before the plows can clear the roads."

"So, there's absolutely no way for us to leave?" Disappointment oozed from Ava's words like caramel from a half-eaten piece of chocolate.

"Not until later this afternoon, at the earliest. But in the meantime, you can enjoy all the outdoor activities we have available. Snowshoeing is always popular."

Ava perked up at that. "I've always wanted to try snowshoeing."

"Perfect! Give me a few minutes," Harold said, "and then I can get you all set up. You'll want to grab your warm clothes, especially ski pants and winter boots if you have any."

Twenty minutes later, the three of us set out along the path that had been cleared by a snow blower at some point this morning. An inch of snow had fallen since then. The parking lot was still deep in snow.

"Snowshoeing is really easy to do," Harold said. "You'll be a pro in no time."

We entered a large shed that stored all kinds of winter and summer sports gear, including a single snowmobile.

An image popped into my head of me riding it with Ava behind me. Her chest pressed against my back, her inner thighs against my hips.

And my cock twitched its approval.

"We have two that we usually rent out, but this one is having trouble starting," Harold said as I checked it over.

"If you want, I can take a look at it. I might be able to figure it out."

"Are you sure? I wouldn't want to be any bother."

I waved him off. "No problem at all." I glanced at Ava. The disappointment was back on her face. "I'll look at it once we get back from snowshoeing." And just like that, she was smiling again.

Harold passed her the snowshoes and helped her fasten the straps. It didn't take us long to master the fine art of walking with what looked like oversized tennis racquets attached to our feet. Harold suggested a path for us to hike; then he returned to the inn.

"Wow, it's so beautiful out here." Ava peered up at the deep blue sky. All around us, the snow sparkled in the sunlight like diamonds had been crushed and sprinkled on the ground. "It's so magical. Nothing like I was expecting."

"Have you ever seen snow before?" I asked.

"Of course I have..." She tilted her head to the side. "On TV shows. But seeing it on TV is nothing like in real life." She puckered her lips and blew out a long puff of air, like a small dragon who hadn't yet learned the fine art of breathing fire. The wispy, white air drifted away in the morning chill.

Both of us were wearing our winter gear. Mine was designed for being practical, perfect for SARs. Ava's black ski pants and raspberry-pink winter jacket were designed to look good on the slopes. She looked even more adorably sexy with the cream-colored woolen hat covering her long, blonde hair.

Grinning, she scanned the area. "You know what I've always wanted to do?"

"Make a snow angel?" Because that sounded like something she would do.

She laughed. "That is on the list. Along with building a snowman." She crouched, picked up a handful of snow, and formed a snowball. "Any idea how you make one?"

Before I could answer, a snowball came hurling toward me...and missed my head by several feet.

"Didn't play much football in college, did you?" I said with a laugh.

She made a face. "That obvious, huh?"

"Yes, that obvious." I bent down and scooped up a handful of snow.

Ava must have spotted what was no doubt a devilish gleam in my eyes when I stood again. She squealed and clumsily turned around and attempted to run. Which under normal circumstances would have been easy to do. But when you had snowshoes attached to your feet, normal didn't apply.

I practically dove at her as she lost her footing and went down...taking me with her. Laughing, she squirmed, doing her best to get away from me. I lifted the snowball, triumphant.

"Don't you dare do what I *know* you're thinking of doing," she said, laughing and squirming.

"And what exactly is that?" I said it as I pushed up the hem of her coat and sweater, exposing her stomach—which was not what she'd been expecting. I could see it on her face. The moment of surprise.

Before I dropped the snow on her skin.

She screamed while laughing at the same time. "You're so dead, Liam."

"I take it you need me to warm you up." I kissed her stomach, then licked the exposed skin like she was my favorite flavored popsicle.

Grape, in case you were wondering.

I don't know about Ava, but I was warming up pretty damn fast.

I moved up to her mouth. If her eyes were any indication, she felt as heated as I did. My mouth caught hers and I kissed her long and hard, with my body pressing down on hers.

The snow around us wasn't melting yet from the heat we were generating, but I was certain it would at any moment. We were like a volcano, ready to erupt.

She moaned in my mouth and made my cock that much harder. But we were hardly in a place where I could take advantage of the situation. Anyone could stumble upon us.

With a sigh, I rolled off her, then helped her to her feet.

I grinned at her. "I can't remember the last time I've had this much fun."

Her eyebrows disappeared under her hat. "Seriously?"

I nodded.

"But you do try to have some fun, right?"

I thought about it for a moment. "Sure. When I play poker with the guys."

"How often do you get together with them?"

"We try for once a month, but it's not always easy. It depends on Travis's and my schedules. He plays for the San Francisco Rock."

"The hockey team?"

"That would be the one."

"Wow. Look at you, Mister Hang-Out-With-Famous-People."

I laughed. "I'm not sure he's really *that* famous."

"Are you telling me other than playing poker with the guys maybe once a month, if you're lucky, you don't do anything else for fun?"

"Is that as lame as it sounded in my head?"

She grinned. "A little bit. But you more than anyone should understand the importance of making the most of the life you have. And that includes having a good time."

I pulled her closer to me—a challenge with the snowshoes attached to our feet. How we didn't end up in the snow again was beyond me. "I enjoyed fucking you."

This time her smile was sad at best. "But I bet you've enjoyed fucking a lot of women, so that doesn't count as fun."

"I've been busy getting my company off the ground and helping with search and rescues whenever I can. It doesn't leave me much time to screw around with women."

Her eyebrows disappeared under her hat again. "So you aren't having sex whenever you want?"

I threw my head back in laughter. "You're the first woman I've been with in..." I did the mental math but then gave up after several seconds. "It's been a long time. Maybe a few months."

Christ, no wonder my cock was such a horny bastard when it came to Ava.

"Really?" she said. You'd have thought from her reaction that I had just announced I ate dragons for breakfast. Every day. "When was the last time you had a girlfriend?"

I looked her levelly in the eyes. "I haven't dated anyone seriously since we broke up."

"You...you haven't? Why not? I can guarantee it's not because women aren't interested in you. Not when you're so hot and you've got the big alpha thing going where you like rescuing damsels in distress."

I chuckled. "Is that what women like? To be rescued?"

She shrugged. "Some do."

"What about you?" I already knew the answer.

She shook her head. "I'm very good at rescuing myself."

"So I noticed. When I found you stranded." I winked at her.

She pushed her lips together into an adorable pout. "I hadn't had a chance at that point to rescue myself. But if you hadn't come along, I would have done exactly that. Eventually."

I could keep pushing my point about Ava needing rescuing, but I was a wise man. And a wise man never antagonized the woman who gave him mind-numbing orgasms. The moment he did was the moment he was demoted from being wise. "So you think I'm hot?"

She rolled her eyes. "Of course you picked up on that. How about we go back to the part where you haven't dated anyone since you dumped me."

I opened my mouth to remind her why I'd ended our engagement. She parked her mitted hand over it, halting the words.

"Why haven't you dated anyone? I mean, I get you were away serving your country, which made dating tough. But you weren't gone the entire time, were you?" She removed her hand from my mouth.

"It's not a big deal, Ava. I just didn't date." After I broke up with her, I wasn't interested in dating again. I had been crazy in love with her, and that wasn't something you could easily turn off.

And then after that, I guess I'd never met anyone who had made me feel the way she had.

She inspected my face, searching for something. "It *is* a big deal. What is it you're afraid of?"

My mouth twisted up to one side. "Aren't you the one who just said I have a big alpha thing going? Obviously I'm not afraid of anything." I turned around—a challenge with the snowshoes on—and began walking in the direction we'd come from.

She snorted. "Of course you're afraid of something. Everyone is afraid of something," she said, calling after me.

I slowed enough for her to catch up with me. "Not everyone is afraid of spiders and snakes and rats like you are."

"I'm not talking about that kind of fear. I'm talking about the fear that keeps you from getting into serious relationships. What is the underlying fear behind your decision to avoid them?"

I shot her a look. "You're not going to drop it, are you?"

"Nope."

"When did you become a shrink?"

"I didn't. And quit avoiding the question. Avoidance is not the solution."

I stopped abruptly. "Fine. You tell me your relationship fears, and I'll tell you mine."

She chewed on her lip for a second, possibly deliberating if it was worth spilling her deep secrets just to hear mine.

She must have decided it was. "I'm afraid that I'm cursed."

I looked at her for a heartbeat...then cracked up. "Let me get this straight. You tell me that you're cursed, and now you expect me to be honest with you? Nice try, Ava." I plodded, plodded, plodded away from her.

"I'm positive I'm cursed, because the men I love—men who claim they love *me*—have a nasty habit of hurting me."

I stopped at her words but didn't bother to look over my shoulder at her.

"I'm afraid of falling in love only to be hurt again." Her tone cut like a blunt knife through Jell-O.

I frowned and shuffled around to face her. "So you never want to fall in love again?"

"I didn't say that. I said I'm afraid to fall in love. It doesn't mean I don't want to. I'm just scared that if I do, the next guy who comes along will utterly destroy me and my heart."

Fuck. I'd done this to her.

I should've trusted Ava to make the choice that was right for her, instead of letting her grandmother convince me otherwise.

But it was too late to play the "what if" game. I couldn't go back and change the past. I could only focus on the here and now—and try to regain her trust.

She took a step toward me. "So there you go. I told you my relationship fear. Now you tell me yours."

I didn't say anything.

"Is it because you're scared of commitment?" she pushed.

"I really don't want to talk about it, Ava. Why can't we just leave it at that?" Because talking about it wouldn't fix things between us. I needed to show her how I felt about her. I didn't need to go all estrogen and talk about my feelings.

"So you never want to find a special woman and have a family with her? Have your own happily ever after like Kelsey has with Trent?"

"I didn't say that."

"So you do want to have your own happily ever after?" Ava seemed surprised at that.

"Yes, when I find the right woman." Yeah, yeah, I know. I should have told her how I felt about her—that I'd never stopped loving her. I just hadn't realized it until now.

She'd given me the perfect opening.

But even though I was a smart man, I never claimed to be a fucking genius—especially when it came to women. Plus, the last thing I wanted to do was break her ground rule about discussing the past.

That didn't mean we weren't going to venture into that territory. I had every intention of discussing it. After Christmas.

Once we were back in San Francisco.

So instead, I went with the other truth. "I'm afraid of losing someone I love."

Her eyes widened. "Because your parents died?" When I didn't say anything, she powered on. "We all die at some point. You can't avoid relationships just because you're afraid the person will die."

"I didn't say I was afraid of them dying. I said I was afraid of losing someone I love. I'm afraid they'll think I'm not good enough for them and they'll walk away."

This had been my fear ten years ago, which was why it had been so easy for her grandmother to convince me to break up with Ava. Deep down, I had been certain that she would eventually walk away from me because I couldn't give her the lifestyle she was used to.

Was I worried about that now?

Not at all.

But that didn't mean the fear didn't linger in the corners of my mind.

9

AVA

"I'm afraid they'll think I'm not good enough for them and walk away," Liam said, his words forming white wisps in the cold morning air.

You mean like how you walked away from our relationship? I wanted to say.

Yes, there was also a slight chance I wanted to kick him in the shin, but I gallantly held back the urge.

"Life is full disappointments," I said instead. "But if you don't take a chance, you never know what you're missing."

With a level of gracefulness that would make a flamingo groan—thanks to the snowshoes on my feet—I turned and ran away from Liam, toward the inn.

By running, think shuffling. And not even fast shuffling. More like the speed a granny would go while pushing her walker. Heck, who was I kidding? She would go faster than me.

What did this mean? Liam, with his legs worthy of a six-foot man, easily caught up with me.

"I guess you've never been on a snowmobile if this is the first time you've seen snow," he said, oblivious to my inner

339

turmoil. The inner turmoil that involved my past feelings for him, which were starting to stir awake. *No, feelings. Go back into hibernation, please.*

"That's right."

"Ever been on a motorcycle?"

I gave him a *What-do-you-think?* look.

"That's what I thought. You want to give it a try? Since you're all about being adventurous." Challenge sparkled in his light blue eyes at the last part.

Challenge accepted.

"I would love that."

Truth? The idea of riding one scared the bejesus out of me. Same deal with a motorcycle. That's why neither had ever been on my bucket list.

But you know who else's bucket list they wouldn't have been on?

That's right—Chris's.

Which meant one thing...I had to try it out. Even at the risk of flying off the snowmobile and slamming into a tree.

"Let's see if I can fix the one in the shed," he said as we continued waddling toward the inn, "then we can hit the trails."

"You know how to fix snowmobiles?" He used to play around under the hood of his car when we were engaged, but that was about it. The man I remembered wasn't a mechanic.

"I tinkered around with motorcycles and trucks while with the SEALs. It was a good skill to have in case you were ever stuck behind enemy lines and needed an escape vehicle. One of my friends taught me everything I needed to know." He grinned at me. "I just can't make a spare tire appear out of thin air."

My mouth tilted to one side. "So I gathered when you rescued me."

Liam and I entered the shed. He got to work on the snowmobile.

And my thoughts went to the mistletoe in my suitcase. Because once Liam and I were finished snowmobiling, I needed to make sure my mistletoe was still okay. It would soon be a very busy piece of foliage—once I arrived at the resort.

That was assuming kissing under the mistletoe after Christmas was still acceptable. Maybe it was against the rules.

Were there even rules for kissing under the mistletoe?

Rules I didn't know about?

I pulled out my phone, ignoring my heart's sudden plea for me to give Liam a chance.

Don't be ridiculous, I told it.

He's happy to settle down and have a family, my heart pointed out, clearly eager to discuss the topic. Clearly suffering from amnesia when it came to what happened ten years ago.

But not with me. He had proven that when he walked away from me a hundred thousand dollars richer, thanks to dear old Granny.

And yes, my grandmother had enjoyed sharing that tasty morsel while we bonded over my favorite dessert. She always had been the party pooper.

I sent Zoe a text.

Me: Happy Christmas Eve Day! I have a
question for you regarding the mistletoe…

A minute later she replied.

Zoe: Have you kissed anyone under it yet?

Me: I'm still not at the resort. Hopefully the road will be cleared later today so I can head out.

Zoe: I don't think you have to be at the resort for the magic to happen. Maybe you're supposed to find your Forever Love at your current location.

Me: No, that's definitely not it. No one here except for married men.

And Liam.

Zoe: Now that would be a problem. So what's your mistletoe question?

Me: Is there a mistletoe expiry date? Like after tomorrow, the mistletoe's power will be null and void?

Zoe: Is this your way of getting out of your promise?

No, it was my way of proving that Liam wasn't my forever.

Zoe: Hey, wait! Does this mean you actually believe me now?

Oh, God. Do I?

No. Because if Zoe's family legend really had merit, then the mistletoe I kissed Liam under had to be faulty. That was the only explanation I had for my body's reaction when we had kissed under the one at the inn.

Maybe it had to be a specific type of mistletoe for it to work. Like the mistletoe Zoe had given me.

That sound? Ignore it. It was only my body cracking up,

reminding me that it had responded the same way even without the mistletoe.

Which just went to prove...I needed to try again but with Zoe's mistletoe.

Maybe that would reverse whatever spell my body was under when it came to Liam.

I didn't answer Zoe's question. I didn't know *how* to answer it.

I returned the phone to my pocket and walked over to Liam. "How's it going?"

"I think I might have figured out the problem. Just give me a minute."

A muffled ping came from my coat pocket. Zoe, no doubt. Since I had a feeling I knew why she was texting me, I made no move to check it.

Another ping.

Liam glanced at the pocket the sound came from. "Did you need to check that?"

"No, I'm good."

A minute later my phone rang. Only it wasn't the song I had programmed for Zoe. It's was "The Imperial March" (aka Darth Vader's theme music).

Liam's mouth twitched to one side. "Interesting choice of music."

"It's my grandmother's." I set the ringtone for her yesterday before heading to Lake Tahoe.

He laughed as I pulled my phone from my coat pocket. "Very appropriate."

I giggled. "Isn't it?" And then I let out a hard breath. "Guess I should get this over with. She'll just keep phoning me if I don't answer." She never bothered with voice messages. She knew I could always ignore them.

"You had better be at the airport, young lady," she immediately said once I accepted the call, her tone as warm as the snow outside the shed.

"I already told you I'm not going to the wedding." My voice wasn't meek like it would have been ten years ago. The pride on Liam's face at hearing it made my insides go unexpectedly warm.

I smiled back at him.

"This isn't just about the wedding." Her voice remained cool and ridged. "Your parents are disappointed that you aren't here to spend Christmas with them. It looks bad that you cannot even be here for your own parents."

"They understand why I can't be there."

"Well, they're the only ones. You're still part of this family, Ava. And as part of this family, there are duties you are expected to uphold. Duties that generations of women in our family have respected."

"Was it expected for them to convince their granddaughters to marry a man who the grandmother *knew* was having an affair? A man *you* knew was still having an affair long after he and I exchanged vows?" *Damn.* Why did my voice have to crack? It couldn't have just pulled up its big girl panties?

I peered over at Liam, half hoping to see him gesture with his thumb that I was doing awesome. Instead, he was frowning. I guess I hadn't mentioned the part about how I'd had my reservations about marrying Chris.

I mean, seriously, what guy doesn't want to have sex before the wedding? It wasn't like he was religious. He believed in God as much as he believed in the Tooth Fairy.

I wasn't a guy but *I* had certainly wanted sex back then.

"You didn't have to divorce him," she pointed out.

"Yes. I. Did. He got to be happy with his mistress. Why wasn't I allowed to be happy?" And because I felt like shocking my grandmother, I went in for the kill. "I had a healthy sexual appetite, but I didn't get to have sex. He got to have all the fun...with Gloria. But since I'm not attending the wedding, how about I send the happy couple a wedding gift? I happen to know firsthand that they're into whips and leather. Or maybe I can spice up their sex life a little more and throw in a studded leather collar for good measure.

"Oh, wait. They already have one. That's right, the day I accidentally walked in on them in our bedroom, the only thing Chris was wearing was his collar. And you really don't want to know what Gloria was doing to his bare ass."

My grandmother gasped—but I had no idea if that was because of my visual description of what I had witnessed that day or because I dared to be disrespectful to her.

Either way, she'd have quite the image in her mind when she watched the happy couple walk down the aisle.

A laugh bubbled deep inside me. I squished my lips together to keep it hidden from her. "Now, if you don't mind, I'm about to go snowmobiling with Liam. You remember Liam, right? My ex-fiancé?" I didn't wait for a reply. I hung up...and burst out laughing.

God, that felt good. Better than good.

"Well, it's official," I said to Liam once I got my laughter somewhat under control. "I think I've just killed my grand-mother. Although I'm not sure which part will do her in first. A new appreciation of what Chris and Gloria's wedding night will be like...or that I'm with you."

I giggled, drunk on an adrenaline high from embracing my inner lioness.

Hear me roar!

I peered into the engine. "Have you fixed this yet? I'm in the mood for speed and danger." I was in the mood for a greater adrenaline high.

"I've almost got it." Liam fiddled with something under the hood. Whatever it was must have been important, because a minute later, he climbed onto the snowmobile and started the engine. It purred like a content mountain kitty.

"So, about that need for speed and danger..." he said, removing his phone from his coat pocket. He texted someone. A moment later, he must have received the reply he was hoping for. He nodded at the screen, typed something else, then put his phone away. "We just need to swing by the inn to sign the waiver and rental agreement, and then we're good to go. And by the time we get back, the road out of here should be cleared. Harold has already contacted his friend who has a tow truck. You might have to wait until December twenty-sixth to get a new tire, but he can drop you off at the resort so at least you'll be there for tonight."

I should've been doing cartwheels at the news. I should've been hugging him and thanking him for getting me back on track with my plans for the holidays. I should've been doing all of that...but instead, my stomach plummeted ten stories.

Wow. That was unexpected.

It's for the best, I reminded my stomach, my heart, my anything-else-that-would-listen. I was supposed to be going to the resort and kissing men under the mistletoe to find my Forever Love.

But what if Liam is the one? my heart asked.

So what? I argued. *I made the mistake of falling for him once before. Money was more important to him than I was.*

Which was funny when I thought about it. Not the ha-ha kind of funny. The kind of funny where something didn't quite add up. In all the time I'd known Liam prior to us getting engaged, he hadn't come off as the type of guy who cared all that much about money.

Don't get me wrong—it was important to him like it was for most people when it came to providing food and shelter and the ability to pay your bills. But it wasn't important like it was to my family. Their lives revolved around money.

Liam was watching me expectantly. I smiled as if I couldn't be happier. "That's great news. And you'll be able to spend Christmas with your family."

Was it my imagination, or did my voice sound a little off? And from the way Liam was looking at me, I couldn't help but wonder if my smile appeared as fake as it felt.

Yep, acting was definitely not my new superpower.

10

——————

LIAM

Was it just me—or did Ava look as excited at the prospect of getting on with her vacation as I felt about going home?

And just so there's no confusion, I was as thrilled about us going our separate ways as I was having bullets rain on me from out of nowhere.

I grabbed the two helmets from the shelf and handed her one. "You ready for this?"

She gave me a dazzling I'm-ready-to-take-on-the-world smile. "Absolutely." Then she looked at the snowmobile. "So how do we do this?"

"I climb on first. You then join me. You'll need to hold on tight around my waist." I popped my helmet on and swung my leg over the snowmobile seat.

Ava sat behind me, her arms wrapped around my waist, her thighs hugging my hips. If it weren't for our coats, I would've felt her breasts pressed against my back.

I gunned the motor...and we were off.

I drove us to the inn, keeping to a slow speed for now.

After we signed the waivers and the rental agreement, I headed in the direction we had been earlier.

It was only a few minutes before we were out in the open. Snowy pine trees towered on either side of us. I slowly accelerated but still kept the speed well below an adrenaline-inducing level. I wanted Ava to be able to appreciate the beauty around us—the stillness that came from the undisturbed, newly fallen snow. She wouldn't get this at the resort where she was staying.

I eventually picked up speed. Ava's arms tightened around my waist. Could I get used to this—the way it felt like we belonged together? Hell, yes. Which meant I needed to talk to her. I wasn't ready to walk away from her once the roads were cleared.

I wanted to find out if she was willing to give *us* a chance.

I steered down a narrow path. The snow-covered pine trees were now only a few yards from us on either side. We kept going until I eventually pulled over to the side and parked the snowmobile in a spot overlooking the valley. A pine tree next to us had sheltered the ground from the falling snow, keeping it from getting too deep.

I removed my helmet. Ava did the same and climbed off the seat. I joined her next to the tree.

"It's gorgeous," she said, taking in the valley in front of us. Her voice was soft and filled with awe. She smiled at me. "Thank you for bringing me here."

I leaned down and kissed her. It was so easy to get lost in her kisses—which was exactly what happened.

When we finally pulled apart, our breaths were ragged puffs of white air. We turned around to face the view again.

"What are your plans once you return home?" I asked.

"Get ready to go back to school. What about you? Any big missions planned?"

"I have some jobs lined up. I was able to put them aside

for a short time while I was helping to find the missing girl, but they still need my attention when I return." A couple of my team members had dealt with the most pressing cases while I was away.

We were quiet for a few more minutes. I opened my mouth several times to bring up *us*. Each time I changed my mind. I thought talking to her about us would be easy. I was wrong. Sneaking into an enemy camp in the dead of night without being detected was a breeze in comparison.

I wasn't sure how to go about it. If there was an instruction manual on getting back together with your ex-fiancée after you broke up with her ten years ago, I'd yet to find it.

Right—I was a guy. When was the last time I'd read an instruction manual?

"What about a boyfriend?" I eventually asked. "Is there someone in San Francisco you're interested in?"

Lame, Quaid. Very lame.

I could practically hear Trent laughing his head off at my lack of finesse when it came to finding out if she and I had a chance for a future together.

"Not really." She released a long, frustrated breath. "Which is probably why my best friend is determined that I'll find my Forever Love while I'm at the resort."

"Forever love?"

"The guy I'm supposed to fall in love with. Due to her family's history when it comes to kissing a man under the mistletoe, she believes I'm going to find this magical person at the resort when I kiss him under the mistletoe there. Her grandmother, her mother, her sister, and my best friend all ended up marrying the men they kissed under the mistletoe. It's like some sort of family legend."

In college, I was a starting quarterback. Which meant the opposition's goal was to knock me down before I had a chance to pass to my teammate. If their defense was successful, I'd get a shoulder to the gut, land on my ass, and have the air ripped from my lungs.

Which was exactly how I felt after Ava's confession.

Did I believe the family legend was true when it came to finding love under the mistletoe?

Fuck, no!

But what did matter was if she believed in that crap.

"Is that why you're so eager to get there?" I asked. "You believe you're going to fall in love with some guy under the mistletoe?"

Her hesitation? Not a good thing.

Because if she believed in it, then it meant she didn't feel the same way about me as I felt about her. If she felt the same way about me, the fucked-up legend wouldn't make a difference.

Another long sigh. "Do I want to fall in love with a man who loves me with all his heart? A man who loves me so much that he's willing to stay by my side no matter what?"

I finally looked at her. She was staring at the scenery, but I had a feeling she wasn't really seeing it.

"Yes, I'm hoping for all of that," she said. "So yes, as crazy as it might sound, there is a part of me that hopes Zoe is correct. But I'll never know unless I go to the resort and kiss some potential prospects under the mistletoe she gave me."

Despite everything, my mouth twitched up. "That's why you have the mistletoe in your suitcase?"

She nodded. "I didn't tell you before when you asked because I knew you'd think I'm crazy."

I hooked my gloved finger under her chin and turned her face toward me. "Ava, I think you're sexy, smart, adorable, and incredible"—*perfect*—"but I'll never believe that you're crazy."

She smirked. "Good to know."

"But what happens if you don't find this magical guy while you're at the resort?"

Did the idea kill me that she would be there tonight, kissing men she didn't know just because of the so-called legend?

Absolutely. For one, she had no idea what kind of asshole might take advantage of her.

"And how will you even know if he's the one you're supposed to fall in love with?" I asked. "Will fireworks go off? Will a gong chime?"

"She wasn't exactly specific on that part. I guess I'll just know. But fireworks or a gong would be helpful."

Well, there you go. I wasn't the one. She would have known last night when we first kissed.

"What about you?" she asked. "You said you're ready to settle down if you found the right woman. Is there anyone you're interested in?" She smiled. It wasn't the smile that usually got my cock excited. It looked plastic, fake.

I had no idea why.

"Not yet."

Yes, my heart might have told me that I was an idiot. Could you blame it? Ava had given me the perfect opening, and I bolted in the opposite direction. But in my defense, the military had taught me how to fight the enemy. Emotions weren't allowed. Emotions got you killed.

Unfortunately, they weren't so forthcoming when it came to teaching soldiers how to tell a woman what was in his heart.

I checked the time on my phone. "You ready to do some more snowmobiling before we head back?"

This time her smile wasn't faked. "Absolutely. Do you think we can go faster? I have a past I need to escape for now." Her smiled wavered slightly.

"This snowmobile is just what the doctor ordered." I

patted the saddle. "It's perfect for escaping pasts involving a shitheaded ex-husband." I climbed on the seat and she joined me.

I started the engine and revved it up, feeling the power between my legs.

And we were off.

The path I was following became narrower and narrower, the trees denser to the point where I had to zigzag between them.

Ava's arms were wrapped around me, but not as tight as before. That didn't change the exhilaration zinging through me from her touch. I couldn't remember the last time I'd had this much fun.

We eventually had to turn back.

Disappointment rolled through me like a tsunami.

I had been through worse compared to walking away from Ava. Hell, I'd survived SEAL training, been shot at more times than I cared to remember, and lived in hellish conditions while deployed.

If I could survive that, then I could survive that this was the last time I'd get to hang out with her.

Now I just had to convince my mule-headed heart of that.

Good luck!

Or there was always option B: convince Ava to allow me back in her life as her friend.

But not her fuck buddy.

And then, with time, I would hopefully regain her trust.

Right—that would be about as easy as convincing her that the earth was made of blue cheese.

Back at the shed, I parked the snowmobile and waited for Ava to climb off.

"Can I see your phone for a second?" Still seated, I held out my hand for it.

"Why? So you can listen to 'The Imperial March' again?"

Her mouth slipped into a one-sided smile, and she handed me her phone.

"Thanks." I programmed my number into it and sent myself a text. I handed the phone back to her. "There you go. Now if you ever need anything or want to go for a hike with me at some point, you have my number." And I had hers.

Her gaze dropped to her screen, and she nibbled on her lip. "Thanks, but I don't do booty calls."

"That's good—because neither do I."

Smiling at me, she returned her phone to her pocket. "Good to know."

We walked back to the inn's entrance. I was tempted to thread my fingers with hers, but I figured we needed to have that long-overdue conversation first. A conversation that would have to wait for another two weeks—until after her vacation.

Assuming she was willing to go there.

We were almost at the inn when Harold approached us.

"Liam, I was wondering if you can help me. One of the families staying here is having trouble getting their car started. I think the battery might be dead. Thomas will be heading over soon enough with the tow truck, but they'd rather not wait that long if they don't have to."

"Sure, I can have a look."

11

AVA

Betsy smiled at me from behind the front desk. Strands of gray hair peeked from under her mop cap. "The roads out of here are finally cleared."

Remember when you were a kid and there was a toy that you wanted more than anything? The commercials made it sound like the ultimate in toys. No toy before it and no toy after it would ever be as great.

But when you got it? It was an epic disappointment.

I think you know where I'm going with this....

"That's great," I said, doing my best to enthuse the proper amount of excitement in my tone.

Betsy's smile brightened. "You don't sound all that happy about it."

I tried to stretch my lips in a replication of her smile. They refused to cooperate. Damn lips. "Oh, I am. I've been looking forward to this trip for several months now."

"And yet...?" She left the sentence hanging, but I had no idea what she wanted me to say. Or more likely I had no idea how to answer the question.

When I didn't say anything, Betsy decided to fill in the

blanks for me. "You're sad that you and Liam are going your separate ways now that you can both leave."

"Possibly. But I shouldn't be. We were once engaged to each other. He dumped me, and we hadn't seen each other for ten years...until yesterday." And now he had my phone number, but that didn't mean anything.

He probably just gave it to me in case I needed to hire his company.

Betsy's eyebrows disappeared under her mop cap. "And yet you're still in love."

Was I?

I was attracted to him. But what female wasn't?

Sure, the sex the previous evening had been earth-shattering, and we'd spent a lot of the night and the morning talking about our lives over the past few years. And yes, while we were talking, it'd felt like we had never really been apart all this time, but there was no hiding from the past. It was still a pesky storm cloud overhead.

The emotions from earlier stirred deep inside, pointing out that despite what had happened ten years ago, there was still a good chance—a *very* good chance—I wasn't completely over him.

Well, doesn't that just suck rotten apples?

My heart voiced its opinion—siding with my emotions.

But it didn't matter what they thought. I had trusted my feelings for Liam once before and look where that had gotten me.

"It doesn't matter if I am or not," I said, "he dumped me ten years ago 'cause he had a better offer."

"Did he cheat on you?"

The laugh? It wasn't so much a bitter laugh as a pity-party one. "No, that honor went to my ex-husband."

"You know what? Hold that thought. It sounds like what you need is a nice mug of peppermint hot chocolate, and then you can tell me everything." Her smile was sweet and held a strong undertone of "Don't even think about saying no" that made it impossible to decline her offer.

She put up a sign saying she would be back in twenty minutes, along with the bell in case someone couldn't wait that long. Then I followed her through the dining room into the kitchen.

A few minutes later, we were sitting in the lounge chairs in the quiet corner of the dining room. No one else was there.

I took a sip of the drink. *Wow.* Betsy had been right. It was the best peppermint hot chocolate I'd ever tasted. The Peppermint Schnapps might've had something to do with it.

"So you were married at one point?" she asked, recapping our previous conversation.

I explained about Chris. Don't worry, I kept it PG-rated. No need to give Betsy nightmares.

"Did Liam ever tell you why he was breaking up with you?" she asked once I had told her about Chris's wedding tomorrow.

"He told me he didn't love me anymore. And then he told me that it was for the best that we ended things because of his job with the military. It was dangerous and there was a good chance he wouldn't come home alive, or as the same man he had left as. But there was one other reason for breaking up with me that he didn't tell me about. It was my grandmother who gladly spilled the proverbial beans."

"What reason was that?"

"My grandmother bribed him. If he walked away from me, she would give him a hundred thousand dollars." I shrugged. "Turns out he loved money more than he loved me."

Betsy's expression resembled how I imagined the real Mrs. Claus's expression would look if Santa announced he was giving up milk and cookies...and hitting the gym and taking steroids.

"You want to hear something crazy funny?" I grinned because I knew this was something Betsy would get a kick out of.

She grinned back. "What's that?"

I told her about Zoe's family legend when it came to mistletoe.

"There you are, Ava," Harold said. I turned in my seat to find the workshop version of Santa in the doorway. "Thomas called. He'll be here in five minutes."

I scrambled up from my seat. "Thank you." I turned back to Betsy. "And thank you for the delicious hot chocolate and for listening to me." I glanced between her and Harold. "I should go get my stuff."

"I'm sorry we didn't have longer to talk, dear," Betsy said. "But I will tell you that love works in mysterious ways. Don't give up on it because of what happened in the past."

I hugged her and Harold. Then I raced upstairs and retrieved my suitcase. When I returned to the lobby a few minutes later, Liam still wasn't there. I went to pay for the room, but Harold just brushed me off, saying it had already been taken care of.

Another thing I owed Liam for.

A man in his forties entered the front entrance wearing jeans and a ski jacket. "I'm looking for Ava Versteeg," he announced to the room, which consisted of just Harold and me.

"I'm Ava," I said, walking toward him.

"I'm Thomas. I've come to tow your car to Mike's Garage. That's close to where you'll be staying."

I waved bye to Harold, and Thomas grabbed my luggage.

Outside, I looked toward the parking lot. Liam wasn't

there. Neither was his truck. Guess he must have already left —without saying good-bye.

My heart squeezed tight and I did my best to reassure it. Next time I fell in love, it would be as real for the man as it was for me.

And the next man I fell in love with would never *ever* meet my family.

Good plan, my brain said.

Sure, my heart mumbled, *brilliant plan—now you just have to forget about the man who you are still in love with.*

12

LIAM

I entered the inn lobby. The only person there was Harold, his gaze on the computer screen. Like yesterday, he was dressed as I imagined Santa would be while tinkering in his workshop on Christmas Eve—prior to traveling around the world.

He even looked like he was double-checking his naughty and nice list...via modern technology.

As if sensing me watching him, he glanced up. "Were you able to get the Jenkins car started?"

"Yes. The interior light was left on and the battery died. But it's all good now. Do you know if Ava is in our room?"

"She left about five minutes ago."

"Left?"

"Yes, Thomas picked her up. Sorry, I thought you knew... considering you and Ava were once engaged to each other." He winked at me as if he'd personally stolen the secret from Fort Knox and couldn't wait to tell me.

Betsy stepped through the dining room doors, a stack of green napkins in her hands. "Although I must say, the kiss you gave her under the mistletoe last night was definitely

360

hot. I would never have guessed you two weren't still involved."

She then shook a head the same way a mother does at her child who ate cookies before dinner. "It's just too bad you valued money over love."

Huh? What the heck is she talking about?

"Money isn't everything, Liam. Just look at Scrooge. He was a miserable old man even though he was rich. Why? Because he valued money over love and family and kindness."

"Not that you aren't kind," Harold said. He lovingly placed his arm around his wife's waist.

Inwardly, I scratched my head, still wondering what the heck they were talking about. "I know money isn't everything. But I also knew if Ava lost her trust fund because I married her, she wouldn't have had the money to attend a prestigious law school. I just didn't realize at the time the money hadn't been important to her. And that she was willing to give it all up if it meant getting to pursue her education degree. Had I known that, I would never have lied and told her I no longer loved her. I wouldn't have let myself believe I didn't deserve her because I couldn't afford to give her the lifestyle she was used to."

Now it was Harold and Betsy who were confused. Both frowned.

"What are you talking about, son?" Harold asked.

"Ava's family is wealthy, but she didn't care about the money like they did. That's what first caused me to fall in love with her. She was beautiful and selfless. She still is."

"But *you* did care about the money?" Betsy said.

"Not at all. I'd rather marry a woman without money than a woman whose family manipulated her every move because of it. That was Ava's family. They saw money as power, and they weren't afraid to wield it like a sword."

Betsy's perplexed frown deepened. "So you never ended the relationship because her grandmother bribed you with a large sum of money?"

"Not at all. Where would you get a crazy idea like that?"

"That's what Ava told me happened."

The realization of what really did go down ten years ago suddenly hit me. Hard. My stomach clenched. If it could have, it would have punched something—preferably a wall.

The fucking bitch. Not Ava. Her grandmother.

"I can't believe it," I muttered to myself. "She played us both."

"Let me see if I got this straight," Harold said, scratching his beard. "The reason Ava thinks you broke up with her isn't the real reason you ended things? You did it to save her trust fund and not so you would walk away a hundred thousand dollars richer?"

Shit. It was bad enough she had thought I no longer loved her, but to think I walked away from her because I was easily bribed....

"I have a question—if I may?" Betsy asked, interrupting my thoughts.

"Sure. Go ahead."

"You still love her, don't you?" She smiled as if she already knew the answer—and hoped it was the right one.

"Yes. I never stopped loving her. But unfortunately, she doesn't feel the same way about me. But can you blame her?"

Betsy snorted a laugh. "I swear, young people these days are too thick to see what's right in front of them."

My gaze shifted to Harold to see if he understood what she was talking about. He just shrugged apologetically.

"Look, her grandmother did a bad thing by misleading you both and manipulating you to end the relationship," Betsy said. "But you can't let that stop what's meant to be."

"And what's that?"

"You two are meant to be together. I would stake my life on it. Did she tell you about her best friend's belief in the power of mistletoe?"

I nodded.

"Maybe there's something to it after all. The sparks between you two when you kissed under the mistletoe were bigger and brighter than Lake Tahoe's New Year's Eve fireworks. And they're pretty impressive.

"The question is, do you want something more between you and Ava? Or are you willing to walk away from her again?"

As if that was even a question. Of course I wanted more. I wanted a lifetime with her.

"If you leave now," Harold said, "you'll make it to her resort before she does. And if I were you, I'd take some mistletoe with you." He pointed at the bunch hanging in the doorway to the dining room. "You never know when it might come in handy."

He winked.

13

AVA

The good news? My poor baby hadn't been smashed by a truck that might have lost control on the icy roads last night.

Thomas examined the front end that had been partially buried. It had taken him half an hour to get my car out of the snowdrift.

The bad news? The tire had still been flat—but at least that was the extent of the damage.

The drive to town wasn't too bad. Thomas was friendly and excited for Christmas. What did we do the entire trip? Sing Christmas carols.

Yeah, yeah, I know—my singing sucked. But Thomas didn't care. He wasn't much better than me.

We could belt out "Jingle Bells" and not give a damn about what anyone else thought.

It was great.

After the garage replaced my tire (which they fortunately had in stock), I drove to the resort where I was staying. But instead of climbing out of my vehicle and checking in, I just sat in the parking lot, already missing the cozy inn.

Who else was I missing?

That's right. But there was nothing I could do about that.

In time, my heart would fully get over him.

Maybe not for another hundred years, when I was already dead and buried. But it would happen.

Eventually.

Did I regret the previous night and the time we spent together before I headed to the resort? Not at all. It had been fun—just like we'd had a lot of fun when we were dating and engaged. Back then, we had enjoyed the simple things in life. The things that my family never noticed or felt were beneath them.

Staring at the building, I released a long, fortifying breath, then grabbed my purse and climbed out of the car. I removed my suitcase from the trunk and headed to the resort entrance.

The pine trees outside it were lit up with thousands of white Christmas tree lights. I approached the sliding doors and entered the lobby. The place was the opposite of the inn. Larger. Busier. Kids of all ages, along with their parents and grandparents, sat on the floor in the center of the room, watching a magician entertain them.

I joined the line for the front desk. While I waited my turn, I glanced around the lobby. It had a modern rustic feel to it, with dark-stained wood. Boughs of pines and pinecones decorated the desk and the wall behind it.

"Can I help the next person?" a woman said from behind the desk.

I stepped up to her. "Hi, I'm Ava Versteeg. I'm checking in."

She typed away on the keyboard. "Yes, we have you in a room with a king-sized bed for five nights."

"That's right." I handed her my credit card.

She did her thing and handed it back to me. "Will you need a second key?"

I shook my head. After the amazing sex with Liam, I wasn't in the mood to do it with a complete stranger.

Not even a hot ski instructor.

Liam had ruined me for everyone when it came to sex. Maybe it wasn't too late to become a nun.

You didn't have to be Catholic to be one, right?

She handed me the key card and told me my room number. "And I have this message for you that you're supposed to read now."

"What is it?"

"It's from another guest."

Weird. No one I knew was going to be here.

Or maybe it was Zoe checking up on me. What better way to make sure I was actually kissing single men under the mistletoe than to come here herself?

Would I be surprised if that was what had happened?

Not at all—if she believed that much in the power of mistletoe.

I moved away from the desk and opened the letter.

For your early Christmas present, go over to the Christmas tree.

The writing didn't look familiar.

I walked to the tree and circled it. My gaze scanned the ground for a present addressed to me.

That was when I came across a familiar pair of work boots. Attached to a familiar pair of legs in jeans. The familiar winter jacket.

And the familiar sexy smile that got my girlie parts excited in record time.

That wasn't the only part of me to get excited. My heart played traitor and began racing.

He's not really here, I tried telling myself. My body and heart and girlie parts chose to ignore me.

"What are you doing here?" I asked, doing my damnedest not to betray my body's reaction to seeing him.

"I came to see you."

"You did? I thought you were heading back to San Francisco to spend Christmas with your family and friends."

"I was. But Christmas is about being with the people you love. And right now, the person I love the most is spending the week in this resort." He brushed his thumb against my cheek as if to wipe away a stray snowflake. "And I'm hoping she'll let me spend it with her. I'm also hoping she'll change her mind about her ground rule from last night. The ground rule that prevents us from talking about what really happened ten years ago."

I blinked. I was hallucinating. That must be it. Why? I had no idea. Maybe the smell of pine needles was going to my head.

The Christmas version of sniffing glue.

I shook my head—partly to clear it, partly to tell him I wasn't interested in abandoning the rule. It was a good rule. A rule to keep Christmas cheer fully intact.

"No, the ground rule still stands." The words crawled out on a whisper, barely heard over the loud *boom, boom, boom* of my heart. "You told me everything I needed to know the night you broke up with me. And what you didn't tell me, my grandmother was nice enough to explain."

I started to walk around him. Another hour and I'd be swooshing down the mountain.

Or falling on my butt.

All right—the latter was the most likely possibility of the two.

Liam gently grabbed hold of my arm. "Except she lied to you, Ava. She never offered me money to break up with you. And if she had, I would never have accepted it. I had no idea until an hour ago—when Betsy told me what had happened—that you'd even believed that."

Ever walked into a wall? I haven't either. But at hearing Liam's words, I had a feeling this was exactly what it felt like. The *Where-the-fudge-had-that-come-from?* moment that caused stars to spin around your head and the ground to sway under your feet.

"Okay, so she didn't pay you off, but you did stop loving me—which, when you think about it, is a good enough reason to end an engagement." Because who wanted to be engaged or married to someone who no longer loved you?

I should know. I was clearly an expert on the topic.

Did I believe him about the bribe? My gut did. But my gut had also once told me that Liam loved me, and look how wrong it had been.

"I didn't stop loving you, Ava. I only told you that because if I had married you, you would've lost your trust fund. Your grandmother had been quite clear on that part. But I underestimated you, thinking the money was important to you, even though I should have known better. Okay, it would have helped if I had known you didn't want to be a lawyer, and you didn't care about going to Harvard." He raised his eyebrow as if to remind me that I hadn't been entirely honest with him back then either.

At his words, it was like the entire world had come to a sudden standstill. *Oh.* "You really did love me?" I asked, still uncertain what to believe. Uncertain if he had even heard me this time.

He stepped closer. "It damn near killed me telling you that I no longer loved you, especially since it was a lie and I knew how much I was hurting you. But her arguments made sense at the time. She convinced me I wasn't good enough for you because I was military, and because I could never give you the lifestyle you were used to. She might have also referred to me as being a leech."

Which Liam would've hated. If anything, my wealth had made him uncomfortable—and that was why his accepting the bribe hadn't made much sense. But despite knowing that, I had ignored my gut and believed my grandmother's lies.

Just like I had ignored my gut and married Chris. I really owed my gut a big apology. *Yes, gut, I promise next time I'll trust you. No more ignoring you.*

It was my turn to take a step forward. "That's where she was wrong. You were always enough for me, Liam. You saw me in a way that my own family refused to."

He let out a long breath. "So you believe me?" There was so much love and hope in his face, it was impossible to do anything but believe him.

"Of course. How could I not? You're forgetting that wasn't the only time she used the trust fund to try to manipulate me into doing what she wanted."

He closed the distance with his final step and traced his thumb along my cheekbone. The look in his eyes was one I'd seen so many times while we were engaged. It was the same look I had seen last night and again this morning at the inn, only I had been too stubborn to notice it until now.

"I still love you, Ava. I never stopped loving you." He voice was low and chock full of emotion—the kind of raw emotion that left my heart singing.

"I love you, too, Liam. Always have. Always—"

I didn't get any further than that. His lips crashed into mine and everything around us—the laughter of the kids watching the magic show, the smell of Christmas, the decorations—faded. The only thing that existed was the man who had his arms around me. The man whose tongue was performing its own magic against mine. The man who owned my heart.

The only man who had ever owned my heart.

"Mummy," a little girl's voice said, "Why are they kissing?" She made a loud *bleh* noise, and I mentally giggled. I would have stopped kissing Liam, but my lips and body didn't agree with my brain.

Not that my brain agreed with that thought either.

"That's because they're standing under mistletoe. You're supposed to kiss under the mistletoe. It's a tradition."

Mistletoe?

I glanced up. The woman was right. A small bunch was hanging from the ceiling, tied with a familiar looking ribbon. "Did you know about that?" I asked him softly.

I swear the smile that spread on his face was brighter than the Christmas tree lights.

"Your friend was right. You did find the man you're supposed to spend the rest of your life with under the mistletoe."

I laughed. "How about we don't tell her that? Or else we'll never hear the end of it."

He chuckled. "Sounds like a good plan."

And then, because we were still under the mistletoe, he went back to kissing me.

And who was I to complain?

EPILOGUE
LIAM

One Year Later

Trent's mom fussed with my tie, doing her best not to tear up. How did I know? She had already sniffed a few times since taking on the task of ensuring I looked perfect for my wedding day.

She might not have been my biological mother, but she was as much a mother to me and my sister Kelsey as our own mother had been. The only difference was that Joanne had witnessed Kelsey getting married and was about to watch me marry the woman I loved. My own parents hadn't been as lucky.

"Your mom would be so proud of the man you've become." *Sniff. Sniff.* "And she would have loved your bride as much as I do." *Sniff.*

"I know." My voice came out gritty, and I coughed to clear my throat.

"Mom," Trent said, standing next to us in the main lobby of Harold and Betsy's inn. "It's bad luck to make the groom cry before his wedding."

She gave him a stern eye. "I seem to remember you tearing up prior to Kelsey walking down the aisle. And look how perfectly things turned out."

She glanced over her shoulder to where my sister was sitting with my five-month-old nephew in her arms. Ethan was busy giggling at three-year-old Lily Hoffer, who was making silly faces at him. Her own little brother was asleep in her father's arms.

The surprise that Kelsey had alluded to the day I discovered Ava stranded on the road last Christmas? Yes, you guessed it. It was that I was going to be an uncle.

I grinned at my sister and my friends sitting behind her: Josh, Travis, and Wes. Josh was sitting with his wife Holly. Next to her was Travis's very pregnant wife, Emma. Wes, the last of my single friends, was busy talking to Trent's father. Trent had already warned him that the love bug was contagious and that it would bite Wes in the ass next.

Wes subsequently declared that he was fine being the last of the dying breed. Of course, it would've been more convincing if he hadn't been staring at Emma's friend, Hannah, at the time.

"You're right," I said, swiveling back to Joanne. "Everything turned out perfectly."

She went back to fiddling with my tie. "I love your choice of color for the tie and lapel flower. Burgundy was your mom's favorite color."

I smiled softly at her. "I know." Yes, there might be a chance that I had told Ava this when we discussed the wedding plans.

"The color isn't the only thing that is perfect. The place looks amazing." She glanced around the lobby, which had been converted into a makeshift wedding chapel. All the available surfaces had been decorated with pine boughs, pinecones, and small rustic hurricane lamps.

The place did look amazing.

It had been Harold and Betsy's idea when I told them a few months ago that Ava had said yes when I proposed to her and that we'd planned to keep the wedding small. Ava had already had an oversized, overpriced wedding, and look how that marriage turned out.

This time she opted for intimate.

Ava's mother was talking to Betsy on the other side of the room. Unlike Ava's grandmother, who was sitting at the back of the room, scowling like she'd sat on dog shit, Ava's mom was laughing and chatting with Betsy. The two of them were responsible for the wedding decorations and for making the day magical for Ava.

Joanne fiddled with my tie once more, then smiled up at me with tear-filled eyes. "You're ready."

Trent chuckled. "I think he's been ready for the past five minutes. Maybe you should go sit with Erin and Darren and all your grandchildren." Erin was Trent's sister and Kelsey's best friend—and practically my little sister by default.

"Good idea." She hugged me, taking care not to squash the rose pinned to my suit lapel.

"How are you doing?" Trent asked after she'd left us at the altar. "Not getting cold feet, are you?" He grinned at me, knowing full well I couldn't be happier to be here.

Harold approached us before I had a chance to respond. "I've just received word that the two lovely ladies are ready." He laughed a deep and jolly sound that really did sound like *Ho, Ho, Ho*. "Should we get started then?"

"Absolutely." Did I mention Harold was our marriage officiant for the wedding? But instead of wearing his Santa outfit from last Christmas, he had chosen a gray suit and a dark-green tie.

He nodded for the keyboardist to begin, and the wedding guests took their seats as the first strains of the music filled the room. A moment later, Zoe, wearing a long navy dress with very short sleeves, stepped through the dining room doors. In her hands was a bouquet of cream-colored roses with small red roses and bright-green leaves mixed in.

She began walking to where Trent and I were standing near the fireplace.

And it was in that instant that I was glad we had chosen to keep the wedding small. I only had to wait for Zoe to finish walking down the aisle before it was Ava's turn.

Zoe grinned at me, then shifted her attention to the doorway she had just walked through. The music changed, and everyone stood.

And my future stepped into the lobby, her hand on her father's arm.

My heart almost crashed through my rib cage at the sight of her. She was the most beautiful thing I'd ever seen. Her white gown was simple and brushed against the floor. The top was cut low, hinting of the cleavage I'd enjoyed a great many times, but her chest and shoulders were covered with sheer floral lace. Under her veil, her blonde hair was long and wavy.

My heart started pounding in my chest, demanding that the keyboardist pick up the pace. The sooner this ceremony was over, the sooner Ava would be in my arms again.

Ava and her father finally stepped up to us. He nodded his approval at me and smiled. Even though Ava and I would've gotten married without her family's consent, we were relieved her parents had accepted me into the family. Turns out, they too hadn't known about the lie Ava's grandmother had told her.

"Who is giving the bride away?" Harold asked.

"Her mother and I are," her father replied. And so began the wedding ceremony that should have taken place over ten years ago.

But like they say, better late than never.

They also say that some things get better with time, and in our case it was most certainly true.

Ava's father lifted the veil away from her face, kissed her cheek, and walked to where her mother was seated in the front row.

Ava passed her bouquet to Zoe, and I took hold of her hands. Harold shared what love is, and indicated for Ava to say her vows. Zoe handed her the ring.

"Liam, you're my best friend, my lover, my sun and my moon. You're my reason for smiling when I've had a tough day. You're my reason for grinning the rest of the time. I can't wait for this to continue as we grow old together. Will you accept me as your wife?"

I grinned at her. "You'd better believe I do."

And with that, she slipped the ring onto my finger, and her lips transformed into my favorite smile. Well, my second favorite smile. My favorite one usually accompanied dirty talk in the bedroom...or the bathroom...or the kitchen.

Trent handed me the matching gold band.

"Ava, the day I found you stranded on the side of the road, just two days before Christmas, was one of the best days of my life. And since then, every day has been brighter and filled with joy because I get to be by your side. I can't wait to spend the rest of our days the same way as we grow old together. Will you accept me as your husband?"

There was a hiccupped sob from the direction of Trent's mom.

And Ava gave me what was now my new favorite smile— my wife's beautiful grin. "Absolutely."

I slid the ring onto her finger, then lifted her hand to my mouth and kissed it.

"With the power vested in me by the state of California,"

Harold said, "I now pronounce you husband and wife. You may kiss the bride."

He glanced upward in an obvious way that made us both do the same. Above our heads was something I hadn't noticed until now: mistletoe.

He leaned closer to us so only we could hear him. "Something tells me you two don't need that magic anymore. You've already created your own."

I winked at Ava. "You can never have enough magic." I lowered my mouth to hers and tenderly kissed her.

Everyone applauded. I shifted forward, my breath spanning across her cheeks. "And in a few minutes, when everyone's preoccupied, I plan to perform more magic on you."

Ava released a shuddered sigh, and I chuckled.

We spent the next hour or so with Kelsey taking wedding photos, followed by Ava and I socializing with our guests. The best part about having a small wedding with only twenty of your closest friends and family? It was easy to talk to everyone without feeling like you were being split in several directions.

It also meant it was easier to sneak away—more or less.

"All right," Trent said, holding his son in his arms. Kelsey was next to him. "You're all set."

"Set for what?" I asked.

Kelsey hugged me and then Ava. "We're guessing at this point you just want to get away for a few minutes and start working on Ethan's cousin. And we're the threesome who are going to help you escape—mostly 'cause you didn't kill your best friend for falling in love with me." She patted my cheek in a gesture that was both sweet and mocking. "It's the least we can do."

"Aww. You always were my favorite sister." I returned the gesture, slightly messing up her hair, on purpose.

She grinned. "I know. Even if I am your only sister. But you better hurry. We can only hold the troops back for so long before they notice you're missing."

"And trust me," Trent said. "You might be thirty-four years old, but that won't make a difference to my mom. She still thinks of us as teens who are up to no good when we're in the same room as our girlfriends. The last thing you want is for her to come searching for you."

"As we learned the hard way on our wedding day." Kelsey made a goofy face.

Ava grabbed hold of my hand. "In that case, we'll see you in a few minutes."

I grunted. "A few minutes? Since when it did take only a few minutes to do what we're about to do?"

Ava didn't bother to stick around long enough to respond. She practically dragged me to the stairs before anyone could notice our disappearing act.

All right, dragging wasn't an accurate description. I was an *extremely* willingly participant.

But because I didn't think we were escaping fast enough, I scooped Ava up in my arms.

"Awww. Are you going all caveman on me again, Liam?" she said with a laugh.

"If that's what it takes to be inside you now instead of later tonight, then caveman it is." I winked at her and she giggled.

"Who am I to argue? Now stop talking and get moving. If you're not inside of me soon, I might explode from horniness. Whoever suggested that we shouldn't have sex for a few weeks prior the wedding needs to have her face smothered with cake."

I chuckled. "I believe it was you, Wife."

She grinned. "I believe you're right, Husband. And I'm looking forward to my punishment. Now if only we had it in our room for a little icing fun. I wouldn't mind licking butter-cream off some your very sexy body parts."

Yep, I might have groaned at that visual.

I didn't bother to look to see if anyone was coming after us. I carried Ava up the stairs to our honeymoon suite. I put her down long enough to retrieve my key card and open the door. Then she was back in my arms again.

I nudged it closed behind me with my foot and continued through the small living room to the bedroom. The final rays of sunlight streamed through the window and lit the bed in their warm glow.

I set Ava's feet on the floor. "God, you're so beautiful." My voice came out low and gravelly and full of heat. "You're like an angel." An angel I wanted to taste every bit of.

I traced my fingers along the lace edging, brushing the skin below her shoulders. She shivered at my touch, her eyes watching my face, her gaze caressing my soul.

"Turn around."

She did as I asked, moving slowly in a teasingly erotic dance.

The lace of her bodice continued in the back, with a diamond shape cut away, revealing her bare skin. I ran my finger along the outside of the lace, down to just above her waist.

"Hmm. No bra," I pointed out. "I definitely approve." I unhooked the button from the loop at the top of the diamond and peeled the fabric down her arms. Once her upper body was free of the material, I cupped her full breasts in my hands. Her nipples were hard and ready for me. I pinched them between my fingers.

"Oh God, Liam," Ava breathed, arching her back and pressing her ass against my thickening length.

"Fuck, I wish we had all night now, instead of having to wait three more hours. But sweetheart, don't expect to get any sleep. There are so many ways that I'm envisioning taking you tonight that we don't have time for with our guests waiting for us downstairs.

"Right now, I want to make slow love to my beautiful wife —even though we don't have time for that either."

The wedding guests would just have to understand.

With her back still facing me, I helped her remove her dress so she was standing in front of me in strappy heels, white lace panties, and nothing else.

My length got that much harder, that much wider. I was surprised my cock hadn't broken through the restraint also known as a zipper.

Ava started to turn around.

"Don't move yet." I nudged her thighs apart. "Just how ready is my bride for me?" With her panties still on, I traced my fingers along the seam of her sex. The heat of her pussy beckoned to me through the cotton. "Tell me, Ava. Are you as ready for me as I think you are?"

"Yes," she gasped and twisted around to face me.

And without saying anything, she undid my tie, dropped it to the floor, and proceeded to remove the rest of my clothes —until I was standing in front of her, naked. Not once did her darkened gaze leave mine.

I hooked my fingers in the waistband of her panties and slowly slid them down her legs. She stepped out of them, still in her stilettos, and I tossed them to the side. "Keep your shoes on."

I backed up to the bed, pulling her with me, and sat down.

Already knowing what I wanted, Ava climbed onto the bed, straddling me. She took my cock firmly in her hand and lowered herself onto my hard length.

We both moaned out loud, and I rested my forehead against hers.

"You think Ethan will get a cousin tonight?" I asked, grinning at her. She'd already stopped using the pill last month, but until now we had been using condoms.

She shook her head, but there was a sparkle in her eyes and a sweet smile on her face. "It will be a little tough for me to get pregnant tonight...when I'm already going to have your baby."

I stared at her for several seconds, digesting her words. Guess my guys weren't unstoppable after all when it came to the condom.

The grin returned to my face, wider this time. I cupped the back of her neck and brought her head down to mine.

I brushed my lips against her mouth, and my free handed shifted to cover her flat stomach. "Are you really having my baby?" The words tumbled out rough and low—with the calmness of someone who'd just found out he had the winning lottery numbers.

"Yes," she whispered. "I only found out the other day. I'm about six weeks along. So too early to announce it yet."

I mentally chuckled. It wasn't like she'd be able to keep it a secret for long. Not when she wouldn't be drinking alcohol tonight.

"Now, about you making love to me..." She left the words hanging, but her tone told me everything I needed to know.

She moved her hips in slow circles, her gaze locked on mine. I slipped my hand between her legs, applying the right amount of pressure to her clit. We continued this way until the pressure began building in my lower region to the point of no return.

Ava came first, her soft heat clenching me hard. I followed soon after as we groaned our release.

"Thank you," I said, once we had both returned to complete awareness, my arms around her waist.

She giggled. "You mean for the amazing orgasm."

I chuckled. "Partly for that. But mostly for giving me a second chance with you, for becoming my wife, and for the beginning of this new chapter of our life. Together."

She smiled my new favorite grin—sweet and sexy and naughty. "You're very, *very* welcome."

READ ON FOR AN EXCERPT FROM
DECIDEDLY BY CHANCE

1

HANNAH

Dr. St. Clair moved the Doppler across the warm gel on my lower belly. In the background, a tiny galloping sound could be heard in the otherwise quiet room.

Even Emma, sitting on a chair near the exam table, was holding her breath, her own little bundle of joy safe in *her* belly.

"Is that...?" My eyes misted like the early morning San Francisco fog, obscuring my vision.

That beautiful sound?

It was my baby's heartbeat—the reason I had endured hormone shots so an anonymous donor could knock me up.

Yep, I know—that doesn't sound very romantic.

But neither was the way Little Bean had become one with my uterus.

There was no candlelight dinner. No quickie against a brick wall.

No husband. No boyfriend. No one-night stand.

Little Bean's start in the world was thanks to modern medicine.

Smiling, Dr. St. Clair nodded. "That's right, Hannah. That's your baby."

I turned my head to see my best friend's reaction. Emma was grinning at me, tears threatening to knock down the dam, her hand resting on her protruding stomach.

I was fifteen weeks pregnant; Emma was five months. Everything about her was glowing, including her curly red hair.

I grinned back at her, then returned my attention to Dr. St. Clair. "And everything is okay?"

"We'll arrange the ultrasound once you're finished here, but things are progressing nicely." She wiped the gel off my still-flat belly with a towel.

The belly that was the result of years of karate as I trained to earn my black belt. A goal I had temporarily put aside to start my own family.

Why not go the more traditional route of meeting a man, falling in love, getting married, and then beginning a family a year or two later? The same path Emma had gone down when she and her now-husband, Travis, hooked up? Although in their case, their relationship had begun as nothing more than a ruse. A way to throw a wrench into his grandmother's matchmaking schemes. She'd wanted to be a great-grandmother. And now, she was finally getting her wish.

Yes, the traditional route was the dream, but it wasn't always the reality.

And my reality wasn't so pretty. Or at least it hadn't been while I was growing up.

Ready for a bedtime story?

Don't worry, it's short.

Once upon a time, a girl met a boy. He got her with child, then disappeared into the yonder, never to be heard from again.

The girl had the baby (me). And met another boy. Who didn't last long.

She then met another boy.

And another.

And another.

None of these men stuck around for long. None were interested in being saddled with someone else's child.

Fair enough.

One day, when the child was six years old, her mother ran off to Vegas with the latest boyfriend, leaving the child on her own.

Neither the mother nor the boyfriend returned. Something to do with a drug deal gone wrong. They went RIP, and the authorities moved the little girl to foster care, where she bounced around from foster home to foster home. Eventually, she ended up with a loving family who wanted to adopt her.

But something changed before she was adopted, and she was tossed back into the system.

There, she met a girl who would one day become her best friend. A girl who'd had similar struggles but had the physical scars to show for it.

I smiled at Emma once more. The scar on her chin had faded over the years—but our friendship hadn't.

Both of us had dreamed of one day finding someone who loved us as we deserved. Emma got lucky with Travis. Me?

Not so much. But I guess that was partly my fault. It's hard to trust your heart to another when it's been beaten down so many times. Before any guy had a chance to walk away, I was already sprinting out the door.

Most guys didn't make it past the first date.

But I was hardly one-of-a-kind in that department. Some women with a similar background to mine married young, yearning for the loving family they hadn't been part of growing up. Others, like myself, ran from those who professed their love to them.

Why?

Because we feared we'd be abandoned down the line— something with which we'd had lots of experience.

The only difference between me and the majority of those women? I never gave guys a chance to get close to the part where they believed they were in love with me.

But not a problem. Thanks to modern technology, single women didn't need a man if they wanted to procreate.

Okay, you're right. Modern technology hasn't gotten to the point where it can create sperm without a man. But I'm sure that possibility is right around the corner.

In the meantime, thanks to a sperm donor's generosity, Little Bean was cozy inside me. No complications. No messy relationship. And no having to worry about the father one day walking away from us—as my own parents did.

Once Dr. St. Clair had left the exam room, I climbed off the table and straightened my clothes.

"Does Travis know you're here?" I asked Emma.

She shook her head. "I haven't told him you're pregnant, if that's what you're asking. But you do realize I hate lying to him?"

"Technically, you're not lying. It's not like he's asked you if I'm pregnant." I felt my eyebrows rise. "He hasn't asked, right?"

Little Bean wasn't noticeable yet. Definitely not to the extent where someone would be posting my photo on social media, a circle drawn around the small stomach bulge with the question "Baby bump?" in block print.

"No, not yet. But he will eventually start to wonder. *People* will eventually start to wonder." Her gaze pointedly dropped to my breasts, which were fuller than they had been fifteen or so weeks ago. Her gaze then continued down to my stomach.

She was right—I wouldn't be able to hide my condition for much longer.

"I just want to wait another week, and after that you can tell him."

"But if he asks me before that if you're pregnant...?"

I opened the exam-room door. "If that happens, you can tell him the truth. I don't expect you to lie to your husband on my behalf." I grinned at her, knowing she'd been practically busting at the pregnant seams to share my news with Travis and our other friends.

All of whom already had babies or little kids of their own.

Except for Wes Chiasson.

Confirmed bachelor and workaholic.

Whom I hadn't seen in several months.

I booked my next doctor appointment; then Emma and I left the medical office and started walking the short distance to the elevators.

"I need to go to the ladies' room first," she said. "This baby is playing hockey with my bladder again."

Did I mention her husband was a hockey player with the San Francisco Rock?

Yes, I had met a few guys on the team because of that.

No, I wasn't interested in any of them. Hockey players weren't my thing.

"Go ahead," I told her since Little Bean was currently leaving my bladder alone. "I'll wait for you here."

She disappeared down the hallway leading to the ladies' room. I retrieved my phone from my purse and checked if there were any messages.

The door behind me clicked open. Without looking to see who it was, I continued reading an email.

"What do you say we go get some ice cream, Everly?"

At the deep sound of Wes's voice, my heart stumbled, and this time I did check over my shoulder. The stumbling heart was a new side effect I'd been experiencing whenever I'd seen him, but I didn't know why.

While my heart's reaction wasn't unexpected, seeing Wes with a little girl hugging a floppy bunny was.

Heck, I hadn't anticipated seeing him at all—especially not in *this* building.

His jeans and Henley top clung enticingly to his tall, athletic body. His short, light-brown hair beckoned for me to run my fingers through it. My lady bits released a dreamy sigh—and not just because I was dealing with pregnancy hormones.

Focus, Hannah.

Without meaning to, I let my gaze dart to the obstetrician's office. It was clearly marked as that. Maybe he would think I was coming from the...

My gaze did another quick dart in the opposite direction to the...orthodontist's office.

Great. Clearly, the building was trying to screw me over. All right, orthodontist's office it was.

Wes looked in my direction, and his eyes widened. "Hannah, what are you doing here?" Non-surprisingly, he quickly surveyed the other two offices on the floor.

And just like that, my explanation vanished from my brain. All I was capable of doing was opening and closing my mouth like a pregnant fish out of water. "I'm...I'm...here to see a therapist." Which was the third office located on this floor —the office that he had been coming from.

Face, meet palm.

But that was okay. I could work with that.

A confused frown crinkled on his brow. "You're here to see a child therapist?"

"Yes...I...I have a date. With one...there." I vaguely gestured in the direction he had come from. It was official. I had pregnancy brain.

That was a thing, right?

"You have a date with a therapist in that clinic?" He enunciated the words slowly as if I was an idiot. Which at that moment didn't feel too far from the truth. "You mean like an appointment or a *date*-date?" His confusion had bailed, replaced by amusement if his voice was an indication.

"Well, not so much a date as an appointment."

Nice save, Hannah.

The corners of his mouth turned up. He really did have a sexy mouth.

I meant a nice mouth.

Not a sexy mouth.

Just a regular old nice mouth.

ACKNOWLEDGMENTS

Writers get inspirations for their stories from all kinds of sources. Emma's love for Harry Potter came from my daughter's love of the same. Yes, I've read each book from the series several times. I was the one who introduced Harry Potter to her. But my love for the series is nothing compared to hers. She's currently reading it for the eighth time. If it hadn't been for her discussing what her future Harry-Potter-themed bedroom will look like, I would never have thought to create a heroine who was equally in love with JK Rowling's series. Thank you, Anja, for your source of inspiration and for being the best daughter a mom could ask for.

This book wouldn't be possible without the help of those professionals who made it shine: Bev Rosenbaum (editor), Hope from Flat Earth Editing (copy editing), and Jessica also from Flat Earth editing (proofreading). My beta reader Brenda St. John Brown was also invaluable for making the story better. She's like my fairy godmother. Whenever I get stuck with a plot problem (or series title), she always has the solution. I look forward to working with you ladies for many more books.

I also want to thank my Facebook reader group, Stina's Sweethearts. Your enthusiasm every time I post about my books always makes my day. And I love it when Lisa Marie posts her Wet Wednesday hotties. She finds the best pictures.

And finally, to my family. Ralph, Anton, Stefanie, and

Anja, you've put up with so much just so I can make my dead-lines. I know it's not always easy. Thank you for your love and support. Thank you for believing in me.

ABOUT THE AUTHOR

Born in Brighton England, Stina Lindenblatt has lived in a number of countries, including England, the U.S., Finland, and Canada. This would explain her mixed up accent. She has a kinesiology degree and a MSc in sports biological sciences.

In addition to writing fiction, she loves photography, and currently lives in Calgary, Canada, with her husband and three kids.

For news about her books and to sign up for her newsletter, check out her website at:

stinalindenblattauthor.com

9 781990 177552